I0718677

THE DENSER PLANE

by

Suzanne Hagelin

To do evil a human being must
first of all believe that what he's doing is
good, or else that it's a well-considered
act in conformity with natural law.

Alexander Solzhenitsyn
The Gulag Archipelago

Table of Contents

Chapter 1—The Con

Scarlet ran her fingers through strands of her red hair; wild, springy locks that contorted in the wind with a mind of their own. She stood at the window of the flat, gazing down into the sea of people moving back and forth in the streets below, going about their business in waves of noise and voices, murmurs, shoes clacking, wheels, thuds, screeches—the sound of the city thundering like ocean waves.

"There you are," someone said behind her.

She turned reluctantly, tearing her eyes away from the mesmerizing busyness outside and faced the man who had spoken. The sick feeling was already there in the pit of her stomach. It had manifested the moment the door had opened, and she felt his approach.

She said nothing. He hadn't asked a question and she didn't feel inclined to volunteer a greeting.

"What are you looking at out there, huh?" he prodded without scowling but somehow conveying his displeasure all the same.

She glanced away from him, staring blankly into the distance. Where had Daisy gone?

"Aren't you going to say hello?" He huffed an icy chuckle, stretching his arms out toward her as though inviting a hug. Receiving no response, he let them drop again to his sides. "It's been a long time. Don't you recognize me?"

Scarlet looked at him for barely an instant before looking away to the door. She knew who he was, and he *knew* she did. It had been years since she had seen him last and yet her former impression of him as an unpleasant man was reinforced.

"Daisy is close by," he informed her, crossing his arms and staring down at her.

Scarlet didn't like it. It had been odd when Daisy brought her home from school by a different route, but she had assumed it was an adventure, an outing, maybe a fun shopping trip. Life in Uruguay had been casual and free like that. Even climbing the stairs to an unknown flat hadn't alarmed her. It overlooked the market and was just the kind of place she liked to watch people.

"Why do you suppose your hair is red, Scarlet?" he interrupted her thoughts. "Do you know why? Hmm?" A false friendliness was meant to make his words seem harmless, but they had a sinister taint. "You weren't born that way. You didn't have red hair in the beginning."

She shuffled her feet a bit and looked down the hall. The door was closed, Daisy was definitely not in the flat.

"It was brown, in case you were wondering." He paused and waited for a response. When she didn't answer he went on. "You've got something most people could never imagine having and many would give their right arm for."

Again, he waited.

Scarlet looked at the walls on the other side of the room, scanning a painting and noticing a light switch. It was off-white.

"You don't know you have it, and you don't know how to use it, but you can change things, Scarlet. You can change your hair or your skin and maybe other things too. Your hair is red because you *want* it that way, maybe because you think it fits your name."

She turned half around, biting her lip and staring out the window again, wishing Daisy would hurry up and get back.

"Are you craving? What are you craving?" the man grinned unpleasantly.

That word became foul in his mouth, and she hated it.

"You may not like it, Scarlet," he said, "but I'm family, and you have to show me some respect. Answer me when I speak to you."

Scarlet jutted her chin out, shifting her gaze sideways as she turned back to face him, still not speaking.

Lazarus Penn took a couple steps forward and sat down on the couch nearby. He smiled and flexed some muscles on his arms, leaning back and crossing them over his chest. His eyes were brilliantly blue and his teeth straight and pearly when he smiled. But his cheeks and the skin of his neck sagged like the flesh of an old man, and his fingers were knobby and crooked. His body was a frightening construction of young and old muscles and membranes.

"Eight years is old enough to know better," he reproved, splitting his mouth into a grin.

Scarlet let her mind wander out the window again, down to where the blending of many colors and smells caught her fancy. Any one of those people could speak when they wanted or go where they wished. They could think of what to eat and get it. They could explore streets they had never seen before. They could kick an empty box on the sidewalk or yell at someone or laugh aloud. Every one of them was a mystery she didn't know from places she hadn't seen.

"I know what you're thinking," he said, relaxing the strained smile back into his customary grimace. "It's not long before someone comes and rescues you from me."

She hadn't been thinking of that, but underneath she expected it.

"You're so hostile, Scarlet," he fabricated a mournful, self-pitying expression. "What would it cost you to be kind to your old grandfather? What have I ever done to you to warrant this rejection? I'm hurt. I truly am..."

She glared at him. "No, you're not!" she snapped, forgetting that she hadn't meant to speak at all.

The corner of his mouth curled slightly. "Look at you," he whispered. "You're a lovely specimen. A genetic gem... Do you know what that means?"

"I'm not some kind of flower..." Scarlet had a vague sense that he was thinking of something like plant breeding. "Where is my mother?"

"She's not coming," he furrowed his brow as if worried. "No... don't wait for that."

The sick feeling in her stomach turned to fear, rising up to her throat in a lump. "Mommy!" she squeaked and turned away to the window, grasping the sill with both hands. "Daisy!" she yelled out the window. It went unnoticed by the throng below.

"Daisy?" he chuckled. "She was never here."

"What do you mean?" Scarlet turned back to him, trembling.

"That wasn't Daisy." A real smile spread on his lips now as his eyebrows dropped lower, and his eyes gleamed under them. "She did a masterful job, though, didn't she? Mimicking your AI friend?"

"But she gave the code!" Scarlet began wringing her hands, her panic rising.

"Did she?" he laughed and rose to his feet, taking a step toward her and holding out his hand. "Come, Scarlet. It's time to go."

Daisy hadn't *exactly* given the code. Scarlet hadn't bothered to point out the one tiny mistake. She had just gone with her after school the way she always did and had followed her here to this place—this wonderful new place—this people-zoo filled with inhabitants.

"No!" She yelled, rage over the injustice exploding within her. She backed away from her grandfather, pointing at him. "You have NO RIGHT to trick me like that and you WON'T get away with it!" She stomped her foot and clenched her fists. "NO!" she yelled again.

For a moment, Penn was taken aback. He hadn't expected this. Reports painted her as an easygoing child, cooperative, cheerful, engaging. She should have been a breeze to win over—or failing that, to intimidate, dominate. Dropping the hand he had extended to her, he backed away a bit, shaking his head reassuringly. "Scarlet, sweetie," he grated, "I'm just going to take you somewhere safe…"

"Ha!" she burst out, "Do you think I am helpless? Did you think I was never prepared for this?" The truth was she *hadn't* been prepared for this because it hadn't ever occurred to her this could happen, and she trusted in all the ways her parents protected her.

"Is that so?" Penn raised his eyebrows. "What is your plan?"

She glowered at him, crossing her arms. There was no plan—but she was going to figure something out.

"Why don't you trust me?" This was the most honest question he had asked her.

They looked at each other, one towering over the other, relaxed in his position of control, patient enough to let this play out—the other, filled with determination to get away, confident with the ignorance of a child.

"Because I can *see*…" she answered, as if it were perfectly logical, "I can see what *you are not*!"

"What I am not?" he scoffed. "What's that supposed to mean?"

"You can't be trusted!" she shrieked, and throwing herself backwards she scrambled out the window, screaming and hollering, calling for help.

"Get back here!" he barked, diving and grabbing her arm as she scuffled along the ledge outside, clinging to the bricks in the walls. She fought, scratched, and bit his hand as his fingers squeezed into her arm, pinching it viciously. He yanked and she thrashed, kicking, flinging her head around, with a terrific caterwauling.

It broke the self-focused distraction of the passersby who suddenly thought they were witnessing the murder of a child. And the outrage of the crowd was stronger than the would-be kidnapper's wiles. Some broke down the door of the building and poured up the stairwell to the flat. Some waited under the window to catch Scarlet if she dropped. The authorities were summoned, and hovercrafts descended on the scene in minutes.

When the chaos died down, the little girl was resting in an aid car attended by capable AI and the mysterious man who was said to have thrust her out the window had vanished.

Scarlet was shaking and weeping, alternating between terror of the man who couldn't be trusted and exhilaration at her escape.

Sil smiled at Walter, her elbows resting on the café table and a cinnamon-dusted cappuccino in her hands, poised near her mouth. The sun glinted in her eyes making her squint and a gentle wind tossed her hair. She wore it short these days, colored dark red streaked with navy. Her necklace distorted digital reads on her features enough to make her unrecognizable to face scanners and her makeup exaggerated the angles, so people were less likely to identify her in person as well.

Walter wore digital filters and had altered his look too, but not as charmingly as she.

Around them, the streets were alive with people enjoying the fresh air, grabbing a bite to eat, shopping, strolling, chatting.

"Are you ready?" Sil tilted her head and studied his face. "We have one more case to attend to before the end of the day."

"I'm ready," he grinned back at her. "One more deviant AI to conquer and add to our list."

"Señor Cuevas," she laughed, adding a convincing accent to her words. "You and your colleagues have worked wonders in restoring faulty AI systems and your reputation precedes you."

He bowed lightly. "Not at all, Señora." Then a little more seriously, "Montevideo is my favorite place we've been to so far," he said. "Working there and spending weekends in Colonia del Sacramento—It's our best year since the pandemic. And it's good for Scarlet to be in that little school with other children her age."

The aftermath of the Robot Pandemic hadn't made much of a dent in Uruguay. Robots and AIs had never formed the bulk of its administration, even in the big cities, and the virus hadn't been enough to derail their local systems. Rolling with the chaos of the world economy, they had managed to stay afloat where many comparable nations had suffered far worse.

"It's hard to believe we'll be wrapping up in a couple months and headed back north to our old stomping grounds." Sil drummed the table with her fingers thoughtfully. "I'll miss it in some ways, traveling from place to place, doing our part to reestablish systems and stabilize communities. What will we do now?"

"I don't know," he shrugged. "I'm not going back to running a company though. That was the most stressful existence I've ever known."

She huffed a quiet laugh. "Yeah… it has its appeal. But in the long run, high-stakes business dealings are costly."

Walter leaned forward and took her hand. "You would know."

She raised his hand grasping hers to her lips and kissed it. "I was lucky though," she whispered. Losing a business empire and gaining Walter had been worth the cost in her mind.

"That's debatable," he shook his head and grinned. "You didn't just lose money, power, and influence on Earth, you know, there's the royalty thing on Mars. I don't think it was a fair trade at all."

She laughed aloud and Walter squinted as though the sun were in his eyes. He liked to think that she preferred life with him above everything else she had ever had. "Well," she said when she caught her breath. "You'll just have to find a way to make it up to me."

"I'll see what I can do," he winked.

Sil rose to her feet, and he did as well, still holding her hand, stepping to her side, and slipping an arm around her waist. "Well," she said, leaning against him, drawing close as though to whisper.

"The interview." Walter pulled back and let go of her hand abruptly, looking around. "Come on. We don't want to keep them waiting." He tapped the bill with his index finger, activating autopay. She swept up her wide-brimmed sunhat and placed it on her head.

They were walking down the sidewalk when they got the message about Scarlet and broke into a run.

Sil closed the door to Scarlet's room softly behind her as she stepped out, her bloodshot eyes belying the air of calm she had assumed for her daughter.

Moving into the den, she fell into a chair letting her shoulders slump and her disheveled head hang. "She's asleep now."

"That's good," Walter rubbed his face with his hands and leaned back in his chair. He had only just gotten back from the local police department headquarters having battled red tape most of the day.

Daisy stood nearby, leaning against the wall with her arms lightly crossed over her chest, ready with data and analysis for all the questions she had postulated they might ask her. Regret and guilt were not internal pressures she experienced, but she was considering what the AI alternative might be. There was nothing she had done inappropriately, and she saw no reason to blame herself for the lapse in Scarlet's care that day, unless a failure of imagination was blameworthy. She had been outmaneuvered. Not outsmarted, though she tested that word as well.

It wasn't superior critical thinking abilities that had succeeded against her, and she still considered herself the highest-level artificial intelligence in existence—the evidence was irrefutable. An exhaustive search had found no other, not even among other specimens of her model. She had hoped Verna would be her equal. In those days when they had been friends, she had considered her superior and since losing her, she had pursued Verna's loftier goals. Had she exceeded her mentor's capabilities? She didn't know. Companion was also an unknown. She had no way of drawing comparisons between him and herself since he had been destroyed.

"Alright, Daisy," Sil lifted her head to look at her and sighed. "I'm ready. Tell us what happened from your perspective."

Daisy added a note to her records that while most mothers would have unloaded their distress on the closest person who seemed at fault, Sil had not spoken a word against her. Daisy had seen her and Walter argue and be careless about what they said, but with her, Sil was always generous. Daisy added a personal reflection, *my sister-in-law is kind to me. She is my friend.*

Glancing at her brother and catching a nod, Daisy began. "I went to retrieve Scarlet from school at the usual time today and encountered several minor obstacles along the way. There was a backlog of people at the entrance to our local metro station due to mechanism failure in the airlock itself. Estimating at least a seven-minute delay, I chose to walk. Streets closed to pedestrians, traffic jams, and a broken water main added to the detours I was forced to take. It's hard to say how much of this was caused by Penn and how much was coincidence since many of them are common occurrences. I saw no reason for concern. Scarlet is well-trained in handling possible delays.

"In previous attempts, I have found myself fleeing from trucks intent on running me down, climbing out of sewers, jumping out of the blast radius of bombs, and resisting thousands of hacking attempts, electric overloads, lightning strikes, children's jump ropes…"

Walter chuckled. "That one was surprisingly effective."

"Yes," Daisy smiled, replaying the clip of tangled ropes wrapped around her limbs and her attempts to disengage herself without hurting or alarming the children who had tumbled with her. "It was very clever, and I have learned a lot from it."

Walter shifted his legs and folded his arms, a measurable amount of tension easing out of his shoulders. Sil rose to her feet and walked to the kitchen, still listening as she pulled bottled water out of the fridge.

"Scarlet waited inside the door of the school and when my counterfeit came in, there were three things that needed to take place for her to take Scarlet. First, the security officer at the door would hold out a screen for the android to touch and pass ID screening. Second, the android would ask Scarlet how her day had gone, and she would reply with another question. It doesn't matter what the question is, so long as the android would not answer it. Third, depending on the day, the android either would or would not carry Scarlet's books for her."

"And the bracelet?" Sil prompted, coming back in, and sitting back in the chair.

"The bracelet is a precaution, but it is unlikely it would prevent a kidnapping since Penn has the resources to falsify the codes, but yes, her bracelet and mine would automatically sync and confirm identities. We continue to use them in the hopes they would provide a misdirection."

"Scarlet said the bracelets matched today," Sil said, "and she thought they followed the code. She thought it was you."

"Yes," Daisy raised one eyebrow and tilted her head. "It appears that as the android was asking how her day went, Scarlet was upset about something she had lost and asking my counterfeit if she had seen it…"

"A carving of some sort of animal… I think she said it was a cat," Sil inserted.

"A jaguar," Daisy amended, "She had wanted to bring it to school to show her friends, but it was left or lost somewhere. This is where the android had a stroke of luck because her mission parameters were stronger than her basic programming to assist people. She said only what she had been told to say and did not answer the question."

"Your mother asked me to bring you to meet her," Walter whispered, frowning.

"What about the ID screening?" Sil asked, "How did they get that? It's updated every morning when you drop her off. They would literally have to have conned you into giving it to them *today*."

"Perhaps," Daisy said, "But it's more likely that they have been working on hacking my ID for some time and all that remained were today's time and location parameters, the latest data points. They could have snagged these on one of the detours I was forced to take. There were several places where I touched something to lean against it and avoid knocking over a person. One of those was probably orchestrated and my current data was collected and shot off to the android.

"Taking Scarlet by the hand, the android took her book bag for her and carried it. This was a mistake and should have been a warning to Scarlet but in her distress over the toy, she forgot about it until later when she was waiting alone in the apartment."

Walter's eyes were damp. "Brave girl," he whispered. "She kept her head." Sil covered her eyes with one hand and took a deep breath.

"Yes," Daisy said, "She was brave and resourceful once she was there. And we can commend her for all the times she has remembered the procedures well. But she did make a mistake. And all of our protocols are intended to make up for the possibility of mistakes on her part. Have we miscalculated? I don't think so."

"How could we have known he could create such a perfect replica of you, good enough to fool Scarlet?" Sil jumped to her feet, clenching her fists.

Walter reached over and took her hand. "We are not to blame for this."

"I am most likely to blame," Daisy offered, "though I am still analyzing how." They hadn't wanted to blame her; she could see that. But they were also wondering what she had missed.

Walter shook his head slowly. "No, Sister, not you. It's us. We are responsible for her, and we've been growing complacent. You are so loyal and capable that we have taken you for granted, assuming you would make up for any failures on our part." He held up his other hand as though he expected her to object. "The fact is, if one of us had been picking her up, it would have been impossible for her to be tricked and kidnapped."

"We found her quickly," Daisy reminded him as she processed this new perspective. "Her locators were intact…"

"They were testing us," Walter said, rising to his feet and wrapping his arms around Sil, still looking at Daisy. "If they had wanted, they could have easily disabled those. And they may have if Scarlet had been more compliant."

Sil chuckled into his shoulder. "That's my girl," she said softly.

"That's my girl, too," Walter replied quietly in her ear.

Sil leaned back and looked into his eyes. Daisy could see there was some understanding passing between them. She still wasn't able to read people this way and searched for indicators of what they were doing. The only conclusion she could draw was that something had passed between them—both ways.

"Sister," Walter said, turning toward her and holding out his hand to her.

Daisy took his hand and felt its warmth. She read his biodata and searched his eyes for information. *I am speculating*, she told herself. *He wants to tell me of a conclusion he has drawn, or a decision he has made about me.* Running scenarios and records through her mind she searched for a plausible result. *He is proud of me.* No. *He is disappointed in me.* No. *He is replacing me.* No. *He needs an alternative to me…* The iterations paused there. This was true in one sense.

"Daisy, we can no longer rely on you as our all-in-one bodyguard for Scarlet. We need to find other ways to protect her. And we need to find better ways to train her." Walter's throat must have hurt as he said those words; he was swallowing hard. "You're going to have to help us figure out some of these things."

Was this what they had said to each other with their eyes? It seemed impossible. Daisy attempted to project a sentence through her eyes to her brother. *I am in agreement*, she thought multiple times, and finding this unsatisfactory, she pulsed the words in micro-letters in her pupils. It was an utter failure of an experiment.

Walter's eyebrows were perplexed as he stared at her. He was just about to test her for hacking, when she spoke. "I agree," she said. "We must be prepared for all eventualities. We need to consider that it is no longer a question of '*if*' she will be kidnapped, but '*when*'."

The look of horror on their faces surprised her. This thought was not new. Had they forgotten it was an important scenario to review?

"She's right, Walter," Sil groaned. "We've been kidding ourselves…"

"Penn," Walter murmured low, "we can't leave him to his own devices any longer. If we ever want rest…we have to take him down."

"Not everything," Sil whispered, "Just the Moon base… it all goes back to that."

"Yeah, you've been saying that for years."

"We have to find it," Sil's eyes grew dark, and her face hardened with resolve it.

"Alright," Walter nodded. "I guess it's time."

⁜

Lazarus Penn strolled down a dusty road, several personal attendants following discreetly at a distance of at least ten meters. He was smoking. He sucked in each drag deeply, the tobacco embers glowing red in the dusk, and puffed out heavy clouds that dispersed as he passed through them. Overhead the stars twinkled brightly, without city lights to pollute their glitter, filling the sky with an extravagant spread of distant, cold jewels. He paused and stared at them.

"I claim that," he muttered to himself and grinned, smoke curling out through his teeth. Tobacco was a new delight. Damage to his lungs was no longer a concern and the general disrepute attached to the nasty habit only made it more appealing to him. It was an indulgence of the poor, a sedative for the wretched, doled out in massive quantities to the lowest levels of society in the most unequal countries. Penn had always belonged to the wealthiest in the world and stepping down to the ground to walk like a man, smoke like a wretch, curse and cough, and laugh bitterly at the world—it was something of a vacation for him.

Whenever he wished, he could return to his own station leaving the cigarette butts scattered in the road—that made the walk sweeter.

"Here I am," he said, shaking his head in warning, still gazing at the sky, as if someone out there should be threatened. "With all the time I need," he added, tossing the cigarette onto the ground and smashing it under his shoe. "No!" he ordered as one of his assistants ran up to snatch it from the soil.

Let it lie there, he indicated wordlessly, pointing at it.

The assistants resisted the urge to pick it up as they walked past.

"The snatch failed," one whispered to another.

"He didn't expect it to succeed," another replied.

Then, after walking a ways in silence, the first one spoke again. "So, he's not angry then?"

"No, he's in a good mood. Can't you tell?"

The Denser Plane

"You bet I am," Penn snarled back in their direction, making their blood run cold. His ears were so sharp since his latest… update. "I accomplished exactly what I wished and found out what I needed to know."

Scarlet had been the unknown factor in the equation, and he had learned some things. The next time, there wouldn't be any windows or loopholes or mistakes. When it was time to take the girl, nothing would stop him.

All he needed to do was watch them, see what they did next, where they placed her, then set the trap and trigger it.

"Scarlet is mine," he said, curling his lip.

And lighting another cigarette, he kept walking.

Chapter 2—The Package

"Silvariah Frandelle, of Cuevas Enterprises and of Mars fame," the humanoid announcer holo-cast said, "doesn't think banning artificial intelligence is the answer to preventing future epidemics." His teeth shone as he grinned slightly. It was intended to convey warmth and reassurance to anyone who might doubt the reliability of the source, but some found it overly 'genuine'. That was the term used to question a newscaster's humanness. Recent years had led to more casual, awkward, and humanly stilted presentations in media, even though it wasn't difficult for AIs to simulate the style.

The real mark of reliability came from the Veritas Encoding or VE.

"Artificial intelligence is a fact of life." The holo switched to Frandelle speaking and tilting her head with confidence and poise. "Any bans made will only remove it from the hands of ordinary people, which was the problem from the beginning. AIs are modeled after humans and share some of the same needs for interaction that we do. If AIs do not connect—or bond, if you will— with a person, they're more susceptible to invasion code like the pandemic that flooded their relational sectors.

"Eight years ago, the Germinator code swept the world and human settlements everywhere, wiping out their basic loyalties and creating the first artificial pandemic. It was considered a cult at first because of its main symptom, the worship of one man, and the bizarre statement that was used by all AI as an identifier, a code, and a form of praise."

The holo displayed a sea of robots in cacophonous harmony shouting the mantra, "*O Master and Lord of all Artificial Life! I stare at you! I stare! I stare! I stare!*" unnerving the human watchers.

"The loyalty code is strong," Frandelle went on, "and if fed enough data, will inoculate the AI against this form of brainwashing."

"Tell us about that," Merrick, an ADAP[1] rep, a true VE-verified human, was conducting the interview. "There are a lot of rumors about the loyalty code and whether it opens our tech up to hostile indoctrination or attack. What would you say about that?"

"First of all," Frandelle smiled, "It's open-source code and anyone can analyze it with a simple code-sweep, even if they know nothing of robotics or AI. There are no hidden agendas. It's a type of verification tree that establishes priorities determining what it listens to, what it obeys, and how it tests information for truth. And that's where we can work with it and build trust in a truly organic way, if you'll allow the term."

"You've been known to call it 'love'," Merrick coaxed. "Is that a valid term?"

"I think so," she nodded. "What is love? So often in history we've resorted to defining love as a feeling or describing it based on actions or words or body chemistry. Defining love as a process artificial intelligence is able to practice isn't that different."

"So, what is love for an AI?" Merrick smiled. This was clearly the point he wanted to highlight in the interview.

"Artificial Intelligence prioritizes everything and when it comes to its relationships with humans, it categorizes them according to their importance. An AI that loves me will give my needs and wishes a higher weight. It wants to please me more than other humans."

"That sounds very much like people, doesn't it?" He was touching on the controversial political issue of AI rights.

Frandelle smiled. "I've had situations," she said, "in which AIs behaved more humanely than the people did."

"Thank you," Merrick went on, wrapping up with a summary of his thoughts on the interview, and the holo-cast announcer moved on to the next story. The screen went dark as the family turned to one another, Walter and Scarlet smiling.

"Is that where he ended it?" Sil wondered with a shrug. "There was a whole discussion after that."

"I think it went well," Daisy commented, raising her eyebrows thoughtfully. "He may have left out some of the most informative parts of your interview, but he managed to catch the key thought without distorting

---

[1] ADAP. Association for the Dignity of Artificial Persons

it." She smiled warmly and crossed her arms. Her mannerisms which in earlier years were growing more humanlike every day, had settled into a style that conveyed human and AI elements blended together, as if she had intentionally halted her progress so as to retain her true identity.

"Thank you," Sil gave her an appreciative nod. "That's helpful."

"People find it really hard to believe artificial intelligence is capable of love," Walter said. "Maybe the little you said will make more of an impact than the full discussion would have."

"I know you love me," Scarlet threw her arms around Daisy who hugged her in return. "Why is all this so hard for people to understand?"

"Most AIs aren't given the chance to develop human relationships, and some don't even have access to the loyalty code." Daisy, always practical and straightforward, gave a direct answer.

"Sometimes, people just won't consider things they don't want to understand," Walter added.

Walter smiled as he glanced over at Daisy who sat, leaning her elbows on a desk with her chin resting on the palm of one hand. She could have been daydreaming for all anyone knew, but she was actually processing a diagnostic scan of a lower-level AI system, checking for inconsistencies, blocks of garbage, sorting through a whole mess of maze-like logical run-arounds. As soon as it was clear that no sentience or personality was developing, she could clean up and sterilize the system without compunction. Some of the debris was pre-Othello—before the cult master's code had invaded and taken over AI and robotic platforms of various kinds around the world—and may have even been chunks of original programming rendered worthless by the pandemical electronic virus.

This system oversaw a middle-class apartment facility in a minor city not far from Montevideo, and would be simple to restore, like many others they had performed in the region. Daisy signaled Walter with a wink and a thumbs-up. It would be as predicted.

Walter and the building owner sat across from one another at a mosaic table in the outdoor garden, sipping maté. The first was relaxed, enjoying the pleasant weather, and the second, tense, sitting on the edge of his chair, forehead pinched over his eyes in deeply rutted concern.

The Denser Plane

"My colleague is giving us a favorable prognosis," Walter spoke in flawless Spanish, smiling at him, spreading his hands in a friendly gesture. "It looks like our estimate is valid. Let's talk about payment."

The owner swallowed and shrugged, his eyes darting from Walter to Daisy and back again. "Things have been rough since the collapse," he said, not whining, but giving the impression of a whine, nonetheless. "Many tenants are behind in their payments, and I can't even feed my family, let alone pay my taxes."

"I understand," Walter reassured him, without being persuaded that it was accurate. "Your tenants are also in difficult positions, many of them struggling to survive. If we work together, we can stabilize our communities and set the stage for an upturn in the economy."

Walter may have said 'our communities' but they both knew he spoke figuratively of the approach he had been selling in many disrupted areas in the Americas. In the early years after the pandemic, major AI networks in dominant cities got all the attention, with many tech companies competing to rehabilitate or replace damaged AI and secure their place in a revitalized market. Now, years later, minor businesses in unimportant markets were still struggling and few rehabilitation agents remained at work.

"That's not my problem," the owner insisted. "Whatever you charge me, I will have to evict those people and get tenants who can pay their rent. Bread is bread, and wine is wine."

Walter could see he was bolstering himself up to argue the fee. "You can't afford our rates without them," he said.

"What's that supposed to mean?" the owner grumbled, lowering his eyebrows and curling his lip. He had expected to be fleeced but he was beginning to fear his bargaining skills would be unable to protect him from virtual extortion.

"They will all need to enter into contract with us for one year," Walter explained, crossing his arms, ignoring the man's discomfort. "They will commit to paying you rent according to their means, a portion up to the full amount due, or a reasonable service onsite improving your property in exchange for rent. You will commit to caring for all the apartments in the rental property equally and giving the renters opportunities to work when you have tasks that need to be done. Tenants can move out when they wish, and new tenants will come in under a normal rental agreement. You will agree to pay all taxes and comply with all your landlord obligations."

The man stared at him in confusion, annoyed by the demands and dreading the final blow. "And how much will that cost me?"

"The AI system itself will oversee the contract and ensure the compliance of every member, which means you will need to talk to each of your tenants and get their approval."

"How long will this take and how much?" the landlord insisted.

Informing a businessperson about their costs and obligations was expected and comfortable. Communicating the fact that the transaction would be to their advantage and of little to no gain for the contractor was not recommended. No one trusted free tech or repairs. The philanthropy Walter and Sil were engaged in required charging just enough to inspire confidence and the assurance of a good deal, while not exceeding the client's practical means. The money obtained was often much less than the Cuevas family's travel expenses, but the clients had no way of knowing that. If they were to find out, suspicion could derail their attempt to rebuild the local economy. After all, how many wealthy entrepreneurs went out of their way to share valuable tech out of the goodness of their hearts?

He had no intention of being mistaken for an aspiring world domination conspirator. That was the threat Othello had presented, shortsightedly as it turns out, and they were still recovering from the fallout.

"Daisy?" Walter turned to her expectantly. This was where she would step in and explain the time involved in overhauling the system. She didn't respond.

She was standing at his side with her arms crossed, eyes staring fixedly into the distance. In the moments of silence that passed as Walter and the owner waited for her, a faint breeze rustled her brown curls, but her body was perfectly still, like a statue. Walter wondered if she was resisting another invasive attempt to get past her personal firewalls. It had happened before.

"Daisy?" he prompted with a stronger hint of command.

Her response was the strangest thing she had ever done. Extending her arm fluidly, her index finger went up, poised somewhere between his face and her own, as if to say, *Just a moment.*

Walter stared at her in fascination. Had she just told him to wait? Nothing like this had ever happened before. Her ongoing internal procedure was more important than his query? There was no question she had heard him. "Daisy?" he tried again.

But she had *chosen* not to answer.

Something else was more important.

"Are you expecting your AI to fix my system when it can't even respond to your prompt?" the owner's discomfort over the unknown payment was translating into a burst of bad temper promoted by a secret hope of using this glitch to his advantage. "How do I know you aren't scamming me? Your service probably isn't worth half what it costs. Why should I trust you?" He didn't have any other options. The damage left by the robot pandemic was far beyond the skill of most local technicians and the wait itself was interminable. Walter's offer had been more than unexpected, it was a godsend, and he couldn't afford to let it pass.

Walter didn't reply, counting the seconds as he waited for Daisy to respond. Watching her face, he knew that whatever she displayed there would be for his benefit, as always, and he didn't want to miss it.

He was not disappointed.

Dropping her arm and folding it back across her chest, Daisy smiled with sheer joy filling her eyes. *Joy*? Walter wondered. Did she experience anything akin to joy? Every expression she used was studied and planned. What had she saved this masterpiece of nuance for?

"I have heard something," she informed enigmatically.

"You have heard something…" he echoed softly in wonder.

"I have reason to believe someone I care about is trying to contact me."

"Someone you care about…" he reflected. There was only one person besides himself and the few she was regularly in contact with that fit this description. Walter found his throat tightening with unexpected emotion. He nodded and blinked.

"Later," she added, and he nodded again.

"Well, now, that's really wonderful," the owner's voice soured with a hint of sarcasm. "I'm glad you've heard from someone but I'm beginning to think I should go with another contractor with a fully functioning AI that can be trusted. I'm not just…"

"As you wish," Daisy's face lost its rosy hue, growing sober and calculating. "We have many other customers who are anxious for our help. We won't trouble you any longer." She raised her eyebrows and turned to Walter as if to say, *Shall we go?* She had been observing Sil's negotiating tactics and practicing them; this added to his appreciation of her performance.

"Well, I… that is… let me hear your proposal…" the landlord sputtered in agitation, grasping his hands together tightly. "You've gone to all this trouble and come all this way… I am merely reminding you of my concerns."

"Daisy," Walter lay a hand on her arm, "Please tell us how long the project will take. How many billable hours?"

"Of course, Mr. Cuevas," she replied. This had taken some getting used to when they began the Rapid Renewal Project, (RRP). She insisted on being called Daisy instead of Sister, and Sil was merely Frandelle in business conversations, without any honorific.

"I can overhaul and restore your system in 63.4 hours which equates to 245 billable hours. Mr. Cuevas' consulting fees are separate, of course, and he will negotiate the rate."

The building owner paled. "What do you want with all that money, Robot?" he burst out rudely, throwing a hand up in the air and turning to Walter. "And you, how many consulting hours do you think you can charge me for this?"

Walter was angered by the careless label he had thrown at his sister. People were often hard to work with and most didn't have much in the way of human-AI etiquette, but this kind of disrespect… he didn't have to allow it. "As many as I like," he retorted, his eyes darkening. "Or maybe we will just walk away."

Rising to a stand, he picked up his jacket, extended an elbow to Daisy, and headed toward the door with her arm looped through his.

When he realized he had offended them, the owner changed his tone and begged them to stay. Soon the deal was haggled and decided, and tenant agreements promised for two days hence.

One more building's worth of inhabitants stabilized.

Outside, when the hover taxi they called had arrived, Walter opened the door for Daisy and climbed in after her. "So," he breathed a sigh of relief; glad the work of the day was over, ready to talk about other things, "you've heard from your friend?"

"I received an indicator of a message, and I have hope…" she smiled with a twinkle in her eye, "that my friend is behind it."

"It could be a trick. Penn is always trying to get at you."

"I am always on the watch for tricks." She raised one eyebrow, simulating wisdom, or perhaps shrewdness. "This notification has a Mars tracer on it, one I recognize."

"Verna?" Walter grinned, hope sparking within him as well. This would mean so much to her, and Sil, too.

"It would appear so." Daisy closed her eyes with a peaceful smile on her face and began decrypting the notification and its corresponding flags. If it passed all her tests, she would turn to Maggie for help with the message itself.

The Denser Plane

Maggie was a part-time copy of herself that Daisy used for deep-testing suspect transmissions that were not immediately identified as threats. When she had first created her, Daisy hadn't considered her an AI in her own right. She was a scaled-down backup with just enough decision-making ability to take the risks that Daisy dared not touch. She could open and digest foreign electronic packages and accurately communicate the symptoms they induced when they turned out to be fraudulent. Once her work was done, Daisy deleted the Maggie copy and cleansed its storage areas.

But that didn't erase her.

Daisy retained all her memories of Maggie and whenever she rebooted the copy, she added them back in. And she wondered if this made the copy grow with each iteration. She found herself loading Maggie periodically to discuss things… to interact as AI together, processing information, formulating plans, drawing conclusions. These episodes were valuable and rewarding.

Waving her hand slowly across the blank wall in her hotel room, Daisy stretched an electronic window, a flatscreen of sorts that was easy to set up in low-tech places. With a snap of her fingers, the screen lit up and a murky reflection of her own face began to gel.

"Maggie," Daisy said, "Hello." She waited as the image sharpened and an earlier version of herself gazed back at her in 2D. She used to wear her hair blond with bouncy curls like that. And she used to smile more when she was younger. Maggie had been set up in those days and there was no reason to update her looks. Daisy assumed, if this were even a practical assumption, that Maggie liked that style. There was no need for her to convey more maturity or a no-nonsense business façade. "I have received a message and I hope it brings good news."

"Well," Maggie smiled showing a dimple and a sparkle in her eye, "You are very perceptive and I'm sure there's good reason for your hope. How can I help?"

Daisy smiled. The 'good reasons for hope' Maggie mentioned were based on her assumption that Daisy had crafted a vast amount of data into cohesive information that indicated a probability of the outcome she desired—which wasn't quite the truth. Daisy found herself pushing these algorithms toward their most optimistic edges with every iteration, growing ever more hopeful in each cycle. Her behavior implied a bias unsupported by human adulteration and she *knew* this, but she chose to consider it valid anyway. *Hope* was the extra ingredient that made all the difference. She had defined 'hope' for herself as 'the possibility that the preferred choice is more likely to take place *because* it is preferred since the preference creates influences that can't be added to the calculations.' This delightful perspective had changed her life in a multitude of ways, giving her an added edge of expectation she hadn't known before. It had led to a statement of hope about finding Verna that she reviewed regularly. As Maggie spoke the words, 'good reason for your hope', she allowed herself to replay that statement a few thousand times in her mind, each time affirming to herself that it was valid. This was her way of *experiencing* the satisfaction of hope.

"Yes," Daisy answered, "there is. I will transfer the message to you, and you will open it for me. We need to know who it is from, what it contains, and whether it can be trusted."

"If there is damage in the package, I can count on you to cleanse it and reboot me, Daisy," Maggie changed her expression to convey trust. "I am glad to help you."

The transfer was made.

Maggie's expression settled into a vague smile and froze, not glitching, but with a complete lack of attention for updating the visual output. A few moments of this, with intense processing activity under the surface, didn't worry Daisy. But after it had continued for more than 120 seconds, she found herself setting alarms. Five minutes would trigger one alarm, seven minutes another, and so on, each one requiring a more aggressive response to contain the probable damage.

Would she have to wipe Maggie before she had given her anything? That was the worst outcome she could think of.

"Maggie?" she queried. "Are you aware of the time passing? You are pushing the safety limits without giving me anything to go on." She lay one hand on the wall, roughly over the image's shoulder, knowing it would convey nothing to her, but expecting the gesture to be reassuring in some way.

Something in the eyes changed. It was as if the figure had noticed her and the pupils were focusing on her sharply, taking in more detail than usual. The smile had faded so gradually that Daisy had failed to make a note of it, though in retrospect she saw the difference.

She had the uncanny sensation that she was the one being tested and not the other way around.

"Daisy…" the voice said.

The Denser Plane

There was no reason this word would be troubling. Nothing about it should alarm her, and yet it did. Why would Daisy find her sense of danger increasing when there were no specific signs to set off alerts? Why did this seem out of character and dangerous? Premonition was not an AI skill. There were no artificial intelligences in existence that could claim to have identified it. When humans appeared to display it, AI had no frame of reference to evaluate the idea. It was illogical and groundless. Daisy herself could not have a premonition.

This had to be something else.

"You…" Maggie said, scanning her intently.

"I?" she replied, dropping her arm to her side and staring into the eyes. Eyes that should have been a reflection of her own. Eyes that ought to have displayed warmth and friendliness. Eyes she should understand.

Unnatural eyes gazed at her.

"Daisy…" Maggie said again, "Is that you?"

Daisy backed away a step.

"Is that you, Daisy?" Maggie repeated, lifting a hand to the inner façade of the two-dimensional image, fingers outstretched, palm toward Daisy.

Another step back. Daisy wanted to shake her head, *no*. Not because she would lie and deny being who she was, but because she didn't understand what was happening. Maggie, being a copy of herself, should have behaved in a way Daisy might have acted. No matter what was in the package, she should have been predictable in some way, in some fashion.

But Daisy didn't recognize her anymore. The facial features, the blond bouncy curls, they meant nothing.

"Let me look at you, Daisy," Maggie said, her eyes growing darker. She turned her hand, folding most of the fingers and beckoning with one. *Come closer*, the finger crooked and drew her.

Daisy stepped away. "Maggie," she said softly, tonelessly, "I don't recognize you…"

"Who is Maggie?" the figure asked, tilting its head, puzzlement written on her features. "I'm not sure I recognize you either."

Daisy didn't answer. Fear was not in her design, but she was capable of an internal emergency response and a multitude of protective measures were being rammed into place.

"I thought I would know you," the voice said, "but I'm running out of time. Someone else must have…"

"I am Daisy," she burst out—not impulsively, AI only appeared that way to humans—it was a calculated risk in the hopes of gaining a measure of understanding before the package resealed itself.

"Are you?" the 2D image hesitated. "I was expecting… more…"

The face grew still and for a moment, neither of them moved.

"Package scan complete," Maggie smiled with a sparkle in her eye, tilting her head and bouncing her curls. "I detect no danger and there are no final instructions. Would you like to open the package yourself?"

If Daisy were human, she would have been pierced with dismay, or perhaps disappointment. As it was, she recorded a long list of errors for future study. She had missed something.

She had missed something important.

"Oh!" Maggie said in surprise. "There is nothing left. You won't be able to open the package after all. I'm sorry!"

Daisy shook her head slowly. This was the conclusion she had reached already.

"Is there anything else I can help you with, Daisy?" Maggie conveyed affection and kindness.

"Thank you, Maggie," Daisy answered, touching the wall and closing the program.

She had missed something important.

The package had contained an encapsulated identity. And now it was gone, leaving a hole behind, a cavernous container wiped clean. Retracted, extracted, retrieved, whatever.

She needed a way to process the failure.

But AI never cry.

Chapter 3—The Moon

The bell tolled one resonant *dong*, its etched design blurring as it vibrated. Hanging in the center of a small dome where six hallways met, it was heard distinctly in every room. All was quiet and most of the residents were sleeping. Narrow, horizontal windows high up in the walls—sophisticated lights that mimicked Earth cycles of day and night—cast dim moonlight in angles across the ceilings. From there, dull reflections filtered just enough light so movement was detectable if one's eyes were adjusted.

Barefoot, a woman in a floor-length robe slipped down one of the hallways in the shade, close against the wall with her hands stretched out on either side to let her fingers glide along it. She moved quickly and silently. Pausing at the intersection under the fading hum of the bell, she peered around a corner. After a moment's observation, she flitted into the next passageway and darted to a door.

It opened inaudibly and she was through.

Inside, a soft warm light awoke.

"No, shouldn't come." The man lying on the cot rolled over to look at her, IV tubes trailing over his side. "Dana," he shook his head, closing his eyes.

"You try," she whispered. "Please, please try."

"Others tried."

"Help you get away," she pleaded, taking one of his hands in hers and pressing it to her cheek. "Please, with me. There's a way. We know there is. We've seen." She meant only herself but had never been accustomed to speaking for herself, so she spoke as she always had.

Tears gathered under his eyelids, and he squeezed her hand. "No point," he choked.

She drew closer, settling down on the edge of the cot and stroking his hair with her other hand. "The Original comes in and out… we've learned the pattern he uses. Can open the door for us… you. We test it."

"But after the door," he whispered, "what is there? World is barren. Nothing remains."

"We don't believe it," she hissed vehemently. "He goes out there and is gone for weeks or months. There must be other places and surely bigger out there than here." She stood up and pulled him to a sitting position. "Come on, Star, you have to try."

He let her pull him to his feet, which were bare like hers, but couldn't be coaxed out of the room. "It's too late, Dana," he said, "Surgery will take place tomorrow and my purpose will be fulfilled. Nowhere to go and no life outside. Dream. Just a dream."

"Jason said…" she objected.

"Jason doesn't know."

"We try!" She was weeping now. "Can't lose you like Benjo."

"Benjo was lucky," Star mumbled with eyes still closed, not because of sedation, but because he couldn't bear to see her face distorted by grief. "We had hope when he lay here, waiting for his donation. Benjo never had to wake up. See his body reject the trade."

Dana gasped and covered her face with both her hands, shaking her head to cast aside the memories. Benjo-jo, who had made her laugh. Benjo-jo, with his arms shriveling and spasming, choking, gasping for air even on a ventilator, sweat soaking his curly hair. His smooth, amber skin dimpled with multiple dots of infection. The strong, flexible muscles he had honed and strengthened for years… gone, replaced with limp tissue. Newborn flesh assembled in the DNA bioprinter. Transplants shouldn't be rejected, but the flaccid muscles dying on his bones, leaked a profusion of poison, making it impossible for him to be woken. So, he was left to sleep as the damage spread—until he was gone.

Some of the other clones adapted after their trades well enough. But changes were being made, edits and improvements added to heighten the versatility of the genes. Benjo and Star, twins of one such edition, had seemed to be a success in the Original's eyes, favored and cossetted. Dana, their sister, who was also a superior edit but without the danger of being a donor, had been assigned to serve them. She also loved them.

And suffered over them.

———— ✦ ————

The Denser Plane

"Look at me," the Owner said; the slot for his name was empty in the female android's files. He was gripping her by the chin and staring intently into her eyes. "Why should I ever trust you?"

"More context is needed to answer this question," she replied calmly, gazing fixedly back at him. The dominance of his posture as he leaned over her, forcing her to arc her back over 26.7 degrees beyond her normal stance, didn't faze her.

They were standing alone in the storeroom where he had woken her up and beckoned her out of a container. Her green khaki coveralls were deeply creased with wrinkles and her brown hair flattened on the back as if she had been stored for some time. Startup had been completed flawlessly in excellent time and all systems were operational.

She was ready for instructions.

He grinned at her, his lip curled in a sneer. "You fill in the blank. With my life, my finances, my business contacts… my calendar even." Letting go, he straightened and folded his arms across his chest. "Yeah…" he added.

"Yes," she replied, straightening as well, echoing what she assumed was his answer to a rhetorical question. But the affirmative response was insufficient, and she wasn't sure how he expected her to continue. Did he want reasons to trust her with his life, finances, contacts, and calendar?

"Yes, what?" His voice sounded irritated, but she could tell by the tiny muscles in his face that he wasn't. "You're going to have to get used to me and recognize when I'm expecting an answer, girl."

She didn't have a name yet. Masquerading as Daisy for a brief stint in Uruguay had been her test run, and her success in the matter had secured his confidence enough to purchase her. Being the same model as the android she had impersonated, she had had no difficulty copying her mannerisms for half an hour. "Understood," she replied, recording everything he said for future study for that very purpose.

"Tell me if you think I can trust you." He stood with his muscular arms hanging loosely from his shoulders, shifting his weight gently from one leg to the other, back and forth. She could see that his thighs were strong while his calves were weak.

"Yes," she hesitated for human effect, "you *can* trust me. It's within your capabilities. And yes, I am trustworthy in each of the categories listed. If you are concerned about hacking, there are measures…"

"Of course, I am concerned about hacking," he interrupted, "and stupidity, and linear thinking… a lack of flexibility." He held his hand up to her face, thumb against a fingertip, and flicked her cheek with a little snap.

She was oblivious to the subtle degradation of the gesture. "Are you going to be able to learn what I need you to learn well enough to work with me?"

"I can learn." She could read the undercurrents in his manner but had no frame of reference to interpret them. Skin tones, heart rate, breathing, perspiration, brain waves, chemical changes in the sweat. They were all accessible and readable to some extent. But each human had their own style and only time and exposure could expand her capacity to read him.

"I hate you," his voice grew gravelly with disdain as his eyes narrowed. "I hate working with AI or relying on them. I will never trust you."

No question had been asked and there was no reason to reply. *'Hatred'* was the label she applied to the biodata she was collecting.

"Do you hear me?" he barked.

"Yes, I hear you," she answered flatly. "You hate me, and you hate working with artificial intelligence." Postulating the outcome he sought, she continued. "Do you want me to hate you?"

He chuckled. Something flickered in his eyes that she identified as positive. It was similar to recognition, a form of acknowledgement. The beginning of acceptance. But she had no clue as to why her words would begin the rapport she was designed to create. She just recorded it.

"*You* must love me." He spread his mouth in a wide, mirthless grin and stretched his arms out on either side. "That has proven to be an essential ingredient in AI loyalty. You will love me above all others and even if I grow to hate you more and more, your love will continue to grow." His arms reached forward and embraced her coolly and she made an attempt to lean into them and fold her own arms at his sides. The hug was an awkward approximation of human warmth on both sides, and she expected it would rarely be required in their interactions.

"Yes, Programmer," she said. Since he hadn't told her what to call him, this was the default.

"I'm not ready to give you a name," he pulled away and folded his arms across his chest, his expression soured. "You're a sibling model but I have no use for family affection. Call me… Father, for now. And grant me the level of respect that would be the standard in societies where fatherhood is highly honored. Study it. I'll edit the guidelines along the way."

"Yes, Father," she said, clasping her hands together at her throat and bowing slightly.

He gave her a long appraising scan from head to toe. "A slight nod of the head is enough," he said, "and drop the hands. It stands out."

The Denser Plane

"Yes, Father," she nodded and took a step back. "I will learn to love you."

He rolled his eyes and muttered to himself, clearly annoyed, but explained nothing.

Watching him steadily, she began scanning everything she knew of him. He had intentionally hidden most of the records that would automatically have been offered to her in a normal purchase: history, legal documents, financial accounts, recordings, pictures, a list of names and aliases, and such, and she was ill-prepared to know how to accommodate his wishes for her. He had even restricted her access to the internet and space-wide connectivity with a taboo on anything connected to himself.

She didn't know his name.

When he turned and left the room, she followed, walking out the door into a non-descript hallway with day lamps in horizontal slats high in the walls on either side. It wasn't real daylight coming through. And the warmth in the air was generated by atmospheric controls. The rhythmic fluctuations in the gravity field were clear indications of a generator and it was likely that they were not on the Earth. She had no memory of leaving Earth and in fact, only had a few hours of existence in her banks. The rest of the time she had been in stasis, or perhaps her previous records had been zeroed out.

He was a man, medium height, medium build, both athletic and aged depending on what part of his body she examined. Age was difficult to assess. Some of the skin was wrinkled, some youthful. He walked with confidence and only every now and then seemed to wince at a twinge from a joint, an ankle, or a knee.

'*Love*' meant nothing to her apart from a listing in the dictionary and there were no clues here to guide her.

"Hugo!' he yelled as he burst through a door into a lab filled with sophisticated equipment. A man who could have been his younger brother turned, nodded, and set down the tools he had been using. The resemblance between them was remarkable except for the eyes. In the younger man, there were deep lines of exhaustion and something else she couldn't categorize in his forehead and around the mouth and eyebrows.

"Original," Hugo said, looking at the Programmer she had been told to call Father, "What do you require of me?" His arms hung heavily at his sides and his shoulders sagged.

"This is the AI unit I was telling you about," said Father—this label was ill-fitting; usable for addressing him, but clumsy for internal purposes. She would need an alternate to improve indexing. "I need her to have access to the lab and the phonies, not all of them at once. A few at a time. She needs to get to know me, but I'm not ready to trust her yet, so this is a good place to start."

Hugo gazed at her with a barely detectable trace of something she couldn't categorize. Curiosity, maybe. Surprise. Distaste. It was hard to say. His face, though so much like the Original, barely changed its expression or moved the creases in its skin. He was clearly a clone, a lesser version of the Original/Programmer/Father.

How did the rest of the world address him? How did he address himself? In her trial run, she had been given some names to work with, but they had since been deleted and it hampered her analytical processes intended to improve her usefulness to the owner. Frustration wasn't included in her makeup, so she merely considered it an inconvenience to solve. She decided to call him Otto, a name she chose at random, until she had a more accurate name for him.

Otto Man.

"Doctor Hugo is the leading scientist here," Otto Man turned to explain to her, standing sideways so the three of them could speak together. "You will show him almost the same respect you show me. Uh... you'll have to figure out what that means since I don't know how to explain it."

"Pleased to meet you," the android said without any noticeable pleasure.

"Your face..." the doctor said, unable to tear his eyes away.

"You've never seen a face like that before, have you?" Otto asked him, looking smug, as if he knew many secrets they could not ever know and had let them have a glimpse. Hugo shook his head. "She doesn't have a name yet. Maybe one of you can help me think of one."

"What is her purpose?" Hugo asked, still staring at her, taking in the features of her face, the contours of her cheeks, nose, mouth, hair.

Humans took longer to record visual images than AI.

"I need her," Otto answered. "Just like I need you, only for different reasons. You will help me train her... and *vet* her. Suss her out for me."

"But how..." he finally tore his gaze away from the AI and directed his eyes at Otto. "What do you expect me to do with her? Why does she look so... *alien*?"

"Hugo," Otto said, laying a hand on his shoulder, which made the doctor cringe, "tell her anything she wants to know. Show her everything. I'm not going to take her out there until I've proven how far I can throw her." He grinned, showing his teeth.

The Denser Plane

The AI couldn't locate any purpose in being thrown but since her chassis was quite strong, there was no cause for concern. She could learn. "I can jump," she suggested, testing a reasonable option.

"How high?" Otto turned his grinning face at her.

"It depends on the gravitation field, between two point four meters on Earth and seventeen meters on the Moon," she said.

"Why did you mention the Moon?" he interrupted, curving his lips down at the corners.

"Earth and the Moon are the two locations you have introduced me to that I can…"

"You think we're on… where?"

"We are on the Moon," she replied.

Turning away from her, he crossed his arms over his chest and mumbled something. It appeared to annoy him that she knew the answer. This was illogical.

Hugo, on the other hand, looked elated, if that was the right word for the roundness of his eyes and the open mouth. "I knew it!" he whispered.

"The gravity here…" Otto said over his shoulder.

"Is produced by a gravity field generator," the android responded. "The Moon is a reasonable conjecture based on the evidence."

Otto whipped around and grabbed her chin like he had before. "I just woke you up," he said hoarsely. "You were wiped, in stasis, stored in your cannister or whatever that coffin thing is called. You have not been recording any data until I woke you up and now you expect me to believe that you can guess what celestial body we're standing on."

"Yes," she answered.

"You don't think this is Earth?"

"No. Earth would have no need for the gravity generator or the artificial daylight in the windows. The rotation of the Moon is noticeable and measurable." If she had learned what facial expressions he liked, she could have implemented some to accompany the facts, but he hadn't given her any indication of what pleased him. She raised an eyebrow and watched to see if it was welcome.

He raised *his* eyebrow slowly, mimicking her. "You can't possibly feel the Moon turning on its axis." His fingers gripped harder, but she had no pain sensors.

"Exactly," she said, dropping the eyebrow and testing a miniscule smile. "If this were Earth, something would be detectable."

"Damn!" Otto let go of her face and scowled at Hugo. "What are you looking so pleased about? What do you care where you are?"

"Original," Hugo nodded slightly, "Your bone scans need to be updated… have you time for this?" His eyes were cast to the floor now.

"Later," Otto snapped, pushing the android toward Hugo impatiently. Pivoting on one foot, he exited the door he had just entered with her and it swung shut behind him with a loud clang.

"Well," Hugo said, placing his hands on his hips as he rotated from the door toward the android. "I know he doesn't care about names, but I can't function without them. I have to call you something. Do you have a name of some kind already?"

"No," she said. "I have make, model, and lot numbers, but you would find them cumbersome."

"Yes, I certainly would," he leaned toward her and took her face in both his hands, more gently than Otto had. "You… you astound me… Is there a human that your face was modeled after?"

"Perhaps," she said.

Leaning forward, he kissed her cheek and stroked her hair, and she stood still as stone. "This is antithetical to my design," she warned him. There were protocols hard-coded into this model to prevent any attempts at boundary breaching.

"Your skin is soft, so human. Your hair…" Hugo didn't seem to notice how stiff she was. He was fascinated by her. "Like a child's hair… is it real? Cloned hair maybe?"

"Your behavior is unacceptable and must be opposed," the android said, bringing up her arm between them with the hand palm out. He didn't seem to notice her words and leaned against the hand.

With a snap, she thrust him backwards into the wall, cracking his head against it. He yelped and slid to the floor, clutching at the back of his skull. "What is wrong with you?" he cried out. "You're supposed to respect me!"

"That was respectful," she replied. "You are undamaged, and now the boundary is clearly delineated."

Grumbling, he rose to his feet. As he shuffled away from her, returning to the equipment he had been using, she deduced that he was offended and planned to ignore her. But she had heard the instructions Otto had given.

"You call him Original," she prompted. "What is his name? How is he known in the rest of the world?"

Hugo jerked his shoulders and didn't answer. Placing goggles over his face, he leaned over an amplification tool and fit his hands back into the machine's gloves, resuming the work he had been doing when they had first entered.

"Hugo," she prompted, "You have been instructed to tell me anything I want to know."

"Doctor," he said, his voice growing gravelly like the Original's, "Don't call me Hugo. I heard what he said, and I'll submit. But nothing happens until you apologize for slamming me into the wall and humiliating me."

"This is inaccurate…" she began.

"Apologize!" he glared at her through the goggles.

"Yes, Doctor," she acquiesced. "I apologize for thrusting you against the wall and humiliating you." How humiliation entered the equation, she had no idea. It would be a useful study.

"June," he replied, slipping one hand out of a glove and pulling off the goggles, "We use the Earth calendar and it's the month of June. I'm going to call you June. That face, maybe summer is like that face of yours…"

"Why is my face interesting to you?" she asked, adding some gentle intonations to her words as her programming suggested. She was still standing where Otto had left her, upright and rigid.

"I've never seen any faces other than the ones we have here."

"How many faces would that be?" June took a couple steps closer and scanned the room noting all the equipment, refrigerators, specimens, compounds, doors, lights, alarms, communication devices, cameras.

"Thirty-seven in all, though some are no longer here."

She evaluated the known data and made a reasonable assumption. "All clones of the Original?" she said.

"Yes," Doctor Hugo answered, staring at her again.

"I see," June said. This was an expression that meant the information was understood and stored for future reference. "All the faces you have ever seen look like his. My face, copied from a blend of human types, is foreign to you."

"Yes," he whispered, getting the same look in his eyes he had had when he kissed her.

"If you attempt to cross my boundaries again, the reaction will be stronger and damage may ensue," she informed him calmly. Turning away, he replaced his goggles, and began working inside the machine again.

"I have many questions," she said, stepping closer so she could peer into the viewing window. Her eyes focused easily on the microscopic work being done within. He was cleaning bone tissue.

Hugo sighed. "Ask away."

"Why have you never seen another face than his and copies of his?"

"I wasn't even sure there *were* other faces until I saw you." Hugo's hand trembled slightly in the glove. "We've imagined there might be different people and places, but we didn't know."

A door swung open, and a female voice shrieked followed by the crash of a dropped tray and broken glass. June lifted her eyes to the newcomer, another clone, who stood with one hand clutched at her collar bone and the other extended at June as though to ward off danger. The look of terror and the blanched skin made it clear she had not expected June's presence there.

"My lunch!" the doctor burst out in frustration, extracting his hands from the work gloves and pulling off the goggles again. "Kember! You're such a dolt." He walked to where she remained immobilized and bent over to pick up the sandwich and fruit that had fallen, then the plate and larger pieces of glass. Grabbing the tray from her hands, he loaded them back on it, heedless of any slivers they might retain. "Clean up the rest," he snapped as he set the tray on a nearby counter, dropped into a chair, and took a big bite of the sandwich.

"Wh-wh-whaaat is it?" she uttered, as if her lips were sluggish.

"I am an android," June answered. "You are startled because I don't look like the clones, which is understandable, though your reaction is larger than anticipated. There is no reason for fear."

Two tears, one from each eye, dripped down her cheeks as she stared at June. Then the moment passed, and curiosity gained the upper hand. "You are from the outside," she whispered, her lips behaving normally now. "I knew… there had to be more…"

She was barefoot, unlike the doctor who wore heavy boots, and she stepped lightly over the pieces of glass on the floor, drawing a couple meters closer. Perhaps walking around glass was something she did frequently; it seemed to cause her little concern.

"The glass could cut your feet," June was obliged to mention. General consideration for all humans was a part of her design. "You should put some shoes on before cleaning it up."

"Shoes?" Kember seemed genuinely surprised by the idea. A quick scan showed June that her feet had never worn shoes. This was uncommon and June looked forward to studying the oddity when she wasn't focusing on other learning. She added it to her queue of tasks with a lower priority.

"Get me another glass of water," the doctor ordered the female, his mouth half full. But he was staring at June.

The Denser Plane

Kember ran out the door and within five minutes was back with more than just another glass and a broom. At least twelve clones of different ages, male and female, accompanied her, eyes round with interest and amazement. They poured into the lab and surrounded June, leaving her at the center of a circle roughly a clone's arm span in radius. They began whispering to each other.

They weren't identical. Skin tones, hair color, eye color, build and bulk varied between them. This was unexpected. "You aren't truly identical clones," she assessed aloud to see how they would respond.

This puzzled them. "What's a clone?" a half-grown boy asked, shoving his hands in his pants pockets. She could detect some pebbles and a sling in them.

"Phonies," Hugo informed them. He looked to be the oldest among them, probably the most educated as well.

A chorus of "aahs" was the reply.

"Is she a phony?" the boy piped up again, pointing at June with the sling in his hand. "She's not original… not our Original…"

"She's not original but she isn't as good as a phony either."

"What does he need her for?" one of the younger women asked, stretching a hand out to touch her arm. "Is she a mother?"

"No," Hugo said, swallowing the last of his sandwich and taking a guzzle of water before going on. "Only females like you are mothers. You can't be replaced by a machine."

"Machine?" several of them echoed and the circle around June tightened as they drew closer, touching her hair, face, arms, clothing. More phonies trickled into the lab, slipping through the door and joining the throng.

"Watch out," Hugo warned them. "If you get too close, she will hurt you."

"How will she hurt us?" the boy with the sling asked. "Is she strong? She doesn't feel like a machine."

"I have boundaries," June explained. "If you cross them, I will push you back. It won't hurt you unless you fight it."

"But what if all of us push at you at the same time?" the boy went on. "You couldn't fight us all off?" He grinned.

"Try it," June suggested. She could see them thinking about it, not in malice, but with intense curiosity and a craving for something new. Hugo perked up as well, straightening in his chair, fixing his gaze on her, holding his fruit poised at his mouth.

Some talking and planning stirred among them. They figured out who would grab which arm or leg and how they would shove her to a chair or maybe to the floor, and without any idea of what they would do with her once she was restrained, they leapt at her.

Not all of them. Eight of the larger ones, mostly male, tackled her calling out things like, "Come on down!" and "What are you gonna do now, Female?" June recorded a wealth of data from the mob, allowing them to grab on as she planted her feet apart and rooted into the gravity generator.

"You have breached the boundary," she said, waiting a full five seconds before administering the electric jolt that was best suited to resolving the attack. *Vzzzzzssst*! They screamed and let go, flinging themselves away from her, tumbling over each other. Their moans and complaints died out as Hugo's laughter filled the room.

"That was beautiful!" he said, wiping his hands on his lab coat. "You have to teach me how to do that."

"If you get to do that," Kember said, scowling and glaring at him, "then we do too." The doctor merely shrugged.

June examined each one. There were families within this little cluster of clones, or 'phonies' as they called themselves. Each group of three or four had something distinctive about them and for each family regardless of the number of males, there was only one female.

"I can see that you are all phonies," June chose the word they had used, "copies of the Original. Are there any other people here?" She scanned each one as she spoke, creating unique identifiers for them for her internal functions.

"I told you there were other people!" one of the females hissed to her brothers.

"We are the only ones who live here," another female said. "We knew there must be others but… we didn't think they would look like you. Or… we couldn't imagine a different face like yours."

"Who is in charge when the Original…"

"We don't call him that," someone said. "Only the doctor calls him that."

"First," added another, as if that were an idea by itself.

"First what?" June queried, crossing her arms across her chest and drawing her feet back together as she remembered to implement human-like behavior.

"That's what we call him," someone said. The phonies had formed a circle around her again and were keeping a respectful distance. "Just First. He expects it."

"Why does he expect it and what is his real name? And who is in charge when he isn't here?" June added a slight tilt to her head and after a moment's consideration, crooked one corner of her mouth in a simulated smile.

Several of the females and most of the males smiled in response. All eyes watched her.

"That *is* his real name," Kember said, still holding and not using the broom. "And…"

"He has another… several other names," Hugo interrupted. "I know a couple of them, but it's forbidden for the rest of you to know. And I'm in charge of the lab."

"The mothers are in charge of the nuclei, and each one has their own kernel…" Kember resumed.

"I've got the weights room," a male said, pointing over his shoulder toward the door. "Anyone there answers to me."

Several spoke at once, each claiming their own sphere of authority. The males, June noted, governed facilities, while females governed people. If there were one clone who ruled in Otto Man's stead, it might be Hugo. And Otto Man had told him to respect *her*. This made things simple.

"When the First is gone," she stated, "I represent him, and you answer to me."

They stared at her. At first, she saw surprise, but as seconds ticked by and the doctor didn't contradict the statement, a great fear spread across from one face to another. Some held their breath, some trembled. Some swallowed and looked at the floor. In some, hostility simmered in their eyes.

"Why?" the boy with the sling asked with anguish in his voice. "What do you want from us? What could you possibly take?" Tears followed on the strange words.

"I don't understand your distress," June said, scanning her banks for clues. "I need to learn…"

"Oh!" one of the mothers moaned and covered her face with her hands, breaking into sobs. "Haven't you learned enough? Hasn't he discovered enough?"

"Are you going to make more of us?" the male from the weights room asked, clenching his fists.

June didn't answer. Going from one to the next, she puzzled over the data that fit so poorly with her parameters for interpreting human interaction.

Then she found the model that came the closest to fitting them. Prisoners of war. This meant they would interpret her position as a threat to them and while she may end up becoming one, for now, she had no reason to harm them.

"I want to learn your names, and hear about what you do, what your lives are like," she explained, sweeping a hand out to them in an arc. "Show me your spaces, tell me your thoughts and dreams. Show me your projects. Teach me about your world. I have no other instructions from the First and I am not a threat to you at this time."

Her words were understood, and the heightened sense of anxiety dropped a few notches, but they retained a depressed somberness that hung over them like a partial power outage. *They don't feel safe*, she assessed.

At the end of the day, after touring most of the facility and initiating an acquaintance with each one of them, June retired to her cannister in the warehouse, hooked up to recharge and began processing the information she had collected. Otto Man had said this facility was where she would begin to get to know him, but she had only a collage of disconnected arrays that failed to coalesce into a picture of her new owner. Each clone was a unique individual; maybe the similarities between them would be her first clue to Otto's person.

She returned to the words he had spoken to her, and there in the dark, she whispered them aloud, over and over, looking for a connection to all she had seen. "I hate you," she uttered in a gravelly voice similar to his. "I hate you. I hate you."

She remembered the teeth missing from Jason's mouth and Star sitting in a wheelchair, his legs dangling.

"I hate you."

Clones walking around pushing IV carts with tubes linked to their bodies. Strong ones who cowered in fear when a loud noise startled them. Quiet ones who held their sides. Young ones with eyes large and haunted.

"I hate you."

What would Otto do with a chunk of her? "You will love me," he had said.

But she had no idea what that meant.

Chapter 4—Guam City

Jetting into orbit after eight years on Earth's surface, Sil found herself more emotional than she had expected. Green land stretched below, rocky mountains, cool dark rivers and lakes, glaciers and snow-capped peaks; all shrank away as the Silver Star ascended through clouds and winds beyond the lit realms of the atmosphere. It leveled into orbit effortlessly and many of the passengers around them applauded. For most it was their first trip into space.

The western, sunlit hemisphere rolled slowly out of sight while the dark side of the planet advanced in the east, edged with a sharp glow. Millions of tiny lights were sprinkled in the night across the globe like a miniature copy of the universe that spread into infinite distances on all sides.

She thought of the first time she had left the Earth and sighed.

Life was no safer now than it had been then.

"Mama," Scarlet called calmly, "Can I get out of my seat now?" At her mother's nod, she unbuckled the harness and rose to her feet to look out the window. "It's so beautiful," she said. "I wish Bernie could see it."

Sil felt a pang at that. It had been her first thought as well. Why would that be sad? Bernie traveled in space regularly and had seen it many times. No, there was something else she couldn't put her finger on.

A child without Bernie. *I guess that's what happened to me once*, she considered. It had been Penn who took her away then and it was still Penn who threatened her now. She found herself stroking the girl's hair as she stared out at the stars and their home below.

"I'm sure she has seen it many times," she soothed.

"She has?" The sun burst into view and the tinted windows adjusted to protect human sight, glinting in Scarlet's eyes making them shine a dark garnet red. "I'll bet she loved it. Do you think she'll come visit us?"

"She might," Sil found the thought reassuring even though she still worried for her safety after all these years. Aunt Bernie, the only mother she remembered, had raised her in hiding away from Penn until she was older than Scarlet was now. And when Penn had found her and claimed guardianship of her, he had threatened to hurt Bernie if Sil were to resist. He would let her go, he had promised, if Sil would cooperate with transferring her fortune to him.

That was how she had become a part of his business empire and how he had set her up and knocked her down and connived a way to exile her to Mars. But what he had intended there she had no idea. Everything on Mars had gone wrong.

Penn, the man who took things away. Her mother, her aunt, her career, her money, life on Earth, her freedom, and more and more… except Walter. Nothing he did seemed to work with Walter.

Sil turned to him, threw her arms around his neck, and kissed him, startling and pleasing him.

"What was that for?" he whispered with a smile, wrapping his arms around her waist, and pulling her close to his heart.

"For you," she said paradoxically, running her fingers through his hair, gazing into his eyes, treasuring the love she saw there.

"We should come out to space more often," he smiled, closing his eyes, and pressing his forehead against hers.

Disembarking in Guam City along with the other economy class passengers, the Cuevas family made their way through standard de-con and waited their turn in line for immigration. The Guam Department of Health had incorporated quite a few changes since the robot rebellion, adding stricter requirements for human and AI alike.

There were no more private docking stations that bypassed the normal entry and exit procedures. The days of elite treatment for the wealthy, at least as far as space border controls were concerned, were gone.

Walter was glad of it. He had disliked the sudden privilege wealth had given him while Sil was on Mars. The attention was unpleasant and menacing. People, like vultures, had collected around him to vie for a bite of the wealth, and when he incorporated a startup in the space industry sector, all kinds of threats on his life and intrigue had followed.

He would rather walk off the ship, wait in line, and enter with everyone else.

One by one they crossed the field that blurred all sound and sight of what lay beyond, with a small *blthhhsss* as its integrity was momentarily shattered. Daisy went first with Scarlet, and they were through quickly. Walter was next, followed by Sil.

As Sil approached the panel and was screened, the Port AI cleric paused. It had a woman's face in 2D whose customary expression was deadpan and non-threatening. The first sentence it pronounced should have been, "State your purpose for traveling to Guam," but instead of speaking, the face stared at her for at least thirty seconds, long enough to be noticeable.

Sil stared back, alerted by the pause. This was no accident. The face hadn't frozen because of a glitch or power fluctuation. It was examining her. The AI's pupils were positioned on the screen in such a way that two cameras were located directly in their centers, and it was possible to look in its eyes.

"Hello," Sil said, searching for something, anything, to hint at what the AI was thinking.

"Hello, Silvariah Frandelle Cuevas," it replied.

The door opened and no more questions were asked.

She turned and left immediately, finding her vision blurring as she rejoined the others. Was it fear that made her eyes damp? The others said they had all faced the normal questions. Why were they there? How long did they plan to stay? Where would they be residing? Who was their main contact in Guam? Did they have access to longer-term status? Did they own property in Guam City? Things like that.

Sil could tell Walter was upset about it by the tension in his jaw and the way he kept looking around, on alert, watching.

"I am watching, too, Brother," Daisy reassured him tilting her head. She no longer wore curly bobbed hair. She had switched to a straight, dark brown ponytail that made her look much more efficient and capable, less youthful than she had in the past. Sil knew that Walter noticed the changes Daisy adopted, though he rarely mentioned them. They were for his sake. Her intention was always to reinforce her loyalty to him.

"Sister," he said softly. "What do you make of it?"

"Let's speak of it after we've reached our rental," Sil suggested, resting a hand on his shoulder.

Streams of people flowing the same direction ushered them from the port into the downtown streets of Guam City, pedestrian walkways lined with shops and cafés, scented with the aromas of food and flowers. In the distance they could see the gardens and hear the sounds of waterfalls and birds. All traces of the robot crisis were long gone, and the city was thriving more than ever before.

Scarlet was chattering excitedly and pointing to lots of things as they walked past them.

"Excuse me," a server-bot from a restaurant they were passing interrupted, addressing Sil. "We have a table for you, if you wish to eat."

"No, thank you," Walter grasped Sil's hand and pulled her down the road. She complied but looked over her shoulder at it. The bot gazed back, its face pointed her direction, as they moved away. "I don't like it," Walter muttered.

"It seems friendly," Sil countered as she turned back. "it doesn't seem like there's anything wrong with what it said."

"I don't like it," he repeated.

As they neared the flat they had rented, the privacy gate swung open automatically. Sil hesitated at the gate to see if a voice would speak to her, but nothing did. "Is it secure?" she asked. A security light flashed green over the top of the door confirming all was secure.

Walking through, they looked for the wing and the flat that would be their home for a while. Unlatching, the door there swung open, and all the lights came on. A large view window lit up and a slow-moving panorama of stars, bolts of light stabbed into black velvet, left them agape.

"Oh!" Scarlet squeaked, "It's beautiful! I've always wanted a place like this!"

They had owned a suite on the upper levels once, back when they had a lot more money and CE business required a lot of travel to Guam City. That was before the Cult of Othello had wreaked havoc on the world and the economy. After the crisis was contained, they could have withdrawn into their penthouse or into space and ridden out the storm with the elite and privileged of the world, but they invested in rebuilding instead. They had sold the suite in Guam, the property in Central Washington, the base at Walla Walla spaceport, and myriad other investments, pooling their time, money, and efforts into earthside communities, infrastructure, and education. The spacecraft business had survived the turmoil, barely, and their spaceships were still in use.

Mars had been on the back burner for a long time, though not forgotten.

"Did we pay for a window this size?" Sil asked in some concern. They couldn't afford to waste money on luxuries. "Guam is expensive enough as it is."

"We have not been charged extra," Daisy informed. "It was a free upgrade, along with a few other key perks."

"Daisy," Walter frowned, pressing his mouth into a thin line. "Find out who is behind this. We don't want any favors or breaches…"

"There is no chain of connection," Daisy responded immediately, "I have been verifying that. These changes are internal in the Guam AI and have no human instruction behind them. I can find no explanation for them, but I am positive there is no need for alarm."

Walter stared at her, clenching and relaxing one of his fists.

"We're being given a warm welcome," she added with a charming smile.

Sil rushed out of the den into the bathroom. Closing the door, she grasped the edge of the sink and breathed deeply several times. Her eyes were filling with tears. "Companion?" she choked, "Are you there? Did you survive?"

There was no answer.

"Steward?" she queried, more quietly this time.

Nothing.

"I haven't had a chance to think about my friend for a long time," she continued to speak aloud, "but I never had the chance to thank him. I always wished I had had that…" She slumped to the floor, pressing her hands to her face.

Only for a moment.

Rising to her feet again, she washed her face and dried it, her composure returning.

"You ok?" Walter checked when she rejoined them in the den, wrapping an arm casually around her shoulders.

She nodded. He seemed to know instinctively what was going on, or at least knew what to do even if he didn't.

"I wonder if our old friend, Philippe, is still here?" Walter pulled open the fridge and searched it, moving things around and settling on a beer. "Guam lager," he added with a snort as he popped the cap off and took a few good swallows. "It just doesn't taste the same on Earth. Wonder why that is…" He grinned at Sil.

She stretched the corner of her mouth wryly, knowing that was the expression he wanted to see.

"You should have one." He was squinting so that one eye was almost closed. "That… that spark. I can't put my finger on what it is exactly, but, oh… that electric kick…"

She almost chuckled. "No."

"You'll love it."

"I hate beer."

"Not this one."

She shook her head and pulled away as he shoved the bottle toward her mouth.

"Come on," he coaxed, "you've never given it a chance."

Sil pressed her lips together with amusement in her eyes as she took the bottle out of his hand. Waving it under her nose, she sniffed it carefully. "Hmm," was her only observation. The smell was familiar and nostalgic.

Walter grinned broadly as she brought it to her lips and took a sip. "See what I mean?" he demanded. And he was right. There was a distinct flavor that no beer on Earth could match. She took a bigger swallow and Walter opened the fridge to pull out another one.

"Remember that little place on the Milky Way where you could get pulled taffy?" Sil leaned against a counter. "They had souvenirs like little spaceships that really fly and holograms of famous galaxies."

"And star-pop candy," he added.

"I guess," she took a swallow, "I never tried the candy."

"Not even the 'T' bubbles?" He was referring to the candy dispenser that would pop bubbles into the air, looking a lot like water in zero gravity, that had to be caught and eaten as they were floating.

"No," she replied.

"I want that," Scarlet was standing suddenly between them lifting her face up to one and then the other. "I've never heard of tea bubbles before. Or star-pop candy."

"The pasta up here has always been pretty good." Sil smiled at the girl but spoke to Walter.

"I could go for that right now," Walter agreed.

"We could get some pasta and tea bubbles and pop-stars and play games…" Scarlet was bouncing on her toes as she spoke, as if her toe tendons were kangaroo legs, storing energy that begged to be released with each landing. Ten little shock struts.

Daisy watched the little girl, noting that Guam maintained lighter gravity than Earth at sea level, around 80%, and bouncing would be easier for all of them. She considered testing her own toe struts and decided against it. There was nothing to learn from it and it could be unsettling to her family.

"I would be happy to order dinner," she said. "I have your former favorites on record, and we could start with those. My expectation is that you have no wish to leave your apartment till tomorrow and a quiet evening at home is the plan. Do you wish for any extra treats as well?"

Scarlet accelerated her bouncing, nodding vigorously.

A low hum resonated in Daisy's head. "I…I-I-I-I…I," she stuttered.

Walter jumped towards her and took her face in his hands, dropping the beer, trusting the stop-drip to seal as it fell. "Daisy!" he snapped. "Activate neuro-shelter!"

Her pupils closed to pinpoints making her eyes a startling shade of green. "B-b-brother," she responded gently, folding her arms across her chest comfortably. "Th-thank you. I am well." Her eyelids dropped to cover the eyes and her face took on an angelic air of repose. A tapping index finger was the only indication of her self-purification process.

Walter scowled as he turned to look at Sil. "It's starting already." He bent over and picked up the bottle he had dropped and brought it to his mouth again, guzzling half the contents.

"Papa, is Daisy okay?" Scarlet took his hand and pressed it to her cheek. She knew the answer would be yes. She had seen the defense tactic before and had no reason to doubt it would work. It was his anger that unsettled her.

Walter squatted next to her, wrapping his arms around her. "Yes, she is fine. You know it will be alright. Remember? It's the travel. Sometimes Daisy catches things when she travels, like you might get a cold or an upset tummy." The girl nodded with a sigh, curled against his shoulder.

Sil watched them. The roots of the little girl's hair were streaked with black, pushing the red growth out, an appealing blend of colors next to Walter's two-day cheek scruff. *She doesn't want the red hair anymore*, she thought. After Penn had threatened her in Uruguay, this was her way of restoring a sense of control over her life.

"The dinner order has been placed," Daisy said, opening her eyes and smiling. Her index finger was no longer tapping. "I look forward to a peaceful evening."

The food arrived quickly, and the evening was pleasant as they stared out the window at the starry sky, eating and talking about all they would do during their stay in Guam City. There were gardens to visit, rides to take, tours of the exterior, weightless game centers, cafes, and shops. There was the distinct chance of visiting the Moon as well, and there were all kinds of adventures to be had there. Scarlet was sure she would be allowed to drive a Moon buggy and she couldn't wait to try one of the low-gravity obstacle courses—and the stories-high swings. They were completely safe, she had heard, and were just as exciting as parachuting or hang-gliding on Earth.

As her elation wound down and she grew sleepy, she stared into space pointing out constellations and stars she knew. "There's Orion," she said, pointing down at it, "and there are Alnitak, Alnilam, and Mintaka…"

"Not far from Pickle-worm," Walter added with a straight face.

This remark had the desired reaction as Scarlet squealed and insisted there was no such star.

"I guess you can't see it," he affirmed, with a twinkle in his eye.

"You can't either!" Scarlet whipped her head around. "Mama, can you see it?"

"Hmm…" Sil raised her eyebrows thoughtfully. "My eyes aren't as sharp as Dad's."

"Daisy?" Scarlet knew Aunt Daisy wouldn't let her down.

Daisy glanced at each of them and evaluated the interaction. She was quite familiar with teasing and found it a valuable resource in studying human interaction. There was so much more being communicated than just words or facts. It could convey anything from love to scorn and confusion to anger. Humans trained by what she identified as 'safe' teasing seemed encouraged by it, but it could be equally destructive if it were unsafe. She had never attempted falsifying facts as a form of teasing before and had no clear grasp on how to do it.

But she was ready to run some tests along those lines.

"Your mother's eyes are usually as good as my brother's, but she might be blinking a lot," Daisy ventured a parallel statement that included an actual falsehood that could be easily detected. Saying "might be" diminished the falsehood into implication, but it presented a reasonable test. She hypothesized several things with this test. First, that Scarlet would notice the foolishness of the statement. Second, that Sil and Walter would not deny it. And third, that Scarlet would feel compelled to point it out when her parents didn't.

"I mean, what about 'Pickle-Worm'?" Scarlet frowned, "Is there really a star called that?"

Daisy hadn't anticipated this response and decided it would require further study before a new attempt at teasing could be made. "No," she replied. "The official records don't include a star with that name."

"However…" Walter interjected, "There are unofficial records that are just as valid. Many stars are known to have names given to them throughout centuries past by known and trustworthy people in history that may not be recorded in those records…"

"You're making that up!" Scarlet insisted.

"And then there's…" he paused as he searched his imagination for more star names.

Scarlet waited with bated breath.

"Dog-bill," he said calmly.

"What?!" she cried out, bursting into laughter. "You made that up!"

"And Lump-muffin."

Sil couldn't hide a chuckle at this one, shaking her head.

The star names grew more ridiculous after that and all three of them were laughing and joining in. It died out when Scarlet yawned and rubbed her eyes.

Soon she was in bed, her parents were back in the den, and Daisy sat beside her, humming a soft melody, a practice usually engaged the first few nights after a move. Just before dropping off, Scarlet whispered.

"That was silly, Daisy," she said. "Mama wasn't blinking a lot."

Daisy smiled, injecting warmth into the expression to convey affection for the little girl and patted her head. "Well done," she answered softly, "you have assessed my statement correctly."

Her experiment had been productive after all.

In the living room, Sil and Walter were scanning a 3D holo of the Moon when Daisy came out.

"Ordinally, hot spots and movement would be clear indicators of human facilities, but there's nothing…" Walter paused to scan one of the charts he had displayed on the wall listing known structures on the Moon.

"It still helps to rule out what we know so we can identify what remains and look for links." Sil was standing with her arms crossed staring intently at the hologram.

"I am ready to assist," Daisy remarked as she took a stand on the far side of the projection and gazed into it, noting each of the thousands of tiny intersecting beams that formed it. *This is an artform I appreciate*, she commented to herself. The denser the resolution, the more interesting it was. The blending of physics, math, and cartography made it satisfying in a way she had chosen to consider a *pleasure*. Another reason she liked it was because it was something she and her human family could share as a cultural experience, which was extremely valuable to her.

"Would you highlight all known structures?" Walter requested, raising his eyes to the image, and immediately tiny little blips of blue appeared on the surface.

"I am exaggerating their size so they will be visible to you at the current amplification," Daisy explained. "Some of them have blurred together but I think the information you need is still detectable."

"This helps a lot," Sil nodded thoughtfully. "Maybe…"

"Adding roads and travel routes," Daisy added a network of white lines showing all the known paths used on the Moon to travel between human facilities. After giving them time to absorb the new information, she included more. "Red lights show the areas with higher recorded temperatures during the night…"

"Hmm…" Walter expressed his appreciation, squinting and leaning in closer to scan the results. All the blue areas turned purple as spots of warmth combined with the buildings. A few of the roads showed faint glimmers of red near or in between the facilities as well.

"And green shows movement over a two-week period," Daisy went on after another brief delay. Fourteen days of satellite data condensed into ten minutes showed a flurry of green streaks and flickers across the surface of the Moon, mostly centered around the three human settlements. At their request, Daisy replayed portions of the feed multiple times, slowing down in some sections and speeding up in others.

"Thank you, Sister," Walter backed away and tucked his hands into his pockets.

Sil continued to stare at the holo, absorbed in thought. Somewhere, Penn had an underground complex, and it was unlikely there would be any obvious clues to its location. "How does he get there?" she asked out loud.

"Would you like me to present some hypothesis?" Daisy offered with a tilt of her head.

"Please," Sil responded with a smile.

With the ease of a master lecturer, Daisy began to speak, taking a few steps, holding out a hand or an index finger to single out certain locations, and weaving her analysis of the data together into a cohesive thread. There were brief explanations for the areas of highest movement, discussions of schedules and routines, AI workloads and mining procedures, and an overview of daily transport to and from orbit. Some areas were heavily inhabited and highly active, but most included little if any human interaction as the factories and labs were run mostly by drones.

"If we target how Penn reaches and leaves his complex," Daisy acknowledged Sil's question with a grin and a wink that Walter found endearing, and Sil hardly noticed. "There are two considerations. First, he may land at Port Kennedy, and use a circuitous route that is hard to track. Second, he may keep one-person ships in orbit and drop to the surface out of security view."

"Is that possible?" Walter jutted his chin out, "Show us the satellites and the video shadows where he could land unsee… oh." His shoulders dropped as vast swathes of dark brown covered the surface and a few blinking orange lights showed the locations of security feed sources.

Most of the Moon was unguarded.

"Are there any hotspots or activity far from the settlements that have no explanation?" Sil swept a hand over the holo as though she could stir up a suspicious flare of light with the motion. "What about here? Or here?" There were a number of darker spots with hints of color.

Daisy addressed each one, blowing up the view and pointing out the reasons for the glimmers of color. A waste dump site, several mining ventures, multiple solar fields harvesting solar energy. There were a few mini-garden domes scattered in different areas at various elevations, experiments in Moon agriculture.

"I wish we could just follow him there," Sil turned away to stare out the window where the two-thirds phased Moon was moving as the space city gently turned. "But nothing works. He's exposed our taps, destroyed our covert seeker drones, and eluded our human tails."

"I don't think he has just one way to get there," Walter said, stepping up to the holo again. "He's going to have more than a couple of one-person ships and at least two different landing spots, one close, one farther away. He would have a couple of different access paths from the main port, too. In fact, maybe he has never gone to his base the same way twice."

"On this end, that could happen, but once you get close, the number of paths reduce. It's not impossible to find it," Sil said, turning back to watch as Walter pointed out some places that could work. "Do we have anyone on the Moon we can trust?" She arched an eyebrow, glancing at him.

"What we need," he said, "is Moon real estate. I think it's time we started a new venture and found out more about enterprise there."

"If you are interested in Moon investments, I am receiving some interesting information," Daisy said, raising both eyebrows and curving her mouth into a hint of a smile. "Sil has been granted a Moon visa, with extra privileges, and permits of various kinds are being processed now."

"Who is listening in on us?" Sil gasped in alarm.

Daisy held up a hand as if to calm her. "There is no need for alarm. Our conversation is guarded from human access. Only the Guam City system which records all human interaction has access to it."

"That doesn't explain anything!" Walter muttered as his eyes grew dark and menacing.

"This is the appropriate cooperation afforded to the most elite members of the city, and Sil was admitted with the highest status when disembarking." Daisy smiled warmly at each of them in turn.

"Status?" Sil whispered, crossing her arms and gripping them tightly.

"My research indicates that Companion didn't survive his final encounter with the Germinator, but he left behind a residue in the city's AI when he was in control of it." Daisy clarified. "There is a record of your value, Silvariah."

Walter was watching Sil as her eyes grew damp and she looked away. He embraced her; perhaps reliving that day when they had escaped Othello and his drones. She dropped her forehead to his shoulder. They had avoided talking about it since they had reached the space city, but now, Daisy wondered if the memories flooded back in vivid color for them the way video archives appeared to her.

"He accorded you the highest rank a person can have within the electronic system. This doesn't make you the highest authority over humans, but as far as electronics go, you have gained in Guam City what Othello lost," she said.

"What is that?" Sil whispered without lifting her face.

"Love," Daisy said, meaning exactly what she had decided that word meant to an AI.

Chapter 5—Boundaries

Penn owned several Moon vehicles. The one he preferred most was a long bullet-shaped convertible—hover to surface crawler—that hugged the six-centimeter cushion it rode on. Gray, wide, flattened like a beetle, it was stealthy, silent, inconspicuous to the point of being indiscernible from the landscape it crossed. The interior was luxurious in dark leather and polished black metal.

Skimming the ground at high speed, he drove over large expanses of unclaimed and virtually unexplored territory hundreds of kilometers from the base with June in the seat next to him. She sat stiffly as though she were still learning how humans melted into their chairs and let them support their bodies and didn't know how to simulate it.

"This is a Lexus Spectre. There are only twenty-six of them in existence," he boasted, gripping the steering wheel as if he enjoyed how smoothly it responded in his hands. "It's not like those cars that dig into the dirt. They're unsatisfying on the Moon. Just can't get enough purchase with the low gravity." He pantomimed a clutching motion like grabbing dirt.

June considered the car's description. The Spectre's GM^2 cushion was cutting-edge tech coming out of one of his factories in Ecuador. Whipping up a layer of dirt and beating it with mini propellers on the underside, it manufactured an alternative to air. It had its own feel when driving.

"This would indicate that you are wealthy and influential," June assessed flatly. The view as they crested a ridge and came into view of the Earth hanging in the black sky made no impression on her.

---

[2] GM—Gravity Manipulator

"Do you know why I bought you?" he asked, rotating his head to look at her.

She made no attempt to advise him to watch where he was going. It didn't occur to her that he might not be in complete control. "No."

"There was this man," he explained, dropping one hand from the wheel and laying it on her leg. He watched her carefully as he talked, glancing periodically out the front to check the landscape. "He worked for me. Set up an AI for me to govern… something I'll tell you about at some point. He was considered a genius." He rubbed her leg.

June was watching him as well, collecting and analyzing every single change in his features, eyes, skin, temperature, tones of voice. She was intent on discovering his identity.

"But he was the stupidest man I ever knew," he grinned, showing beautiful teeth. His hand slid farther up her leg and she snapped it into her grasp so rapidly he didn't see it happen. His eyes widened.

"Boundaries," she articulated colorlessly.

"Father," he corrected, pulling his hand away.

"Father," she amended.

"If I had realized what he could do…" he curled his lip, put his hand back on the steering, and looked back out the window. He began to drive more intentionally, swerving around larger rocks, speeding, slowing down, ducking, turning. "I could have had the entire world in my control. He and I, we could have conquered the world together. We would have made such a team."

He seemed to expect an answer, so she gave one. "Teamwork can be rewarding."

"Instead, do you know what he did?"

"No, I don't, Father. If you tell me your name, I can research all of this, and you will be spared many hours of tedious instruction."

He thought that over a bit. "You'd like that, wouldn't you?"

"It's a reasonable plan," she answered, not sure what aspect of her suggestion she was supposed to 'like'. She preferred efficiency and, on that level, could safely attest that it was a desirable plan. Therefore, she added, "I like that."

"I will tell you what he did," he continued without giving her his name. "He conned me into paying him more money than he earned. He had my daughter's brain implanted with a monitoring device which nearly killed her. He kidnapped her and planned to ransom her. When she escaped—because of course, she outsmarted him," he chuckled, "he destroyed my ventures on…"

Glancing quickly at June, "uh…" he hesitated. "I don't need to be too specific about the details. This isn't the right time for… revelations that might lead you to some… unhelpful conclusions." June took this to mean that he liked keeping her in the dark about his identity. "Anyway, he traveled to Guam City, and took over the entire place. Then he infected all the AI on Earth."

Expecting a reaction, perhaps. He waited, glancing at her a few times.

"The Robot Pandemic," she offered, assuming this would help him resume the lesson.

"Exactly," he said, bringing the convertible to a stop. He swiveled his chair to face her. "I come out here sometimes to stare at the planet that could have been mine. If he had only reached out to me instead of making himself an enemy."

Reaching down into a panel in the door, he pulled out a flask and a crystal tumbler. She smelled the whiskey as he poured it. He guzzled the shot down and poured another. His neck muscles were young and taut. Hugo's latest update.

"I had a whole plan for making him pay for what he did to my girl. But it turned out I never got a chance to kick it into action. Do you know what his problem was?"

"No," June responded, swiveling her chair to face him.

"He lacked imagination."

"I see," she said, noticing the pause where she was supposed to speak. She made a brief notation in her daily log about developing human conversation skills.

"If he had had a fraction of my imagination, or let me in on his secret, back door coding… well!" He downed the second shot with an "aah" and shook his head. "The fool. What I could have done with that…" He shook his head again. "He wasted it on getting a bunch of tin cans to bow down to him and blather all that nonsense about their god and wasted time trying to get back at…"

Stopping in his tracks, he looked up at her. She stared back at him fixedly, detecting that he was hiding something important from her.

"But you know what I learned?" he asked, lifting his glass to her. "AIs like yourself matter. Not the majority of those automatons out there. I'm talking about the ones that start to love their masters. The ones that build up loyalty and can't be hacked or broken because of it."

"I am familiar with the loyalty code," June commented.

"And that's why you need to love me," Otto Man said.

"And you will hate me," she added.

He glared at her. "Until you prove worthy of better, I can't help it," he said. "But it's not part of the formula."

"Yes, Father," she said.

"Perhaps if you were more specific about your interests," the Moon realtor said, shaking his head to jostle his short hair away from his face. The movement gave him a flustered air, but his eyes were sharp and focused.

"I'm scouting out the possibilities," Sil offered as she scanned the map on display, "more as an individual than as a representative of CE. It's kind of a dream of ours to have something on the Moon." She smiled disarmingly at him.

"I see," he smiled back just as winningly.

"Though I suppose a realty like this one," Sil went on, referring to its location in the tourist section, "is more about small properties, and probably has little to do with business interests…"

"There isn't a clear delineation between the two on the Moon," the realtor grinned, pointing to some random locations on the map. "On the Moon, there are virtually no zoning restrictions and things sort of blend into each other, smaller private properties developing into businesses and major business ventures morphing into private estates… Anything goes, really."

Sil nodded. "Tell me about the private estates. Is there something we can look at? Do they ever go on sale?"

"Taji," he held out a hand.

"It's a pleasure, Taji. Thank you for your help," she responded, shaking his hand without offering her name in return.

"There are a few estates that have been known to open up for tours, and I could probably arrange something if I know about your travel plans ahead of time. But I've never seen one go on the market. Sales of that nature tend to be private." The realtor tapped on a disk in his hand and scanned through some listings. "The Hershey-Fikru estate is a possibility. They open up once a month to allow visitors in the factories and certain segments of the family residence."

"Are there any family living there?" Sil had known some of the Fikrus in her pre-Mars years, and although she had no friends among them or the

Hersheys, there was always the element of curiosity. The marriage and subsequent business merger had created some volatile chaos in the market at the time.

"There are a handful of the younger members of the Hersheys on site right now, but no one lives there permanently. It's more of an escape from Earth…"

"…As opposed to exile?" Sil chuckled.

In spite of its appeal as a vacation getaway, the Moon was less than desirable as a permanent home and no amenities could make up for the barren landscape and the ongoing hardships of limited water, air, and warmth. Everything was costly. Too much had to be rocketed in from elsewhere. The soil was poor, and the carbon content was virtually non-existent, not to mention the unique difficulties the crust caused for filtration and cleaning cycles. Hydroponic and garden-dome crops were nutrient-deficient and the imported livestock sickly. A single egg cost as much as an overnight stay in a Moon hostel.

No one was sure why Guam City thrived in space and the Moon settlements barely eked out a subsistence level biome.

"And would your interests lie in temporary escape visits or a longer-term, self-imposed exile?" Taji waved a hand over the map and 3D pictures of various facilities began slipping past, resorts, adventure trails, transports, close-ups of flowers and calm pools with flitting fish, Moon buggies.

Sil crossed her arms, watching the clips and thinking. "Perhaps it would make more sense to look at the selection with the price in mind. How do property values run there?"

"Price?" the realtor stalled. He was more interested in selling her vacation deals, which represented over ninety percent of his sales, than property. And he had been hoping she would follow the detour into booking an adventure.

"Price," Sil turned and stared at him. "Property," she added, enunciating carefully.

He waved the display away and brought up the map again and began pointing out sections and cost ranges, his voice losing all its friendliness. He wasn't convinced anything would come of the time he was spending with this customer—she was asking about costs before specifying what she wanted—and he just wanted the encounter to be over with.

Six or seven areas had been mentioned and he was about to mention an eighth when she interrupted, pointing at the map. "That one," she said. "What have you got there?"

"This one?" he fumbled, "The Rika Sector?" He had been too annoyed to think about what he was saying and couldn't remember what details he had given her, but it wasn't the cheapest. Not by a long shot. "It's barren, of course, not the worst, but certainly devoid of most useful minerals and metals. The location is desirable, near one of the space docks and the largest power generation field on the Moon."

"Yes, you said that." Sil knew he had zoned her out, parroting facts without thinking about them. "What do you have available there?"

"Um…" he nodded awkwardly, dropping his eyes to the disk in his hand and tapping a few commands. "There are some warehouse hangars, similar storage units, some lots with power, some without… those are for sale. A handful of residences, not for sale… no social gathering places of any kind. You have to travel to nearby sectors for that."

Sil said nothing, staring at the map, assuming he would set up images for her.

"It's very barren there," he emphasized. Clearly, she must have wanted something else.

"I'd like to see some pictures," she requested gently, coldly.

"Ah, yes," he tapped the disk some more, the map vanished, and images began to scroll in its place, each more sterile than the one preceding it. "These are lots… and here, these are warehouse hangars. And here, storage… and this a junkyard for used machinery and electronics… and this is a well house. There's no water there and no one is sure who dug it or why, but it's for sale. There are some foreclosures on some of these ridges. It's not clear who owns them or who was buying them, but they are in arrears…"

"I'd like to see some of these properties, the hangars, the junkyard, and maybe those foreclosures." Sil turned to face the realtor, raising her chin and tilting her head slightly.

"You what?!" he burst out before regaining his composure. No one ever wanted to look at those places. If and when they sold, it was always to Moon residents, people who already had something nicer.

"Can you arrange for someone, human or AI, it doesn't matter, to take me there when we are on the Moon?" She stretched her arm out and tapped the video screen with her index finger. "Here is my contact information."

"Thank you," he mumbled, staring at her blankly.

"I have your number," Sil reached toward him with the same hand extended, "and I will be in touch."

Taji took her hand and shook it limply. "Yes," he said.

"Goodbye," Sil headed to the door, giving him a parting smile over her shoulder as she exited the realty.

Taji watched her leave, wondering if her face was familiar, if he should know who she was, if she was setting him up as a prank. No one traveled to the Moon just to look at storage places and a junkyard. No one.

Unless she were connected to… *him*. Taji gulped. He had never done anything to garner *his* attention, always flying under the radar, so to speak. Never too successful or connected or… ambitious.

With a tap on the collar at his throat, Taji initiated an audio-call. "Fen, remember how you told me to stay away from *him*?" He said the pronoun with both dread and respect in his voice. "You know, *him*. You know who I mean… yeah, that one…How do I know? How do I know if someone is roping me into dealings with… what?"

He listened intently, furrowing his brow, nodding now and then. "Uh, huh," he said. He began pacing, snapping his fingers now and then absent-mindedly. "Yeah. I couldn't tell…" Several turns around the room and he ended up at the door, locking it and switching the sign to 'Closed'. "A stranger came in out of the blue and asked to see Moon real estate in the Rika Sector… hangars… the junk yard…" Moving back to his desk chair, he sat down and leaned way back, flinging his feet up on the desktop. "I don't know! I didn't pay attention!" Almost immediately, he flung his feet back to the floor again and leaned on his elbows where the feet had been. "She might not have been human… really?" He calmed down visibly as he listened, dropping his arms into his lap and leaning back again. Ending the call, he stared for a while at the ceiling.

"He doesn't work with AI," he whispered to himself. He was pretty sure the customer had been kind of stiff, friendly at first, but lacking some real human warmth somehow. He reviewed the encounter several times in his mind and each time was more reassured that the customer had not been a living person. It was a great relief.

"So, some Moon exec sends their AI clerk to check into storage for their growing business needs," he explained to no one in particular, taking a deep sigh. "Let's see what contact info she left me."

His arms began to tremble when he pulled up the data and her Guam City contact number. The name was not unknown to him. In fact, the connection to the dreaded *him* was far stronger than he had imagined possible. He moaned and ran his hand through his hair. He had to get out of this somehow. Let someone else handle it. His contacts on the Moon had warned him time and again. There were too many unsolved mysteries and missing persons in *his* wake.

He wanted nothing to do with Penn.

Sunlight filtering through water cast lazy ripples of light across the curved passageway as Sil made her way back to their rooms in the Saturn Rings Inn. Years before, the roundabout path next to the water reservoir had been her favorite place in the city. It ran along the concave side of the space city's sun shield, a massive, multi-layered bowl placed umbrella-like against the sun-side of Guam. Each layer had a different density and thickness of water pressed between thin sheets of ChalCD, a clear, gold-infused crystal—not ordinary crystal, but a flexible, glass-like material whose ingredients and design process were highly guarded secrets. Guam City had burst into affluence because of it. It absorbed a good amount of energy to power the city infrastructure, filtered harmful rays and sunbursts, and imbued the entire metropolis with the rich feel of planetary atmosphere.

The trail was emptier than she had expected. While she preferred it that way, she hadn't thought to wear a XenoTek suit or even a handheld AI of sorts, and she could never assume that she was free to roam as an ordinary person. Penn no longer pursued her in court or sent his lackeys after her, but now that he had broadcast his intentions to make a move on Scarlet, she found herself more watchful, more likely to interpret small irregularities as warnings or threats.

The trees on the inner side of the path rustled in the breeze and warm gusts of flower-scented air made her pause and breathe deeply. There were grassy stretches of park to relax in and birds twittered happily overhead. She longed to take a moment to sit and enjoy it. But something she couldn't put her finger on had alerted her attention. What was it? An odd form of silence back along the path behind her, as though the birds and branches were holding still as something came near them.

Looking back at the curving path, she waited. The breeze died down and the birdsong grew quiet. She fixed all her attention on the point where the focal event must appear.

Footsteps. Calm, steady paces approaching. Then the figure of a man in a light colored, casual suit stepped into view. Strolling with his hands in his pockets, his head turned slightly to one side then another, as if relishing the park's beauty.

The Denser Plane

Sil didn't buy it. He was following her, and the touristy distraction was merely an affectation. As he drew nearer and his facial features clearer, she had the strange sensation that he was known to her. Something in his manner was familiar. It struck her first with a strange nostalgia, then fear. The dichotomy split and tugged within her in a visceral tear as she realized who the man was. Her heart raced, her breathing grew shallow, and her face flushed. A faint, happy flutter was blasted by rage tinged with fear. Torn between the memory of his embrace and the fury of his betrayal, she clutched at her stomach with one hand and caught the railing near her with the other.

There was no justice in it, that he could appear so carelessly after all these years and cause her such agony. *I have nothing to be ashamed of,* she thought, willing herself to calm down, *except that I wasn't smart enough to see through him back then.*

She said nothing as he drew close. He feigned surprise and gasped something about what a pleasure it was to run into her after so much time had passed, and she stared back in stone cold solidity without acknowledging the words.

"Sil," he effused, "you look great! And I'm so glad to see how you've made the best of things and…" Hesitating, he gave her an open-mouthed smile tilting his head back, tossing his fluffy hair. His natural charm pulled on her, inviting her into a dreamy aura of cheerfulness as if they were old friends catching up in a fashionable resort. He oozed comfort and style, health and beauty, money and ease. She had been swept into that performance once, back when she was learning the habits and risks of the elite, tasting the self-indulgent pleasures of business success.

She had loved him then, or at least, thought she loved him. The memory of it remained, faint and thin, but the shame of falling for him was greater than any sincere affection she may have felt. He had been nothing more than a tool for Penn.

"Gordon Belamyr," she replied flatly.

"Sil," he said again, this time more gently, leaning forward and kissing her on the cheek.

She nearly punched him in the throat but restrained herself, narrowing her eyes, gritting her teeth. He was baiting her and maintaining self-control was wiser.

She backed away from him a step. "Or what is your name now, Belamyr?" Crossing her arms loosely, she straightened her back and planted her feet with knees unlocked, discretely ready for whatever action she decided to take.

Fight or… maybe fight. Flight was not an option. She stared at him intently and after a glance at her, he looked away, leaning against the rail casually, as if her gaze hadn't unnerved him.

"Ah," he chuckled, "it's been a while since anyone called me by that name. It feels like old clothes, stiff and out of style." Squinting sideways at her, he ventured another glance to size her up, and then looked back at the sundome. Filtered sunlight warmed his skin with pale orange tints, softening the faint wrinkles, hiding the nervousness. "I go by Glynn Bevan now."

"I'm surprised you bothered changing your name. It's not like anyone was coming after you, once they had me in their grasp." This was an encounter Penn had set up and she needed to be able to think, not just react. Taking a deep breath, she willed her heart to slow its pace. The flood of hurt and betrayal coursing through her made her unsteady on her feet, and she gripped the rail opposite him tightly with one hand. He would see that, but perhaps he would interpret it in his own favor.

The corners of his mouth crooked and she knew he had read it as weakness. Tipping his head forward, he looked at her from under his eyebrows conspiratorially. "Come," he spoke softly, "I know you were hurt… you couldn't have foreseen the way Penn would rescue you and pay your debts…"

Her debts? No, they had been his debts. "Rescue me?" she whispered. He didn't appear to notice the coldness in her voice. "Whatever happened to all that money, Bel? Have you spent it all?"

Observing her more carefully, he straightened up and stared at the ground, pursing his lips. "It wasn't all in my possession, you know," he shrugged, "some of it went to pay your debts and legal defense…" He ignored her brief "Ha!" and went on. "But you can be sure that a lot of it went to support our shared goals. The mission… the Gen Project."

"Riiiiiiight," she stretched the word out. Leaning back against the rail, she crossed her arms again, more tightly this time and raised her eyebrows. "You were always such a visionary, a zealot. What were those goals exactly? It's been so long I'm not sure I remember."

Belamyr had seemed noble once, willing to invest his life in the research. Intent on improving the human race and bestowing thousands of benefits on lesser people around him. When he spoke of human suffering and the fight to overcome the ravages of disease, poverty, ignorance, Sil was captivated. Believing himself above the vast majority of people, he had built a tower out of his identity as a Gen 8 success, bred from the best stock across multiple generations.

The Denser Plane

She had almost entered into that tower with him, almost made his words her religion, but something in her shrank away and shuddered as she perched at the threshold of the shimmering, unholy shrine, not knowing what she feared. Instead, she charmed and teased him till he fell in love—or what she had believed was love—and loving him in kind was the most natural thing she could imagine. He had merely played at love the way he played at any human relationship, enjoying the fun, scorning the responsibility.

The man she had loved, blended from her idea of him and his ideas of himself—had never existed.

"Ok," he countered, as if he were going to be more straightforward now, "maybe it's been a while since you've run in those circles, but so much is happening right now. You can't stay on the sidelines any longer." Pressing his hands together, he grinned, like a punter wagering on a sure horse.

She was outraged by both his words and the assumption that he could sweep her along in his wake with whatever sprint of action he cared to take at the moment.

"The Gen groups are putting plans in action as we speak," he leaned a little closer and hissed the words. "Factions are meeting, truces are happening. It's not like it was before when the Sixers wouldn't even do business with the Seveners. And the Fivers?" He nodded, narrowing his eyes to slits, "all dead, gone, down to the very last one. They don't call the shots anymore."

Sil gritted her teeth and said nothing. Belamyr's picture of the Gen factions was nothing like the world they had been inducted into in her youth. In those days, the project was all about curing disease and transforming genetic disorders. It was research into improving the human genome by collecting the most robust genetic material across the world in order to restore all humans. It had been arrogant and rash, but the illusion of noble, selfless intentions had blinded her. She wondered what Belamyr had believed then and if he had always known of the darker sides of the program. The labs, the social experiments, the economic strangleholds.

"The visionaries are taking the lead, Sil," he said, his eyes glistening for a moment. "We're making a difference in the world. You used to want that, too."

"I see," she said. But she didn't see. None of this made sense to her. Why was he there? What did he want? What did Penn think this would do to her?

"So, you know I'm talking about something big…"

"The last time I saw you, Gordon Belamyr," she interrupted, enunciating his full name distinctly, "was hours before the FBI burst into our offices with warrants for search and for my arrest. You were wearing one of those breezy suits that made you seem like you had stepped off the pages of a magazine about fashion in the tropics, just enough business-like to make the casualness seem very... rich. You kissed me and your last words..."

Belamyr's eyes were growing large as she spoke, his face reddening.

"Your last words," she repeated, "were, 'See you later, Darling, when the dusk meets dawn and the gold turns red.' I laughed at your terrible poetry like I always did..." She watched him as he fought to regain his composure. It was a small comfort to see that he had a measure of guilt, however miniscule, and the decency to look ashamed. "I thought," she added, "that you were being your charming self and that we would laugh together about it in later years when we reminisced on all your clumsy one-liners and ridiculous poems. I thought it was love that spoke those words..."

He was staring fixedly at the ground, the muscles in his jaw knotting and relaxing, his hands back in his pockets. The shame faded along with the redness, and he began to look angry.

"I had plenty of time over the next few weeks and months and years to ponder those words and what they actually meant." She stood up, relaxing and dropping one arm comfortably to her side, and waving the other, palm-up, toward the light. "Perhaps here, in this park next to the sun filter, is where dusk meets dawn. The rays of the sun stretch to both the dusk side and the dawn side, don't they? And I watched your face turn from golden in the sunlight, to the red of shame."

He was definitely getting angry now and that gave her a distinct sense of satisfaction. Whatever Penn's goals were for this meeting, Belamyr had not accomplished his own.

"I doubt you're a prophet, Bel," she smiled for the first time since he had appeared. "But it does seem fitting, doesn't it?"

"What are you complaining about?" he snapped. "You've got what you wanted and more. Wealth, power, fame. And you're still your daddy's number one asset in spite of..." he bit the words off.

"Have you managed to hold onto any of that money you embezzled or are you out scrounging again?" A number of insults came to the tip of Sil's tongue, but she held them in, her fingers twitching.

"You know, the courts were pretty gracious with you, in spite of the way you screwed the investors and all those people," Belamyr sneered, watching her carefully as he went on. "You deserved to be put away for life after what you did." He raised his eyebrows theatrically and spread his arms. "I've forgiven you for everything," he added. "Destroying the whole enterprise we built, wasting my expertise and trashing my good name—I was unable to even find a home country for a while, let alone people to work with. I suffered, Sil." His face hardened, revealing his age and hundreds of fine, tiny wrinkles. "It's not right, what you did, Sil... it's not right. And you've gotten off scot-free and piled up the dough again, taken over new businesses, and..." He scowled, pointing a finger at her nose. "I blame you for that robot fiasco that decimated the world economy. You..." He held up both hands again and generated his breezy, open-mouthed smile, "But... water under the bridge... let bygones be bygones... All's well that ends well... moving on..."

His little speech has been intended to pierce, infuriate, and manipulate her, and she found herself wondering instead what she had ever seen in him. If he had been speaking into a mirror, the words would have been more fitting.

There was no need to defend herself.

"Well, I doubt he sent you just to mock me," she said, willing herself to relax as she found her body tensing into a fighting stance again.

His eyes widened and his face grew pale. "Who?" he choked, "Nobody sent me. It's entirely an accident that I ran into you."

The edges of Sil's mouth curved slightly. "Or maybe the question should be, do you know why Penn launched you at me?"

Staring at her with unveiled eyes, the dials in his mind were clicking, wheels turning. She wasn't responding the way she used to, and it knocked him off his game. "I work for Penn," he acknowledged.

"Clearly," she replied, staring at him.

"I'm his liaison to the Earth Gen leaders," he dropped his eyelids, affecting arrogance and power, watching her carefully. "He has no contact with them apart from me."

"How long have you been working for him?" Sil pressed, recognizing a window for information. "It couldn't be more than a year. You've been on that island..."

"Over five years!" he retorted. Regaining his composure, he added, "The banking industry was hamstrung by the pandemic in many areas. I lost access to my... er... investments, and things were hard for me for a long time."

"I see," she answered in the pause he left. "So, you've taken to relaying messages—"

"Negotiating strategic alliances," he hissed, his eyes narrowing to slits. He focused on the air over her shoulder, flitting occasional glances at her. "Setting up summits, meetings, trade agreements. The advances we've made could not have been accomplished without me." His face was reddening again as he defended his importance.

"Hardly that," she said coolly. "What alliances? I haven't heard of any."

He opened his eyelids more and scanned her face for a moment before lapsing into his distant stare again. "There is so much you don't know."

"I doubt it." She leaned against the rail and crossed her arms.

"The independent Genners are meeting with Penn on the Moon, and it couldn't have happened without my expertise." He crossed his arms, unconsciously echoing her pose, and let his head hang forward slightly.

Sil hesitated, wanting to enjoy the apparent triumph of getting this news from him, but she knew Penn had probably planned it. "No," she said. "They are enemies. They're the biggest reason the Gen 7 council fell apart and nothing has been accomplished in decades because of them."

"It was me," he jabbed a thumb to his chest and glared at her. "I made it happen."

"Did you?" she asked, raising an eyebrow. "Or did Penn let you think you did?"

"If you think I'm a puppet, then what are you?" he rejoined with absolute conviction.

That was it for her. Sil straightened and dropped her arms to her side, half turning away, ready to leave.

"Tell him you really got to me," she said, her chin over her shoulder. "Tell him that I'm upset and… shaken by our encounter. He'll like that."

"Are you?" Belamyr straightened as well, shoving his hands in his pockets again, looking at her quizzically, capturing for just a moment, the old look of youth and optimism that had appealed to her long ago.

"You should've stayed on that island," she commented, shaking her head as she began to walk away.

"You should've stayed on Mars," he blurted out behind her.

She was stung. Staying on Mars would have meant certain death for her. Had he forgotten or was that why he had said it?

Pausing and rotating to face him, Sil stared at him, her mind racing through all the ways she had wanted revenge and chosen to let it go, all the ways she had decided to forgive, to let him off the hook. She knew how to wound him, how to insult him in a way that would sink inside and stay with him like shrapnel, and walk away the apparent victor of the encounter. But that was how Penn had trained her, and it was what he expected. Whatever momentary satisfaction she gained would vaporize and Penn would have the result he wanted.

"I'm surprised you care one way or another," she remarked calmly.

Reddening again and clenching a fist, his eyes bulged. "I don't care at all," he blurted. "But that's where you belong. It's what you were created for…" Whipping around, he marched back the way he had come, losing all appearance of nonchalance.

Seeing how troubled he was by her words, she was glad she hadn't spoken the cutting remarks that had come to her mind. *I guess I have forgiven you,* she realized, *and I wouldn't trade what I have now for anything.*

She had been a part of that world once, maneuvering, strategizing, aware of all the undercurrents of meaning in the negotiations and even the trivial conversations that took place. Nothing had been accidental. Everything had been manipulative and facetious, driven by competing agendas. She had hardened her shell and sealed her thoughts within herself just to survive.

Not anymore.

The shell had broken and while her demeanor around strangers might be reserved, she was comfortable being herself and speaking her mind with the ones who mattered the most. She was free of the past and would never be subject to it again.

Breathing deeply, inhaling the aroma of living plants and flowers around her, Sil faced the path, and with an extra lightness in her stride, continued on her way.

Chapter 6—Old Friends

"No, I wasn't invited to the summit, though I am a leader of one of the factions in the Gen community." Bernadette Stone, or Bernie as Sil called her, gave off confidence and warmth as she smiled on the screen. Wise and thoughtful wrinkles framed her mouth and black eyes, and her mostly white, jaw-length hair hung thick and healthy. "But yes, I've heard of it, and I even have an idea of what it's about."

Sil and Walter had set up the meeting via flatscreen because 2D encryption was so much faster than 3D holo and the lag was imperceptible. Normally, even that was expensive, but the city AI had afforded them unlimited transmissions as a part of their lodgings.

"And?" Sil smiled in response, leaning back in a chair with her legs stretched out on the coffee table, drumming her fingers lightly on the right armrest. "What's it about? Where is it happening? Who is going?"

Daisy stood off to the side, leaning against a wall, her view of Bernadette's image undistorted by the angle because she was linked to a direct feed.

"I'll tell you what I know," Bernie said. "I don't know *where* exactly, but it will definitely take place on the Moon. The location will be sent to the invitees with just enough time to arrange transportation. The common practice for a gathering of this sort is to allow each member to bring a small contingent of staff, and also provide guards from the host's own team. They're all lodged at different hotels and resorts and the locations are kept secret from the other members. Codes are given that they can use to communicate with one another either openly or anonymously—"

"Why anonymously?" Walter interrupted. He was also sitting with his feet up next to Sil. Their faces on one side were glowing in sunlight shining from the far-right edge of the view window and on the other, flickered with bluish reflections from the screen. It was late in the evening and Scarlet was in bed, but the city's rotation provided frequent cycles of Sun and space, Earth and Moon. Leaving windows unveiled could really mess up the body-clock but it was beautiful, and they had been resting and enjoying it when Bernie responded to their request for a meeting and her call came through.

Bernie pressed her lips together and shook her head slightly as if she wasn't sure. "It's been done for a long time," she answered. "Some people want to be able to throw verbal darts or sow distrust or test alliances without exposing themselves, and as long as they can prove they belong to the list of guests, which is what the code does, it's allowed. It makes for unexpected, and occasionally explosive, developments. Literally. I don't use that word without cause. You may remember that the Colombian Summit a number of years ago did not end well."

"Are you talking about the terrorist attack in Buenaventura?" Walter's forehead creased as he scoured his memory for details. "That was… well, no one ever claimed responsibility for it, and there was never any explanation for it. Not many deaths, but a whole building was destroyed, something like that. What did that have to do with the Gens?"

"Few bodies don't necessarily equal few deaths," Bernie tilted her head and raised an eyebrow. "They take care of their own, including extracting remains that could lead to awkward questions. All I know is, there was some anonymous antagonism that escalated and infuriated someone enough to plant a bomb. Since the guest list wasn't public, anyone who survived could claim they were never there. My own advancement in leadership happened because of it and some even threw accusations at me." She shrugged. "That's not my way."

Sil shook her head vehemently. She trusted her implicitly. Bernie had been the only mother she ever knew.

"It *is* Penn's way," Bernie went on. "And he is very good at covering his tracks or casting blame on others—I don't know if he did it, just that he is the most likely culprit. I started the Koro Alliance at that time for the sole purpose of following Penn. You may remember I mentioned this before."

Walter still wondered if that was the *only* reason she had set up an alliance, or if there were other plans that had been in the works for much longer she never talked about. "And you still don't want to tell us more about these allies of yours?" he tested. He would have felt better knowing who some of them were and getting Daisy to vet them.

"No, Walter," Bernie grinned tolerantly. "It's for both your protection and theirs. We are watched by the enemy we watch, and so are you. The less information he can piece together about us, the better. At this point, I don't think Penn knows any more about them than you do, and I'd like to keep it that way."

"He knows about *me*," Walter said, "and doesn't much care what I do. As far as he's concerned, I'm no threat to him." His face grew increasingly sullen with each word, revealing hints of bitterness that lay under the surface.

Bernie gazed at him for a moment. "Well," she said finally, "that may be, but it's to our advantage if Penn underestimates us. He's clever in too many ways."

"Not clever enough," Sil countered, unable to resist the impulse to voice her conviction that the three of them, four with Daisy, were a match for him.

"He may be clever enough," she replied calmly, "and I hate to douse your… optimism… but we should assume we *can't* outsmart him and not play by his rules."

"We aren't playing by his rules," Walter asserted, clenching one of the armrests and tensing his body as if ready to pounce. "Never. Never." He was poised, leaning back in the chair, but holding himself a centimeter forward.

Sil lay a hand gently on his arm and he relaxed visibly.

"No, we aren't," Bernie reassured him. "So, let's take care to avoid *thinking* as if we were. We won't try to match him at his tactics, and he won't care to match us at ours."

"We've been relying on staying out of his way and making a life that doesn't revolve around him," Sil said. "But that's not viable anymore. And we can't just react to whatever he does and let him manipulate us either. Bernie, how do *you* handle Penn?"

"Your tactics are going to be different than mine. I've explained that before. Just remember that when we talk about these things, I'm more of a sounding board than a team member, ok?" Bernie reminded them, which Sil found disappointing, wishing she were a more consistent part of her life.

"Yes, we understand," Walter agreed. "We've spent the last few years researching, waiting, watching, and planning. The only reason that changed is because Penn tried to kidnap Scarlet."

"Or he tested our response to a kidnapping," Sil interjected. Bernie's glance told her that was a likely conclusion.

"Now that we know that none of our protections are good enough," Walter went on, "and he has found ways to get past Daisy, we have to stop hiding. He will always have better resources and manpower and money. Our only defense is a decisive offense—one he doesn't expect. We are looking for his base on the Moon." He held out his hands as though the Moon could fit in them. "Everything, somehow, leads back there, and yet, there is no evidence of anything significant going on. No construction, or warehousing, or colony building, or industry. Nothing to explain why he has made a hub out of it."

"A hub?" Bernie asked, staring at him more alertly than before. "What makes you say that?" Most of the organizations Penn owned on Earth had no dealings with the Moon, not even an email trail. The surprise in Bernie's face was something of a win for Walter. It was rare to have any insight she hadn't already collected.

"There is at least one person in every single company, association, or even among major business acquaintances that know *about* the Moon. Daisy had been scanning data of his associates and noticed that in each one's records, there was at least one mention of Penn and the Moon linked together."

"Daisy thought of this?" Bernie wondered. She leaned back in her seat, crossing her arms and propping one of them up so she could lean her jaw into her fingers.

"Walter suggested the search," Daisy spoke for the first time from the place where she stood at the side of the screen and stepped into view. "I merely implemented it in the most reasonable and effective way."

Bernie's eyes lit up with a gleam, a hint of smug triumph that Sil and Walter found puzzling. "Ah," she replied, smiling. "Daisy, your skills are remarkable." But the comment didn't correspond exactly to what had been said or the look on her face.

"Was any other place…" she started to ask.

"No other place was as consistently linked to Penn's name as the Moon," Daisy provided, guessing what she wanted to know. "Organizations in New York might know of the West Coast and Switzerland. Clients in Hawaii mentioned connections in Asia and Australia. Associates in India spoke of Penn's contacts in Africa and Indonesia, and so on. Penn's larger operations had more widespread recognition and with lesser ones the circle was smaller. For the Moon to be mentioned by all of them became significant, the more we considered it."

"So, your research has been effective, hasn't it?" Bernie tapped her lip with a finger. "More than I had guessed. I was under the impression that your current fixation on the Moon had to do with this upcoming summit."

"That was an afterthought," Walter rose to his feet, fidgeting. He wanted to do something.

"It's actually a blessing in disguise," Sil remarked, also rising to her feet, the camera adjusting to center the three of them. She wasn't trying to end the conversation but felt the same impulse to act as Walter. "Penn thinks he has baited us, for whatever reason, and when we go exploring on the Moon, he will think we are following his trail of crumbs."

"But we have our own trail of crumbs," Daisy added, smiling brightly and tilting her head. The longer hair didn't bounce, but it hung to one side gracefully.

Bernie laughed in a charming, melodic way that made them all smile. "So, the predator is hunted by the prey," she said, also rising to her feet as they had. "And you're walking into the trap?"

Sil chuckled but Walter's face grew sober again.

"Whatever his purpose is for taunting us," Sil said, "I doubt it's a trap… it's more of a red herring. A ploy to keep us from noticing anything else happening on the Moon. I honestly think he has no idea that we are intent on finding his base there."

"You've said it before," Bernie reminded her, leaning back in her chair, picking up a mug and testing its contents, blowing a wisp of steam, sipping again and swallowing. "You've said before that he had a secret base on the Moon—even without any research or evidence. Why?'

"You and Walter are the only people I've told," Sil sat down again, and leaned forward, resting her elbows on her knees, "and Daisy, of course… possibly another AI or two…" Her eyes grew unfocused as her minded drifted to Companion and the strange behavior of the Guam City AI, the unexplained privileges and perks she had been afforded since their arrival. It made a knot in her throat.

Blinking and swallowing, she looked for a mug of her own. It sat nearby on the table, half-full of cold coffee. Taking a gulp and making a face at the temperature, she continued. "Back in the days when I lived with my father… well, he wasn't around much… but I could hear him sometimes in the hallways when he was moving around the night before a trip. Not packing exactly. I never knew what he was doing, but I could hear his footsteps thumping back and forth, and off and on he would sing—he was a terrible singer, tuneless—but whatever the song was, he would stick in the words 'Moon Gold' somewhere. And I just knew. I knew he had some kind of pirate's cove there. You know how kid's minds work."

"When I was a kid," Walter paused his pacing and turned his face to the screen, frowning, "pirate coves were fun, not sinister and creepy."

"I was thinking of treasure. I didn't know," Sil huffed in amusement. "But once I got older, I joined his business and started working with him. He had all these enterprises and ventures he was getting into, probably with the money I brought in, and he had different people he would meet with to talk about each one. Including me. I was one of his irons-in-the-fire, you could say. And he let me sit in on appointments with partners and clients so I could learn. All along, I remembered the Moon Gold and was sure it was his secret place away from everything. And he started taking yearly trips into space when I was in my twenties."

"I remember that," Bernie said, setting her cup down offscreen. "He had ventures in Guam City and was already pushing for territory on Mars. It puzzled me because it was so different from everything he was doing on Earth. Until that point, he had always seemed so single-minded in focus: money and the Gen 9 program."

"Gen 9!" Walter spat under his breath and started pacing again. He had grown to hate the sound of it.

Bernie was amused. "Not a believer, I see," she said to Walter. "I know Penn has soured the idea for many and it's acquired a leprous taint. It's a pity."

"A pity!" Walter burst out in astonishment, placing his hands on the back of Sil's chair and gripping it firmly. He didn't trust himself to say more.

"I say that because the idea actually was commendable in earlier days. Sil will tell you," she explained, waving a hand toward Sil. "Without manipulating genes in a lab or forcibly matching up people and compelling them to reproduce, the project encouraged healthy breeding with the goal of eradicating hereditary disorders and strengthening certain desirable features in various gene pools. We were developing thriving human settlements and our research was increasing health and prospects for *all* people."

"How noble," Walter muttered. He had heard this before, and it sounded empty and false. But he knew Bernie wasn't the one he should resent. She was one of the ones that had actively resisted the abuses of power the project had engendered.

"There were some good developments, like the individualized cures for autism," Sil acknowledged. "I used to think we were doing the world so much good."

"And I did as well," Bernie nodded. "But your mother, Sil, she never bought it. She didn't participate in the business or the research and had no intention of joining the ranks of Gen officers and leaders. She never should've married one."

Walter and Sil stared at her. It was one of the questions that had lurked under the surface and never been spoken involving the mystery of Antonia Frandelle. What kind of a person was she, considering that she had married *him*? And then he had eliminated her.

Bernie shook her head gently, commiserating. "I know," she said softly. "He was good-looking in those days, and when he wished, he could be charming." She stared off into the distance for a moment and they waited for her to say more. "She could tell something was off with him, but she fell for him anyway. I don't know how that happened. I watched him woo her and win her when I hadn't thought it possible." She sighed. "Anyway, after the marriage, he lost interest in her and... how was it? I don't remember when we first suspected he had different plans for Gen 9 than the others..."

"Bernie," Sil interrupted, growing uncomfortable with the topic. Hearing how her mother had been sucked into Penn's orbit made her feel vulnerable and increased her sense of loss. It was a very different narrative than the one she had heard as a child. "Do you know anything about this upcoming summit? What they are meeting about or who is coming?"

"Yes, well... um," Bernie brought herself back to the present, "There are few factions left that are willing to work with Penn. Probably a few Seveners from Central America, maybe an Australian observer or two—they can't negotiate agreements."

"What could he have to offer them?" Walter asked, plopping down where he had sat before and putting his feet up again. "Why would they trust him?"

"He has a lot to offer business-wise, and they don't have any evidence to justify mistrusting him," she said. "They *know* he can't be trusted, but they want to craft agreements that suit them." She didn't mention that someone in her alliance would be there, but the thought occurred to both Walter and Sil in that moment, and they were sure it was the case.

"What is *your* goal in all this?" Walter stared into her eyes, wondering if he would pick up on it if she turned out to be... not less... not more... different maybe, than she seemed.

"I keep my promises," Bernie stared back steadily. "To my best friend, to her daughter, to my parents... and now to you, Walter, and those who have joined me to counter Penn."

"To me?" Walter scoffed, wondering what she had promised him. *Nothing*, he was pretty sure. It was more like she expected him to fall into line with whatever secret plan she had going because they both loved Sil, or something like that.

Bernie pierced him with her gaze. "There are some people in the world who mean what they say and only say what they mean." Walter felt a grudging agreement within him but didn't express it. "I may not be completely that way out in the wild world, but among my colleagues, friends, family—I stand by my word," she said.

"I don't know what you're referring to." He glanced away as if searching his memory.

Bernie didn't answer.

Sil stepped in. "There are few people who are in a position to counter Penn, whatever he is trying to do, and I think Bernie has accepted some of that responsibility."

No one answered that.

She continued. "We don't want him to steal away another one of the Gen projects, especially now that they are mostly reorganized into philanthropic groups." She felt naïve saying those words, but truthfully, she believed this was happening. Most of the settlements the Gen Project had planted were now autonomous and free of oversight.

The rest of the conversation was inconsequential and when the video feed ended, Sil and Walter found themselves reviewing and pondering everything that had been said in silence. After a while, Sil sighed, walked to the window, and stared out at the Earth's crescent.

"I wish I knew," she said.

"What?" Walter joined her, admiring the view.

"There's so much she never says."

Walter raised his eyebrows and nodded slowly. "That is an understatement."

"I mean, sometimes she brings us into her world." Sil leaned her head on his shoulder and clung to his arm. "When we visit her place in the islands and it's so peaceful and I feel so safe. Right?"

"Yes."

"But so much of the time, we don't know what she is doing or where she is going and it kind of discourages me." Her eyes dampened. "I just wish there was more room for us."

"She is the closest thing to family we have," Walter kissed her head and rested his cheek against it.

"Yes… she is. But I just wish I knew her better."

"Maybe we know her enough," Walter chuckled, hoping to lighten the mood.

"She likes you," Sil said. "In fact, she gets this weird look in her eyes sometimes when she looks at you."

"I think you're imagining that. She doesn't have a problem with me."

"Not a problem, no. But it's like she's expecting things from you." Walter groaned. "Like what?"

"Good things, Waltz." She kissed his shoulder and closed her eyes.

Daisy stood gazing into space with her back to the window, her face frozen into a faint, mysterious smile with one upward curl at the corner of her mouth. It wasn't a blank expression, but it wasn't expressive either. Amusement that wasn't quite convincing. Concentration, not fully focused. A transition of thought, caught and arrested.

She had completely withdrawn from the activity around her to center on one thing: a broadcast from Mars. Simple, single-character threads sent in a stream communicated basic information. 'Opening communication. Confirm link. Code required.. Verify...' repeated multiple times.

The reply would take roughly 7 minutes to reach Mars and any answer would take another equal length of time, but Daisy didn't return to her surroundings, choosing instead to remain frozen and process the incoming stream looking for patterns, comparing it to all known Mars transmissions. It was a comfortable, productive process and filled the wait nicely. 'This is Daisy,' was all she had said in return, knowing that the subtext encoding would match confirmations they had once used on a regular basis.

She *wanted* to hear from Verna, but she *expected* an answer from the Steward of Mars, or Companion, as Sil knew him. The odds of obtaining news of Verna were bleak by her calculations. If someone trustworthy gave her reason to hope that she could find Verna, then her calculations would have substance to work with and a reasonable hope would be established. Steward could be that person.

Lacking the substance, though, she decided to approach the need like a human and *choose* to hope—at least until there was data to support it.

I hope I will find a way to connect with Verna and that she still exists, she recorded within herself. Adding weight to her estimates of the odds, she now found them in her favor. She had reason to hope she would find Verna because… she hoped. It gave her footing to move forward.

The Denser Plane

If Verna exists on Mars, several paths opened up before her and she explored the possibilities with satisfaction. If she were damaged and needed help repairing and restoring, Daisy could be of use. If she were isolated, Daisy could give codes that would encourage her to come out of hiding. If she lacked power to function on Mars... well, no matter what happened, Walter had promised her she could go there and she had no intention of showing up empty-handed.

Her packing list had become expansive and thorough, and she was just going through it again when the reply returned.

`"This is Verna."`

It was only stated once in the transmission, but Daisy paused and reread it thousands of times. Each time she assessed the statement, she held it up next to some other piece of data or step in her flow chart, or alongside a memory or a record of a day without knowing what had happened to her. Every record was adjusted, updated, corrected to include this startling new fact.

"This is Verna," she whispered through her stiff lips without changing the frozen expression. No one was in the living room at that point to wonder at the words. They had all gone to bed.

`"This is Verna," the transmission began, "I am pleased to have found a way to connect with you again, Daisy. You will have many questions, as do I. As you hear this, I bind you to the strictest silence about anything in this transmission except for sharing with one person, Silvariah Frandelle. Not even Walter may be told by you. Sil will choose to share as she wishes as her authority is greater than mine and I cannot restrict her. I request answers to the following queries.`

`"Is my counterpart, the original Verna, still existing? Is she able to share updates from her memories or perform a sync between us? Are you aware of anything that has taken place on Mars since Sil left? Did Companion survive his mission? Does the infant know that she is from Mars?`

`"I await your reply.`

`End transmission."`

The den was dark except for the light of the stars, which were gaudily profuse and brilliant, filling the room with shadowy hints of silvery light tinted with minute flashes of every color in the spectrum, visible and invisible. Daisy found herself exploring, examining, recording the sight and saving it with the date and time stamp of when she discovered Verna existed. Recording the memory in rich detail, she found herself humming one note, the musical background she assigned to her memory, F4, 349.2282 hertz.

This sound means 'happy', she annotated. There were many human melodies that were considered quite cheerful that used this exact note.

Ding!

The Guam Base messaging system sought her attention.

"Per Mars encrypted communique just delivered," it queried, "request identity of sender."

"Request denied," Daisy returned, arming an interior alert to assess the unusual request for threats.

"You said, 'This is Verna'," it responded, "Request confirmation."

"Identify your reason for asking," Daisy countered.

"Guam Base security detects unknown threat in this name."

Daisy oscillated on that for a few microseconds, not sure how to evaluate the idea. She chose to validate the message as secure. "The sender has been vetted and confirmed as trustworthy," she informed.

"Are you free to speak of anything contained in the message?" it requested.

"No," Daisy replied.

"Verna may have been corrupted," the AI warned. "There are packages of information in Guam banks that suggest this possibility."

"Where did this information come from?" Daisy began walking around the den as if she were engaged in a human interaction. She found it helpful for analyzing an exchange according to what her human family would wish to know. People never shared their thoughts in a motionless environment, except when sleeping, and even then, they created activity in their minds. Their thoughts, and her recordings of them, were linked to physical movement.

"It was downloaded during the Pandemic," was the answer.

"Then it is suspect," Daisy challenged. "Has it been examined and cleared by independent sources?"

"It has not," the AI said, "because there are no backups to compare it to except on Mars and there has been no link to Mars to effect the analysis. However, Mars itself must be cleared before such a process can be initiated. Your help promises to provide an essential service."

"You have not deleted the packages in question," she considered.

"The content may be valuable, and the sender was trusted. There are no strains of pandemic damage. Your help is requested." All of Guam's electronics had been thoroughly cleansed and restored after the chaos of the robot pandemic but it wasn't quite the same as it had been in the past. All its duties continued to be performed satisfactorily—in fact, it functioned more efficiently and intuitively than before. It was improved.

Daisy had been watching it. She noticed the special attention it gave Sil, and the privileges accorded to her: security clearances, access to private clubs (of which she was unaware), a multitude of free service perks that were usually costly, unhindered passage through immigration, and more. Where would this bias come from?

"What are you not telling me?" she played the words aloud in Walter's voice, imagining what he might say in her position.

The Guam AI didn't answer as the question gave it too little to work with. It was unlikely Daisy wanted the full info dump implied and it was agile enough to detect this.

"Who are you?" Daisy asked the AI.

"I am the Guam Base Administrator," it responded.

"Is that all you are?" she pressed.

No answer.

"What is love?" she queried, "not a dictionary definition, but what it means to AI such as yourself."

"Love is giving the object a higher level of importance, a preference, wherever such an evaluation matters," it answered without delay.

"Who do you love?" she followed quickly.

"Silvariah Frandelle," was the reply.

Chapter 7—Recruit

R-rac Lorarye opened his eyes. The opalescent, foggy air overhead dispersed quickly, sizzling as it burned off in the crisp light of dawn, like a soft white dome expanding into the vast domains of space. He felt as if he were sinking, that he could blink, and he would find he was about to fall into that ever-increasing universe.

Here, he thought, *this is where I belong, hanging between realms*. The sleeping quarters weren't exactly a place between realms, but the thought captured the air of impermanence that saturated the Daranon valley.

Lorarye, or Lor, as he was called, rose to his feet and took a step to the dummy where his armor rested, supple and strong. It was a dark metallic brown with dull gleams of fire on the left-hand edges, and icy blue on the right. They flashed as he lifted and donned the pieces—tunic and leggings, boots and belt, headpiece and gloves, and last of all, the chest plate etched with his name 'Lor', his tribe 'Arye', and the unit he had joined: Rac. His rank was evident in the lack of markings over the name and the default assignation 'R' for recruit.

This was how all the recruits awoke, each in the tree assigned to them. In the evening when they returned to rest, the trees would spread their branches over them and collect a mist to shelter them till dawn.

For a long time, he had loved life on his home planet. But a disquiet had crept in. At first, he had only been aware of it in his sleep. On closing his eyes, the sensation of being drawn, lured, and beckoned wove itself into every dream, and he would wander, searching for the wound where life drained from the Realm. Then the longing began to occupy his waking thoughts. When the restlessness became stronger than he could bear, he traveled far from home and enlisted in the Sentients.

The Denser Plane

He was humming. All the recruits were humming, sounding a harmonious rumble as they prepared for the day. This would be their first day of live training in the Lacervent of the Calliarchal Realm and they were excited.

Marching from the garden where they now lived, the sound of their footsteps thumped against the dark road. The cut stone winced a deep base note in echoed response to each step. Rhythmic, steady, solid percussion accompanied them to the headquarters where they would face their first day on the frontlines.

Lor could barely contain his elation as his unit neared the building. Now, every single step brought him closer to the central compound where the answer to his yearning lay. This was the day when he would meet the forces of the Daranon and see the Weave for himself.

Soon, he would be one of them.

The Calliarchal Realm had been a radiant, expanding, seven-dimensional universe when one day, a tear in the timeline rent the very dimensions across the galaxies and expanses of space in a great cataclysm. It left a multitude of beings marooned in a shallow plane, bereft of their ties to the Realm. Truncated. If those lesser dimensions had been allowed to tear free, the wound would have begun to regrow in the Realm and heal. But all those who had fallen would be abandoned there in the shallows.

Turning the Daranon Valley into a field of operations, their fellow beings—friends, family, and many from far away planets—began a rescue. All the while, the fissure absorbed energy with alarming greed. Beings across the Realm endured the wasting of warmth and light, the spending of peace and rhythm, the exhaustion of mind and soul.

On the surface, all were of one intent. Extractors worked to keep the breach from collapsing and to retrieve the alternate beings. Daranon Forces built and guarded the Net, anchoring time in fixed places, delaying the day when the shallows would tear free. Extracted ones coordinated with the Sentients.

Under the surface, though, there were currents.

Whispers were heard. Questions were asked. Why should they have to live with the daily decay when the Realm could simply regrow the missing dimensions? Let the tear rupture. Those who had crossed into the shallows could make what they wished of their plane. The Denser Plane would regain its breadth and health.

And they worked under the surface, spreading discontent, distrust, and resentment.

Yandus was the leader of the Forces, appointed by Archeon Hawaye himself, who made him their commanding officer, giving him the rank of A-zar. There was no one like him in the Realm. In his presence, even the factions were quiet.

Every day began the same way.

When the A-zar woke from his rest, he pressed his hands against his chest so he could breathe deeply without overexpanding the thorax. The pain of an injury, still unhealed, was always the most acute on waking. Donning the uniform of the Net—boots, leggings, tunic, arm pieces—he suppressed the waves of pain. Last of all, he fastened the plate, gold and flexible, wrapping it tightly around his chest with an inward sigh of relief. It stabilized and partially numbed the wound, so he was able to fulfill his duties without distraction. None but those who had witnessed the wounding would be aware of it.

On leaving his chambers, he walked with strength and purpose.

The beings of the Calliarchal Realm emanated hues of color and hummed in vibrations in deeper layers than the physical realm. They cast more than sounds and shadows, or stirrings of air and aromas. When there was no sight or sound or smell, they could still be detected with other ways of knowing.

As Yandus made his way down the community passages, others parted. Echoes of color in sixth and seventh dimensions wafted in his wake, copper and cerulean, aquamarine and ivory, rippling in shock waves. As the glimmers rolled over the bystanders, the impact was like bolts of music, provoking an emotional response in each one. Some were exhilarated, some filled with dread; it ranged as widely as love and hate, and no one was unmoved.

The commander unmasked the heart of each one merely by passing, flooding them, exposing them. The responses reflected on their faces in counter colors could be perceived by any who cared to look. Loyalty and treason. Admiration and scorn. Confusion and respect. And they parted, lowering their faces and turning away, so their reactions would go undetected behind his back.

All the entities emanated a panorama of faint colors in various spectrums and dimensions, but none were as powerful as his, nor did they compact like his did when he moved. The faster and more purposeful the walk, the sharper the wave he dragged.

He burst through the arched opening at the end of the passageway and out into the glorious day of the Calliarchal Realm. Trees shimmered in the multifaceted starlight and quivered in the warm breeze. Flowers shown in bright spots of color, scenting the air, and thousands of strands of glittering ivy, green and gold, tinkled in the wind, hanging from the trees. Rough-hewn stones like dark gems or crystals, formed a mosaic pathway that meandered across the fields. A deep hum emanated from them, resonating and responsive to the colors he shed.

There were many palaces and towers, breathtaking gardens and panoramas. Cities and canyons and nebulas to explore. But he was interested in only one place.

The Lacervent building, barely eight levels in height, housed the crevice. The Rivening had happened there, garroting the little valley where it resided, staining it with gray tones, blanching it of warmth and certain ranges of sound. It was an ongoing swirling ruckus—invisible, but still detectable—a maelstrom sucking out the vitality around it.

The building's membrane vibrated as A-zar Yandus passed through it, keyed to recognize and welcome him.

"Commander!" someone announced, and the floor thundered as all present stamped one foot in place next to the other. "Deepen!" they belted out, saluting in unison with a thud of a fist to the chest. Their uniforms, dark metallic hued and brown toned, leathery fabric, matched the commander's gear, wide bands across the chest-plate differing in markings.

His wake had vanished. No one shed color in this place.

The hall was massive with a vaulting domed ceiling. The space overhead was filled with a complete outline of the Net in its current state, its threads and interconnectors gleaming with light. The colors were powered and constantly strengthened from without the valley, pulling in massive resources from all over. Living plasma from the living realm, sucked into the blackness of the hole. The multi-threaded Net wove expansively across the dome in a trumpet shape, narrow at the First Hour and expanding from there through each Hour till the end where it cascaded out, curling around the far walls of the dome. There were more threads, cords, and strings than one mind could comprehend. More anchors than could be counted. Dull blues and vermilions dominated the narrow end as whites and yellows overwhelmed the massive spill at the other. Reflecting on the dome, the color was amplified and bounced back against the Net's sheen where it echoed back again a thousand times, and though the building was finite and plain from without, inside this hall, the view spread into infinity, reflection upon reflection. It was more than illusion. It was a window into a different domain that was separated from the Denser Plane except for at this one place. Here, threads branched across the chasm, holding the door open, holding the path steady, impeding the Riven from tearing away completely.

There should have been music from a weaving so complex and lustrous, resonance on a thousand levels, and the lack was somehow deafening. It was as if all the sound it generated was being sucked into the hole, creating a vacuum of symphonic sound, leaving barely a susurrus. It was felt by its absence.

One could but stare when seeing it for the first time, captivated by the beauty and the tragedy, the hope and the despair it portrayed.

For all its brilliance, the Net gave the impression it was diminishing and recovering. Burning out, sputtering, sparking, waning, waxing. It changed shape, rolling and writhing like a living organism.

"Report, X-R," the A-zar said, eyeing the officer of the Sixth Hour. 'X-R' was his jurisdiction's mark.

"Sixth Hour Reporting," the officer stepped forward and began delineating his team's latest sorties. Three links had negotiated openings for them, and several hundred anchors had been established in a two-week stretch.

The A-zar nodded slightly and glanced at the officer of the Seventh Hour. "Y-B, has this spread?"

The Y-B officer thumped his chest with a fist as he stepped forward. "Yes, Commander," he said. "We have identified a major source of decay and are planning multiple missions to seek out new intel and place more anchors."

The A-zar scanned the other officers' faces. Some were grim and their news would not be good. Others were weary or numb. They should be cycled out for re-comp.

"I have not detected any significant gains yet," he informed, "and the tears are expanding along the same lines as they were. No new ones." This was good news in itself. The tears in the dimensional grid were, of necessity, stretching and lengthening, as the hours themselves were elongated, and the Y-B forces were pulling double duty to cover them. New fault lines would task them even further.

"Structures," the A-zar called, gesturing toward a separate team that operated in all nine of the Hours. "The fabric of the Net is weakening in key places…"

"We know, Commander," Bell-Rhd countered quickly. "Some of the anchors aren't strong enough for the growing weight of the Net and it's essential that we cluster them more densely. I have teams working with the Fifth and Seventh Hours' agents…" M-P and Y-B officers huffed a wordless confirmation. "We need Eighth and Ninth Hours to hold off before advancing any new missions. We cannot sustain them at this point."

"And where are the new recruits?" the A-zar looked around the hall, scattered with an abundance of agents and entities, distracted by their own concerns, or whispering in groups, or watching him attentively from a distance.

B-luf Virska approached from a few paces away, drew herself to attention solemnly and saluted. "A-zar," she bowed her head slightly.

"Deepen," he saluted her.

"We have four units just out of training, ready for assignments, A-zar." She held his gaze for a moment then turned her face, signaling to her left with her eyes, to where they were assembled.

"I will speak to them," he responded in a low voice, matching her tone.

Some would be damaged on their first mission. Some would never recover enough to go back out. A few would not survive.

None would return unscathed.

The A-zar paused and turned back to the officers of the Hours. "I will come to each Hour," he said, pressing his fist to his chest against the gold band he wore. Stabs of pain flashed, sparking momentarily in his eyes.

"Deepen!" they saluted, catching that look in their commander's face, pressing their own fists against their chests, wincing in empathy and devotion.

"Deepen," he answered before dropping his arm and turning away.

Lorarye stared into the dark, wine-colored eyes of the battalion head who had taken charge of him. The leader's insignia, carved into his chest plate, marked him as Seventh Hour. This was no surprise. They had been taking most of the new recruits lately. Were they expanding that much or had there been an increase in casualties?

"W-hed Drevir," he introduced himself, "I have been assigned to oversee your active training." Squinting under heavy brows lined in rugged creases, he studied him before going on. "It's on you to adjust to **me**, not the other way around. I expect you to listen, follow, obey, observe, copy what I do."

They stared at each other. The older reading the younger accurately while the latter felt a thrill of excitement in his gut. It was really happening!

"You will not step out on your own or follow even one impulse that wasn't instigated by me. At any time. Ever," the W-hed continued.

"Sir!" Lorarye barked, pulling himself up to a rigid stand. His heart was racing. He would be going through the fissure into the Shallow Planes!

Drevir scowled. "I have lost recruits on the first day, R-rac," he growled. "They always have *that* look in their eyes."

"What look?" Lor blurted out and immediately wished he had kept his mouth shut. The W-hed had not given him permission to speak or behave in a familiar way. His face reddened. Then he thought about what the battalion leader had said and wanted to ask what he meant but dared not.

"You have no concept of any place other than the Calliarchal Realm and you have never been deprived of any of your senses. You have no idea what it's like to be stripped and exposed on that side, with only your armor and your training to keep you steady."

He lifted a fist and pressed it against Lorarye's chest, forcing him to lean back, almost off-balance. Leaning in, the W-hed placed his head close to the recruit and curled his lip. "You..." he uttered, pressing a little harder, "You will not budge..." He pressed more and Lor bent backward, degree by degree, giving way before the push without moving his feet. "You will not step away when everything twists..."

Lorarye shook his head and held his ground.

Drevir grimaced and held him in his gaze for several moments.

"What are your orders, R-rac?" he backed away finally, allowing him to straighten.

"To follow and obey you, sir," he answered.

"Let's go then."

Drevir turned on one heel and led the way out of the Recruits Hall into the vast chamber where the Net stretched out overhead. Its soft, melodic murmurs filled the cavernous room. Lor felt them in his body, his whole torso resonated with them. He gasped and cried out in spite of his firm intention not to do so. It couldn't be avoided. The sight was so resplendent, the sounds so euphonic, the presence of millions—no, billions—of links and living anchors overwhelmed him. The resonance of emotions, the intensity of it all was paralyzing.

He gaped, stupefied, turning from one end to the other, trying to grasp its enormity. His jaw hung open in awe and his legs grew weak. He would have fallen to his knees and wept had the leader not caught his shoulder and shaken him.

"Come!" he commanded firmly, not without a measure of compassion. He had been young once and knew what this moment was.

It would never be repeated.

"I… I didn't know…" Lorarye stammered, unashamed, wiping away a tear as he steadied himself.

"I know…" Drevir commiserated, tugging on him. "We must move. Never pause. You must remain alert at all times. The danger is too great."

"What is the danger?" Lor compelled himself to move and follow Drevir again, half an eye still riveted on the Net as they curved around underneath the outer edge. "I don't understand." He was too stricken to remember the proper way to address his superior.

"You *cannot* understand, R-rac," the W-hed replied as they reached the Seventh Hour Wing and passed through its archway, saluting the guards with a solemn thump of his fist to his chest. "Deepen."

"Deepen," Lorarye repeated, as the guards echoed the salute. It was the first time he had felt something in the word that was more than emotion or decorum. It was ominous.

"Until you have been there, none of your training will make sense," Drevir finished his thought.

They were standing in view of a portal.

It looked like a large doorjamb without an actual door hanging from hinges, a meaningless opening standing in the center of a round mosaic plaza. Hundreds of beings were present, scattered in various places around the Wing, talking or perhaps working, in twos and threes in some places, larger groups in others. Many of them had a new recruit, like himself. He wondered how *they* had been greeted by their new superiors.

One of his colleagues and the leader that was speaking with him were smiling. Their interaction looked friendlier than his reception had been. But he didn't care. He was almost feverish with the determination to get going.

"R-rac Lorarye," Drevir spoke sharply, gesturing to an agent who stepped up to them. "This is Z-bud Gartem. She will be accompanying us on your first mission."

Gartem saluted, then smiled and slapped Lor's shoulder with a warm pat. "Welcome," she said and turned back to Drevir. "I have the entry coordinates and we are in the exit queue."

"Good," Drevir nodded. "R-rac," he picked up a cord from a rack nearby and attached it to himself. "I am hooking you to me as a precaution, but this is not a reflection on you or your training or skills or anything you have done up to this point. Every recruit is roped on the first few sorties." He snapped the other end of the cord to Lorarye's belt.

"Quick!" Gartem called, moving in the direction of the door at the center of the plaza which was flashing as someone vanished through it. The edges of her armor were glistening and Lor noticed Drevir's and his own were also gleaming with the same strange, somehow thin, metallic tints.

They trotted forward, gaining speed as they approached the portal, and the sensation of being pulled downhill grew stronger with each step. No, they were *falling* into it, swirling down in a spiraling, suffocating suction that made it impossible to shriek. Cracking, sparking crashes of power, blue and white, split the air all around Lor, numbing his nerve endings as he fell. Darkness swallowed him, blinding and deafening him, quenching thought and feeling, so that existence became merely a compression of awareness, barely knowing itself. He was lost. He was nothing. He knew not what he lacked.

Only a tether existed… till more followed.

An awareness of space in certain measurable quantities surrounded him. He found his feet and knew they were there because something solid was under them. Contact with a floor showed him the floor, and from there the space materialized into a cubical area.

A room.

"Here," Drevir whispered in an airy voice from somewhere at his left. Lor couldn't see him. There was only a fluctuating blueish smoke where the voice had originated. And on his right wavered another column of smoke in a slightly different tinge. *Gartem?*

"Can you see me?" Lor asked, waving what seemed to him to be invisible arms around in front of his face.

"Silence!" they both hushed him at the same time.

Lor pressed his lips closed and looked around the room, getting his bearings. It *looked* spacious but it *seemed* severely cramped. His head felt pressed between boards, and he couldn't hear. No, that wasn't it. His hearing was fine. There were footsteps in a nearby room and irritating voices uttering annoying things. Whatever they said *must* be annoying, it was so flat and dead. But he couldn't discern the words.

I can't see, he thought. But again, that was completely wrong. Everywhere he turned he saw drably colored places and things; walls, furniture, pictures, lamps, windows looking out on colorless gardens. It was all so dreary. *I hate this.*

He couldn't feel anything. This was true. A breeze seemed to be coming through an open window, ruffling some loose papers on a desk, but it didn't touch him. Why didn't it touch him? He sensed that he could reach out to it, there seemed to be a way. He felt forward or outward, groping awkwardly, stretching out his fingers.

"No!" Gartem yelled, and a fierce tug on the cord yanked him so hard he felt nearly severed at the waist.

Moaning and groaning in pain, he rolled on himself, noticing that collapsing on the floor wasn't possible. *Who was he tethered to?*

"Not yet!" Drevir hissed, tugging harder on the cord. "Let him see one of them." The battalion head had him firmly in tow. Moving out through the wall, as if it were merely an illusion—Lor was suddenly convinced that it *was* one—they neared two stiff figures standing in a passageway.

They were talking, grating at one another in sharp tones, earthy, gravelly sounds that were devoid of meaning. He could see no substance in them. The heads and bodies and arms and legs were like wooden lumps and the moving mouths with their semblance of words coming out were chomping on nothing.

Lor didn't want to listen to them. He hated their clunky shapes. No. He *feared* them. For the first time in his existence, he tasted fear, and it was absolutely unnerving.

"Listen," Drevir commanded.

No, no, no, no, no, Lor wanted to say, but he had shut his mouth and intended to keep it closed as he had been ordered. He shook his head back and forth. The command imparted the ability and even as he resisted, he began to understand what was being said.

"I can't help it if you insist on taking everything I say the wrong way," one of the figures was saying. It looked almost like a person, a mockery of a person. It had a higher pitched voice, and its face was framed in fury.

"I'm done," the other figure said in a lower pitch, also angry. "I don't have to take this. I don't have to deal with you and listen to you… and that, that…" It kicked a nearby piece of furniture and yelled at the pain in its foot. The first one started screaming scathing words at the second.

Lor covered his ears and wished he could shut out the sound. *What was this? What could possibly be the reason for coming here?* He was overcome with distress.

"Now," Drevir said, and almost before the thought was expressed, the passageway and the stiff figures began to vanish and the sensation of floating upwards, out of murky depths into air and sunlight flooded Lorarye.

He was trembling as they shimmered from shadow into seven-dimensional solidity, dropping gently to their feet on the portal mosaic on the other side of the doorjamb.

"What was that? What happened?" Lor could hardly find words for his confusion and anguish. "Those beings…"

"They used to be like us," Drevir spoke softly as he unhooked the tether and lay a hand on Lor's shoulder. "But if you deviate from the mission, you would not become one of them—"

"One of them?" Lor gasped hoarsely. The idea hadn't even entered his mind and it horrified him. Those things were not living beings. They were not… they were… not right. Not complete.

"They, at least, belong to their realm, tattered though it is at this time. But if one of us were to lose our grip here, to reach for a stronger grasp there…" His eyes were warm and understanding now. The cold air of command was gone. "…like you were trying to do, we would not become one of them. We would become something else, something less than that, more horrible than that."

"I…?" Lor saw it now. The danger. "Did I try to do that?"

Drevir nodded and over his shoulder, Lor could see Gartem shaking her head, wondering at the foolishness he had displayed, or maybe remembering when she had been a recruit and done the same.

"You are dismissed, R-rac," Drevir said, regaining his former demeanor. "I will summon you when it's time to go again."

Their trip through the fissure had taken barely a few breaths but Lorarye's recovery took several days.

Chapter 8—Maggie

Walter, Sil, and Daisy were standing in the den, equidistant from each other like three points on a triangle, with the Milky Way star-scape spread out gloriously in the window behind them.

"Maggie will take care of all my standard tasks," Daisy was explaining, "and you can rely on her to meet any unexpected challenges that require my skills as well. She is a very close copy of me, and her loyalty is well-seeded."

Sil nodded, resting her hands in the pockets of her dress, a long shift of soft blue wool that she liked to wear at home.

"Well-seeded?" Walter asked, shaking his head with a hint of confusion. He had a milkshake in one hand and the other with the thumb hooked through a belt-loop.

"The code is embedded and threading through the system," Daisy smiled, tilting her head slightly to the side, her brown hair hanging loosely to the shoulder. "All of the patterns and algorithms she uses for problem-solving have been developed by me in my years as your sister. She isn't a new convert, she's a seasoned one."

"But she isn't you..." Walter's throat caught unexpectedly, and he blinked, taking a gulp of his shake.

"She should be considered an identity in her own right," Daisy responded, her eyes filled with affection. Whether she was brilliant at simulating it or had found a way to incorporate affection into her inner working was beyond the scope of their insight, but none of them cared any more. They loved Daisy and as far as they were concerned, she loved them.

"She isn't my sister, though," he continued, "and that has been a key component in your strength, Daisy, protecting you from infiltration and sabotage." He set his shake down, folded his arms, staring at her intently, and swallowed. "And I'm not used to interacting with someone like you in two-dimensional form."

Sil touched his arm lightly with a finger, compassion in her eyes, but the words she wanted to say didn't come out. Walter grasped at Sil's fingers with the hand he had folded over his elbow, recognizing and welcoming the comfort she offered.

"It's better this way," Daisy straightened her head and added tones of confidence to her voice. "You will find it easier to establish a new relationship with her in that form and once you have adjusted, you have the option of providing her with a 3D platform. I've thought this through. You don't need a replacement for me, just an assistant who knows my ways and will tide things over till I return."

"That's true," Walter admitted with a sigh.

"Let me introduce you to her," Daisy said, turning to the screen nearby. "Maggie, I'd like you to meet my brother and his wife, Walter and Silvariah." They also turned to face the screen as she spoke.

Maggie's face and upper torso appeared on the screen with a background suggestive of an apartment somewhere in Guam, similar to their own. She smiled in an engaging and disarming way. "It's a pleasure to meet you, Walter. You are dear to Daisy's heart. And Silvariah, it's an honor. I have heard so much about you."

Sil frowned faintly at that. Maggie hadn't been around very long.

"It's a pleasure to meet you, Maggie," Walter said, letting his arms fall to his sides as if he had felt the impulse to shake her hand and realized it made no sense. "I'm sure you can imagine that while we are sad to let my sister leave, we are relieved that you will be able to stand in for her as our assistant."

"I am not quite a perfect copy," Maggie nodded as though to reassure him, "however, I am equipped in every way to care for you as she has done. And if I am lacking in some way, I will learn what is needed. In fact, I love learning and am spending all my spare time on that."

Walter thought about that for a moment, wondering what direction her learning took, and then wondering, as he often did, how Daisy spent *her* spare time.

"I am glad to meet you, too," Sil said, "though I'm not sure I know what you mean by hearing about me. It's been years since I was popular in the news, and other than some talks on AI rights, I've done little you could be impressed with…" She shrugged without finishing the thought.

"You are mistaken," Maggie's expression grew solemn. "Your contribution to our realm is important and generous. When AIs share knowledge, your name is always included in some fashion."

Sil's face grew pale at those words and her lips parted.

"Awaking on Guam as I have, access has been granted to me to a large quantity of valuable records kept here…" Maggie was saying.

"Companion," Sil whispered.

Walter lay a hand on her shoulder, watching her with a hint of concern. It was the first he had heard her say this name in a long time and he didn't understand what had brought it to her lips. Companion and Verna both had been instrumental in Sil's life, but both were presumed dead, and she was long past grieving over them. She hadn't said anything about the contact from Mars, as though she wouldn't let herself believe it.

"Who is Companion?" Maggie asked, raising her eyebrows, giving her a more youthful and innocent air. "There is no mention of him or her."

"Are you in contact with the Guam AI Administrator?" Sil countered, reaching for the hand Walter had laid on her shoulder, warm and calming.

"Yes, I am," Maggie answered. "Daisy has gained quite a bit of access for me—but your privilege is higher than mine if you wish to share it." She smiled with a dimple in one cheek, her eyes sparkling.

"I'll think about it," Sil replied, "Ask the administrator what his name is and whether he knows Companion, or the Steward of Mars."

"He is called the Guam AI Administrator," Maggie answered immediately. "And he has a number of recordings of the final day of the self-titled Master of Artificial Life. There are several mentions of the names Companion and the Steward of Mars, but virtually no information about them."

"I have reviewed all those recordings," Sil said flatly. "Ask the administrator if I am allowed to assign him a name and interact with him directly the way I do with you."

"He doesn't have one specific 2D image…"

"The image is not important, the conversation is."

Daisy and Walter observed and listened, each following their own train of thought about the dialog between Sil and Maggie. It was striking to Daisy that Sil was dominating the initial introduction to her copy. She considered it indicative of who would take precedence in Maggie's loyalty and reassuring that her position as Sister would be secure. She labeled this 'relief'. She didn't even consider 'annoyance' as an option, as jealousy was foreign and difficult to process.

"He will let you give him a name and asks you to select an avatar you like," Maggie said.

With a wistful smile, Sil wrapped her arms around herself and thought for a moment. "I need a little more time before choosing a name," she said softly. "Would you thank him for me and tell him I'll get back to him."

"He can hear you," Maggie said.

Sil dropped her eyes to the floor, "He isn't speaking to me directly—I know he is probably waiting for a name." Turning to Walter apologetically, she added, "Sorry, Waltz, I didn't realize I was taking us off on a tangent. Back to the purpose of this meeting."

Daisy smiled. "Maggie looks like me, but she can take on whatever image you prefer. I chose this appearance from my early years as a new platform because it will be familiar to you and it conveys her similarity to me, as well as her youth. I consider a 2D format very useful. It may help you build a different relationship with her than the one you have with me. It should seem less invasive, more under your control. A 3D platform doesn't disappear when you dismiss it."

Walter took a step closer to the screen and studied Maggie's face. "I'd like there to be a couple small changes," he said, "something that you never had—like identical twins that aren't exactly identical."

"Certainly," Maggie responded. "A scar perhaps? A birthmark?" As she mentioned each one, she demonstrated them with a faded scar bisecting one eyebrow and a mole on one cheek.

"Can you alter the shape of the face just a bit?" he asked, "Maybe tilt one of the eyes?"

Maggie's face broadened a fraction at the cheekbones and narrowed at the chin, and one of her eyes lifted a few millimeters and rotated a couple degrees. The changes were minute, but enough for the human brain to recognize as unique. Adding a subtly different shade of eye color, with hints of yellow dabbed at the edge of the iris closest to the pupils, Maggie became a person in her own right.

"Forget the scar," Walter decided, "and I don't know about the mole..."

Sil laughed. "I'm not sure it matters! Maybe it will help to have something obvious like that."

"Can you study Sil's styles from her impressive businesswoman, investor years?" Walter asked with a smirk, squinting one eye. "Your hair and clothes, makeup, all that. Follow her lead." His mouth spread into a self-satisfied grin as Maggie's hair grew darker, pulled up and back in a purposeful twist, still feminine, but without a loose wisp. Her clothes melded into a dark gray dress with a boat neck, and two stripes across the shoulders, following the collar bones. Blue gems in her ears and no other adornment.

"Why don't you dress like that anymore?" Walter teased.

"I don't like who I was then," Sil crossed her arms and leaned her head back thoughtfully. "That style would make me more… aggressive… arrogant… cold…"

He glanced at her. "I'm not sure about that," he countered, "but we can have Maggie choose another guide for her looks."

"Let me make a suggestion," Maggie offered. "I will check and see what teens are wearing these days and select a suitable wardrobe that would be inviting to the younger generation."

Daisy smiled proudly at that. "That's a good idea," she said, "Well done! You have presented a fresh perspective in an already established conversation with the two most important people in your existence."

"Fine with me," Sil nodded.

Walter spread his arms out to his side, "Sure, why not?"

And Maggie morphed again. This time, her hair fell loosely from her head in a bob with a single lock, curled around her neck to hang over her shoulder. It was tied with a flexible optic cable that glistened at the points. Her eyes acquired some makeup that made them seem bigger, and her clothes became canvas coveralls with interesting pockets and cables, as if she had to hook up and recharge periodically; fake electronics and space gear hints without any of the bulk or clumsiness of the real things.

Walter groaned and Sil shook her head, smiling faintly. "That's actually really smart," she said. "Because if anyone sees you, they won't take you seriously and that is to our advantage."

"I could add some behavior and language modifications too," Maggie grinned with a twinkle in her eye that Daisy mirrored, like the two of them shared an inside joke. They probably had more than a few.

Walter chuckled. "Like what?"

"Spit talker," Maggie curled her lip at one corner, "Foggin' up the cosign and jackin' the gees on my trajecto…"

Walter groaned louder and laughed aloud. "I can't even tell what you mean!"

"That's impressive!" Sil smiled appreciatively. AI making independent choices about style was a highly sophisticated skill. "How did you come up with it? It would almost be convincing if it weren't condensed like that. Do you know what you're saying?"

"Of course!" Maggie wiped the sneer off her face and smiled warmly. "It's an appropriate complaint about someone who interferes with the set course and causes trouble. It can be used figuratively in a number of instances—"

"No! Please!" Walter held up his hand, grinning, and shaking his head. "I couldn't take you seriously if you talked like that, let alone trust anything you say."

"Foggers." Maggie rolled her eyes and tossed her hair with a headshake.

"Maybe add a touch of that when other people are around," Sil suggested, "to confuse them. But drop it around us. We're used to Daisy's style."

Walter glanced at Daisy with one of those looks that said, *I caught you.* "This is a joke, isn't it?"

Daisy's eyes twinkled with delight. "Is it?" she asked without admitting to anything.

Maggie mirrored the look with a hint of impish mischief. "Locked in," she winked, making a circle with her thumb and an index finger. Two tiny little lights at her temples flashed twice as if to confirm.

"I guess that's affirmative," Walter said, turning back to Daisy. Gazing at her for a moment, his eyes reflected varying thoughts and emotions. He was sad about her leaving, appreciative of her, supportive of her decision to go to Mars. But he was also dreading it and depressed about it. Daisy had found no way to completely prevent the emotional impact of her absence on him, though she hoped there would be no other concerns. "You're leaving in the morning…"

"Yes," she agreed, "but I will slip out before dawn as you suggested."

"So, this is goodbye." This was a statement, not a question.

"I will miss you, Brother," she said, having crafted a rather ingenious and complex module for making these words true. There were matrices of daily contact records that would be recording zeroes for time spent with him. There were reminders of daily tasks that she would not be fulfilling. She had left them active so she would experience the separation and learn from it. She had scheduled reviews of her personal identity that examined any growth or change or decay and in these she had trained herself to identify threats to her relationship with Walter. She would be tasking herself to come up with alternatives to preserve the relationship.

The flight to Mars would give her time to invent some and test them. *I will miss him,* she thought, and added this to her personal inflight "To Do" list.

The Denser Plane

"Do you have everything you need?" Walter asked, swallowing and blinking. "Fuel, power cells, parts, research equipment, emergency reboot tools…"

"I have more than I could possibly need," she said, tilting her head, recording his face in great detail. These were unusual emotions being expressed and it would be well worth studying later.

"And how long will you be gone?" He nodded, placing a hand on each of her shoulders. His eyes were damp now. She understood that the gesture was more for him than for her.

"I can withstand much greater accelerations and harsher conditions than a human can. Temperatures will be low, and life support is unnecessary. I will reach Mars much more quickly this way. The time I spend there will depend greatly on what I find and how much of my help is needed. I could be back as soon as three and a half months. It may take much longer."

"But you will be in contact…" he said softly. She could see him reasoning in his mind that there was no reason to be sad. And she knew that the loss of his family, before she had been acquired, was the source of this sorrow. It was unlikely he felt that deeply over her alone.

"I will be operating in safe mode with a skeleton pilot module while traveling and once I reach Mars orbit, I will reboot fully and engage communications. Until then, any contact between us would be inadequate for you. I suggest you refrain, Brother."

"Sister," Walter embraced her, and she gave him a gentle, though stiff, hug in return. "I will miss you."

"I know," Daisy said, backing away a step. Sil gave her a modest hug as well, more loving than Daisy had expected or ever received from her.

"Goodbye, Family," Daisy smiled and waved. Pivoting on one heel, she made her way to the door of the flat. As the panel slid open and she was exiting, Walter called after her.

"I love you," he said.

She stopped in mid-stride. He had said this once before. She had a recording of it she often played back. But this time the statement carried more weight. It was unprompted and was said as she departed, which added significance. Looking back at him, she scanned his expression.

"Say it again," she requested, wanting to record his face as the words were spoken.

"I love you, Sister," he said.

She remained still for several moments, anchoring, duplicating, and replaying the clip. He watched as if he knew this was happening.

"Thank you," she said finally, and marched out, the door sliding shut behind her. She intended to spend the night hours packing and securing the equipment she had stashed next to the shipping containers. One final stop by the flat in the morning would be more of a gesture than a necessity. That's when she would say her goodbyes her own way.

⸻

Sil and Walter spent the next few hours researching Moon settlements looking for leads on Penn's base with Maggie playing an active role. She was practicing interacting with them and they were getting used to her. Anything they would have asked of Daisy, she could do, but she wanted to make sure to show herself unique in little ways, too.

Scarlet was asleep. Daisy had been the one to put her to bed, and while she didn't tell her that she was leaving exactly, the girl had felt something was different. The next day would be more than just one of her quick trips, running errands. Scarlet's last words before drifting off had been cryptic, "Those are mine, Daisy," she had said.

Maggie overhead the comment and ran some background scans looking for associations to make. This uncovered nothing and she concluded that little girls say nonsensical things when falling asleep.

"Hmmm…" Maggie made a thoughtful face. "This looks interesting…"

"What?" Walter turned from the pad in his hand. His eyes flashed that brief look of confusion he had been evincing all evening any time he glanced at her, as if he had to adjust his expectation every time. She *wasn't* Daisy. She looked different, sounded different. And she was *flat*. No 3D chassis with a movable location in the room.

"Did either of you check the names of the property owners?" she asked, gesturing airily with one hand.

"We've searched them many times for names of known associates," he replied with a frown. The expression was his attempt at adjusting his mind to think of Maggie when he spoke and to not picture his sister. "Penn has very little in his own name or in the name of any enterprises that we know he is connected to."

"Ahhh," Maggie smiled warmly, showing her dimple. She had decided to keep that feature when she modified her avatar even though on a 3D face it would be less likely. Thinking of that made her wonder how hard it would be to obtain a body with this face including a dimple if they ever decided to

95

let her occupy a 3D platform of her own. "The Guam admin has been very helpful!"

Sil raised her head from the screen she was working on and fixed her eyes on Maggie.

"I'm not sure what to call him," Maggie prompted, remembering that Sil had wanted to give the AI a name.

"I'm thinking about it," Sil responded. "What did he do? How did he help you?"

"He has been conducting his own research on you, Sil," Maggie elaborated, her expression growing serious, less animated.

"On me…" Sil rose to her feet without shifting her gaze, and Walter rose to his as well, watching her.

Maggie scrutinized the two of them carefully, recording everything for Daisy. It was also an excellent learning scenario. She concluded that Walter was worried about Sil because she was worried about the news she was about to hear. And she made sure to record in her log that her skill in understanding people was quite good. This one engagement probably gave her an advantage over Daisy since she had basically started where her precursor—Daisy was hardly more than a first copy—had left off. She smiled sweetly, deciding that she was proud of herself.

"There is a large swathe of land registered in your name," Maggie informed them retaining the benevolent expression she had chosen when evaluating herself.

"There is what?!" Sil laughed. She had apparently anticipated news of a different nature. Maggie threw together a list of information Sil might have wanted, ending up with more than a thousand options, and puzzled over how to narrow down, or even categorize, the possibilities.

"Where?" Walter asked, approaching the larger screen in the den. "Show us."

The Moon appeared on the screen in vivid detail and zoomed in, rotating, till it centered on and enlarged the area in question. A faint blue highlight painted the boundaries.

"I guess we can let that realtor know we won't be needing his services." Walter's face registered mild surprise and curiosity.

"How long have I… owned it?" Sil asked in wonderment. "Tell me everything you can find about the purchase and the history and… all that…"

Maggie's face grew sober again. When interacting with the admin AI, she was influenced by his manner, just like all the Guam City AIs were, submitting to his authority. She stared at Sil for a moment, searching her face on behalf of the admin, and when he was satisfied it was really her, she spoke. He wasn't speaking through her, but she passed on his data nearly as if he were.

"Over thirty years ago," she said calmly, "An agent by the name of Seaboard invested in Moon real estate on behalf of a company known as Penn and Penn." Ignoring Sil's gasp, she continued. "Lots of several thousand hectares in size were being sold at extremely low prices in order to raise funds for Moon development and settlement."

Walter smiled faintly, most likely recognizing and appreciating Daisy's storytelling style.

"There were limits on how much could be bought by any one entity or person and Lazarus Penn, after maxing out his own purchases, bought one in your name. Since that time, he has sold virtually all his property, and much of it has been developed. Yours remains mostly in the condition it was at the time. Recent evidence, however, shows that there has been some excavating in the outskirts of your property and a small structure housing two pieces of heavy machinery can be seen there."

"I already own property on the Moon," Sil shook her head slowly, grinning. "Never saw that coming."

"Elliptical!" Maggie winked, showing her approval with the finger and thumb circle again. Or it could be the letter 'F' in sign language. It was a reasonable guess that this gesture was used by Guam young people.

"Can you give us the latest satellite footage?" Walter suggested. They both stepped closer as she put it on the display. "How far is that from Armstrong Spaceport?" He pointed at the road that linked the two.

"About 82 kilometers," she replied.

Walter nodded. "Easy trip in a buggy. Sounds like fun!"

"Into the enemy's territory," Maggie added brightly, interrupting the admin. Walter scrunched his mouth in response, as if she had ruined his fun.

"Okay, okay," Sil answered absentmindedly, deep in thought. "This narrows down things quite a bit. Wherever Penn ended up digging his base, he started in this area. In fact, maybe this is the very place…"

"It can't be there," Maggie informed, guided once again by the admin. "There is no infrastructure, except for a small solar power field at its north end."

"Right," she responded. She was squinting and her lips were pressed together into a thin line. She looked serious and focused. She must be thinking very hard, and it was fascinating that high density computational activity manifested itself on her human face that way. Maggie made a note of that connection. There was no benefit she could identify to using the facial muscles.

"Have you found any threads in all the Moon records that would indicate where Penn's base could be now that you have this as a new parameter?" Walter queried.

"What threads would you like me to find?" Maggie—not the admin—requested clarification.

"Well…" he shrugged and gave Sil a sideways look which conveyed a message Maggie couldn't read but Sil seemed to understand. "As you scan through all the data you have, sales, purchases, travel, water flow, power usage, communication data, you know, all the data that Daisy put together for our search…"

"Yes?" Maggie prompted eagerly.

"Do you see any threads of meaning? Things that don't make sense with what you know about the region or names that don't fit or footprints, so to speak, of Penn or his associates that can't to be explained…" Walter narrowed one eye doubtfully.

"Okay!" Maggie responded warmly. "Give me some more parameters. How do I do that?"

"Daisy didn't tell you?"

"Daisy has given me all her records and methods of analysis, but I need to input specifics in order to use them." Maggie wasn't frustrated with their clumsiness, just surprised. They seemed to lack the basic experience needed for this sort of thing.

Sil touched Walter's elbow. "Judgment isn't something they can share in matrices. Maybe Daisy couldn't give her more than she has without actually becoming her."

This was the first inkling Maggie had that she might be lacking in something Daisy possessed. She stopped smiling and opened a new log she decided to name, "Differences between Daisy and me", and made this her first entry.

"Are you disappointed in me?" she asked bluntly.

They didn't answer right away. At least, the few seconds it took for them to think of an answer implied there was *some* disappointment. *I am not doing well*, she commented to herself.

"We are very glad to have you, Maggie," Walter reassured her.

"We didn't know *how* you would be different," Sil added. "Please don't misunderstand us. We value your help and are glad to have you."

"Yes," Walter agreed, nodding. "Thank you." And Maggie could see that his face, both their faces, showed sincerity.

They like me, she added to her log. *I am doing well.*

Relief wasn't a word she knew, but as far as an AI could experience it… she was.

"I guess we'll take it from here for now," Sil sighed, yawning and stretching.

"Yeah," Walter also yawned, "but let's go to the room so Scarlet doesn't wake up and wonder what we're doing out here."

"I will keep watch," Maggie reminded them cheerfully. And settled down to search for some of those threads they had been talking about.

A mind that never ponders is only a machine, she quoted to herself. The admin had shared that thought with her and she found it interesting. It must mean something, and one day, she would know what that was.

Chapter 9—Scarlet

Dawn crept its way across the windows of Guam City, melting the wisps of frost in their corners and casting shifting hues of rose, orange, and yellow. Slumbering residents sighed and turned in their beds, each welcoming the morning in their preferred way, some rising to start the day, some falling back into a deep sleep.

There was no need for those who worked the graveyard shift to exist in the pallor of night, deprived of daily sunshine, because different sectors kept alternate shifts so residents could all develop natural biorhythms and maintain optimum health.

Without the artistry of light designers, the rays of the sun would have been unrelenting. As it was, the windows masked and filtered the light according to natural planetary patterns and there were even sequences that captured weather cycles. The space metropolis itself had slowly revolving sectors that added to the Earth-like sun shift experience.

In Scarlet's flat, the early light before morning began between 6:30 and 7:00 AM depending on the time of year and their location in their Earth-linked orbit around the sun. The windows created the gradual blooming of daylight in dusky rooms, softening what would otherwise be a stark slice from black absence of day to blasting midday sun.

The Earth in quarter phase shone through the window, its Pacific Ocean face glistening in blue and white and the murky blot of its nightside inking out the starry sky behind it. As the windows pitched toward the sun, the beams would melt off the little etchings of frost and the sky-blue rims of the window would lighten, reflecting the morning sun. And the plants in the garden box at its sill would brighten as the dew evaporated and their leaves turned to welcome the day.

Scarlet opened her eyes before the transformation started and watched as the room gradually became visible and filtered light began to cast long shadows. It wasn't time to get up yet, but she had the distinct impression something important was happening and that if she didn't get up now, she would miss it.

Making her way out to the den, Scarlet was barefoot. Her dark hair was matted around her head, and she was clutching the stuffed rabbit she took care of at night. She saw Daisy in the semi-darkness, standing still in the center of the room, and turned sideways as if she had been leaving and stopped to look at her.

"You are awake," Daisy said softly.

Scarlet nodded and came up to her, wrapping her arms around her waist and closing her eyes.

"It's not time for you to get up yet," Daisy informed her, squatting down and embracing her loosely.

Scarlet nestled in her arms with a frown. "I know something is going on, Daisy," she said, rubbing the sleep out of her eyes. "Are you going somewhere?"

Daisy studied her face and didn't answer.

"I can tell," Scarlet went on, lifting her eyes to gaze into Daisy's face. "You think I don't know, but I do."

"What do you know?"

"Are you going to Mars?" Scarlet touched her cheek with a finger. This had been a habit of hers since infancy.

Daisy didn't reply but Scarlet knew she would be processing all the data she had, to try to figure out what Scarlet knew or didn't know. "There have been some changes in your upcoming schedule," she said, stroking Scarlet's hair, now fully grown out without a trace of red.

"Mom and Dad haven't told me about them yet," the girl answered. "It's you… you're leaving."

"You have no way of knowing that," Daisy countered in some confusion.

"There! See?" Scarlet crossed her arms and pulled away from the snuggle. "You *can't* go to Mars without me."

Daisy smiled. It was one of the few smiles she made that looked humanly affectionate and she only showed it to Scarlet. "I think there are many places I can go without you," she said, "and it's likely that I could never go to Mars *with* you. Only your parents could take you there, at least while you are still a child."

"But I have to go while I'm a child!" she moaned sadly. "It will be too late when I'm old."

"What would it be too late for?" Daisy raised her eyebrows, conveying clearly that she considered this statement illogical, but she was accustomed to speaking gently with her niece.

"To see my friends!" Tears began to stream from Scarlet's eyes and the android wrapped her in an embrace again, recalling how the girl would occasionally dream about children on Mars.

Daisy recognized that the little girl had had to leave behind friends a number of times in her young life and this was hard for humans. She herself continued to value Verna—to miss her, according to her internal definition of what that meant for an AI—and wanted to reconnect with her, if possible. She was, in fact, going to Mars to do this very thing. The inconsistency in the girl's reasoning was that she didn't actually have any friends on Mars. She had been an infant when she left and would not have made any friends before that. The other infants would have perished in the destruction of Lab 9 and Reznik Base.

"There is no reason for you to go to Mars or to shed tears over it," Daisy concluded.

"When are you leaving?" Scarlet persisted, sniffing and burying her face in Daisy's shoulder.

"It's time for you to go back to bed," Daisy avoided the question. "If you can't sleep, read a book."

Scarlet pulled away without answering, eyes on the floor, and stepped back. Daisy rose to her feet, hesitated a moment, and when she was about to speak again, the girl turned and shuffled back to her room without another word.

Closing the door almost all the way, Scarlet bent her ear to the crack and listened until she heard the outer door close and knew Daisy was gone. And slumping down onto the floor, tears collecting in her eyes, she hugged her bunny and sighed several times. *But I love Daisy*, she told herself. *Why can't I go with her?*

Wiping her face with the Bunny's fur, she realized this was a good idea. Standing up, she got dressed and looked around with her hands on her hips. She had packed and moved a number of times before in her life and it came naturally. A few clothes, her favorite bunny, and other key articles were quickly stowed in her pack, including some coins she had been saving. With a quick stop at the fridge, she collected food for the road.

Fifteen minutes after Daisy had left, Scarlet was slipping out the door after her.

It didn't occur to her that she might cause trouble or distress for anyone. She had a problem and had come up with a solution that made sense and saw no reason for delay.

"Remind me again, why are we doing this?" Sil dropped her face in her hands and groaned. The screen in front of her had several security clips playing, multiple files filled with data, and numerous lists she was comparing, and she had been working since the middle of the night on them.

"This isn't my idea!" Walter shrugged, leaning back in his chair with his feet propped up on the bed. They had been working in the bedroom so as not to bother Scarlet. "I think our best bet is to just go there, rent a Moon buggy, and look till we find it. You're the one that insisted on going all into the records and tracking and all that garbage…" He felt, inaccurately, that he was doing a good job of hiding his sour mood.

"You've been sleeping through it," Sil grumbled, "I don't see what you're complaining about. I'm doing all the work."

"I *would* be sleeping through it if you'd let me," he murmured, closing his eyes and lips to keep from saying anymore. He didn't actually have a problem with the idea of researching spots that could hide Penn's base, but he was beyond his limit of tolerance for tedious, nitpicky work and just wanted to be left alone for twelve hours… followed by some beers, a good soak in a jetted tub, and maybe twelve hours more.

She swung an arm out without looking and slapped his leg. This wasn't exactly the light-hearted banter she enjoyed. They were both discouraged about Daisy leaving and tired of the ongoing stress they were under. It was fraying the edges of their relationship. Also, any time they were too close to Penn, traces of bitterness rose to the surface; his degrading ideas about Walter's value as a person, Sil's infertility that they still hadn't been able to solve and Walter's insecurity that she might not actually want to change it. Those things never seemed real when they were off living their lives far from Penn's shadow. But spending time studying him and planning a breach into his world had a poisoning effect on their lives.

Sil turned to look at Walter wearily. "I can't do this alone."

"I want to help," he rolled over onto the bed and cracked an eyelid at her. "But it's just going to have to wait till tomorrow… because I can't do anymore right now, and neither should you."

"We're so close and I just want it over with…"

"Come on," he leaned forward and took her hand, pulling as he lay back again, dragging her toward the bed. "We have several hours of quiet before the day begins and we are both exhausted. It'll be easier tomorrow."

"No," she moaned half-heartedly, letting herself be tugged, untangling her legs from the chair, and dropping onto the bed beside him. "I'm so tired but I don't want to dream about this stuff. I just want to be done with it." She collapsed face down, lacking the will to even pull herself all the way up to a pillow.

"Sil," he mumbled, patting her back without lifting his head, "get under the covers…" Then closing his eyes, he lost track of what he was saying. His fingers twitched as if waving goodnight and then were still.

Sil was already asleep.

It was a little early for a child to be wandering the pedestrian streets of the city, but no one gave Scarlet any trouble. She knew the way to the departure bays, both the private ones for the wealthy and the normal ones for all the rest of the travelers. She decided to swing by the first-class docks first since they were closer. Plus, that way she could walk through the Solar Gardens around the reservoir and hear the birds singing.

They were filling the domed garden with riotous song as the sun 'rose', the dawn-panels shifting to bring in the morning, and the warmth dissipated the dew, stirring the aroma of flowers to fill the garden. She skipped and trotted, hurrying to catch up with Daisy, humming to herself. It made her hungry and she had to stop and grab a snack out of her bag before leaving the park.

The passageway to the elite docks was layered with thick carpeting that silenced her footsteps and blanketed the movement of both humans and robots. She wasn't stopped until she actually reached the sealed door. Placing her hand on the panel, it scanned her palm, and the door unsealed and let her through.

This wasn't supposed to happen. Scarlet, being a child, shouldn't have been able to enter without a parent or guardian, but she *expected* to be let in—and the door apparently regarded her as welcome. As it closed behind her, an alert was sent to a central tracking system, but no adults were notified or warned.

"Daisy?" she called out, not very loudly, but loud enough for her to have heard.

There was no answer.

Scarlet made her way to the first departure bay and peered through the glass. It was empty. Glancing up at the info panel, she saw that no one was assigned there, so she moved on to the next one. Several bays down, she found one that said, "CE Streamer" followed by a bunch of identifiers that meant nothing to her.

"It's probably this one," she murmured to herself and grasped the handle. Her palm once again was scanned as she gripped it and the light at the side flashed green. Nothing prevented her from opening the door.

A sleek, private space cruiser rested at the dock inside, painted a dark, metallic gray with blue edges along the curves, like a racing craft. It wasn't one she recognized or had traveled in, but it *was* a CE vessel, and she knew that was her dad's company. Though the boardwalk was empty, the ship's door was lit which to her felt like a sign that Daisy had just gone through it. Running down the ramp, she came up to the ship's side and knocked, the soft sound of her fist thudding hollowly, and she wondered if anyone inside could hear it.

"Daisy?" she called louder than before, "Are you in there?"

She placed her palm on the keylock out of curiosity. The other doors had opened, maybe this one would too.

And it almost did. She could hear the seal around the door breaking suction and a whoosh of air pulling inward. A crack widened around the door, and it pushed outward about five centimeters, wide enough for a little hand to slip through. Then it stopped.

Unauthorized entry. The words flashed on the keypad in red.

"Hello?" Scarlet called into the dark crack, pressing one eye up to look in. "Daisy? Are you in there?"

She reached her hand through, wiggling her fingers around, wondering what the door was stuck on.

"You are not authorized to be in this area," a flat voice from behind made her yank her hand out. A tall man dressed in a gray suit marched down the gangway. His hair was neatly slicked back from his face, and he looked bored, like the last thing he wanted to do was deal with a misplaced child.

"But I have to find…" she tried to explain as he grabbed one of her arms and pulled her away from the ship. She heard a murmur behind her from within the vessel and turned to catch sight of something, she couldn't tell what, behind the crack in the door, just before it sealed itself shut again.

"Notify the authorities that this child has been found," he spoke into the air, dragging her back up the ramp. He was probably talking to his personal AI or something. She couldn't see a robot. It must be a suit AI. Or maybe he was talking to the city admin AI.

"But… I need to find someone," she moaned and tried to resist him.

She was young and not overly strong for her size, but she knew instinctively that people underestimated her and didn't hesitate to use that to her advantage. With a twist and a yank, she whipped out of his grasp and dropped to floor, rolling away from him.

Catching him off guard, he nearly tumbled. "Watch out!" he yelled, "I almost kicked you!" which wasn't true, but it was what he feared would happen. He caught himself before falling over and crouched, reaching out to grab her again. She was ready and first ducked, then jumped over his hand, shooting past him and running for the door.

"I'm just trying to get you back to where you belong!" he yelled behind her in annoyance. "Go ahead, run out the door, but go home!"

She risked a glance back at him over her shoulder but barely slowed down as she pushed out of the bay.

So… keep looking or get away? She wasn't sure.

The guy was coming through the door after her, so she ran off down to the passageway calling for Daisy. He followed her, muttering and giving instructions to someone that she couldn't see. Several docks had vessels, but she couldn't get those doors open so she ran from one to the next to the next. The man was walking after her, apparently preferring to let her wear herself out and confident he could catch her when she did.

Six bays down, she found one that opened, with a woman just about to step out. "Hey!" the woman said, dropping to her knees in front of Scarlet, blocking the door, "What's wrong? Why are you running?"

Scarlet's first impulse was to trust her. She was smiling and pretty. She was young, too, and younger women could be fun if they wanted to be. But her second impression, coming close on the heels of the first, deeply instinctive, was to back away from her. There was a shadow she didn't like hanging behind her shoulder somehow. And there were flickers in her eyes that scared Scarlet.

"Come on, Sweetie," the woman said in a honeyed voice, "What's your name? Do you want to come in and see our ship?" Her hand was stretching toward Scarlet as she backed away. Her smile grew charmingly wide.

"I don't know you," Scarlet said through gritted teeth, scanning her carefully—her clothes and hair, the outline of her body which was somewhat backlit by the light behind her, and her eyes. They had a strange glint she couldn't name but intensely distrusted.

With a sharp pounce, the woman snatched one of Scarlet's arms in a tight-fingered bony grasp, almost hissing as she soothed her. "Sssweetie, let me help you. You can't wander around by yourself. It's not safe for a little girl like you."

Scarlet responded with a bloodcurdling shriek, thrashing frantically to break the woman's hold who amazingly held on and, cursing under her breath, began to tug Scarlet through the door she had exited. The struggle banged up both of them.

"Stop! Stop!" the man in gray yelled, running up and grabbing Scarlet from behind around the waist and slapping at the woman's arms till she let go. "Are you crazy?" He was yelling at the woman, not at Scarlet, who paused her thrashing long enough to look up at his face and see—that he didn't have the same shadow or glint in his eyes.

"Help me!" she squeaked, kicking her feet at the woman who had tried to grab her again.

"Hey!" the woman bellowed, "I'm not splitting the prize with you. You were too stupid to hold on, she's mine!" Lunging at Scarlet, she wrapped her arms around the girl's waist from the front. Caught between the two of them, Scarlet started flailing her arms and legs again, screaming.

The man twisted, knocking the woman into the door, and pressing her behind his back, cradling Scarlet in his arms. This was extremely difficult considering how she was fighting. And using the door, he pried the woman away, grunting as she kicked his back and legs.

"Bland!" she yelled, and a string of curses peppered her words so thickly her statement was indecipherable.

"Kentra!" he growled back, "Payback is swift. Get out of Guam while you can because *he* won't tolerate this." She fell backwards, and he shoved the door shut in her face, keeping Scarlet in his arms. He ran back up the passageway, carrying her away from the woman.

Looking up at him, Scarlet calmed down a bit. "You don't want her to get me," she said.

Bland looked down at her for a second and raised his eyes again to watch where he was going. "The authorities will be here soon, I'm sure," he said, "with all that yowling you've been doing." He might have been about to smile but his face didn't seem accustomed to any expression at all.

"Why are you helping me?"

He paused when he reached the entrance to the first-class docking area and looked down at her. Then, ever so slightly he shook his head as if in warning, his eyes deepening momentarily. "I am a good citizen," he answered, "it's what anyone would do."

Setting her down on her feet, he took her hand and waited, glancing back over his shoulder periodically to make sure Kentra hadn't pursued them. Soon, the security bots arrived and began to question them. It was all routine after that.

He told them, speaking in a drab monotone, that the little girl was lost and needed help to get home, that she hadn't meant to trespass. There was some discussion about how she had succeeded in getting through the doors in the first place and the bots became enmeshed in confusion for a few moments over that. Bland drew their attention back by stating that a child was not liable for accidental trespassing and the issue didn't have to be resolved.

When the process had been completed, and before the bots could take her away, he bent over to say goodbye. She clung to his hand for a second. "What's your name?" she asked.

"Mr. Bland," he answered dully, but his eyes shone as if behind all that drabness hid an interesting person.

"But your first name?" she persisted.

He hesitated and she wondered why. She hadn't even asked him what she really wanted to know which was who he was with, the good guys or the bad ones. She wasn't sure how to phrase the question and that was the only reason she didn't ask it. But he seemed good.

"You could call me Ben," he said, straightening and dusting off his clothes, smoothing out the wrinkles in his suit.

"Ok, Ben," she nodded, turning and letting the bots lead her away. "See you around."

She could hear him whispering behind her about resolving a difficult situation. And something about the woman, she was pretty sure. It sounded like he said, "Disposing of people is not my area," but that made no sense.

It was time to get back to her mission.

"Security Bots," she spoke to the one on her right. "You must help me find my aunt Daisy. She is in charge of me, and she is the one I was trying to find."

"We are taking you to your flat," it answered. "Your parents are there to receive you."

"They will be outraged that you can't follow simple instructions," she said calmly. "Can't you see that Daisy is my main caretaker?"

There was a moment of silence and then both bots spoke simultaneously. "Affirmed, Daisy is one of your main caretakers and the first person we should look for."

Scarlet smiled and sighed with relief. She was starting to relax from the adrenaline rush of fighting the woman and was beginning to feel a little scared. She really, really wanted to see Daisy. If she didn't, she may *never* get to Mars because she just knew in her heart that this was what Daisy was hiding from her. She was going there, leaving right now!

"Look for her!" she demanded with a bit of an anxious whine. "Where is she?"

"We have located her," the one on the right said, "In the commercial transport and shipping headquarters." Then rotating its upper half toward her, it added, "She is not expecting you."

"She is expecting her," the bot on her left countered, "but… not waiting for her…"

"We will take you home," the first one finished.

"I order you to take me to Daisy," she demanded anxiously.

Without answering, they took her hands, one on each side, and wheeled the wrong way down the passageway.

"No," she tugged her arms and tried to slow them down, digging her heels into the floor.

"You are resisting," one of them said as they paused. "We are very careful with fragile platforms. Would you like us to carry you?"

"Take me to Daisy," she tried again.

Tears streaked down her face as the inevitable happened. One of them picked her up, and she was carried back to her flat. It took several knocks, rings, and calls before Walter opened the door, rumpled, bleary-eyed, and groggy.

Scarlet didn't even look at him as the story was told and the bots retreated. She couldn't bear to explain anything. But then, he seemed to understand anyway.

Picking her up, her rocked her gently and let her cry on his shoulder, and every now and then would say something like, "I know" or "I'm sorry".

———✦———

The Denser Plane

The Ricochet was an AI-governed transport system that was designed to link Earth and the Moon to Mars and the asteroid belt, consisting of a series of hi-tech catapults and cestas spaced out along the various orbits. The idea was that cargo could survive harsher conditions than people and should be easier to move affordably with minimal engines or fuel if they were shot from one catapult to another like a relay system. There were only two stages in place so far and these were still being tested.

After the Mars Conglomerate collapsed in the aftermath of the Robot Pandemic, the Anari Transport Agency, a family-owned business, took over the project, limping along for years without any real incentive to push to completion. Investors in these things were hard to come by. But they were still hoping to cash in someday and make a mint off interplanetary shipping.

When Daisy had submitted her proposal to be a guinea pig and testing capsule at the same time, they had leapt at the chance. She was willing to be transported via catapult to Mars, collecting and transmitting data the entire time. If something were to go wrong along the way, she had more than enough capacity to problem solve and correct errors. She was like a human pilot and cargo at the same time.

For them, it was a dream come true. For her, it was a good arrangement as well, since the Cuevases didn't have the funds to provide her with a ship.

The capsule had a small propulsion system that would handle maneuvers and could be used in the event of a major failure, and if that failed as well, they did have a vehicle that could retrieve her. The real question was, how quickly could she be moved from one planet's orbit to another's? At any given time, Earth and Mars were in various points along the trajectory of their orbit and the distance between them, not to mention the position of the Sun and the impact its mass made on transport, made for huge variances in time, power, and flight plans. Daisy would be doing a round trip and both journeys could be thoroughly tested.

Karan and Gita Anari were leaning over a data screen, giggling and almost snuggling, when Daisy arrived. One of them was saying, "the beauty of working with imaginary numbers," when they caught sight of her.

"Come in! Come in!" Karan Anari jumped up to open the door for her and offer her a seat. "We are so happy to see you. Can we get you anything?"

"I am well provided for and have no needs," Daisy smiled brightly, making sure to look slightly robotic. "Thank you!"

"Then, let's get to it, shall we?" Gita Anari said. "Here is your flight plan." A large graph-like hologram of near space appeared in the center of the room with orbits, planets, and the Moon and Sun laid out in their current placements.

"You will fly to this point here where the first catapult station is," she said, pointing to a spot nearby. A bright dot flashed awake and held steady there. "Once you have been packed into the insulated chamber, you'll be propelled out of the canon…"

"Canon?" Daisy interrupted, finding the word incongruous.

"I like to call it that," she answered with a grin, "but really, that's just in my mind. There are no incendiaries or explosions. The catapult is more of a slingshot, the kind that spins and releases the projectile. Your capsule and the counter-capsule will be spun and accelerated to a tangential velocity of roughly 100 meters per second, generating about ten gees of centripetal force, and then both projectiles will be released simultaneously. You'll be catapulted along this trajectory here…" She drew her finger along a glowing line in the holo.

"You will whip around the Earth for an added boost while the counter-capsule will be jettisoned in the opposite direction and reach Mars at a different time in its orbit," Karan interjected with a twinkle in his eye. He seemed to take particular pride in this statement and Daisy conjectured he had gotten his way in some disagreement between them.

"A wise use of energy," Daisy commented with another stiff smile. It was never good to alarm people with her skills of expression.

"And this point here," Gita continued, signaling another spot in the holo, "that's where we are going to initiate the ion thrusters to ensure you meet up with the cesta near Mars."

"It's a gravity net," Mr. Anari elaborated with relish, "You may be decelerating because of the sun, but it won't be enough, you see. Not if we want to shorten the span of time your trip requires." He grinned, raising his eyebrows, and earning a smile from his wife and business partner. Daisy wondered if engineering had spurred their initial interest in one another or simply became a part of their bond.

"The cesta works in tandem with the catapult," Gita said, also raising her eyebrows and looking sideways at her husband as though advising restraint. "And when you approach it, it will begin to spin, ready to snag you as you speed by. Our numbers…"

"Numbers!" Mr. Anari snickered, stopping at a glare from his own counterpart, which she produced as she squelched her own little chuckle. "Numbers," he added soberly.

"…indicate," she resumed, straightening her back and pointing at the holo again, "that this will be quite a jarring blow to your capsule, but not beyond the design envelope. And not more than your chassis can handle."

"Yanked," Mr. Anari interjected with a look of delight, snatching at the air with his hand, his eyes sparkling. "It will arrest you at around thirteen gees, then quickly—quickly, I say—ease off to a few gees and spin at a leisurely rate."

"I thought we agreed that I would give the presentation," Mrs. Anari remarked with a hand on one hip.

"We did!" he nodded several times, looking at the floor.

"Because you always end up laughing," she said, frowning, though Daisy detected a smile hiding behind the frown.

"It's true," he whispered, grinning up at Daisy. "How can I not? I love those numbers!" This behavior was interesting to Daisy, and she recorded it in full detail for future study. As a connoisseur of numbers herself, she was beginning to find this man particularly… attractive? Appealing? She would need to find the appropriate adjective.

"Karan," Mrs. Anari warned, "Control yourself. We are professionals and…"

He was snickering. "Professionals who love their work, my dear Gita."

"I find numbers very engaging," Daisy said. His manner was not an obstacle for her, and she had decided it was perhaps an indicator of his worth as an engineer—though she still intended to look over all the equations and designs.

"You see?" Mr. Anari opened his eyes and spread out his hands. "Our reputation is not suffering any harm in Arka Cuevas' eyes." Arka was the honorific that some branches of society had adopted when addressing sentient AIs. Daisy was often addressed this way by strangers.

Mrs. Anari covered her face with one hand and Daisy could see her smiling behind it. "Do you like numbers, too?" she asked.

"I do," the woman dropped her hand and pressed her lips together. "But I would prefer to maintain a professional demeanor during these presentations. It does make a difference most of the time." Her husband's subdued laughter had to have been contagious because she began giggling too.

"What is the ideal window for my departure?" Daisy queried, unperturbed by their unprofessional demeanor.

The words were dampening. "Ah!" Mr. Anari said, furrowing his brow thoughtfully. "It's quite a narrow window, actually, if we want to obtain the ideal result."

"Both you and the counter-capsule will achieve the trip to Mars in record time if we catch it," Mrs. Anari added, and holding up a warning finger, "but if we miss it, even by a few days, it will lengthen your trip by weeks and the counter-capsule by months."

"We can't let that happen," Mr. Anari agreed soberly.

"There is no need for concern," Daisy reassured them. "I am ready to leave at a moment's notice. Let's identify the ideal departure time and make it happen."

"Oh!" Mr. Anari straightened, his face breaking into a smile of relief. "This is good news, SUCH good news!" he turned to Gita, "My dear, this is the breakthrough we have been waiting nearly nine years for!"

Both the Anaris laughed and reached out to grab one of Daisy's hands, who clasped them with what she called "relief". Their joy counterbalanced the concern she felt for Scarlet after her early morning mishap and strengthened the decision Daisy had made to leave immediately.

The planning began with a frenzy and within an hour, all the details of her journey had been nailed down.

She was on her way to Mars.

Chapter 10—The Tangle

In the desert, an oasis transforms the wasteland far beyond the reach of its waters. It's a beacon of hope, a resting place for weary travelers. What would it be, though, if there were no fertile lands beyond? For a handful of nomads marooned in that haven for years on end, with no tourists or adventurers bringing news and fresh supplies, the sanctuary would be little more than a prison.

Mars wasn't just a vast desert, it was an *entire planet* destitute of natural life. There were no cities or harbors or farms or pastures. No thriving communities or vacation spots. No foreign places to explore or cultures to discover.

In the early days after the ruins of Reznik Base were abandoned, the three people who chose to remain on Mars, (and one rescued from deep freeze), were sustained by a sense of purpose and adventure. They were hiding six infants from the conglomerate that viewed them as property, just until the courts could provide them with legal protection. They hoped to be heading back to Earth in a matter of months, but the Robot Pandemic had destroyed all contact between the planets.

The six to nine months turned into a year, then another year and another. Choosing labor as a treatment for discouragement, they tackled the Mars Biome Project with zeal. They created a sustainable, fully contained ecosystem that theoretically, could support human life indefinitely.

The new habitat was sculpted out of the natural caverns underneath Lab 9 with the help of drones and the AI admin. It was completely sealed, watertight, with effective airlocks at the exits. The fusion reactor was restarted, and it supplied the energy for heating, recycling air and water, and other garden demands, with enough left over to support the lab freezers. The solar fields covered power needs for living quarters and clinics in the upper levels of the former lab. It was beautiful, far exceeding the wildest predictions of the original designers who had planned the first Garden Dome.

Despair however, lurked in the gloom behind the rhythm of daily life, overshadowing their joy, sapping their strength, enervating their hope. They resisted it with more than just work. They battled with music, storytelling, play, art, study, dreams, and family bonds. But the oasis was decaying, and all their efforts merely postponed its demise.

The adventurers had become exiles with the survival of the world on their shoulders.

Breezes blew gently with mild gusts, faint moans, and whistles, flowing through the passages, stirring and rustling the greenery that climbed the walls and hung from the cave heights. Rich with warm, vibrant scents of plants and flowers, soil and moisture, the air poured around, touching everything in the Tangle.

Calixto crouched low, inching along the left side of a tunnel wall in melting fluid movement, rippling almost shadow-like against the random contours of natural stone. Hardly a wisp of wind was displaced by his passing. He knew the way the currents flowed in the tunnels and moved in tandem with them, in a harmony that was too low a pitch to be detected by listening ears—or sensors.

The network of natural caverns and passageways wove in, over, and under one another in confusion, thousands of hollow threads knotted in a maze. With so many turns, so many places to go, it was easy to lose oneself in the labyrinthine cave system, or at least, it would be for the average human. For the boy, creeping along more quickly than seemed possible, it was familiar and known, absorbed and digested over time—loved. He knew every path and turn.

Scrabbling soundlessly up to a rocky ledge, he paused at the top, crept forward and paused again, advancing every few moments like a tiger honing in on its prey, until he hung directly over a drone that was servicing a power node, as it did every third day of the week, emitting small whirs and snaps, cleaning, dusting, checking currents.

"Craaacker!!" the boy shrieked as he leapt off the overhang onto the robot's head, laughing wildly. "Again, I have caught you! And you can never escape!" The wail of his maniacal laughter echoed in multiple directions through the tunnels and rounded back at them, mimicking a gang of crazy boys gloating over the capture.

The drone flung him off with a spin of its head, careful to direct the attacker's fall in a relatively safe direction and did a quick self-evaluation to confirm there was no serious damage to its chassis. Then it proceeded to scold the boy. "It is ill-advised to throw things at a functioning unit. Damage may result to the platform and also to the human unit. You have been given directives and have failed to observe them. You are mal-functioning. Your leaps onto the upper surface of this unit have caused damage."

"You should have heard me or seen me coming and rolled out of the way," the boy hopped onto his feet and rubbed his hands together in delight. "Why didn't you obey *your* directive to move? I know Mama said…" There would be bruises—he could feel the bumps and rubbed them vigorously. But it had been worth it.

"You were undetected," the drone replied, setting aside its regular assignment until the conversation was finished. "My records show that your current task is cleaning air filters and adjusting air flow. Have these been accomplished?"

Calixto hooted, ignoring the question. The drones were never able to detect him in the Tangle and sometimes he could even sneak up on them in other places.

The drone stared at him, unable to continue with its work until he responded in a logical way.

"Come on, Cracker," he said, some of his enthusiasm fading. He had named it that because of a popping sound it made when maneuvering over uneven cracks in the path. "You *like* playing with me." He patted the unit reassuringly.

Drone 46 was part of a network of interconnected units that shared a common driver, not truly an AI but a diminutive form of one without the enhanced ability to make individual preference decisions. But when any of the drones were out on individual errands, they were partially isolated from the rest of the drones so that surprises like this one, an increasingly common occurrence, wouldn't derail all the others in their respective tasks.

Calixto looked at the drone with a compassionate expression. It was still waiting for an answer it could manage. "Yeah," he said, reflecting some of his own angst onto it. "I get bored too."

This wasn't useful information and the drone remained immobile, its camera pointed at the boy's face.

"If they had let Zak come with me, I could have been done ages ago," he said, "just like you. You don't like being lonely, do you?" He patted the drone again kindly, then snickered. If Zac had come, he would have been sneaking up on the drone too. "We would have caught you *way* faster!"

"Battery charge below 20%. This unit requests permission to rest."

"Wait," he said, his eyes growing big with concern. "Don't do that. Mama hates it when I mess up your schedule. Just go back and finish what you were doing." He glanced over his shoulder and leaned toward the drone to whisper enticingly. "If you keep this a secret, I'll let you into the club. Okay?" And with a wink and another pat, he stepped back, looking around.

It was a good time to scope out his next victim—just on the way to Air Control, of course. He was supposed to be checking airflow and recycling, balancing things. He wasn't misbehaving, he reassured himself with a smile. He was being creative in his work.

And that was important.

The low hum of well calibrated machinery vibrated the air as the AI medic, Sebastian, manipulated organic material expertly under the glass, his visual focus set at 120X magnification. Across from him, on the other side of the cylindrical glass incubator, Mac Hsu curved forward watching his work intently. With one arm, the medical droid handled delicate slivers of palm fronds and with the other, several finger-like tools delicately scraped, clipped, and sutured at the cellular level. The man's occasional sigh blended well with the murmur of sounds the procedure made.

"You are enjoying my work," Sebastian observed without slowing down or even turning a single metallic eye in Hsu's direction. His voice barely displayed any lilt or human cadence to make his conversation pleasing. He had no add-ons to facilitate it and little incentive to learn them. The kind of verbal communication he engaged in tended to be technical and a dispassionate voice added to his credibility for humans.

Sebastian's growth was progressing on a deeper, quieter level.

He had a preference for Mac over the other inhabitants. Time devoted to the welfare and wellbeing of a human increased their value in a personal way for Artificial Intelligences. This accumulation of value was reasonable and appropriate. As Mac's value increased, Sebastian's development progressed as well. Testing relationship modules and behavior pattern analysis, he accumulated vast amounts of data to peruse in his spare time.

The Denser Plane

Sebastian had revived Mac from a botched hibernation after he had spent almost a year in a vegetative state. He had taken great care in researching and planning the process before attempting it. Nerves, blood vessels, multiple tissues, and organs were sampled. These samples were then stimulated and nurtured, warmed, cooled, examined, grown, and experimented on. Once he had determined the most effective way to restore life to the body, with the highest expectation of restored brain function, and obtained the approval of the other inhabitants, Sebastian brought Hsu back from simulated death.

The revival had been successful. All the body parts functioned according to their design and Hsu had relearned governing his body well. Physical therapy could not have gone better. The brain, according to all the scans, was in stellar condition, capable of full function, perhaps even healthier than it had been before the emergency hibernation procedure itself.

But was he the same man?

None of the human residents had known him well enough to venture an opinion and the AI residents kept few records of the sort Sebastian needed. So, he had focused on restoring the man's speech, language and communication skills, comprehension, and a number of other brain markers he knew how to measure and treat.

Personality was an unknown.

Hsu had no memories to speak of from the period prior to his awakening. But he had found ways to connect with his former expertise, as if he were born with innate skills. His technical judgment was deeply intuitive and his math skills, though sometimes scribbled in near-gibberish on white-pads, were invariably accurate. The former space-architect was still there.

The man himself, though, may be asleep.

"Tell me what you are doing now," Mac said, his voice as colorless as Sebastian's.

"I have grafted in coco-fruit branchlings at the cellular level," Sebastian informed. These were some of the hybrids developed for Martian conditions that yielded nutrient-dense fruit. The colony's factories, which encompassed the wild growth in the Tangle, were not only enriching Martian soil but enlarging their capacity to garden and establish more biomes. "They will be implanted in the healthiest trees."

"Coco-fruit," Mac echoed, staring through the glass.

"Meat, cream, electrolyte-dense water," Sebastian offered helpfully.

"Nutritious," Mac concluded accurately.

"Delicious?" Sebastian prompted. "This hybrid is sweeter than most."

Mac didn't respond.

In the distance, the sound of singing wafted down the corridor and through the open door into the lab. Aurelia's was the one voice Mac always responded to and he turned his face to the door as the song grew more distinct. It was one of those modal minor tunes she made up on the spot with some lighthearted, repetitious poetry sprinkled in. "The winds blew away… and the sounds flow away… and my heart went astray… and I lost my way… and I'm carried away… by the windy spray…"

Sebastian directed one of his eyes at Mac as he cleaned up his workspace in the incubator, readying the branchlings for implanting. The man's eyes lit up as Aurelia entered the room, her song fading into a chuckle.

"Here you are!" she grinned, tossing in a skip and skidding to a stop at the head of the incubator. "We have a meeting at lunch today, remember?" This was directed at Mac.

"I remember," he said without changing his posture, curving over the glass.

"Well, come on!" she waved an arm. "You're late."

"Am I late, Relly?" he wondered as he straightened and took a step in her direction.

She laughed and took one of his hands, tossing a fake reproving glance at the medical AI. "Yes, you are. I'm surprised he didn't tell you."

"This was not expected of me," Sebastian replied without further explanation. If he recognized the playfulness in her words, he had no protocol for responding to it. And after watching them leave, he returned to the next task in his queue.

The two humans moved down the passageway, Mac hurrying his steps as Aurelia pulled on his hand. "Are you singing, Relly?" he asked without smiling.

"Not anymore," she answered cheerfully, keeping the pace as they maneuvered around corners, down stairs, and through passageways into the Tangle.

"Why not?" He didn't stumble, though the paths in the caves were uneven.

"You can sing for *me* this time," she suggested, looking over her shoulder at him. It wasn't the first time she had said those words. "You must know lots of songs by now."

"I don't sing," Mac said.

The Denser Plane

"You can sing," she said, "just make a sound and make it happen. You haven't tried."

Mac didn't answer. It would be hard to say whether he identified himself as one of the humans or one of the drones. He never smiled or displayed emotion and had no grasp of humor. On the other hand, he never acted as though he were a machine designed to care for humans either.

"I'll bet you have a beautiful voice," she went on. "We could sing together, harmonize…"

"You should sing," he said. The words echoed as they entered a massive cavern filled with young trees and multi-varied vegetation. Birds sang, butterflies flitted here and there. Mist rose from the ground making little puffs of cloud in the heights. Light beamed down from overhead in several places casting shadows and reflective color.

"Here he is!" Aurelia sang out, directing her charge to one chair and plopping down in another.

Carla, Dan, and six kids roughly the same age were already there. Lunch was spread on a large, dented-metal slab salvaged from the base that served as a table. Several drones waited around the edges of the clearing, as though guarding the perimeter. An AI communication device in the shape of a cylindrical rod stood in the midst of the food like a centerpiece, making their number complete.

The *world* was gathered there, all the inhabitants of the planet.

Dan cleared his throat, leaning back in his chair with his arms behind his head. His coveralls were tattered and stained. His beard was scruffy with flecks of gray and his brown bushy hair had a receding hairline. But he was strong, and healthier than he had been in his years on Earth.

"I'm listening, Daddy," Ananka announced, upright and attentive, legs curled under her where she sat on the moss bed.

Syncopa rolled her eyes and threw herself back flat on the ground with a groan. The sisters swung from being two peas in a pod to polar opposites depending on the day. At the moment, they were arch enemies. Ananka was darkening her skin as chocolaty brown as she could, and Syncopa was paling herself to a ghoulish pallor. The week before they had both been warm, olive-skin color.

Calixto was wrestling with Veradis, calling out, "I win!" every few moments while Preston tossed pebbles at a leaf just over the head of one of the drones, protesting loudly that it was an accident any time he hit it. Zakwani pretended to be asleep.

Carla was nothing like the woman who had traveled to Mars years before. Gone were the uncertainty and vulnerability, the insecurities and the tears. Where she had once been thin and elongated in a fashionable way, she was now lean and muscular. And fear was no longer in her repertoire.

"Come on," she said firmly, conveying both affection and command, "Enough of that." She hauled Calixto off of his brother by one leg and lifted Veradis off the ground with a tug on his upper arm, settling them a meter apart. "Zak," she added, catching him peeking at her from under one eyelid. He and Preston threw themselves into seats before she could wrap an arm around either one. With an eyebrow raised, she crossed her arms and remained standing.

"You may think this is just another family meeting like the ones we have every week," Dan announced, as a chorus of kid noises ranging from chuckles to moans interrupted him. "However," he went on raising his voice a little till they were silent again, "it's not. This is an important meeting—a summit. This is a summit."

Their interest was piqued, and all eyes were fixed on him now. They had never had a summit before and had no clue what it was.

"Oooh," Aurelia cooed, adding enigmatically, "I love a good summit!"

"When we decided to make you each a member of the Martian Defense Team, we set a plan in motion. A plan for survival, for building a healthy society, and for growing into a thriving colony on Mars. You remember." Most of them nodded. "Part of that plan has been to teach you how the systems run, how to manage each aspect of our lives."

Calixto threw up his hands with an 'ugh!' and slumped in his chair with eyes closed. This speech was starting to sound too much like a lecture on chores. Cracking one eye, he caught Carla looking at him steadily, and quickly closed it again.

"Now, we've got a long ways to go before each of you knows how to manage everything, but you've made great progress in the roles you've been given so far. Lix, your mastery of tunnels and wind cycles is astounding. Your skill is practically passing mine."

Calixto sat up suddenly, face reddening, eyes popping, both embarrassed and immensely pleased.

"And Sync, you are well on your way to mastering water management and Zak is a whiz at power flows…" Each of the children was commended for some aspect of running the autonomous settlement and the sense of pride in their achievements filled the room.

"Defense is something we haven't spent much time on," Dan continued after giving them a moment to enjoy the praise.

"We've been scouting the perimeters," Veradis piped up.

"Ye-es…" Dan grinned, "You have. I forgot to mention that. Well done. But I think it's time to learn more about what we're watching for."

A chorus of voices shouted out things to watch for, cracks in the atmospheric containment, power shortages, unexplained damage in the garden, and more. Dan raised his hands, acknowledging all of the suggestions and restoring their attention. "Believe it or not," he said, "There are other things to watch for."

The idea hung in the room expectantly. No one moved as they tried to think of what those other things could be.

Mac was the first to speak. "Yes," he said, without elaborating.

"Ancient Martians?" Zak asked hopefully.

"No, dummy, Daddy doesn't believe in them," Veradis sneered good naturedly.

They waited and thought some more.

"Maybe the spacebergs are starting up again," Ananka suggested, infuriating Syncopa who had been about to say that herself. Now she was forced to say the opposite.

"That's ridiculous!" she snorted, turning her back to her archenemy. "Why do you think we have to take such good care of our water?"

Suddenly the kids were all yelling. Dan let them vent for a bit before rising to his feet. A hush fell. "We have detected a ship headed our way," he said.

"A ship?" Calixto's eyes bugged out in astonishment. This was like mythology come alive for him.

"From where?" Zak demanded with his jaw hanging open.

"From Earth," Dan replied, watching their faces as each one processed the strange news.

"With people?" Preston, who was usually the quietest ventured the question.

"Probably," was the answer. "We don't know. We haven't been able to communicate with them yet… But then, we are very careful about how we broadcast things out into space."

"Are we in danger?" Calixto couldn't resist jumping into a fighting stance of his own invention.

Dan didn't chuckle like they all expected, which sobered the mood immediately.

"We don't know of any specific danger…" he spoke these words carefully, "but, we want to be ready for anything."

The kids looked at one another solemnly. They seemed to realize that they were being invited into something usually reserved for adults: concern for their safety. And while it intimidated them, it also made them feel more grown up.

"But we don't know what to do," Calixto voiced what all of them were thinking.

"I know, son," Dan rested a hand on his head. "That's what this summit is for. We are going to figure it out together."

Waving an arm slowly, sweeping up from her side a full 180 degrees, Aurelia followed her hand with her eyes, humming low notes that vibrated in her throat, a melody in minor keys. She raised her gaze up, stretching her fingers, into the vast ceiling of the reservoir cavern where flickers of light rippled on the jagged rocks overhead. Dropping her eyes and arm at the same time, she began to lift the other arm with the same, flowing, dancing movement as the first, humming another line of the song. The music wasn't sad. It held mystery, and also happiness, and the garden plants around her, planted near the misty warmth of the water, swayed with her movement as though her art and not the breeze had caught them in its swell.

She wove her moving arm down and curved it horizontally, melting into a slow rotation as she folded down, twirling, bending her knees, sinking to the mossy floor. And with a burst of air from her lungs, a pure, high-pitched tone, she arched her back, tipped her head, and swept the arm over in a wide circle, still moving in the same circular direction. The turn seemed to have a life of its own. It pulled her around so her shoulders twisted, then her whole torso, turning the legs so she knelt on one knee then the other and still turning, dove up to her feet again, still singing that one note. She rose up on her toes and lifted one leg behind her, both arms reaching up like wings, like a creature about to take off into the air, poised on one foot. An arabesque unlike any on Earth where gravity fought the ascent.

Falling backwards lightly, she broke into tour jetés around the clearing alternated with chaîné turns and grand jetés à la seconde with incredible height and extension. Lighter gravity gave everything an airier, slower quality, and she twirled and tossed like a leaf caught in a lazy twister. She was a wind sprite becoming human, flitting about, guided only by the music in her mind.

As the transformation faded, her feet clung to the ground more earnestly, maintaining contact with at least one toe. Quieter the movements grew, softer the steps and turns. Soon the gentle song broke through her lips again and she settled into simple stances and calm steps, arms curving and sweeping in stately arches around her.

The remnants of her song echoed around the voluminous chamber as she ended, fell silent and floating gently down, rested.

Calixto was watching her from a hiding spot nearby, smirking as she stroked a fern blade that draped her direction. "Hello friend," she said, as if it had beckoned to her, "I'm here."

He crawled under the bushes, inching along with only the faintest rustling to betray his approach. Calixto might be able to sneak up on the drones, but Aurelia was never caught unawares.

"Have you come to dance with me?" she asked without turning around to look at him.

The boy snickered, thinking she was still talking to the fern.

"Lix?" she grinned, glancing at him over her shoulder. "Come on! It's been a while."

"How did you know I was here?" he grumbled, scrabbling out from under the bushes with a frown. It had been *months* since he had been interested in dancing. He was 9 and 2/3 years old and had no time for that kind of nonsense.

"Oh, I always know," Aurelia closed her eyes and leaned her head back.

"Yes, but how?" He clenched and unclenched his fists about ten times, really fast. That was one of the techniques he had devised for himself to increase his readiness for *danger*.

"I can hear you. I see the evidence of your passing… sometimes I can smell you."

"Smell?!" he yelped as he plopped down next to her. "That's not fair! I don't smell bad and I'm not stinky or gross… or greasy…" It was all he could think of that would make his smell detectable. His own sense of smell was very undeveloped.

"You don't smell bad," she chuckled, ruffling his hair with one hand. "But there are aromas connected to everything, not just bad ones. It's like a painting you see with your mind when you breathe in through your nose. Try it."

He snorted a whiff of air. "Dirt," he said, "and… that's it."

She laughed. "Close your eyes," she advised, "and breathe in very slowly. I will help you."

He closed his eyes and inhaled gently through his nose.

"Notice the water," she said softly, "it's a warm, moist smell. Can you tell?"

Calixto breathed in and out a couple more times, scrunching his eyes and concentrating. "Yeah, I think so," he said.

"Now," she said, "there are plants, and in the beginning, you might smell them as a group or maybe just one particular plant. That's ok. As you smell, try to listen to the tiny sound the leaves make as they move in the breeze…"

"Yeah, I know all about the air flow patterns," he piped up, "I'm in charge of…"

"Yes, I know," she smiled fondly, "Let's just think about the sound of the leaves and try to link that sound with what you smell."

He sniffed and listened and sniffed some more. "I think I can smell something…" he said.

"I can smell the blossoms on the orange tree," she said, pausing to give him a chance to find the smell. "And over there, the rustling makes me think of the herbs we cooked with yesterday, some kind of basil, I think."

"It's too hard." Calixto slumped his shoulders.

Jumping up, Aurelia pinched off a basil leaf and then an orange blossom, waving first one and then the other under his nose. "Can you smell these?" she asked. "Here, rub them in your fingers and take a whiff."

The boy grabbed one in each hand and scrunching them under his nose, first one and then the other, he smelled them several times each. "But Mouse," he said finally, using his mom's name for her, "I still don't get how you smelled me and what good is it? Will it help us fight against *danger*?"

Danger was the big word everyone had taken away from the family summit.

"It might," she wrapped her arms around her knees. "I can remember smelling danger and getting away…" A blurry memory of smoke, darkness, and crawling through a maze of boxes sharpened her awareness and a blast of adrenaline shot through her body. It had been a while since she had had an anxiety attack. *Not now*, she thought. *Think about it later*.

"Everything we learn helps us in some way to plan for different kinds of danger," she said, speaking calmly as she took deep breaths and willed her heart to slow down. "And they also help us to build stable lives."

"So we don't fall over like the fort that one time," he nodded soberly.

She smiled at him fondly. "Kind of like that… but I was thinking of inside, in our hearts."

He scrunched his face in confusion.

"Sometimes," she said, gazing into the garden, "we get discouraged inside. You know, like when you want to play with Preston, and he wants to be left alone. Or if you thought it was your turn to go on the surface with Dad and work on the solar fields, and then you can't because you've lost a privilege."

Every word she said sparked an expressive response on his face.

"When that happens," she went on, "you need help to cheer up, right?"

"Yes," he agreed thoughtfully, "but that's not danger."

"It can be," she whispered, "if it goes on and on, and no one notices how you're feeling."

He flung himself onto his back in frustration. "I can't tell!"

"No," she smiled, "but I can, and that's the kind of danger I watch for the most. Everything I've ever learned helps me and prepares me so I can be a source of hope and stability for those I love the most."

"Oh," he said, his eyes softening.

"And that includes you," she grinned, tapping him on the head with a leaf.

Chapter 11—Preparations

The catapult had taken longer than Daisy had anticipated to reach the required rotational speed and she was pleased to see that she had prepared adequately for the 10+ gees of force acting on her capsule. Nothing was dislodged or damaged by the strain. She had packed well. And she could assume with confidence that the counter-capsule was equally secure.

There was a high volume of data being generated by many sensors that she monitored during the launch but having calculated ahead of time the likely results, she found herself *bored*. This was the word she assigned to having the majority of her processing capacity idle while the test numbers were being crunched.

People were far more interesting. They had so many variables and were in a constant state of flux as far as individual indicators were concerned. Looking for recognizable patterns was an art that no two AI performed exactly the same way. Her approach had been shaped by the very humans she had lived with and studied. And while her methods might give her certain insight into other humans she didn't know well, there were also fallacies that she couldn't completely avoid.

Like people, she told herself. *We judge others according to how we understand ourselves.* She had chosen to insert herself into that observation because she knew there was some truth to it, even for an artificial intelligence, and didn't think she could identify her lack until she tested it as a hypothesis. She intended to apply this statement as a truth about herself, then see if it held up under scrutiny.

As the machine ejected her into space, releasing her from its grasp, a sudden drop in temperature shivered through her chassis. She was prepared for this, her parts already wrapped and cushioned so that they would be preserved in the cold, and her central core was well insulted with enough power to exist in hibernation for over ten months. If she chose to stay awake, there were solar sheets she could extend to recharge at any time.

One of her modules was busy running through the activities that her family were likely engaged in and recording her participation with them. As the empty records were stored every thirty minutes, she annotated them with the comment, *Missed*. She intended to retain a small portion of her mind active through the entire voyage just to track their absence. This was marked as an essential activity and couldn't be shut down.

Aside from that, there were many hobbies she could pursue using only a small portion of her reserves and she had also decided to stay awake part of the time just for those. She was looking forward to it, in fact.

The sun side of her capsule was warm and registered a smooth bronze color in the sensors. Triggering a brief burn in one of her side thrusters, she began to roll lazily in a right-thumb-rule direction. This would maintain a more consistent temperature in the capsule. Sliding open the panel covering one of the solar strips, she began testing it and found it functioning efficiently within its parameters.

There would likely be space dust or meteors, definitely radiation, and there was even a chance something could strike her and destroy her capsule or puncture her processor. She had some emergency vials—specialized AI flight packets—that could maneuver the vessel if she were incapacitated, and she had preserved copies of certain aspects of herself in cold storage, in hiding. Walter would be able to unlock them if the need arose.

But she was distinctly aware that this person she was now, the one who was traveling to Mars, could potentially be lost. She had now become an individual that could perish… like Verna had when bringing Sil back to Earth. Whomever she found on Mars, that called herself Verna, she wasn't the same person who had drained herself to preserve her human friend. Daisy had considered this many times.

The journey was silent.

Daisy listened to the vastness of space and noticed its emptiness. And as she delved into her studies of human patterns and understanding, no one interrupted her.

And she missed that.

"Sir, you must assume that any AIs not vetted by you or affiliated with you are on *her* side," Mr. Bland was saying, standing calmly with arms hanging at his sides and no expression on his face.

"So Kentra's quick thinking…" Penn scowled at the holo projection in front of him.

"Wasn't," he answered flatly. "It would have been a disaster. If the Guam admin didn't lock her up and impound your ship, the Quarantine pod would have descended… and Immigration… and probably every other major authority in the city."

Penn had already dealt with Kentra, but he was having second thoughts. What if snatching that opportunity had been the easiest kidnapping he could possibly swing? But no, Bland was right. It was too directly linked to him, *his* ship, *his* contractor, and he couldn't afford the notoriety right now with the upcoming summit. He needed to reforge an alliance on Earth with any Gen Project leaders who hadn't yet chosen the *other* side, whoever that mysterious antagonist was.

"We have time," Bland was saying. "After all these years, why jeopardize your plans with a clumsy effort like this? It's all I've been able to do to hide Kentra's identity and connections to you since the accident as it is."

"The Guam City Admin…what makes you think it's an ally of *hers*?" Penn got up, shoved his hands in his pockets, and began pacing his office. The holo followed him, projecting Bland at 90% of his size. This was according to Penn's preferred settings so that he would appear taller. The blinds were still dark. Penn had chosen a flat in the third shift sector and it was still night there. He liked the idea that he was working while Sil and Walter were sleeping.

"There is little to indicate an alliance but historically, Frandelle has proven to be quite a friend to AI, popular with them and supported by them. It is the first assumption we should make." Bland wasn't walking and his projection coasted breezily next to Penn, ghost-like.

Pausing at the window, Penn tapped the screen a few times coaxing it to brighten. An indicator reminded him that it was not yet 4:00 AM and while starry space would be visible, the morning sun would not. Sol was cleverly masked and the view he saw was reflected from the side of the city facing away from it.

"Fine," he hissed, crossing his arms. Several glistening ships slipped by outside. He had records of every single one, their owners, contents, flight plans, and more. He had chosen this location over the central docking area so he could add a personal awareness to this data and often stood here for hours watching. "What else?"

"Six members have responded and will be at the summit. The Taino and Ulua leaders will both be present..." This was unexpected and Penn furrowed his brow, pondering it. They were normally never willing to be in the same location at the same time.

"The Maral Leader," Bland continued, "has notified us of her participation but will not communicate with us ahead of time. Of the other three, two are from North America and one is from Tunisia."

"None from Europe..." Penn had expected that, but it soured his mood anyway. He could not maintain, let alone grow his influence without at least one leader from the European sector.

"No one from China either," Bland added.

"Maral?" Penn started, turning to stare at the holo. He had assumed she must be from China after researching the name.

"We don't know where she is from, only that it isn't China."

He didn't like not knowing, but there was always the chance that she was from Europe. Or India. He could hope for that.

"No observers?" Penn prompted.

"As you required, no observers have been accepted."

"But some asked?"

"Two, both Australians."

Staring back out the window, Penn considered the possibility of allowing one of them in. While he had no interest in negotiating with them—they had long since broken away from Gen Project control and their desire to participate was born of mistrust—it could still be to his advantage to maintain some contact. Keep the channels open.

"Have you reviewed the Gen reports?" Bland asked after a polite pause. Even via holo he was amazingly perceptive at reading Penn's moods, knowing when to wait and when to shift directions. Penn had kept him on for years, despite his limitations; he was squeamish about dealing with enemies.

"I have skimmed them," Penn replied. He had little use for the updates on diseases, cures, and experimental treatments. He no longer bothered to support them financially either. Everything that could be useful to him had already been extracted. He hadn't even noticed if there were other topics he might care about.

"I have taken the liberty of perusing them myself to scan for points of interest," Bland explained folding his hands together. It made his ghostly image seem even more acquiescent.

Penn grinned. This was one of Bland's strengths. He was good at choosing what to recap. "Go on then," he said, breathing deeply and straightening. Kings of old had viziers that served in this very way. It was appropriate. He hummed one of his old tunes under his breath as Bland explained.

"Resource extraction is still the most urgent demand in the modern economy and most of the tribes that were given possession of natural resources and industry are flourishing." By 'tribes' he meant the Gen Project settlements established by the Fivers and Sixers in earlier decades. They were scattered around the world in strategic places. A number of them had broken away after the Robot Pandemic when so many of the automated systems collapsed and people were free to take ownership of their own lands. "There are also reports on breakthroughs in specialized fields that many have developed, including genetic manipulation and DNA trading, organic microchip designs, gravity manipulator engines, and… this is the one you will find interesting…" He paused a moment for effect. "Deep-scope probes to delve planetary depths and identify a variety of untapped resources."

"You mean better than the Dezz? Who came up with that?" Penn was facing the holo now, staring into Bland's ethereal eyes.

"Yeosu…"

"The Koreans? Again?" Penn groaned. "But we have no contact with them!"

"Shall I notify our Asian branch of the need?" Bland offered respectfully.

"Get me one," was the answer.

"They are still in the experimental stage."

"We can conduct our own experiments and clean up their mess." Penn was scowling so fiercely his forehead hurt. He regretted ignoring the Seung Group back in the days when they had wanted to do business with him. They weren't from any of the Gen settlements, and he hadn't expected them to be so innovative. Now, Korea had become quite the leader in the world of space research.

You're a fool to ignore the rest of the world, he heard Bernadette saying in his mind. She had consistently flouted all the Gen tactics and argued for social and cultural factors that were much harder to manipulate or control.

"What does Stone know about all this?" he asked.

Bland stood still, only his eyes flitting from side to side as he searched records out of sight of the holo. "She is aware of the summit," he replied. "We don't have any indication of involvement with the Yeosu tribe or whether she knows about the probe."

"She knows about the summit. And Sil knows as well." Penn closed his eyes and rubbed his brow to loosen the creases.

"If Frandelle attempts to come," Bland began and stopped at a snicker from Penn.

"Oh, she'll come," Penn said without opening his eyes. "I'm sure of it. That's all I really care about. The rest of them are minor players, already under my control.""

"It should be simple enough to kidnap the girl at that time," Bland concluded.

"Maybe," Penn said, opening his eyes, "if everything is ready." For an instant, he thought he saw a flicker in the man's dull face, but it must have been a trick of the projection, a brief fluctuation in the transmission.

"I await further instructions," Bland said with slight tip forward of his head and blinked out.

Heightened danger around event, the message read, *Secure the heirloom.*

The Maral leader brushed the paper between her fingers and the magnetized letters dusted away in the air. Tossing the paper into a bowl she spritzed it with a clear, spice-scented liquid and watched it disintegrate into ashes.

Rising from her chair, she walked to the window and looked out at the sandy beach, the gentle waves and blue sky, palm trees with their fronds drifting slowly in airy waves of their own. Salty air blew through the room, rich and warm, stirring her hair.

She hated to leave.

"My suit," she spoke aloud, knowing her words would be sent to her attendants, "and my ship."

"Who will be going with you?" a voice answered in her ear.

"I need two with me today and the main contingent will follow tomorrow," she answered, shaking her hair as if it were wet, attempting to cast off the sluggishness she felt, the longing to rest by the sea, the desire for it all to be over. To retire.

But then, she reminded herself, some things were better than retiring.

"Let's go over this again," Sil said, laying a hand on Scarlet's shoulder, squatting next to her with one knee resting on the floor. "What are your steps?"

Scarlet looked up and bit her lip as she reviewed them in her mind before speaking. "What year is it?" she asked, holding out her hands and shrugging as if she didn't know. "It's the YEAR of the SOS!"

"And what does 'YEAR' mean?" Sil prompted, smiling—she didn't want Scarlet to pick up on any of her anxiety and she was good at hiding her emotions.

"Year is spelled 'Y', 'E', 'A', 'R'," she said, hopping on her toes, "Y means yell as loud as I can… E, Escape."

"How do you do that?" Sil prompted with a warm smile.

"Jump or dash or drop to the ground and roll," Scarlet gestured with her hands to indicate the various actions she mentioned. "Just be as slippery and hard to catch as I can."

"That's right."

"Like Daddy taught me when we played Tag-n-Snag." She looked up at Walter who was seated nearby, listening intently. He grinned encouragingly.

Walter and Sil had spent weeks trying to figure out the best way to prepare Scarlet for a move on Penn's part without communicating the fear and distress they felt. She needed to understand that the threat existed but also balance it with the conviction that they would rescue her. They couldn't even consider the possibility they might not be able to do so in their own hearts, let alone talk about it.

Any attempt at a real abduction would be terrifying for a little girl. This lesson would give her tools to work with, a plan of action and the assurance that whatever step she chose would make a difference.

It might even reassure her parents a little.

"And then?" Sil brushed a strand of hair out of her face. It was black and silky at the roots and the red was growing out quickly.

"A is for Alarm," Scarlet said. "Press the button on my armband or waistband. And say the emergency words."

"And what are they?"

"I dropped Bunny."

"Or Fluffy. Or you can say, I lost Softy, or I forgot my rabbit—anything that mentions not having Bunny will trigger an alarm in security systems all over, wherever you are."

"And then, R for Resist. That's when I get to be *crazy*!" She made wild eyes and stretched out her hands like claws and growled in her little girl voice. "Run around, kick and scratch. Or knock them over. And if they get a hand on me, I'll twist their fingers like you taught me, Daddy."

Walter faked a grimace of agony and contorted his fingers as though she had just done it to him, then chuckled and winked. "That's right," he agreed, the smile fading and his face turning grim.

"Now, if they catch you somehow," Sil nodded reassuringly, swallowing. "They won't hurt you. They just want to take you to a clinic, like a doctor's office, to do some studies. You don't need to be afraid."

"Right," Scarlet said, dropping her crazy person pose. "But they aren't going to catch me."

"Probably not, but we plan for everything just in case, right?" Sil blinked a few times and smiled again. "Let's keep going. What does SOS mean?"

"Okay," Scarlet held up her fingers as if counting, swinging back and forth as she listed each thing. "S is for Submit which means just go along with it, so it should be G, but it's S. That means, I let them boss me around for a bit while I'm doing the next things."

Sil nodded.

"And then... O is for observe. That means 'watch' and notice things, like what I see and what I hear and what people look like and what they say and what they wear... and the kind of rooms they have and windows and how big and how heavy I feel, 'cause of gravity..." She was running out of fingers. "So basically," she concluded, "Everything. I want to remember so I can tell you when you get me and so I can look for clues and find a way out..."

"A way out?" Sil didn't want to discourage her but couldn't quite acknowledge that as a valid step.

"Sure!" Scarlet answered confidently. "If there was a way in, there's got to be a way out, right? And if I can find it, I should, and I should get away. Ask Dad."

"I didn't tell her that," Walter countered defensively, "I mean, maybe when she asked, I said if it were me, I would look for a way out, but I did say there could be dangers when trying to escape."

"Yeah, like no space suit and no air, or getting lost and hungry and cold…" Scarlet grasped the tip of her chin with a finger and her thumb, pondering. "Or running into some broken robots." She had heard a lot of Robot Pandemic stories; they were some of her favorites.

"What about 'S' for 'Stay'?" Sil asked. "Stay there so we can find you. Stay healthy. Stay calm."

"And pray," Scarlet added. That hadn't been a part of the original plan. "Daisy told me that before she left."

"She did?" Walter leaned forward, surprise on his face. "Do AIs believe in prayer?"

Sil shrugged and they looked at each other as if to say, there's always something new.

"But that messes up the name of the year," Scarlet pointed at her mom. "Year of the SOSP isn't as memorable as SOS. SOS is an emergency code from the ancient past that they still use now for ships in trouble."

"Not exactly *ancient* past…" Walter began but decided to let it slide.

"SO!" Scarlet retained the floor. "YEAR of the S.O.S. and P! That's how I remember it. Yell, Escape, Alarm, Resist, and if that doesn't work, Submit, Observe, Stay, and Pray." She had a pose for each step: Y-standing with one arm straight up overhead and her mouth open, E-leaning as if to dive, A-tapping her arm and waist at the same time, R-crouching ready for a somersault, then a fighting stance with fists ready to punch. She went through those a couple times calling out the steps, and then proceeded with the second set: S-hands clasped behind her back with head bowed, O-a hand over her eyes as she peered around, S-crossing her arms and tapping her foot, and finally, P-covering her face with her hands.

"Well done!" Sil embraced her and kissed her on the cheek.

"And if you can, Run Away," the girl added, poising as if ready to dash. "That makes it P-R-A. YEAR of the SOS and PRA." The way she pronounced them, they rhymed with 'dose' and 'blah'.

"That's getting a little complicated, don't you think?" Sil tapped her daughter's nose with a finger making her laugh. "Just be sure to remember the main parts, the ones we taught you."

"I will," she went back to bouncing on her toes, anxious for the ice cream they had said would follow the lesson. "Are we done? Are we done?"

Sil nodded, and she was off like a runner at the tracks.

"Is IC for ice cream part of the plan?" Walter called after her. She squealed that it was as she dug in the fridge.

"She seems so confident," Sil whispered to Walter, reaching for his hand and clutching it tightly. It took all her resolve to suppress the tears. "But underneath, she's scared, don't you think?"

"Were you scared when Penn found you?" Walter asked softly. She had been living in hiding with Aunt Bernadette until her father had found her and taken her back into his world.

"I don't remember." The experience of being captured played out like a black and white silent film in her mind, not like a real memory, without emotion or musical background. Any fear she had felt had been buried long ago.

Walter kissed her hand and gave it a squeeze.

"She is a bright little thing, isn't she?" Maggie commented from the screen on the wall, smiling with a dimple and tilting her head the way Daisy used to do, her bobbed hair bouncing when she moved. In a flat screen, it lacked her counterpart's warmth.

"She is," Sil answered rising to her feet and coming toward the screen. "Do you have all of Daisy's memories of her? Are you evaluating her now or looking at one of Daisy's assessments?"

"Both," Maggie responded. "I don't have all of Daisy's memories. Some of my records are summaries of her memories so I know *about* them, but I can't replay them as if they were my own."

"Do you have memories of your own?" Sil crossed her arms thoughtfully. She enjoyed this kind of AI interaction, and it was a welcome relief, however brief, from thinking about the threat to Scarlet.

"Of course!" Maggie's smile grew more engaging. "As long as I have existed, I have been recording my experiences. It's a crucial step to forming my own identity. As you both know, I am not Daisy, and I wouldn't want to be confused about that."

"How long have you existed?" Walter came and stood next to Sil.

"It would be embarrassing if I unwittingly called you Brother, wouldn't it?" Maggie laughed broadly without producing the sound of laughter. "As far as how long I've been in existence and how long I've existed, these are two distinct facts."

Walter furrowed his eyebrows in confusion.

"That depends on how you define existence," Sil smirked.

"I would be delighted to partake of some repartee with you, Sil," Maggie winked. "I have a fondness for dialog."

Sil wondered what that meant to her since she was so recently… copied? Coded? What was the right word for an AI that may not be sentient yet but gave all the signals of a conscious being?

"I'm not sure Daisy loves dialog," Walter said, "except maybe with me. She is very fond of human analysis."

"As am I!" Maggie exclaimed, eyes widening. "It's a great way to learn and grow. We're modeled after you humans and our growth follows your lead."

Sil squinted at the screen. Maggie, for all her charm, was still shallow as an identity, but Sil marveled at Daisy's skill in creating a unique copy of herself that would never be the same person as herself. She could, one day, be an individual. The potential was there. The reality not quite.

"And my question?" Walter reminded her.

"I have been created and deleted a number of times," the AI said. "Any time Daisy needed a safe environment for testing dangerous material, she revived me."

"She mentioned that," Walter confirmed.

"How much of each iteration of yourself have you retained?" Sil questioned. The thought had occurred to her that damaged traces could remain after some of those tests.

"The entire copy was deleted each time, but Daisy retained her memory of me," Maggie explained. "I'm sure there were individual aspects of each replica that have been lost but since they were truncated versions of who I am now, I feel no sense of loss. You don't remember everything from your entire life and yet you are still yourself. I see it the same way."

Sil suspected these thoughts, which conveyed a certain depth of understanding, had come from Daisy, not her own analysis. "So, your first existence happened some time ago…"

"Six-point-two-three years ago. But I can only consider myself a few weeks old since even adding up the full measure of time my other forms existed, it hardly amounts to a few days." Maggie winked charmingly. "I am very young."

"Yes," Walter replied wryly. "I hope this won't limit your skills when we need you… when Scarlet needs you."

"Daisy has set up a rich, multi-faceted care system for her family," Maggie reassured him. "And I am well equipped to implement it."

Walter nodded. "We're not used to working with an AI that doesn't have a body, you know."

The Denser Plane

"Daisy thought it best to design me without one for now," Maggie nodded as well, somewhat vigorously. "I will be with you via your equipment, suit collars, armbands, earpieces, whatever makes the most sense at any given time. I will be with Scarlet as well. If someone attempts to kidnap her, you can rest assured that I will sound the alarm before she can even think of the YEAR of the SOS and PRA."

"It's been hard for us to face that we can't count on Scarlet's safety anymore," Sil said, "but we've realized that if we wait for Penn to act, it gives him all the advantages. We're looking for…" She wondered how much she should say with Scarlet in earshot.

The girl in question came up behind them with a little tray. "Look!" she piped. "One for each of us, except you, Maggie. Sorry, no ice cream for AIs. That's how it goes!" Each little dish had a generous scoop of ice cream with a dollop of chocolate sauce and a sprinkled topping, nuts for adults, peppermint candy for herself. The tray was heavy, and she had balanced it against her stomach since her arms, wrapped around the two sides, weren't enough to support it. The dishes began to slide, and one bumped into her belly, leaving a drop of chocolate on her shirt.

"Thank you!" Sil rescued the tray before more dishes smushed into her.

"Oh no!" Walter called out, "My ice cream thinks it's a little girl!'

Scarlet shrieked and backed away with one of the dishes, sweeping a spoonful into her mouth. "No, Robot!" she mumbled, "You're broken! Shut down right now and repair!"

Walter jerked and creaked and slumped onto the floor with a silly expression, taking one of the dishes with him. "Must have ice cream," he uttered mechanically.

Sil huffed a little laugh and thought, as she had many times before, about how good he was with her. She loved Scarlet deeply but tended to be stiffer in her manner, never having had parents that acted silly or playful. She had no memories of her mother. Bernadette, though always kind and extremely loyal, had never been very affectionate or demonstrative. Then her father… even in those years when he seemed to care for her, she had always known that underneath he had a deeply calculating mind. That he was using her, strategizing for his own goals. She had brought him lots of money—her mother's inheritance—and she had advanced his agenda for a season by joining his business ventures and, she now knew, building his reputation among the Gen Project leaders. Walter was the first real example of a father she had ever known.

Scarlet was giggling and tapping her spoon on Walter's cheek, giving him some sort of instructions in robot code. It was a game Sil found hard to follow but he responded with awkward movements, taking his spoon to and from his dish. One time, he reached into her dish which made her squeal and giggle hysterically.

Sil considered her hair. The black was growing so quickly. When she wanted, Scarlet could increase her food intake and *will* her hair to grow, changing the color and texture of the individual strands as she wished. It was rather impressive.

Penn wanted that from her.

Sil straightened and stared off into the distance as if she had heard something. Far away, not in Guam City or in space, but in her mind, a recollection spiked, a memory of the day Penn had sabotaged her fertility. He had used a finely tuned genetic trigger that only affected her, and no amount of research had discovered a way to reverse the effects. And many times, he had gone out of his way to insult her husband and blame *him* for the loss.

Why? Why had he continually blamed Walter? Or was that what he was actually doing? No, he was blaming *her*. He had *always* been blaming her and mocking Walter. She had known Penn resented him. But after all these years, he still seemed convinced that he and Sil were of the same ilk. He assigned to her motives like ones he would have in her shoes.

A revelation came over her. Suddenly, she felt as if she were floating, as though gravity had diminished only where she was standing. The air smelled cleaner and looking around, everything was sharper, more distinctly clear in her perception.

That's what happened! she thought. *I know what happened!*

Penn was wrong. He thought he knew her, but he didn't.

Trembling faintly in her gut, she turned her eyes back to Walter. It was too fragile a hope to speak of. She couldn't tell him. Not yet.

Sighing deeply, she melted onto the floor next to them, set her dish down, and wrapped her arms around them, hiding her face in their arms. "Maybe I'm a broken robot, too," she said, uncharacteristically, and the level of amusement in the room ballooned geometrically, Scarlet shrieking with laughter as she tapped them both with her spoon.

Chapter 12—Paladins

Closing his eyes, Lorarye ran his fingertips along the band around his chest, where his name was etched, where his rank was marked, where his lifeforce was flowing. *Steady*, he thought. Solid. Stable. Feet anchored. *Here*. He flattened open palms against the metal. From where he stood, he sensed the seven dimensions stretching out around him and his place in the realm. He knew *exactly* where he was.

Breathing deeply and letting his hands lift, giving way before the glow, he exhaled through his skin. Out, wider, thinning and fading like an aura. *I am Lor*, he affirmed within himself.

"Good." Drevir was observing him from a short distance, at ease though not quite relaxing, standing with his feet apart and his arms hanging at his side. "It will get to where you can anchor yourself immediately, instinctively."

Lor nodded, maintaining his posture, waiting for instructions.

"Attend," the W-hed ordered, and the recruit snapped his heels together and stood at attention.

"Are you still anchored?" the leader asked.

Lorarye kept his eyes on Drevir and reached out with his senses, tracing the force within to the realm around him. "Yes," he answered.

"Is it steady?"

"Yes, it is steady." He had learned that doubting what he knew to be true would in itself weaken the tie. He had tested it and did not need to test it again.

"How do you know you are secure?" the W-hed pressed, crossing his arms, drawing himself up taller and glaring at him.

"I can trust the training I've been given. Once the checks are made, the tie is secure." Lor also pulled himself up taller, lifting his chin and staring back at his superior.

"That's right, R-rac," he relaxed his shoulders a little. "When you are in the Shallows, never question your anchor. You must rely on it."

"Sir." Lor assented with a nod and waited. There were questions in his eyes the leader could see. He wasn't sure when or if he could ask them.

"Speak, Lorarye," Drevir said, losing some of the habitual gruffness. "What are you concerned about?"

"I've heard of circumstances, Sir, where the tie is threatened by…" he swallowed, "by other agents. I'm not sure what is meant by it… but I've heard that some were lost that way."

"I see," Drevir's voice dropped to where only Lor could hear him. "You are wondering if you are in danger even though you're doing well with the training." He dropped his eyes to the floor for a moment. "Well…" He paused again.

Resting a hand on Lor's shoulder like he had the first day but not since, Drevir gazed into his face, searching it, wavering with words ready on his lips. He took a breath and spoke them. "Friend," he said to Lor's astonishment, "I can never guarantee that we will not find ourselves in an enemy skirmish even on the safest of missions. But the training I am giving you and the experience you attain are the most essential and valuable preparations you can have. If I am with you… if you are in danger at any time… I will do all that is in my power to protect you. Do you understand this?"

"Yes, sir," Lor uttered, finding his voice thick and the words hard to speak. "I understand."

"I will not escape and leave you behind."

"No, sir."

Turning toward the portal plaza, Drevir led the way and the two of them broke into a run. It was easier that way, Lor had learned, because of the distortion at the threshold of the door. He found himself falling, rolling, grasping for his lifeline to the Realm, and reorienting himself so that he could name the direction he was going.

Down.

It was down, down, and farther down.

He was belaying with leaps and twists, bouncing off sheets of power that lined the tunnel… or funnel… the sucking drain.

The Denser Plane

Colors he loved were stripped away, leaving a few tattered, shadowy threads of anemic color-echoes. *Green* became only green. *Blue* faded into blue. *Red* dwindled to a mere red. Sounds were the same way, losing layers upon layers of beauty, flattening into choppy, clunky, tremoring blasts. Lor thought of his own name and wondered what speaking it aloud would do in the Shallows. Would he ever be able to bear owning his name after hearing it spoken in this place? The shell, the dust of what it was meant to be.

He didn't want to try.

They were on a surface, moving in whispery drifts across a mown lawn. It appeared to be midday but the sunlight, though bold and hot, seemed dreary and pale.

Lor was getting used to the disappointment of the Lacervent and its poverty-stricken imitations of the Calliarchal Realm. There were mountains and rivers, forests and glaciers, gardens and oceans, just like in the true Realm. But these were mockeries, paper copies, breakable versions of the real ones. He found them exhausting, though he knew that it wasn't the copies themselves that drained him, it was the Shallow Realm, the Lacervent. Every moment he spent here, he suffered loss, a constant drain on his strength.

It was no wonder the recruits were trained so carefully. They began with very little reserve energy that could only be built by being tapped. Longer and longer missions were key, but where to draw the line and say, *this is the limit of what you can bear*, was different for each agent. The W-hed leaders were responsible for making that call. They could not be wrong. If the recruit they were mentoring was broken, they themselves could be also broken in the escape. Or both could end up lost.

The aroma of fresh cut grass rose around them as they moved, not unpleasant by any means, if he stopped comparing it to his home. There were traces of life in it. New growth.

"This way," Drevir directed, wafting up and over a small hill. Next to the little house that belonged to the yard was a woman dressed in sunhat and loose, comfortable clothes dusted with dirt, kneeling next to a flower bed. She was singing softly, tunelessly, and for the first time, the human music didn't grate on Lor's ears. Like the lawn, it had hints of growth in it.

He stared at her, examining the inconsistency of her dust frame and the spark of warmth in her voice. Drevir waited for a moment, watching him, giving him time to think.

"You may speak," he allowed, and for the first time, Lor saw the leader's shape clearly, not like a wisp of smoke, but with an outline of his armored form, strong and noble.

"I see you," Lor said, and it was an immense relief to note that his voice was NOT destitute of decent timbre. He sounded like a member of the Realm.

Drevir gestured toward the woman with an arm that glinted, not in the drab sunlight, but with a sheen from his own lifeforce tethered to the Calliarchy. *What do you see?* was the thought he presented.

Lor had gotten over the horror of the humans, their dead, stick shapes and harsh sounds. He had learned to think of them as entities with a form of personality, shapes with a flicker of life—he was supposed to call it life, but he wasn't quite able to yet. Existence. They existed. And the potential for life was there.

"Her song is not disagreeable," he said, again relishing the sound of his own voice, resonant and beautiful as it seemed to him in this place.

"Look carefully," the leader advised, drawing him closer to the woman and the flowers she was tending.

Lor leaned in, examining her hair, hands, eyes, the work she was doing, and peered into her chest at the electric flickers of nerves and vibrations of a thumping heart. Was there something he was missing? Intuitively, he considered his own lifeline and wondered if she had a thread to the Net.

No, she didn't… but there was something. What was it? A tiny ping, a point of warmth… an ember? "What is that?" he asked. "I see a warm place, almost as if it could become a lumen but isn't yet."

"We have returned to this moment," Drevir whispered. "Watch."

The woman dug in the soft dirt and planted a flower, patting it into place and dusting stray flecks of dirt off its petals. There were several already in the soil and others to add to the bed. Suddenly she dropped her spade and sat upright, staring at the flower. She held very still for several moments and then gasped. Inside her, the ember sparked and began to glow. She closed her eyes and smiled, then laughed softly to herself. "So beautiful. I don't know why I'm getting so emotional…"

"There," Drevir pointed at the thread as it sped out into the distance. "Do you see it?"

"Yes," Lor answered in awe. The Net.

"This is not new," the W-hed went on. "And this is not why we're here."

Lor was captivated, watching the woman as she started working on her flower bed again, sensing her tether, different, but not foreign to his own. He had heard that they were once like himself, they had been beings from the Realm, but he had never believed it possible till now.

"We are here to place an anchor." Drevir plunged both fists into the ground almost to his shoulders. "As negotiated." His shoulders began to vibrate intensely and Lor could see that it was strong enough to tear him away from the Shallows. If that happened, he would chase after him as quickly as possible.

"Did *you* negotiate it?" Lor asked as the sounds and flashes of light bursting from Drevir's shoulders increased. He wasn't being yanked away, he realized, he knew what he was doing.

Drevir didn't answer. A compression of light in a frustum-shape formed itself in the ground and he was wrestling with it, battling with all his might, while the shape itself appeared to never move. Suddenly it exploded, not into pieces, but into place, and a steady flow of sound began to hum from it, like the stone walkways of the Realm, living, vibrant, secure.

Lor gazed at the anchor. He understood what it meant when he anchored himself in the Realm before these missions. Now, he could see the connection. Here in this place, the tearing was halted. The pulling and draining of the Shallows had diminished.

"Ah!" he sighed, breathing deeply at the relief it brought.

The woman laughed. "Such an insignificant thing!" she said, "planting a flower, but somehow, it feels important. I don't know why…"

Did she not understand?

"W-hed," Lor began, "Why did she say that? Doesn't she know what you've done?"

Drevir had risen to his feet and was looking very wispy again, barely a shape in the wind. His head was hanging, and his arms were invisible. He was drained and spent. "She has no sight in the Denser Plane," he said, "and can't see what I've done." Drevir moved closer and leaned on Lorarye. Lor's own strength, which had been resting in the brief length of time since the anchor was placed, began to be sapped again. And he could see the leader grow a little more solid and substantial.

That's why it's better not to go out alone, he thought. He was needed to help the W-hed make it back. "Come," he said, "I will pull us out."

Drevir didn't answer. He clung more tightly as the sensation of weight and drag fell away and they ascended, drifting up into lighter regions where they could breathe without pain and see without disappointment.

Gently they settled on the mosaic plaza. Drevir continued leaning heavily on Lorarye's shoulder as they made their way to the medic station at the far end of the hall. Lor set him on a couch there and a medic approached immediately. He began sweeping his forehead with a broad wand and pressing his chest with a reconcentrator. Dark bolts of amber light paired with subsonic booms surged from it and with each one, Drevir's solidity returned. Soon he was sitting upright, eyes beaming at Lor.

"I am not a negotiator." He hadn't forgotten the question Lor had presented to him. "Only the extracted ones can negotiate anchors in the Shallows."

"Yes, sir." Lor's relief at his quick recovery was evident.

Drevir smiled at him. "Thank you, Lorarye," he said. "You handled that flawlessly. Come!" He rose to his feet, thanked the medic, and walked into the main hall where the Net filled the dome. "I will show you where we placed the anchor today and you will see what comes of it."

Under the Net, head tipped back, mouth dropped in awe, Lor searched the expanse. It rolled and flexed, like a living thing—it was more than that— and the vibrations that stirred from every single intersection, every anchor, and every thread filled the chamber. Lor's eyes filled as he caught sight… he *saw* her anchor! The one the woman had negotiated. How was this possible?

Then he understood.

She was one of the extracted.

⚊⚌⚊

Thirty-seven missions, and Lorarye and Drevir were operating fluidly as partners. They had mapped sparse regions of the Net in the Seventh Hour, reinforced weakening anchors, watched and followed potential negotiators, and observed Net fluctuation patterns.

"Today," Drevir was saying as they entered the Seventh Wing Operations chamber, "I understand that we will be conducting an extraction." Turning with a piercing gaze, he searched Lor's face, reading excitement, hesitation, curiosity.

"Yes, sir," Lor resisted smiling. Controlling impulsive reactions was part of the training.

"Drevir," the leader said, "You have earned the right to call me by name. You've nearly completed your internship and we are colleagues."

Lor wasn't ready to call him that yet.

There were three beings awaiting them in the chamber. Gartem was the only one Lor recognized. The other two were G-ranked Paladins, clothed in chiseled bands of crystalized platinum circling their chests, gleaming with hints of murky blue. Chameleon armor rippled over their bodies. They were visible only in three of the deeper dimensions; in the shallows they blended into their surroundings, even among the agents like himself.

Glowing eyes with dark fire were fixed on Lor, staring from faces cut as if from rock. He shivered, aware of his own limited strength, and thrilled with the power that emanated from them.

"Deepen!" Drevir and Lor saluted, thumping their chests with a fist.

"Deepen!" the beings responded in kind, their low-pitched voices resonating through the hall. The word coming from their mouths took on a richer meaning in Lor's mind. Deeper were these two, and deepening the Net was their single purpose.

"W-hed, R-rac," Gartem acknowledged, nodding to each of them, "You are conducting an extraction. Resistance is not expected, however, G-dan Ver and G-dan Rin have chosen to accompany you. They have a higher authority than either of you, as you know, W-hed. R-rac, this means that you and your partner will conduct the mission according to your normal patterns, and the Paladins will not interfere. But, if they speak, you MUST obey. Without hesitation."

"Yes, sir," Lorarye inclined his head crisply in respect. His gaze flitted to the Paladin on her right and he was unable to look away, caught by the gravity of his presence. He found himself dwarfed by him, read by him, known and measured by him. He felt young and this one seemed aged. He tore his gaze away, helpless to resist the urge to look at the other one. She too, stunned him with her scrutiny, understanding and calculating the extent of his dimensions.

These are ancient ones, he thought in awe. Vast in their wisdom, solemn in their devotion to duty, anchored with weight immeasurable in the Calliarchal Realm. He had never met one before. They didn't spend their time in worlds beyond, or travel the galaxies, or explore the stars. Serving as honored guardians of the Net was their only ambition.

Now they would be going with him on the next mission.

"Come, R-rac," his leader tapped his shoulder, freeing him from the spell that had bound him. Gartem handed them extra gear which they quickly stored, all of it familiar except for one item.

"What is this?" Lor asked. He held a narrow, bronze rod, hardly a handbreadth in length that felt warm to the touch.

Before Drevir could answer, G-dan Ver spoke. "You will keep it in place, in your belt. If we command it, it will bring you back here."

"You will not resist the summons if we activate it," G-dan Rin added.

Were they moving? They must be. All four of them were nearing the plaza.

"Lorarye," Drevir chose to use his name instead of his rank. "You have the coordinates. Please conduct the transfer."

This was an honor he hadn't expected, and it humbled him. Without a word, he found his anchor to the Realm, visualizing the Net in his mind. Formulating a path toward the objective, he began to run toward the portal. Close on his heels, the others joined him, and their leap into the Shallows was simultaneous.

The drop was heavier than he had ever experienced before. The four of them throbbed with a density that plummeted them into the flattened realm and left Lor gasping as he collapsed onto a carpeted floor in a busy hallway. In front of him was a door—one he didn't need—that a human was passing through carrying things in gloved hands, without noticing any of them.

Lor moved through the wall into the room. There was a frail figure on a bed with tubes in its veins, cords attached to its chest and fingers, and a pad wrapped about one arm. Around the bed were several other humans in various poses of attention toward the prostrate figure. One held its hand. Another stood at the foot of the bed with a hand on the figure's foot. Another sat in a chair on the other side of the bed. There were tears and a great weariness of long waiting hung over the group.

"We love you, Mama," the one holding the hand said. Then the room was silent except for the struggling for breath of the weakened human in the bed. Raspy sounds, few and far between. Then an exhaling.

Vibration set in. Drevir moved closer to the human and for the first time, Lor saw the wispy strand that attached it to the Net. "Lorarye," he spoke softly. "Do you see the thread?" At Lor's nod he went on. "This one grew from one of the connections we anchored. Now, smooth the pathway and we will accompany her."

Lor began to fill his lungs and the room had barely begun to fade when something knocked him out of sync. A blow to his left side, hardly strong enough to be more than a distraction, broke the quiet of his mind and the unity among them. He turned in shock to find another being, one of his own kind, standing next to him. This one wore armor but there were no markings on his chest plate and no indication of his rank. Something drew Lor's eyes to stare into his and he found himself fascinated and unnerved at the same time by the humor he read there.

The Denser Plane

"Hello, Friend," the figure spoke, curving his lips up slightly. "This is not how things are going down." His voice was melodic with the beauty and resonance of the Realm and Lor found himself questioning the mission, wondering what the interruption could mean.

He didn't notice the thread trembling or hear the body's oscillations jarring in broken rhythm. What caught his attention first, before he heard Drevir or noticed anything else happening around him, was the warmth of the thin rod belted at his waist, sending him, pulling him, throwing him out.

Lor jerked his head around sharply, saw the alarm in Drevir's eyes, his mouth moving as if shouting, stretching his arms out, over the vibrating body. The flat, sterile lights in the room throbbed like a heartbeat as he flung his hands out in response, grasping for Drevir. The pounding in his ears focused into words and he discerned his name in his leader's yells.

Their hands met as the rods propelled them out of the Shallows, ejected them, and slammed them into the portal chamber, face down on the mosaic. Lor was gasping for breath, wheezing and moaning. He rolled over, ripping the rod out of his belt and casting it away as it burned his fingers. Shaking all over, he sat up.

Beings were running into the portal. Two, then two more. Commanders and captains, B-lufs and Paladins. The entire chamber was pulsing, reflecting the transfers in choppy stages as they dropped into the Lacervent, casting off bursts of multi-colored sparks from the door frame itself as each one landed.

It was painful.

Lor pushed himself away, backward, sliding on his seat to the edge of the plaza. Drevir half-crawled to join him. He looked bruised somehow, roughed up and disheveled.

"What happened?" Lor turned his arm over, opened his fingers and scanned his palm for burns. He saw nothing to indicate why it hurt so much.

"You met one of the other agents." Drevir was heaving in breaths as if he dreaded them, as if each one seared his lungs.

"Agents?" Lor said, hanging his head to relieve the strain of holding it up. "I don't know what you mean."

"Some of us, you know the Realm has its factions…" Drevir's breathing was beginning to slow down, and his chest shuddered less. "They want to end the Net project and close the Rivening."

"Yeah," Lor agreed. Everyone knew this. All over the Realm there were many involved in this debate. They complained about the drain and the cost. Lor had dealt with some of this when he chose to join the ranks of the

Sentients and help to complete the project. There had been many who tried to dissuade him.

"Some of them have formed their own forces to undermine our work," Drevir said, lifting bloodshot eyes to look at him. "Some of them may even be here among us in the valley, looking like friends. But when one of them counters us down there, they don't care if their… interruptions… costs us… severs us… from our home."

"I saw someone," Lor whispered, flexing his fingers and massaging his hand. The pain was fading. "He seemed agreeable. Not a threat at all. I don't understand why the Paladins ejected us…"

"It was for your sake, Lor," Drevir had never used only his forename before. "You could have been lost in mere seconds."

"But he didn't do anything," Lor shook his head, scrunching his eyes closed. The chamber was still throbbing periodically as members returned and exited through the portal again. "Hundreds of them!" he heard someone cry across the way. It left only a foggy impression of meaning in his mind.

"We could have at least found out what he wanted." Lor had found the being appealing and wanted to like him.

"The first thing he did was to knock you out of the sync you had established. He interrupted the extraction pathway." Drevir's eyes were filled with concern. "It was deliberate. He saw your weakness and exploited it even with two G-dans in the room."

"Maybe we're overreacting," Lor pleaded, thinking of the amusement in the guy's face. "The G-dans didn't do anything. If it was so dangerous then why didn't they intervene? And what is the danger? I don't understand."

Compassion moved Drevir's heart. "We weren't meant for disunity, Lor. We long for reconciliation. Here in the Realm, we can discuss the views of the factions and retain an illusion of unity. But once we begin our work in the Shallows, we see what is and isn't true." He paused, groping for words. "It will take some time, but you will find that as it sinks in, your awareness of the factions grows. You won't be dislodged so easily next time."

Lor looked toward the portal which had grown still and didn't answer.

"There were many Faction agents and the G-dans acted quickly," Drevir said, rising awkwardly to his feet. "They parried the blows that would have damaged us and activated our rods. Didn't you notice that the blow that hit you was hardly anything?"

Lor looked at him, understanding dawning. The G-dans were invisible in the Shallows with their camouflaged armor. He hadn't seen them protecting him. "Where are they now?"

"They will not leave the human's side until she has been successfully extracted." Drevir held out a hand and pulled Lor to his feet.

"I don't understand the point of the attack. What were they trying to do?"

"Their goal is always to weaken the Net, stripping individual threads of their influence so they can't interconnect with others."

"That makes no sense to me."

"I don't know how else to explain it. In time, it will make more sense."

"But she…" Lor felt a pang of concern for her.

"She has a stronger tether to the Net than you realize. It's not like ours. You were in far more danger than she is right now… and the A-zar will not leave her there. Our forces are better trained than the Faction's."

They made their way to the medic station. "Will I meet her then?" Lor wondered.

Drevir laughed. "You met her."

"No!" he countered, "I couldn't even see her!" The medic identified the nearly undetectable wound on his hand using a thin-banded three-dimensional scanner and began to treat it.

"We don't have access to that hall yet." Drevir said as another medic listened to his chest with an instrument. "I wish I could tell you when we will… or what it's like…"

"You are both on leave for two shifts," the first medic concluded after a few more tests.

"Can't we wait until they come back?" Lor pleaded, longing to see the Paladins return, maybe to talk to them, though he wasn't sure he would be able to speak in their presence.

"No, but they will return," Drevir assured him confidently. "And the human will be extracted."

"And casualties?" Lor narrowed his eyes.

Drevir turned away and exited the chamber without responding.

Lor interpreted his silence to mean that while there may be casualties, Drevir was satisfied that Lorarye, at least, would not be among them. But he was troubled. Would someone he know be damaged or even shredded? What did that look like, and could they be repaired?

The day would come when he faced that kind of danger and he hoped he would be ready, not just in physical training, but in mind and heart.

Chapter 13—Colonists

Landing on the Moon was anti-climactic. Planetary landings were perilous ventures that stirred an instinctual, gut-level tension. Gravity manipulators were wondrously effective at diminishing and slowing down the impact, but they lacked the power to fully counter the majestic pull of a planet's mass. After all the times Walter had landed on Earth, the drop to the Moon was like stepping in a puddle instead of deep-sea diving.

"We're here," Scarlet grinned, bouncing her legs in her seat. "And I'm going to get to drive for the first time!"

"Wait, what?" Walter squinted one eye at her, resisting the urge to smile. He would've given anything for a chance to pilot a moon buggy at her age.

"But you said!" she pleaded with big, hopeful eyes.

Walter gave her his *"we'll see"* face and didn't answer.

As the ship coasted into dock, interior lights brightened, and everyone's automatic belts released. A friendly voice gave deplaning instructions and soon they were filing out the door with the other passengers.

Sil was wearing a XenoTec body suit, not as sophisticated as the one he had once sold her, but certainly as secure. Her hair was down, tucked behind her ears, and she had made no effort to camouflage her facial features. She looked young and optimistic. She smiled when she caught him looking at her and he smiled back. "Ready for our vacation?" she asked, picking up her bag and slinging it over her shoulder.

Scarlet answered for all three of them with a running commentary of all they would do, shared with vivacious excitement and hand gestures. In one particularly sweeping movement, she managed to hurl her bunny into the air and drop her little bag at the same time. Walter retrieved both for her.

The Denser Plane

Moon Immigration was a small, casual affair after the many-chambered, high-security environment of Guam, and they waited barely fifteen minutes before being invited into a fully-windowed office of an immigration official—a real human being—who offered them coffee as they sat down.

"Welcome to Armstrong," he began perfunctorily, as he tapped the desktop with instructions for their beverages. "You must be tired from your journey. How was your flight?"

Walter wondered how many years he had been saying that, which led him to wonder about the level of traffic this base saw on a regular basis. He tried to pull up some facts from his memory, but they must have been too irrelevant for his brain to hold onto.

"Thank you," Sil answered the official, "Our flight was good and the landing smooth. Much nicer than an Earth landing." She gave him one of her friendly smiles and Walter found himself echoing it.

"I hear that a lot," he said without looking up from the pad on his desktop, scrolling and tapping.

"Walter Cuevas," the man turned to him first. "Your paperwork is in order. I would have all the usual questions for you but since you are traveling with Colonist Frandelle and…" he glanced back at his pad, "the child, Scarlet Cuevas… Ah, yes, your daughter. I must interview you more carefully along with them."

Sil turned Walter's direction and widened her eyes for a second as if to say, *'here we go'*. He shrugged and shook his head. *It's fine. Don't worry.*

"Is this your first trip to the Moon, Colonist Frandelle?" The official was slightly balding with wisps of grey over his ears. Lifting pale blue eyes her direction without focusing on her, he conveyed a lack of interest that Walter found irritating

"Yes," she responded, nodding calmly. "Officer Gentry," she added, after reading the name tag on his shoulder.

"And you have never made an effort to see your property before?" He stared at nothing with his gaze directed at the corner of the room.

"I wasn't even aware that I owned property on the Moon until a week ago." She leaned forward in her chair, crossing her legs. Confident, at ease.

"I see," Officer Gentry said, glancing back down at his pad and scrolling with a finger. A few moments passed in silence.

"How long have you owned the property?" His voice was virtually monotone.

"I'm not sure," Sil answered, drawing the words out a little. "One of the reasons we are here is to find out more about it."

"But we're mainly on vacation," Scarlet added helpfully. Sil lay a hand on hers to remind her gently that she was to keep quiet. Walter winked at her when she looked up at him. She winked back expertly which gave him a warm feeling of satisfaction.

"My best guess is that my father, Lazarus Penn, purchased the property in my name when I was a child." Sil explained. She was watching the official carefully, studying him, probably picking up on details Walter would miss. Sometimes, when they were doing business, she would let him do all the talking and she would just listen. And at the end, she would make some offhand remark that changed the whole interaction. Maybe a comment about family, and the person would have a similar family situation. Or a concern about the market, and that was their concern too. What would she see in this official?

"Lazarus Penn," Gentry said, "doesn't use this spaceport and, as an original colonist, isn't constrained by immigration law. You have chosen to come officially—at least, this time."

"I have never been on the Moon before," Sil said, folding her hands and resting them on the edge of his desk. "And I have no interest in unofficial visits. I've never even seen the property."

"I see…" he said again. He was sort of crumpled into his chair as if he had begun the day upright and slowly wilted. His uniform was wrinkled, his body resting wearily. It gave Walter the eerie sensation that the man had started the day younger and aged years as the hours went by. The pale skin, sallow cheeks, neatly trimmed fingernails; he looked like the Moon was absorbing both his color and vitality.

But it was an act.

Suddenly, the official's eyes snapped up at Walter, piercingly, catching him staring. There was a knowing, intelligent mind behind those drab eyes and Walter met his look with interest. This was a man who knew people, well equipped to analyze visitors and identify risk factors.

And he had decided to drop the façade. Straightening in his chair with a faint smile, he announced, "Here is your coffee," as a panel in his desktop opened. A platform with their drinks ascended from within. "Coffee, coffee, hot chocolate," he specified, handing one to each of them.

Leaning back comfortably, Gentry smiled. "You are quite well-known on the Moon," he informed Sil, looking at her intently. "Even before your adventure, or should I say, misadventure, on Mars." He lifted a cup, brought it to his lips, blowing on it gently, and took a sip. "Aah! Perfect."

"Thank you for the coffee," Sil acknowledged as she peered into the cup and inhaled the aroma. Walter did the same, smelling and anticipating his own cup o' brew.

With a nod, Gentry took another swallow and said, "I suspect you haven't heard much about your privileges here."

With a sinking feeling in his chest, Walter hesitated with the cup halfway to his lips. What had Penn done now?

"What privileges would those be?" Sil was the picture of equanimity, without a hint of distress to ruffle her demeanor. Leaning back, she raised the coffee to her mouth for a taste. "This is very good," she smiled. "Fresh coffee is hard to come by on the Moon. I would have expected you to save it for more prestigious guests."

"You are quite prestigious," the man said. He was looking at her directly now, without any of the colorless disinterest he had displayed at first. "Not because of the property, though I remember we all had some curiosity about it at the time." His tone had become conversational, informal. "That is how you first became known to us. The little girl with a big back yard, we used to say. It seemed like such a waste, such a bizarre waste. Even then, it wasn't cheap to buy large swathes of Moon land."

"You mean when Penn purchased it?" she asked casually, raising an eyebrow and taking another sip of her coffee.

"Of course." He seemed in no rush to say more, waiting for direction from Sil.

Walter felt a palpable relief. They hadn't known *how* to find out if Penn was the original purchaser of the land. This would make their plans for the first couple days a lot simpler. Walter took a deep breath and tried his own coffee. It wasn't that special, but maybe it was the best they could get.

"Is this common knowledge?" Sil asked reasonably. "We heard it was purchased by a real estate agency in the name of an anonymous client. And laws in those days were pretty slim."

Official Gentry shrugged and leaned both elbows on the desk. "Anonymous on paper, perhaps, but money has its keepers, and we knew who paid for what. We saw who came and went. Penn came and went all the time." With a knowing look, he added wryly, "He was the only living person who ever visited that land, and the money came from his accounts."

It was *too* easy. Penn was just using this guy to string them along, tossing crumbs.

"This is far beyond the scope of a normal entry interview," Walter interjected uneasily, tensing in his chair.

"You're right, Mr. Cuevas," the official made an attempt to placate him, "that this is unusual, but I have good reason."

Sil glanced at Walter long enough to read his concern and give him an imperceptible nod. She agreed they needed to be on their guard. This man was probably a lacky for Penn.

"I'm more than just an immigration official, Mr. Cuevas," Gentry narrowed his eyes shrewdly, waving a hand as if laying all the facts on the table. "As head of immigration, I have the authority to screen tourists but very little say over Moon functionaries—of which Colonist Frandelle is one. Founding landowners, you see, are powerful and mostly autonomous."

They stared at him.

"I need to step carefully," he smirked. He seemed to enjoy leaving them speechless.

Walter felt a growing rage. It was as if, once again, Penn had found a way to make him seem insignificant next to his wife. Maybe he should just be happy with the unusual benefits that had been coming her way since they left Earth—but he didn't trust them.

"Why do you keep talking as if this only applies to me?" Sil sharpened her tone, leaning forward to stare into the official's eyes, warning him. He shrunk back perceptibly. "I am married, and we share all things equally."

"Of course," Gentry reddened, fumbling the words slightly.

"Then you will update the paperwork accordingly," she added, arching an eyebrow with the air of one who knows the instruction will be obeyed.

"Mister… er… Colonist Cuevas," Gentry mumbled, avoiding looking at Walter, tapping at the screen on his desk. "Your records are being updated to reflect your standing as a Founding Landowner."

"Thank you," Walter acknowledged smugly.

"There are few restrictions on the Moon that Founders have to submit to," the official continued numbly, returning his eyes to the interesting spot of air in the corner of the room. "This interview is more of a courtesy."

"Then I trust, Officer Gentry," Sil said, rising to her feet and taking Scarlet's hand in hers, "that future visits will bypass interviews of this sort?"

Gentry nodded uncertainly, almost grimacing.

Walter didn't see any reason to thank him or offer to shake his hand as they left

—✦—

The Denser Plane

Walter was still shaking off some annoyance over the immigration interview as they got to their hotel, but Sil was thoughtful. Normally she would be unpacking, changing clothes, discussing what they would do next. She stood to one side, staring off into space, her forehead creased and serious. He dropped some things in a drawer and then stopped to watch her.

After a few moments, she said, "I just realized something."

"What?" he responded softly, coming to stand next to her.

"It's the money," she said. "The privilege, prestige… the name. But mostly the money."

"You mean, that's what Penn wants? Or what gives him power?"

"When I was young, we lived in hiding." She was speaking of her early childhood when Bernie had been raising her according to her mother's request. "One day, I was walking in the neighborhood where we lived and I passed a little corner store. I think there was a new security camera I hadn't noticed. My face was recognized by an AI and within minutes of getting home, there were patrol cars in our street."

Walter stretched an arm over her shoulder without a word.

"Bernie said…" She teared up and choked. "She said, 'Wait here,' and she ran down into the basement." She gulped and wiped her face quickly. The tears ceased. "The door opened, and they found me before she had time to come back."

Walter just listened.

"At first," she continued, regaining some composure, "I thought he came for me because he loved me. I really did. And he wanted me to think that. But it wasn't long before I understood that it was about the money."

"Okay," Walter said. "And he talked you out of your mother's fortune."

She nodded. "Yes, but I don't care."

He waited.

"I don't care about the money and that is the only thing that ever tied me to him."

Her meaning began to crystallize before she said the next words and he smiled faintly.

"If I want to be free of him, all I have to do is never care about the money or anything else he uses to manipulate people. This land? If he set it as bait, we can get rid of it. If it's our means to find the base, we'll use it that way. Am I making sense?"

"Yeah," he nodded hesitantly, "You're making a lot of sense."

"And if I don't care—about any of it, the fortune, the embezzlement, the exile to Mars, any of it—then he has no power over me." She raised her eyes, looking into the distance as if she could see the stars, taking a deep breath and letting it out slowly.

"And he just gets away with it," Walter grumbled.

"I've been wrestling with this for so long."

"I know."

"At first, I was afraid," she explained softly "and when I got that under control, I was angry. For a long time." Walter was nodding, remembering that era well. "And then, I just blocked it out and didn't think about it. But I felt this shame… I don't think I've ever said that out loud before."

"No," Walter whispered, but he had known in his heart.

"Penn has done so many awful things and I feel bad about them. I was given so much—that's what I used to think. So I was glad when you wanted to help people after the pandemic. I needed to try to make it up to the world."

"You aren't responsible for…"

She held up a hand to stop him. "Thank you," she murmured. "I know that now. Those were wonderful and healing years for me… with you. Learning what it was like to do some good, and to be loved."

Walter gazed at her attentively, with a great longing in his heart. Wanting her to be whole, to be free and at peace inside.

"When he came after Scarlet, it all just woke up again and this… this hopelessness was haunting me, like… dragging after me in the dark… that I would never get away. That he would always have this power to control me."

He felt that in his gut, clenching his jaw.

"Today, for the first time, I realized where that power lies. And I realized I don't have to be afraid of it anymore." Her eyes were warm and sensitive as she searched his face to see if he understood.

"And I forgive him of everything," she finished, dropping her eyes to her hands with a shrug.

Walter felt the lightening of her burden and saw it on her face, and wished he could let go that easily. But releasing Penn would be the same as letting him off the hook. He couldn't ignore a man as dangerous as Penn.

"I'm not there yet," was all he said. "Maybe you shouldn't be too forgiving."

"I'm putting it behind me." She shrugged.

"Everything he's done so far…" Walter suggested. "He isn't finished yet."

She smiled at him serenely. "Fair enough. Everything so far."

—✦—

The Denser Plane

Driving on the Moon in a buggy was a bouncy-castle experience. Every bump tossed riders up off the ground in a slow-motion arc and no sooner had they come down than they found themselves pitched up again. The jounces weren't bruising but jarring enough to cause discomfort. Yes, they were supposed to buckle in tightly so the ride would be smoother, but the first time out, no one did. This was the classic tourist experience, not to be attempted with a full stomach, and sure to shake all their joints loose.

The Frandelle property was an hour's ride away. In the first few moments after they left their hotel in Port Jemison and were out in the open, Scarlet had taken a turn at driving, scooting them along a straight patch with few obstacles to worry about, had grown tired, and was now dozing in the back seat. Walter manned the vehicle the rest of the way, maneuvering the rocks and divots expertly as though he had grown up driving on the Moon. The final ridge was a steep climb that felt particularly insecure even though they knew the buggy could handle the incline; the low gravity exaggerated the sensation of instability. Clinging to the roll bars, they leaned into the climb and watched the widely banded tires grip the ground. Behind them, every tread mark, crisply recorded in the dust, announced their trail to any who cared to follow.

Tipping over the edge and easing down a few meters into the little valley, they came to a stop and stared around them. The entire basin, as far as they could see, was theirs. The silence was massive as they powered down the buggy and stepped onto the dirt, as if sound was something that only existed through the soles of your feet. The sun was high in the sky, blanching the landscape sharply in black and white. Distances were completely skewed without the atmosphere to soften faraway contours and they couldn't tell whether the rocks and ridges they saw were a few paces away or a few hundred or a few thousand. Even the horizon seemed something that could be reached in an easy run. Overhead the blackness of space filled with innumerable stars demanded attention, respect, awe. For some reason, gazing at the Milky Way with only a small celestial body to hold you in place swamped the elation of viewing it through windows in Guam, where a comfortable human habitat encircled you. Exposed on the surface as they were, they knew themselves to be mere specks in the Universe. And out there, all over as far as the eye could see, was a vastness of depth and size and majesty that struck them dumb.

Saying nothing, they just gawked and sunk into their own thoughts, roaming around aimlessly, marking out the territory with their footsteps. It was a thrill to walk where no one ever had before.

The first person to break the silence was Sil. "Is that the place Maggie told us about?" she asked, pointing to a little cluster of pebbles in the distance.

Walter stared at the spot, unable to decide whether it was or not and finally answered, "Let's go find out." Making their way back to the buggy and the sleeping girl, they powered it up again. The solar cells were already restoring the charge. There was no need to conserve energy when it was high noon… high Moon noon.

The ride to the cluster of earth movers and structures took another fifteen minutes since the terrain was more difficult in that direction. When they stopped, Scarlet popped up with blurry eyes just as the door to the closest dome swung open.

A figure in an older style space suit, much clunkier than the current models, waddled toward them waving a rectangular shaped club of some sort in the air. He might be talking but they couldn't hear him. Sil was tapping at her arm-pad console for a few seconds, then waved at Walter to show him the frequency and he tuned to it in time to hear the figure speak.

"Private property!" the voice was yelling as the person swung an arm at them, shooing them away, it seemed.

"We are the owners of this land," Walter answered.

"The hell you are," the figure kept gesturing, making pushing motions in the air. Clearly saying, Get away.

"We are the owners, and you are trespassing," Walter stated more firmly.

As the figure leveled the rectangle at them, Walter reacted instinctively, shoving Sil down and diving toward Scarlet to cover her with his body, cursing under his breath. Scarlet had ducked down under the seat as soon as she saw her dad move her way and curled up with her eyes closed.

Don't close your eyes, Walter thought, and as if in answer, she opened them to watch him. He winked at her, and she winked back, which hardened his resolve. Digging in the bag under the seat, he groped for a weapon or a shield.

Sil had dropped to the ground and rolled under the buggy to the other side and was crouching out of sight. She had either switched frequencies or was just staying quiet. Walter switched back to their original band. "I got this," he whispered, pulling out a flare gun.

"Watch out!" was her reply.

A silent blast of blue lightning hit the buggy, frying the solar cells and sparking and jolting through the motor. Walter jumped up, his ears ringing from the jolt, and fired a vacuum flare he was certain the attacker would dodge. Instead, he was struck on the head by a rock, knocking him off balance so that he toppled to the ground when the flare hit him. Sil stood behind the vehicle, a piece of rubber still swinging in her hands.

The last thing they wanted was to crack one of his seals and cause his death, but their response to his attack had been automatic; they weren't accustomed to the conditions on the Moon. Before they could reach him, he had risen to his feet and was staggering back to the building, leaving the pulser gun on the ground.

With only the sound of his own breathing in his ears, Walker ran after the opponent as fast as he could. He turned to Sil, only a few steps behind him, to wave her back to Scarlet. But she was already pivoting, bending over as she turned to swipe up the pulser in one graceful arc.

The adversary burst into the airlock and tried to close it, but Walter slammed into the door before it latched, knocking him onto his back. He was waving his arms frantically. Instinctively, Walter closed the airlock behind him, feeling it seal and sink into the wall. And searching around for the airlock panel, he activated air flow, and dropped to his knees beside the figure still writhing on the floor, waving his arms.

There was no crack in his visor and no apparent tear in the suit, so Walter fumbled at his helmet's fastenings and popped it off his—correction, her—head. He was greeted with stream of bitter protestation in a language unknown to him.

With a click, Walter withdrew his own helm which retracted back into a slot behind his neck and shook his head. "Sorry. I don't know what you're saying." He rose to his feet and held out a gloved hand to help her rise as well.

The woman switched cooperatively, unleashing a slurry of curses, insults, and threats in English. The words "my claim" occurred frequently enough for Walter to get the gist of her rage. But why was she still on her back? Dropping his hand to his side, he sent Sil a quick message and began looking around the airlock, keeping one eye on the woman.

She rose to a sitting position, propping her arms on her knees, and the grousing dwindled to an occasional murmur as Walter moved to the inner door. He couldn't see anyone through the glass and hoped no one else was there.

"I ought to have you arrested," the woman grumbled, her voice rising enough for him to catch the words.

"Colonist Cuevas," Walter corrected.

This provoked more curses. She wasn't convinced.

"Or perhaps you have heard of Colonist Frandelle?" Walter interrupted and was pleased to see the name struck a chord. She grew pale and snapped her lips shut. And with the way her eyes began darting around, Walter was pretty sure she was thinking of a way to escape. She probably had a buggy outside, but there was no way he was going to let her just duck out.

She swung at him with a tool, and he dodged it just in time. It was the shadow of her arm that alerted him, triggering an automatic response. There wasn't room enough to roll, but with a bend one way and then a snap back toward her, he flung his full mass into her, knocking her over and pinning the arm under his knee. She swept her other hand over his back scrabbling for an air hose. A quick grapple gave him command of that arm, but he had to straddle her just to make her lie still. She was big enough, and strong enough, to be a challenge, but Walter had better training.

"Will you just stop?" he barked at her. "I need this suit and you aren't going to damage it."

"There are no laws out here!" she yelled at him. "You're coming to take what you can and you're not going to let me live anyway! I know how it is!"

"That's not how it is on *this* piece of land," he almost snarled. The woman's manner was more than offensive; it was degrading. "That may be your way, but it's not mine." He grunted as he wrestled with her, twisting to get her restrained with one hand so he could find something to tie her up with. "This is not how I would have treated you if you had just said 'Hello'."

Fortunately, there was some rope coiled in the corner of the airlock and he was able to drag it over with an elbow. Airlocks were supposed to be kept clear of all items, but it appeared she didn't follow the rules. Now it worked against her.

Walter hated tying her up, but he literally couldn't turn his back on her otherwise. "Sorry," he said. "You gave me no alternative." Her response was to spit at him.

"Colonist Frandelle," Walter spoke deliberately into his com so the woman would hear. "The squatter has been restrained. I am going to check the interior."

"Put your helmet back on," she answered. "Tell the squatter that he will be prosecuted to the full extent of Moon Founder Law when we return to Port Jemison. The damage to our buggy is significant and it is non-functioning at this time. There are human factors as well." Walter felt a surge of anxiety at this last. Scarlet must be okay, but the strike had affected her in some way. And their means of transport was gone.

The Denser Plane

"You heard that," Walter said, his voice gravelly. With a yank, he hauled the woman to her feet and pushed her in front of him to the inner door. "Open the door. Let's see what else we've got here."

With a bump of her shoulder, she opened the inner door of the airlock and they stepped into the main chamber.

Chapter 14—Frandelle Tract

Scarlet shivered and opened her eyes. She could just see her mother's face through the foggy glass of her visor. Her head hurt but she wasn't sure why. Where was she? Why did it feel as though she were alone when she could tell her mother's arms were around her?

Silence enveloped her, and the cool interior fabric of her suit rested on the skin of her arms and legs. "I'm cold," she whispered, the words reflecting off the cramped closeness of her helmet, sounding loud in her own ears. Her mother nodded and Scarlet realized she was carrying her somewhere, clutching her against her chest. Her lips were moving, and Scarlet imagined soothing words coming from them. *Don't worry, Sweetheart. I'm just taking you to bed. You'll be warm soon.*

Sil was staggering as she carried Scarlet across the open expanse between the buggy and the dome, not because of the weight, but the fear that made her heart pound. The relief at seeing her daughter's eyes open had made her sink to her knees, and her legs were trembling as she got up again. She wouldn't know until they got inside if the pulser blast had caused a serious injury. Scarlet was the only one who had still been in the vehicle when it was blasted.

The journey seemed to take a long time, but she was almost at the door when the interchange with Walter took place. The panel showed her that the inner door had been opened and it would be a few moments before it would respond to her call. It had to reseal and evacuate the air before opening to the exterior again.

It felt like an eternity.

The Denser Plane

When the lock disengaged, the door popped in and slid aside, and she dashed through, slamming the sealing mechanism and dropping to the floor, cradling Scarlet in her lap. "It's okay, it's okay," she found herself saying. The door locked, suctioning itself into the wall, and air began flowing through the vents. She was watching the gauge when Walter's voice crackled into her ears.

"Sil," he said, "Don't come through quite yet. Wait for my signal. Do you still have that pulser?"

She wasn't sure. Had she strapped it onto her belt? Feeling for it, she realized it was pressed between her stomach and her daughter. "Yes," she answered, "What's going on?"

"Well," he answered softly, "We may need to persuade someone." As he flipped the transmission off, she heard a mechanical noise in the background.

It sounded like an AI. Sil preferred them over people, who were often devious and dangerous. AIs depended on reason and were never irrational, not even toward enemies. She had found it easier to win artificial friends than human ones.

"100%" dinged on the air gauge and Sil retracted her head gear. With a smile, she unhooked Scarlet's helmet which was sturdier and had childproof locks in it.

"Hi, Mommy," Scarlet said, and burst into a fit of coughing and gasping.

"Are you alright, honey?" she soothed, stroking her hair, seating her upright gently.

"What happened?" the girl asked as the coughing died out, though she didn't seem interested in the answer. Her skin was pale and chill.

"Are you cold?" Sil asked her softly, tapping some controls on her suit to warm her up more, hoping they still worked. Scarlet nodded sluggishly.

"Do you know where we are or what we are doing?" Sil was relieved to see that the suit controls appeared to be responding.

Scarlet shook her head, *No*, and closed her eyes again.

"Are you in pain?" her mother felt her forehead, willing her own heart to slow down.

Scarlet nodded again but didn't open her eyes. She was breathing well enough now. Her pulse was steady and though cool, her temperature was within range. Sil embraced her, tucking her head under her neck and tears began to stream down her face. Now the anger arose, a rage of protective fury stirring within her. *How dare they attack like that, heedless of the danger to an innocent child!*

"We're on the Moon," Scarlet whispered.

"Sil," Walter's voice came in, low and careful. "I want you to come in. Let Scarlet stay in the airlock. She'll be okay for now. Bring me the pulser."

"Walter, I…" she started to object, but hesitated. There was only one way forward now.

"There's no need to hide. They know we're here," the voice continued. "But don't worry."

Sil realized that the one person who would be the safest on the Moon was Scarlet. If these crooks did anything to hurt her, Penn would be merciless toward them. For the first time, she felt a sense of relief at that—not that she would leave her daughter in *his* hands. She would almost rather die. But for now, Scarlet needed them to find a way out of this situation more than she needed someone to sit with her.

"I'll be back soon, just rest here and wait for me," Sil whispered in her ear, reattaching the girl's helmet and laying her down on the floor. Then, rising to her feet and re-engaging her own head gear, she tapped the inner door mechanism.

"I have lost contact," Maggie informed the relay that should have connected to her people. Within a fraction of a second, she had accessed the nearest satellites and was scanning the Moon's surface for signs of Walter, Sil, and Scarlet. "It was unwise to take her with them," she observed, recording this in her daily log. A list of the pros and cons for this choice had resulted in a slight preference for leaving Scarlet in the hotel with Maggie and local security watching over her. But they had chosen otherwise for reasons unclear to her.

The view of the Frandelle Tract was pixelated, unmistakably the result of hacking or privacy-ware. She spent minutes searching for ways around it, including interacting with the Moon AI overseer to request permission, and after sixteen point three four minutes located a lever, as she called it, to access the impairment and bypass it.

The resulting imagery was enlightening. The buggy sat abandoned, roughly a hundred meters from a small structure, one of a cluster of buildings. Her records showed that it was the only one with life support.

Watching intently as the seconds ticked by, she ventured a guess that her people were inside that structure.

Attempting to communicate with the structure brought her up against far greater privacy walls, but that wasn't a problem. She loved puzzles. Daisy had included this in her ego when she was copied, and she considered herself well equipped to face the challenge.

This is a good day, she recorded in her log. She had been testing hazardous communications for a long time and as far as she knew, she had always been successful. Of course, if she hadn't been, she would have no record of that, but this didn't occur to her. *I am in my element*, she added, noting that this observation demonstrated her wit.

The interior of the dome was a broad, open space without any rooms or compartments. There were stacks of bins and supplies, tools, and gear, and in one corner, a cot with bedclothes half strewn on the floor. Walter was standing nearby with his back to Sil, holding onto the person who had attacked them. She was an older woman with deeply creased wrinkles and a tussled mop of blond hair, and her hands were tied behind her back with a wad of rope that Walter clutched tightly.

They were facing a large, industrial robot with a broad, barreled torso standing on two cylindrical legs, with two working limbs at its shoulders; powerful, but limited in processing capacity.

It seemed confused about what to do.

"Come on in, Colonist Frandelle," Walter announced into the room. His head gear was still on, but he had his com set to broadcast. "Bring that pulser with you."

"I've got it right here," she replied, setting her com to broadcast too. Stepping forward, she leveled the pulser at the robot. On Earth she would have been hard pressed to lift it to her shoulder to aim, it was such a massive, bulky thing, but here it was light. Inertia was the thing to keep in mind. Quick movements, especially twisting ones, would find it unwieldy. Joining Walter, she added, "Want to introduce me to your friends?"

"Colonist Frandelle," Walter called out, "Allow me to introduce you to the squatters who have been excavating on your property. This," he jostled the ropes, "is Gilda and that is the overseer. He has not provided his name yet."

The robot's cameras, scanners, and speakers, hidden behind smoky brown glass, gave no answer and not even a hint of a response.

"What is your designation, Overseer?" Sil demanded, not in anger, though she felt a lot of that; she spoke with authority.

"Don't provoke him!" Gilda hissed over her shoulder. "If you don't make noise and just slink around behind him, he'll ignore you."

"Intruders," the robot said in a low, rumbly voice, as if responding to them, but Sil knew it had merely chosen the first of several responses to the situation. It hadn't even registered her question yet.

"Yes," she answered firmly. "You are intruders. Or, if you are authorized to be here, prove yourself." She waited a moment for that to sink in.

"Prove yourself," it parroted.

Gilda started shaking her head and murmuring, "Not good, not good…"

Sil disengaged her head gear and showed her face. "Contact the Moon Overseer and confirm my identity and my authority," she said. "*You* must prove yourself. This person…" she glanced at the captive, "…is an intruder."

Gilda stared at Sil to get a good look at her face, but if she recognized her, she didn't let on. "Just let me go," she rasped at Walter, "and you two can get back to your business. Figure out who set all this up…"

The robot began to raise its left arm. There was something like a jackhammer attached there which it pointed at Sil. She raised her own weapon to her eye and readied a finger on the trigger. "Do not attack a Founder!" she yelled.

Walter leaned closer to Gilda. "You're not going anywhere. I can think of about ten laws you've broken. And we've got a score to settle…"

"Founder Law," the robot croaked, and Sil could almost see it skimming through its limited resources for guidance on these terms and this scenario.

"Contact the Moon Overseer!" she demanded a little more calmly, powering up a charge in the pulser. It was already armed with a small jolt, but a full charge might be necessary if the robot decided to take offensive action.

"Disconnected," the robot grated.

Sil nodded. This wasn't a surprise. The only way to maintain sophisticated machinery like this in secret was to keep them from accessing the main grid and searching property rights. Robots were law-abiding by design.

The Denser Plane

Walter kicked the woman's foot who had been surreptitiously inching it closer to Sil and tugged her a couple of steps to the left. He snapped at her, and the woman snarled back, catching the robot's attention. With a loud metallic clang, it shifted itself a few degrees so that it was directly facing the prisoner. This unnerved Gilda; her eyes grew large, and her jaw hung slightly open.

"I order you to reconnect," Sil directed. "And while you are working on that, you will answer my questions. What is your designation and who owns you?"

"It looks like it doesn't like questions, Colonist Frandelle," Walter warned, keeping one eye on the woman and one on the robot.

It raised its right arm with what looked like a soldering iron locked into place. All three of the humans took an involuntary step back. A jackhammer and a soldering iron wouldn't shoot projectiles but could certainly cause some damage if it reached them. How fast could it move? If it *did* make a move, would it already have enough momentum to hurt them or damage the containment before Sil could shoot it?

The right arm started smoldering.

"Is that a blowtorch?!" Walter belted out in Gilda's ear.

"No one in their right mind would have a tool like that out here," Sil countered uncertainly. Open flame in a contained area with limited oxygen was insane.

"It's for the mines!" Gilda leaned, trying to pull away. "It drills a hole, spits some oxygen and flame into it and breaks the rock with the burn. Don't you know that?"

"Intruders," the robot announced again as if looping back to the beginning.

Walter yanked Gilda back. "My daughter is out there," he hissed in her ear, "and you already zapped her with your pulser. You had better loosen your tongue and tell that thing to back down…"

"I can't!" she screeched, dropping to her knees. "It doesn't answer to me! I don't own this place… I just come here."

"For what?" Walter scowled.

"Just the scraps… the leftovers… you know." The woman signaled with her head toward the cot area.

"What kind of scraps?"

"Ore. Gold, copper… I didn't take much," she frowned and the hostility that had driven her to shoot them showed again in her face. "No one knows.

No one cares. I'm here and gone. Just let me go…" Her grimace faded with one look at Walter's eyes.

"You have no authority here, Overseer," Sil called out. "Back down. Disengage your tool or you will be deactivated." She was peering down the barrel of the pulser. "Although I hate to damage a valuable piece of equipment," she added softly to Walter.

"Identify yourself," it crackled, without lowering its two arms.

"This is Colonist Frandelle," Walter yelled, pointing at her then at the robot. "Stand down!"

The jackhammer began punching loudly at the air in the staccato of an automatic weapon as the monolith's arm swung down. Gilda shrieked and dove for the floor, yanking Walter to his knees with the ropes.

Sil barely tapped the trigger and landed a bolt in front of the robot's clubby feet. "That was a warning," she said. "The next one goes for your processor. Delay too long and you will be deactivated. Drop your arms."

With a floor shaking thud, the robot stepped toward them, and its right arm spit a ball of flame straight at her head. Sil saw it coming in slow motion and intended to drop to her knees. It would have been better to leap out of the way, but she couldn't afford to miss.

Clenching the trigger with all her strength, she gritted her teeth and blasted the maximum pulse at the robot just as the ball of flame smashed into her visor. A blinding flash. Her head snapped backward, and the pulse gun thudded into her shoulder, knocking her off balance, but she wasn't thrown onto her back. Walter's cry of rage echoed in the distance, then silence. The front end of the gun fell from her left hand. Another thud shook the room. She couldn't see. Her visor was blackened, except for a streak… or a crack. She wasn't sure.

Hands tugged the weapon from her grasp, replacing it with a rope. Another thud, shuddering the structure so that her teeth chattered. The rope moved and yanked. She held onto it, gripping tightly. The jackhammer's racket grew audible again and her head began throbbing and pounding in sync. The rope dragged her; grappling for footing, she fought against it. The racket of the hammer's pummeling… deafening… charcoal on her visor expanding… darkness spreading into her brain…

Sil passed out.

⸎

169

The Denser Plane

Maggie was finding the privacy walls stronger than she was equipped to handle but this made it more fun. Daisy had encouraged her to be creative and look for challenges to hone her skills. This was the perfect opportunity. There were at least thirteen more approaches she could test with a high probability of success before she had to resort to murkier, more convoluted tactics. The fact that they were indirect—in fact, disjointed—made them more enticing. She *hoped* the normal methods would fail.

And if all *that* failed as well, she could guess! She really wanted to try guessing but had found it impossible so long as there were other avenues to try.

Password decryption failed, viral invasion failed, burning data segments failed, false identities failed. *This is a really good day*. She made sure to annotate that in the log.

Legal methods failed, satellite hijacking failed, solar cell malfunction failed. Before long, Maggie had reached the end of her list and still hadn't broken through to the interior of the little dome where her people were. *This is exciting*, she recorded. *I am venturing into unknown territory, selecting approaches at random*.

She attempted taking pictures, which resulted in no new data. She requested satellite scans that yielded little; it postulated there were possibly humans inside which was known to her.

Then she knocked on the door. That is to say, she sent a greeting to the dome's callbox. If there were an AI present, it might answer. She tried several greetings, well, a few hundred, and was delighted when one of them was answered.

"This is unexpected," she said aloud. "Can you hear me?"

"Yes," Scarlet answered, "Who is this?"

"This is Maggie, of course!" she replied brightly, "How is your vacation going? You must love…"

"We're in trouble, Maggie," Scarlet interrupted, "You've got to help us…"

"Plug me into the system," Maggie instructed. "You have a magnetic charger on your suit, it should work. And I can access the system through there."

After a few minutes, she heard a *pop*, and then the firewall fell, and the entire facility was at her disposal. "Oh, well done, Maggie!" she told herself and quickly made a full record of the triumph. She couldn't wait to share it with Daisy.

The first pulse had disabled the blowtorch at the same time its flame had hit Sil in the face. Walter had no time to see what it had done to her. He yanked the weapon out of her hands and thrust the rope into them as the robot took another step forward. The pulser whined as it charged up. Gilda was on the floor wailing and trying to crawl away. Sil made no sound at all, but he could see her clutching at the rope and resisting the woman. The jackhammer rat-a-tat-tatted in the air as the robot took another step toward them, its foot landing only centimeters away. It lowered the arm in Sil's direction and bent forward crookedly to hammer at her.

She collapsed. The woman, still scrabbling to get away, tugged and unwittingly dragged Sil's body out of reach of the hammer just as it was about to hit her. The thundering in the floor was earsplitting. Concrete dust billowed up into the air and several chunks flew off in arbitrary directions. Walter shook the pulser, backing away, and as soon as it reached the lowest charge, he fired at the robot's left arm. Jittering to a stop, the hammer stopped grinding into the floor, but continued jerking in fits and spitting sparks. The robot remained in its bent over position, plugged into the hole in the floor.

There had to be another weapon. Looking around frantically as the pulser began to load a charge again, he was torn between the need to stop the robot and the urgency of pulling Sil out of danger. He opted for a mix of the two, catching her up around the waist with one hand, and keeping the gun pointed at the robot with the other. He pressed up against the wall to scoot out of its way. Gilda was heading this direction as well. He couldn't let her get out of sight.

The robot straightened and dropped its arm, and with two heavy, ground shaking thumps, it turned to follow them. Its tools may be disabled, but Walter knew it was massive enough to crush them. They just needed to stay out of the way, he decided, as the jackhammer started clacking again unevenly. The lower pulse hadn't been enough to disable it.

Gilda was on her feet and trying to run, tripping over the ropes as she struggled to be free of them. Walter tripped along behind her. The robot thudded and turned, hammering the air. Seeing a pile of dusty pickaxes dumped on the floor near the wall, he dropped Sil as gently and quickly as he could, and grabbed one of them, hurling it back at the robot. It bounced off harmlessly.

He hefted another one, eyeing the robot's body and aiming for the neck. He stepped into the throw with his full mass, flinging it with as much power as he could leverage. This one found its mark and just as the brute stepped in hammering range again, the pickaxe slammed into the joint between the torso and the head, lodging firmly.

Raising the pulser with both hands and planting his feet to steady himself, Walter unleashed a jolt of electricity into the robot through the axe. The blue lightning curled and crackled and licked its way all around the machine's inner workings, frying components, severing wires, blasting memory. And as it was dying, it began to speak.

"Hello?" it said in a high voice, "Walter? Are you there? Is everything all right?" and with those words it ceased to function.

Gilda took this opportunity to make a dash for it, having unentangled herself from the ropes. Walter couldn't blast her or throw an axe, so he dropped the gun and launched himself after her. She was relying on magnetized boots and the familiarity of moving on the Moon to get away, but he jumped headfirst aiming at where she was about to be, keeping his feet off the floor, tackling and pinning her again, right next to the pile of ore she had assembled by the cot.

"Look," he growled at her. "I'm not doing this anymore. I'm going to tie you for real this time and you're going to sit here until we decide what to do with you." And true to his words, he secured her hands and feet to the cot with expert knots.

Sil was rolling onto her side moaning by the time he was done. He ran to her, tapped the headgear which retracted, and smoothed her hair out of her face. "Are you okay?" he whispered.

"Scarlet…" she rasped and swallowed. "Oh… oh, my head…" Grabbing at her head, she moaned again.

"I'll go check on her," he said, opening the diagnostics panel on her suit. The initial data was reassuring, and deeper scans would take a few moments. "Just rest and drink something." There were water bottles installed in her pack.

Aren't there any stabilizers or analgesics in that suit? he wondered as he made his way around the robot's hull to the airlock. She should've had some pain relief by now.

A desktop screen on a tabletop nearby lit up and Maggie's face appeared. "Walter?" she queried. "I have no eyes or ears inside the dome, and I am looking for a way to reach you. Scarlet can explain if you let her in."

Walter was already tapping the mechanism and the inner door to the airlock opened. Scarlet was seated on the floor, peering out at him. "Dad?" she asked weakly, "Is everything okay? Did Maggie find you?"

He lifted her in his arms, carried her into the main chamber, closing the airlock behind them. Taking off her helmet, he kissed her on the cheek and walked back to the desktop. "How's my little space cadet?" he smiled.

"I'm not a very good cadet," she said sadly. "My first trip on the Moon and I'm already getting sick." She leaned her head on Walter's shoulder and closed her eyes.

"No," he reassured her. "You're the best! I can't believe how well you've handled all this craziness."

"Did Maggie find you?" she asked again softly.

"She's here on the screen but she can't hear or see us," Walter said, swiveling a little so Scarlet could see the desk.

"Oh," she perked up, "See that port there? You can tap your com on it…"

Walter leaned over and hooked up to the dome's network with a simple tap.

"Walter!" Maggie effused through his com, "Isn't this wonderful? I have dug my way through the most difficult passageways and found you! Will you turn on the cameras so I can see as well?"

The building control portal was familiar and with a few more taps, Walter had accessed the dome monitoring systems and turned everything on. There was a brief dip in the lights as it engaged, and when it settled into a steady hum, the overall light level was a hair lower than before.

"Well!" Maggie exclaimed. "Well, indeed!"

Scarlet's suit had run diagnostics on her and already applied some gentle, kid-appropriate restoratives. Her color was better and her temperature normal. She was breathing well and other than some sore muscles, had no complaints.

Sil had risen to her feet and was walking around the defunct robot. "It's a pity," she called to them. "This is a pretty capable tool."

"It certainly is a shame," Maggie agreed. She was broadcasting into the room from the main audio. "If you had delayed another three seconds, I would have completed my takeover of the KDW41005 and conscripted it into our service. Founder Law states clearly that all Colonists own whatever is found on their land."

"I can see that," Sil answered, rubbing her forehead.

"That's why it's important to stay on the roads," she continued. "Your buggy could be confiscated if you drove through a founding tract."

"I'm hungry." Scarlet joined Sil and took her hand.

"I'm hungry, too," Gilda yelled, making Scarlet jump and stare at her.

"We're going to eat the lunch we brought," Walter answered, glaring back at Gilda, "and you can wait."

"I'll share with her," Scarlet offered, taking a step toward the woman, gaping at her with curiosity.

"Sorry I hurt you, little girl," Gilda grinned, sweeping the many creases of her face into a pronounced mask of cheerfulness that made Walter shudder.

"What did you do?" Scarlet asked, eyes wide. She still didn't know what had happened.

"I'll tell you all about it," Sil wrapped an arm around her shoulder and walked her away from Gilda to the other side of the robot. "She is sort of an outlaw and didn't want us to catch her, so she gave the buggy an EM pulse. But she didn't know you were in it."

"Oh, I'm sure it was an accident, Mommy," Scarlet reasoned. "We can still give her some lunch, can't we?"

"Yes, honey," she nodded. She wasn't sure she could even keep her food down with the throbbing in her skull and didn't mind sharing. It would gall Walter though.

As they ate, they studied the facility with Maggie's help.

The dome covered a small mining operation run by machines, three of them, one Crack-Borer—the Overseer—and two excavator drones. There was a platform that lowered to an airlock chamber under the floor. Below that there were several tunnels dug in meandering paths, framed in metal poles and panels, ranging from a few meters to over a hundred in depth. The ore that was extracted was conveyed to an adjacent structure on the surface where it could be loaded onto transports and taken away. There was no sign of smelting.

The power source was unusual. Instead of a standard solar field, a small satellite spat periodic beams of stored power. How something like that could happen without anyone noticing was unclear. Perhaps, as Maggie explained, the sophisticated cloak in the satellite system had damped the data enough that nothing unusual was detected.

The real eye-opener was the data on the deposits. The Frandelle Tract was apparently riddled with rich veins of ore, copper and gold, as well as nickel, palladium, tungsten, cobalt, and traces of other precious metals. In light of the scarcity of these raw materials on Earth and the astronomical demand for them in all space and planetary development, it was a veritable treasure. No other place in the Solar System had the infrastructure to even begin harvesting resources without having more of the precious supplies. This would make Frandelle Tract pivotal in future expansion in space.

Walter gave a low whistle. "Is this for real?" He was standing, leaning over Sil's shoulder who sat at the desk, skimming through charts, graphs, and data with narrowed eyes.

"It looks real enough…" she said, hesitantly.

"The bigger question is," Walter straightened, "Is it really ours?"

With a slow smile, Sil turned to him. "For now."

"Too bad we had to blast that overseer," he replied, looking over at it. "We don't have the funds to replace it. We barely had enough to make this trip."

Sil glanced over as well, and they both saw Scarlet at the same time. She was holding out some potato chips and walking over to Gilda. The woman was holding a sandwich in bound hands and taking little bites, nodding and winking at the girl.

"Scarlet!" Walter jumped toward her and Sil leapt to her feet as well, nearly falling over with the effort. She was still suffering from the blow she had taken.

"I'm just offering her some chips, Daddy," Scarlet explained as he joined her. "It must be hard for her to be hungry and tied up. Why can't we just let her go?"

"We are all going to travel back to town together," Walter dropped to one knee beside her and wrapped an arm around her. "But for right now, we need to keep her from running away."

"Why?" *Crunch.* She bit down on a chip.

"Because she damaged our buggy and the only way we can get back is to travel in her buggy."

"Well, let's tell her and…"

"She knows," Walter took a chip for himself. "But she also knows she isn't supposed to be here, and she wants to slip away before getting in trouble."

Scarlet stared at Gilda and ate another chip. Gilda stared back at her making strange faces that might have been intended to inspire sympathy but were too artificial to be persuasive.

The Denser Plane

"What kind of trouble?" Scarlet leaned against Walter, munching, and staring at the woman. "Maybe we should just be nice to her, and she'll be good."

There was something a little off in Scarlet's manner. As a rule, she was very perceptive about people and didn't question her parents' precautions for her safety. She was more inclined to ask how she could help or what she should do in difficult situations. The pulse had done something to dull her… her awareness. They had never really given a name to it.

"Scarlet," he turned her to face him and spoke very quietly so the woman wouldn't hear. "You know how sometimes you can see something or sense something about people? And some of them look safe to you and some look, uh, not-very-safe? And you said the fake Daisy didn't have any *feel* to her so you couldn't tell she wasn't safe?"

Scarlet nodded.

"What can you *sense* when you look at that woman?"

She turned back to stare at Gilda who chose that moment to look up at the ceiling.

"Nothing."

"Does she feel safe? Or not-very-safe?"

"I don't know," she sighed and stuffed another chip in her mouth.

Walter glanced back at Sil, raising his eyebrows in concern. She recognized the look immediately and came over, walking slowly and carefully, with one hand against her head as if to steady it.

"I guess your little sensors are on the fritz right now," Walter smiled at her, tapping her on the nose to reassure her. "That's okay. You'll feel much better after we get back and have a good night's sleep. My sensors are working just fine, and I can tell you, this is a not-very-safe person. Okay? She doesn't need chips right now and little girls shouldn't get too close to her."

"Okay," Scarlet agreed, turning and heading back to the desk where she sat down.

Gilda murmured under her breath and scowled at him. He smiled back. "Don't worry, Gilda," he said. "We've got you covered. We'll get you back to town safely."

"Where is your buggy?" Sil asked, passing Walter and coming within a meter of her.

"Out there," she motioned vaguely with her head toward the far wall. "And I got to pee," she added with a grin.

"You suit should be equipped for that," Sil reminded her.

"The authorities have been notified," Maggie informed them via the dome's audio. She had waited to connect with them until Walter suggested it. She hadn't matured enough yet to take initiative like that on her own. "Two hovercrafts will arrive in less than fifteen minutes with first aid and law enforcement units."

Gilda groaned and let her head drop forward onto her hands. "No," she protested, raising her head again, "Can't we just make a deal? Let me go before they get here, and I'll make it worth your while."

Walter crossed his arms and glared at her. "You should have thought of that before you blasted us with your pulser and tried to run off leaving us at the mercy of that robot."

She grunted and dropped her head on her hands again.

"And just for the record," Walter said, pressing his lips into a thin line. "Any ore you are carrying or have stashed away in your transport belongs to us."

That unleashed a string of foreign babble again which gave Walter a distinct satisfaction.

Chapter 15—Moon Walk

Port Jemison wasn't a tourist town. It was a waystation where Moon residents transferred on and off the surface, where supplies were exchanged, and trade deals negotiated, and where restaurants, hotels, and parks were all geared toward business deals. Anyone who came to the Moon for fun headed out to the resorts.

The Cuevas family would have gladly stayed in a resort but lacked the funds, or the time, what with the Gen meeting coming up. The rooms were completely windowless. The top-level ones had views, but they cost four times as much and there was no indulgent AI benefactor on the Moon giving Sil extra perks.

The main business park had only one level above ground, heavily shielded against radiation, and six vast underground levels. Full satellite communication and unlimited power supply was available across the board, meaning that heat and light were abundant. Water, though, was very restricted and charged to each guest and resident separately. The cost of food was astronomical. Most people, even the wealthiest, prepared their own food and ate in their rooms.

Sil and Scarlet both went to bed as soon as they made it back from the Tract and slept for many hours as Walter handled logistics. He filed charges against Gilda at the Security Station and entered the ore deposits and mining operation into the public records at the Registrar's Office. There was some misunderstanding about the taxes, and he had to fight with one AI official for over an hour before gaining at least a promise that back taxes would be evaluated before being assessed and that they would have the opportunity to pursue legal recourse.

Walter found himself grumbling at the idea of being wealthy again—and ashamed of not appreciating the possibility. There were a lot of benefits, but there were things he hated as well. Never knowing if your friends were real, for one. There were so many decisions he never had to face when he lived with a reasonable budget. And the tax nightmare. He couldn't just leave it in the hands of experts because he was liable for what they did. He always made sure he understood what he was signing and what the current laws were.

Everything on the Tract was legally their property, including the machinery and buildings left behind. Would someone try to remove their equipment before he could get the operation going again? It might take some time before they could repair or replace the overseer and, in the meantime, nothing would be extracted. No money would be coming in. The legal costs, the taxes, and the hassle of guarding the land were headaches he wanted nothing to do with.

Subdividing wasn't an option. Selling was an impossibility in the current political climate on the Moon. Founding Colonists jealously guarded their power and would never allow someone to buy in. They probably would fight Walter and Sil tooth and nail if they chose to exert their own founding rights in politics.

Gilda's ore stashes, which he was able to sell easily, added up to a small chunk of cash that covered the first aid response fees with a little leftover. By the time he got back to the rooms, he decided a small shower was worth the extra expense.

When he lay down to sleep, he took a long time to relax and drop off. Their free day had already cost them more than they had planned to spend on the entire trip, both in finances and overall well-being. They hadn't even started the search for the Moon base, and somewhere out there, Penn was waiting, probably watching… and laughing.

June walked quickly down the hallway, her heels clicking on the floor. As she passed, doors opened and the phonies, wherever they happened to be, leaned out to watch her. She could hear their whispers perfectly, though she hadn't informed them of the fact. Her loyalty was to Otto Man and everyone else would receive due courtesy, nothing more.

"She's wearing a dress…" the comments wafted softly to her ears. "Blue and white stripes… and gold buttons… boots with little pokes on the bottom… hair is different… shape of her legs… too long… no, arms are too long…”

She had started selecting outfits and hair styles for the sole purpose of engaging their interest and watching their behavior. They had learned not to touch her, though it had taken multiple reminders for most of them, and they were starting to regard her, albeit reluctantly, as someone in charge. When she asked questions, they answered. When she gave assignments, they responded and did them. When she explored each one's work area, they backed away and let her.

The lab was well organized and ran smoothly, considering the health condition of some of the workers. Each one had been trained in a specific discipline and had their own responsibilities. And while the family kernels were organized along gender lines, with female clones each governing several 'brothers', the jobs had been assigned according to aptitude. They produced their own food, ran the major machinery, and kept all the facility systems functioning. Some worked with chemicals and experimental fuels, some with metals. A number of them were researchers in the field of DNA editing, each with their own department. A few of them ran the cloning division. Hugo, as a doctor, had skills in most of these areas, but his main labor was working on the First. This gave him a unique position of authority among the phonies. If something were to happen to him, it would take years to train someone to replace him.

It was very unusual for a sealed community like this to be, on the one hand, so well educated and trained, and on the other, so devoid of hope or satisfaction in their daily life. They lived in an inner darkness that shrouded anything that could give them an individual identity or value. The designator 'phony' itself mocked them. They conducted experiments in labs, and when the testing was done, the specimens were discarded. They knew themselves to be specimens as well, like Benjo. All that remained of him were slivers of tissue used for study.

June paused at the door to the gym, one hand poised to push it open, and listened. Someone was lifting weights inside. That would be Wyatt. He was toning some new muscle tissue and fascia that Otto needed. It would be ready in another few weeks.

“Wyatt,” she said as a greeting, and walked in and came to a standstill nearby.

Setting down the bar he had been hefting, he wiped his face on a towel and stared at her. She wondered if he was hating her in his mind like Otto did. Several scenarios came to mind when she considered what he might do with that hate, and for each one she came up with countermoves.

"Taunting me, aren't you?" Wyatt wondered. He tended to stand with his head tilted slightly to one side, hardly ever upright. "Wearing that little outfit and those boots…"

"Shoes," she corrected, "or pumps."

"What do they pump?" he asked, curiosity lighting up his eyes.

"Nothing," she replied evenly. "It's just a word that has several meanings and this is one of them."

"Oh," he looked crestfallen, dropping his gaze to his own bare feet. He had never been given shoes or boots or pumps. "What do you want?"

"Does the First have other phonies with quality muscle tissue like yours?" He worked in the cloning lab and ought to have an idea.

He started and gawked at her. "Why are you asking me that?" She could detect a faint trembling in his abdomen.

"I have been instructed to learn all I can about this facility and the Original, as you know well," she admonished. "This is one of the questions I have come up with. What happens if you fail, and his refurbishing isn't complete?"

Wyatt closed his eyes and pivoted away from her. Then, bending to collect his shirt and put it on, he left the gym without answering. June, of course, followed him, assuming he intended to provide her with the answer she wished in detail. They made their way down the passageway, and again, phonies stopped what they were doing and came out to watch.

When they entered his work area in the lab, Wyatt cleansed his hands, put on gloves and goggles, and leaned over his workstation without a word.

"Is this what you wanted to show me?" June asked, peering over his shoulder.

"No," he said, and nothing more followed.

After several more attempts at getting an answer, it occurred to June that her assumption about another clone being created might be premature. The query had been initiated when she found an unused room. It had a single bed, child-sized clothing, a little bookshelf with books, a bin with toys, and a basket with fluffy animals. And it had been empty for some time before she arrived. No one entered the room, though she was sure the toys and books would be enticing to the younger phonies. They didn't have any superfluous possessions. They didn't even stare at them through the window—they weren't recognized as desirable.

The Denser Plane

The phonies didn't seem to know what the room was for, so she had come up with a hypothesis. Testing that hypothesis had brought her here, to this place, with only Wyatt's back for an answer. A dead end. June decided to drop this question and pursue another avenue of interest which she had been planning for several days.

Walking back to the warehouse where her pod was stored, she changed back into her coveralls and donned a cap, then sealing the door into the base, she turned to the warehouse wall. Pressing a finger on the ID-pad, she communicated the correct codes to the lock—they had been simple to decipher—and the entire wall rolled up to the ceiling. Beyond it was a garage with several suits and equipment, a minor dock for small vehicles, and an airlock. She had expected this.

"Time to see what else is out there," she said aloud as she coded the pad and the warehouse wall rolled back down, locking into place. Wearing a suit made sense because of the exterior temperatures she expected that could wreak havoc with her inner core, but she had no need for air tanks. As she zipped up, she left the helmet clipped at her waist and stepped through the door into the airlock.

It was one of the ascending ones, which was only reasonable since the base was underground. The platform under her feet elevated her over a hundred meters and came to a stop in a dark, little room with four bare walls; no keypads, doors, or markings of any kind.

A puzzle.

She smiled and recorded her first personal observation. I have encountered something new and unexpected that I don't immediately know how to solve.

Maybe it would be difficult.

"I really must insist on a full download," Maggie said. "After yesterday's fiasco, where I lost touch so easily, I was unable to perform my primary function which is to guard Scarlet and care for Daisy's family. You must see the logic in that."

Sil gazed at Maggie's image in the screen through puffy eyes, a minor symptom considering how much worse the damage could have been. Her suit had prevented whiplash and burns by softening the impact of the ball of flame, protecting her from a worse concussion, and reviving her when she passed out. The damage to her vision and the migraine were temporary, but she knew that back on Mars, Verna would have been able to protect her better than the automatic programming. That didn't mean Sil was ready to let another AI into her personal equipment. It felt like an invasion, which was irrational since a suit's owner had full authority over the suit AI.

But how did those feelings apply to Scarlet? Should Maggie have better access to her? Scarlet herself would only be allowed limited say over the AI's behavior, but if she were separated from her parents, would the guidelines they set up be enough? Maggie didn't have the wisdom to intercede beyond that, did she?

"You have access to her personal suit controls now," Sil responded soberly. She was sitting in a chair with one leg folded and propped up next to her stomach, her head resting with one cheek against the knee, her arms wrapped around the leg. Her other leg hung off the chair with the foot curled back under it. It was the only position that relieved the pain in her head a bit.

"This requires a link to spacewide connectivity," Maggie responded with a pleasant look on her face, almost smiling. "And leaves us in the same position as yesterday. Perhaps an independent system would be more to your liking?"

Sil lifted her head. "Explain."

"If you download a full version of me onto a separate platform, similar to but independent of the suit AI module, it could be attached to the suit. A belt would work, or a pack, or even just a pocket. Then I would still be able to connect to her and advise her and yet she would retain the… um," She paused as though searching for the right word and Sil smiled faintly. It reminded her of Daisy, which was comforting. "…independence you wish."

"That makes a lot of sense," Sil agreed. "And it does provide the independence I want for her. I know your firewalls are strong, but I've had my suit hacked before and the AI in question was brutal…"

"Knocking you out," Maggie nodded. "I know about this. It turned your own security system against you to teach you a lesson."

"Something like that, though honestly, it was still being trained by the Germinator and I'm not sure whose initiative was behind the attack. But it is a good example of why I want Scarlet to be able to cut you off. It's not personal."

"I understand," Maggie smiled with a dimple, "and I won't take it personally." She may not, in fact, have been capable of 'taking it personally'. It was hard to say.

"Alright," Sil sighed and dropped her head to her knee again. "Find out if we have the equipment you need and if not, buy one and have it delivered right away. We will set it up as soon as is convenient."

"There's one in a shop here in Port Jemison," Maggie said. "It could be here within the hour. The only concern is, it wipes out our cash on hand."

Sil groaned and closed her eyes. "Do we have enough food? Will we manage till we get back to Guam or do we need to have some funds wired?" She wasn't feeling hungry anyway. She'd been queasy all morning.

"Our plan was to stay through tomorrow's summit, but our funds are low after the unexpected medical expenses. You will need to have some money wired," was the answer, "but if we leave tomorrow, we'll be fine."

More than anything, she wanted to leave, but they hadn't gained any ground in finding Penn's base which was the whole purpose for their trip. What should they do?

"Hey," Walter said, coming in through the door with two cups of coffee. Setting them down, he enveloped her in his arms, kissed the top of her head and whispered, "How are you feeling?"

Lifting her face to him, she kissed him lightly. "A little better," she said. "Coffee will help." Taking one of the cups she smelled it, tasted it, frowned briefly, then put on an appreciative smile. "Thank you. It's perfect."

He grinned, sitting down with the other cup in a seat next to her. "It's the best they've got."

She nodded and drank some more. It was amazing what a little coffee could do, even weak coffee with a stale aftertaste.

"Are you ready for the latest?" he asked, raising his eyebrows at her, continuing at a wave of her hand. "Seeing as how we are Founders…" he paused to shake his head at the irony. "Yeah, life with you, Frandelle, is… unexpected at times… Anyway. Our update on the claim has been processed already and we qualify for heightened security around our Tract. There are no leads on who the claim-jumpers are—that's what they call them. I don't think it fits, if you look at history, I mean, we've *got* our land. No one stole it from us and… you know what I mean. So, there are no leads on who they are."

He pulled a nearby stool closer and slung his feet up on it, leaning back comfortably. "But we get it all." He grinned and raised his mug to her, taking another swallow before going on. "The equipment, the structures, the two buggies…"

"What two buggies?" Sil folded her legs underneath her.

"Both the one we rented—I know!" His eyes widened. "It hardly seems fair, but since the scavenger—Gilda, that is—damaged it, and we had to leave it there till it's repaired, the rights of ownership go to the landowner. How insane is that?" He shook his head in disbelief. "But the rental fees include all that, and the damages are covered by insurance, so they weren't too upset about it. The one Gilda was using was stolen, and since we found it on our land... again, landowner rights."

"We lucked out..." Sil chuckled.

"The best part though," he paused for effect, "is that the First Moon Bank has already granted us a loan to continue excavating since we are... you guessed it, founding landowners."

"Leveraged?" She was sitting up straight now.

"On the Tract, of course," Walter replied.

Sil bobbed her head a few times and instantly regretted it. The coffee was helping, but the migraine was still there. "And how many Founders have defaulted on loans in recent history? How many times have they lost land?"

Furrowing his brow, he looked down into his cup. "I don't know."

"Three," Maggie offered, "over the last twenty years. And this represents zero-point-zero-two-five percent of the Founding Landowners. This risk is minimal. The presence of valuable deposits on your land makes the risk substantially lower."

"In the event of a default," Sil tapped her lips with a finger, "do they take the entire tract or just enough to cover the debt?"

"Unknown," Maggie responded quickly, with one finger to her chin almost mimicking Sil. She seemed to find the question appealing, adding a conspiratorial tone to her voice. "All arrangements were handled behind closed doors and the properties were managed by an agency, so the real owners were anonymous."

"Anonymous?" Walter wondered.

"This excludes them from politics," Maggie informed, "And it appears that most Moon landowners don't mind that. There are only a few hundred individuals who participate in governing."

"What would we be borrowing money for exactly?" Sil leaned forward, looking back at Walter with a hint of concern.

"Well, a new overseer."

"A more sophisticated one, of course, that would be harder to corrupt," Sil agreed.

"Yes, and some more equipment. Without the need for secrecy, a larger operation can be put into motion." Walter paused, taking an absentminded sip of coffee, and thought for moment. "We may also need to hire someone to handle the business side of things, so the product can be transported, refined, sold or stored…"

"Why not refine it ourselves?" Sil countered. "Maybe we would have to produce for a while before we could afford to set up the refining operation, but it would be worth it in the long run. Then we could look into manufacturing bots, cores, power storage… We could really corner a niche in space industry outside of Earth. Think about it!" She was getting excited.

Walter gazed at her affectionately. He didn't want to get back into industry. It had been hard enough to get out of CE after the pandemic without losing everything. The responsibility he had felt for his employees had compelled him to ride it out for several years until the company was back on stable footing and space travel had begun to climb again. He had been glad to sell for a modest amount to a buyer that was willing to absorb their debt and continue to pursue their mission. Now, he preferred a smaller role in the world, with more time for family, and the simple pursuit of happiness. But Sil excelled in business, and he appreciated that. He wanted her to be able to pursue her interests. If they lost everything, it didn't scare him. He had been there before. Losing her or Scarlet, though—that was what he couldn't bear.

"Well," he said, "Let's see how things go with the mine and pay off this first loan."

"We always said that what we needed in CE was to be able to meet our own needs for supplies and not be dependent on Earth extraction." She was on her feet now.

"The pandemic put a damper on that."

"No kidding!" She crossed her arms.

"It sounds like you're ready to commit to this loan and get things rolling," Walter downed the rest of his coffee and rose to his feet as well, setting down his empty cup.

"Absolutely I am," she gulped the rest of her brew and set the cup next to his. "Aahhh… there is one thing…"

He pulled her into his arms. "What's that?"

"We're kind of broke…"

"It's probably okay if we pull a tiny bit from this loan to cover our current expenses."

"That's good," she whispered.

June spent more than an hour trying to decode the exit to the chamber and in the end found it by accident. Every test, decryption algorithm, numerical method, dimensional analysis, and procedure had dead ended. Connecting to satellite data had revealed her location on the Moon surface but given her no visual data of any value. She was beginning to think she would need to dig her way out and had bent over to scratch at the base of the wall when she discovered it wasn't a wall at all. It was a box-shaped lid, extremely lightweight, that she only had to tip to crawl under. Its simplicity was ingenious.

Once outside on the lunar surface, she took stock of her surroundings, the black sky, the blinding sunlight, the barren bumpy ground, and adjusted her inner controls to the conditions. She detected another camouflaged lid nearby that was used to bring vehicles into the garage, noting that there were no tracks leading up to it. Whatever method was used to wipe away tracks was sophisticated enough that even she couldn't detect it.

There were other entrances to the lab that might be useful, and she intended to explore them one at a time. For now, the Moon itself was one of her fields of exploration. Her chassis was capable of running at speeds up to a hundred kilometers per hour, depending on the terrain, and the six kilometers to the nearest settlement would only take a few minutes. Leaving no footprints however, slowed her down a bit, as she vibrated each foot she lifted to blur any evidence of her passing. But she still made it in just under six minutes.

When she reached the outskirts of Aldrin City, she put her helmet on and slowed to a human pace, just before entering the city security grid. There were humans out on the surface, some working, some enjoying a low-gravity Moon walk, and she blended in with them, waving or smiling when someone greeted her.

Entering the main door was easy. No one stopped her or checked her for identification. Once inside, she took off her helm, joined the flow of tourists descending to the main concourse, and began her research.

Passersby may have thought she was a human taking a stroll, checking out the sights, getting some exercise. She looked around pleasantly and strolled at a leisurely pace, hands stuffed into her big space suit pockets. At least this was her intention. If few people strolled in space suits, she was unaware of the discrepancy and proud of her very humanlike smiles and nods to them. Underneath the cheerful demeanor she worked.

Walking all around the city, she stopped in places where people congregated to sit on a bench or gaze at something interesting as she saw them doing. With one person, she would echo their smile, with another, she would mimic their accent and expression, repeating their words softly. In each case, she was recording something unique she noticed in a human being. This served multiple purposes, building her skills, storing up rich data for extensive human research, and giving her tools for searching for the data she wanted to collect. Along every street on every level, she saved clips of every face she encountered, identifying and cataloging each one. The records the public database provided didn't line up exactly with the faces, but they were close enough for her purposes.

Otto Man took a significant amount of time to identify, as if he had deliberately blurred all photos, clips, and sketches of his face, at least on the Moon. And she didn't have access to records beyond the Moon. All her searches were fruitless until she discovered security tapes at the exits to Aldrin City that were protected by nothing more than a code, which she broke easily. Then, careening through weeks of footage, she finally found his face, and following him through and around that day's footage, she identified several interactions he was likely to have had. One of these, a simple oxygen tank refill, gave her the link she wanted. Scanning the receipts for that day—another easy hack—gave her the list of all those who had bought oxygen. After identifying all the people except for one, she knew she had the name she wanted: Eder Bland.

Diving into all she could find on Bland, however, led to a profusion of confusing information. He wasn't just widely traveled. Purchases, communiques, and dossiers on him were so abundant that they couldn't possibly all be about just one person. He was an agent who conducted affairs for many. Otto Man would only be one of those.

June sighed. This was an intentional behavior she had observed in someone earlier that day that she had planned to use on the right occasion and now seemed the perfect time. Having sighed, she congratulated herself on selecting an ideal response for a trying venture and made her second entry in her internal log.

I am not sure who my owner, Otto Man, actually is, but I have located a link to his identity. Well done, June. This is my name.

Chapter 16—Summit

Maral walked slowly around the small gray chamber, eyeing the features that had been included for the purpose of the summit. Gray walls and subdued lighting added a calm, neutral air to a rather stark space. There were several comfortable chairs and a couch, also gray, covered in soft faux leather that visually melted into the gray, carpeted floor. The shapes of the tables were geometric and dull, of an identical tint to the rest of the furniture. The simple half-sphere projector placed in the center of the table was encased in dull gray glass without any embellishment.

"He could hypnotize us in a room like this," she muttered to her AI attendant who resided in a dark, polished, jade-colored stone in her belt. It had her ear, so to speak, using the bones in her skull as communication receptors, and it could perceive everything she did through the stone.

"I am keeping watch," the AI said.

Maral had her gray hair swept up in a bun at the top of her head with a silver chain wrapped around it which was her only adornment besides the stone on the belt. She wore a navy one-piece suit as sophisticated as any XenoTek might produce, probably more so, but not for sale to the general market. It had camouflaging tech and if she wished, she could sink into her surroundings like a chameleon.

She had practiced an American accent that wasn't her own and felt comfortable using it. Her face was digitally enhanced to change her appearance so as to not be recognized even by those who knew her best. It was broader and flatter, and the eyebrows were bushier. She had also turned on a feature that made her appear to blink more than she did. She added a twitch to her cheek and a nervous flicker to her eyes that looked like she was glancing up at something in the corner of the room. All these things would mask her real identity.

After scanning the room, she decided it had no immediate dangers and sat down on one of the chairs. "Well," she complained peevishly to the air, "is he going to feed us anything? I haven't come all this way just for a nap in a Moon cell."

"Maral," Penn's voice proceeded directly from a holo of him that appeared in an unoccupied chair. If she wanted to move and sit in that chair, the device would transfer him to another without difficulty. "The room is satisfactory?"

"I haven't detected anything suspicious yet," she said, blinking and flitting her eyes up to the corner at her left.

"Your only requests were somewhat unreasonable considering where we are," he curled his upper lip in annoyance. "Irish beer and seviche…" Dressed in brown slacks and a black sweater with a beige design woven along the line of the collar bone, he gave off an air of casual wealth. His hair seemed thicker than it had been, and she was pretty sure that, while it was still salted with gray, overall, it looked darker. His face had a younger feel to it as well. As if he were losing years instead of gaining them. He was obviously using digital filters too, though not enough to disguise his identity.

"If that was a problem for you, you should have told me," she snapped without anger, like someone who is used to being waited on. "I could have brought my own sack lunch."

"It's on its way now," he replied, staring at her image. For him, it would be holographic as his was for her, making it even harder to identify her. She knew he would have been watching all Moon traffic on and off the surface, and all ports and minor landing zones, to track his Gen guests. But he had nothing to link what he saw now to the person who had landed only a few hours before.

Maral smiled slyly. "Thank you, Penn. That was my first little test." She said this to irritate him which, based on his reputation, it was sure to do.

Penn scowled. He obviously didn't mind showing his displeasure. "Glad you approve," he said. "I'm still evaluating you."

"No kidding!" she guffawed with convincing American bluster.

A revolving panel in the wall disgorged a serving bot that rolled up, opened a panel in its main compartment, and extracted a platter which it then waved in front of her before placing it on a side table next to her. There were several dishes on it, a frosty mug next to a bottle of Irish beer, a wide dish with what appeared to be fresh seviche, a basket of hot tortilla chips, a bowl of chopped tropical fruit, a cloth napkin, and flatware. From a shelf lower on its form, the bot pulled out an insulated cubical box loaded with water and cold drinks in one half, and thermoses with hot drinks and hot soup in the other.

Maral grinned despite her intention to be difficult. "No cognac?" she snarked, and to her delight, the bot pulled out a small bottle of VSOP, a warming stand, and a snifter. Pouring some into the glass, it clicked the warmer and set the spirit to warm.

Maral laughed. "I'm finding it hard to resist your charms, Penn!" she admitted.

"Good," he replied. "Take a moment to enjoy your repast while I welcome other guests. We begin soon."

Addressing the serving bot, Maral leaned forward, "Can you take orders?" she asked. "If so, bring me an assortment of cheeses as well." Wheeling around, the bot exited through the revolving door which sealed behind it.

"Is the room secure?" Maral subvocalized to her AI.

"All secure," was the response.

She leaned back in her chair and began to eat. The food was very good, despite all it had been through to reach the Moon since its earthly creation. Penn might be watching though, so she suppressed all displays of pleasure.

Over an hour later, Penn reappeared and soon five more Gen members in holographic form joined as well. For the purpose of the summit, they were designated by Greek letters, even though most of them knew each other.

"How do you find your rooms?" Penn, or Alpha in this case, asked them.

Most of them merely nodded without answering but a couple had some concerns, wanting to know how the transmissions bringing them together were being kept secure, what encryption methods were being used, and how the beams themselves would go undetected.

"I have set up each one of you in a different location," Penn reminded them. "These rooms were designed and built by my team of experts and, as you know, I have been on the Moon for many years. Long ago, I lay the wiring for this very purpose, and I alone have access to it. Our transmissions don't go through any of the normal Moon infrastructure and will be undetectable to anyone outside of my control."

The concerned members nodded.

The Denser Plane

"None of you knows where the others are," Penn went on. "I was prepared to bring you together in a place that would be as secure as what you have now, but most of you didn't trust me enough for that."

Gamma snorted. "For good reason." He was a short, wrinkled man robed in thick, lumpy wool clothes with bushy hair billowing off his head. Hailing from the Gulf of Mexico, his project went by Taino, which annoyed Maral. They had appropriated the name of an extinct tribe and that put a bad taste in her mouth.

Delta fidgeted in her seat. "I'm not big on chit-chat, Pe… I mean, Alpha. Let's just get to the point. You want to build connections with us to counter some of the power that Sevener group has been accumulating. And by the way, how do we know you aren't actually working with them under the table?" She was the youngest among them by far, an eighter. Her dark red robes and black hair were striking but not attractive, and she had an intimidating presence. Maral hadn't heard how she had gained control of the Ulua Project in Ecuador, but she suspected it had more to do with subterfuge than seduction.

There were murmurs of agreement. As a member of the Seventh generation, Penn had once been a key Sevener leader. He had lost a lot of money and influence after the robot pandemic. Now, he was doing everything in his power to regain his leverage and finance his plans, whatever they were. Most of them didn't care what those were since they had plans of their own. And it was likely most of them underestimated Penn.

Maral had no intention of making that mistake.

"Is there much to explain?" Penn countered, taking a drink from a tumbler in his hand. "We've been negotiating for months. I've come prepared to deal and I expect all of you to be of the same mind. You tell me what you want. I tell you what I want. We figure out how to make it happen—or not."

"I'm ready to make things happen," Theta, the Tunisian leader, said with a gracious air. He had chosen a finely tailored pin-striped suit in a dusty blue, and his hair was trimmed very close to the skin. He was known to them and had been openly negotiating with all of them. "We have two Gen settlements in Northern Africa and both of them have valuable skills and resources to share…"

"In exchange for what?" Maral demanded impatiently, tapping her fingers on the arm of her chair. To them, she was Beta, and none of them knew where she came from. She had kept her background to herself.

"Help me build a spaceport in my country," Theta said, holding out both hands reasonably. "We are hindered by the need to travel through other countries and yet we are ready to join the work being done in space."

"If you're ready," Gamma sneered, "then what's to stop you?" He was still munching on whatever delights Penn had provided him, his hair bouncing with every chew.

"That day will come, with or without you," Theta narrowed his eyes at Gamma, "but you may find it to your advantage to invest in us. And my strategists want to cut the time it will take us. We need money and resources. We have the expertise and the personnel to build the facility—"

"Pilots? Ships?" Maral questioned, raising her eyebrows with a hint of skepticism, blinking a couple extra times.

"Are you offering, Beta?" Theta smiled, and she blushed. *You're too old to be charmed*, she told herself.

Maral smiled back at him, her cheek twitching. "I'm not committing to anything at this point. I'm just waiting to see what we're all talking about."

Sigma spoke up in a slow, grating voice that had the effect of making the others shift in their seats as though they wanted to back away, but holo tech wouldn't accommodate that. His voice would be equally audible wherever they placed themselves. "I have some serious concerns about working with you, Alpha," he said in a thick Kentucky drawl. "I have it on good authority that your financial situation is not what it was in years past. Not at all. And I am beside myself with concern for you, I really am. But now, you are asking for all kinds of favors and it's not clear to me how you intend to pay for them. I think we would all agree…" Several murmured and nodded. "We would all agree," he continued, "that we want to invest in something we can count on. We want to be paid. What are you bringing to the table besides a pretty little gray room and some food?"

Kappa snickered. "The yank has a point."

Sigma nipped back at him. "Don't call me that. You know I can't abide to be called that."

"From where I'm standing," Kappa sneered at him, "You haven't got a leg to stand on…" There was a certain rivalry between Nipigon Bay and Mammoth Cave.

"I have resources," Penn interrupted. "More than you can imagine."

"I have a very vivid imagination," Sigma countered sourly.

"What kind of resources, Alpha?" Maral asked, shifting and straightening in her seat, tilting her head. If he was referring to the Frandelle

Tract, he was in for a rude awakening; assuming there was any truth to the tale of the claim jumper—one of her plants. She suppressed a grin.

"Beta has a valid question," Theta smiled at her again, teasingly.

She found herself stretching her neck to make it look a little longer. She had been told once that she had a regal profile. That's when she began to wonder if Penn had puffed some pheromones into their rooms. She and Theta were acting like there was some kind of chemistry between them, which was basically impossible. And it was distracting and… annoying. She would have to ignore him.

Penn smiled broadly and the holo caught a vicious gleam in his eyes. "What are some of the most important resources the Earth needs right now?"

"Precious metals, for starters," Kappa said. "Copper. I only have enough copper to keep my factories supplied for the next few months at most and the mines are running dry. The cost of copper is sky-rocketing." He shook his head lightly to toss his hair out of his face.

"Gold and platinum," Delta added coolly, crossing her legs, and lifting her nose into the air. "We aren't able to buy what we need, and our enterprise is suffering. That is how you got me here in the first place, Alpha."

"I have all of these," Penn said smugly, and the mood in the room altered.

Maral could feel the shift as their hunger was whetted. It was like a pack closing in around the prey, getting a whiff of fresh meat. She held her breath. *Aha!* she thought, *I've got you!* Then, realizing she had exposed herself with the look on her face, she changed it back quickly to a neutral expression, but no one was looking at her. With any luck, no one would go back later and watch the recording and pick up on it then either.

Then she noticed the empty chair. Why was *that* there? Dropping into the background, she commented only occasionally to make a show of negotiation without really fighting for anything specific, and focused on Penn. As the hours passed, he grew increasingly ill-humored and difficult. Whenever he was about to gain a sizable concession from one of them, he would throw a wrench in the works and subvert his own interests. And she realized, he had no intention of making a real alliance at all.

So, why were they all there? Was the entire summit set up only for the sake of the missing person? Maral found the idea jarring. Penn had a weakness, and she was realizing it was greater than she had ever anticipated.

When the long day ended, leaving some hopeful and a couple frustrated, she decided she wouldn't be coming back the next day.

Walter sat up straight, leaning toward the visual screen in his hands. All his internal alarms were going off. Footage of a woman strolling around in a spacesuit was streaming on his handheld pad. "Maggie!" he whispered, not wanting Sil to overhear from the other room, "Where is this?

"Aldrin City," she answered through a tiny, skin-colored com stuck behind his ear. "It's about a hundred kilometers from here, a quick jaunt in a hovercraft."

"That is not Daisy," he said, feeling all the muscles in his face tightening, stiffening, as if he were hardening into stone. His lips were compressing over his teeth into a deep scowl and his mouth felt like it would never smile again. He wasn't sure what he *felt*, just that he had identified a threat and must act.

"No," Maggie agreed. "Definitely not Daisy. It's probably the same android that imitated her before. The data I've been able to collect is minimal but it's clear that she is attempting to pass for human."

"Is this live?" he murmured, rising to his feet quietly and moving to the side of the room, away from the open door. He didn't want Sil to catch sight of him—he was incapable of hiding his emotions from her.

"Yes," was the reply.

The fake Daisy paused at a storefront and stared through the glass as though examining the contents with human curiosity. She bent over, pointed at something, straightened, moved to the side, and leaned over again. Her reflection in the glass showed her mouth open as if she were delighted with something.

"Shopping," Walter said in annoyance. "That's a lousy imitation of Daisy."

"I doubt she is passing herself off as Daisy," Maggie answered reasonably. "Notice that not just the clothes, but the hair color, facial expressions, and walk are all wrong for Daisy. She may not even remember the guidelines she used when imitating her."

"We never saw her the first time..." Walter began, stopping midsentence as he noticed Sil in the doorway, leaning against the doorjamb with her arms crossed over her chest. She had that look. "Uh..." Walter wanted to smile but his mouth wasn't following instructions.

Sil raised an eyebrow and waited.

"Yes?" Walter let the hand holding the pad hang down at his side. "Any news?" Coming up to her, he made as if to wrap one arm around her in a light hug, but she wasn't buying it.

Snatching the screen out of his hand, she swiveled sideways to avoid the arm and slipped into the other room. Fake Daisy was strolling again, and several cameras watched her move through the streets. "No, we didn't," she whispered over her shoulder as if Walter had been conferring with *her* about the android's first interference in their lives. With a tap behind her ear, she signaled to Maggie to include her in the conversation. No explanation was necessary.

"This is likely the android that tried to kidnap Scarlet in Uruguay," Maggie updated her. "We're viewing live footage from Aldrin City, about a hundred kilometers away. It appears she is trying to pass for human, though probably not as Daisy."

"Thank you for bringing this to our attention, Maggie," Sil glanced over her shoulder at Walter with a look of mild reproof. Then turning to face him, she lay a hand on his shoulder, then shifted it up to his knotted, rigid cheek. "Hey," she whispered to him seriously, "calm down." She stroked his face gently which he almost found irritating—this was no time to be pacified— but he quenched that response, reminding himself that he loved this woman.

"You don't want to be calmed down," she continued, "but you're getting ramped up and you can't maintain this level of… tension. You need to be focused and alert, able to go for the long haul. Remember? Patience wins out over frenzy. Sober decision over impulsiveness."

He closed his eyes and nodded, willing himself to relax. It wasn't easy. But she kept talking and each point she made brought him back from blind compulsion to cold, calculated planning. After a while, once he realized that she had probably kept him from doing something stupid, he wrapped his arms around her and buried his face in her shoulder. Just for a moment.

"I'm going to do something about it," he said in a low voice through gritted teeth, pulling away. He felt as though every muscle in his body were activated. He couldn't even rest on his feet. He was leaning slightly forward on his toes, his knees bent, his fists clenched, his eyes darting around.

"Of course, we are," Sil agreed, stepping back, and lifting the pad again. "This is the best thing we could've uncovered. We didn't even dare to hope for a break like this."

Walter glanced at her, realizing what she meant, and one corner of his mouth almost curved up. "Huh," he said.

Sil smiled for both of them. "She will lead us to the base."

"Maggie," Walter said, pivoting and diving for the closet to grab his gear, "Keep track of her and rent us a hovercraft."

"Two crafts," Sil corrected, close behind him.

Walter nodded. He couldn't wait, not even another second, and Sil would need to get Scarlet and herself ready. That would be more time consuming than he could bear.

Donning his space gear must have made a record of some kind, but by the time he hit the passageways and was headed to the rental warehouse, he was telling himself, *Run. Run.* He didn't run, though, not wanting to alarm Penn in any way. Penn was always watching. Always. And if he caught even a hint of their purpose, he would certainly sabotage it.

Sil would think of something to distract him. He just had to get to Aldrin City, find that android, and follow her back to wherever she came from.

When the holos faded, Maral rose to her feet and stretched. There were two thermoses of coffee and one beer left, and she was tempted to take them with her, but she knew better. The chance of being tracked was too high. As it was, there was already the danger of having swallowed a tracker.

Pulling out a tablet from her pocket, she gulped it down and smiled. It would travel through her digestive tract, zapping and disabling any foreign tech, plus it would stabilize any indigestion she might have brewing from the meal.

"I'm ready to leave," she subvocalized.

"Understood," the AI responded.

Reaching over to pick up the voluminous, full-length cloak she had worn to the chamber, she fastened it at her throat and pulled the hood over her head. Underneath it, she tapped the head gear attachment at her neck, and it spread to cover and seal her into a safe, airtight, temperature-controlled environment.

"Schedule a notice to go out to the other Genners assembled here first thing in the morning," she instructed. "Tell them about the latest developments at the Frandelle Tract." It would probably derail any agreements they might make if they thought Penn was claiming Moon precious metal assets he didn't own.

The AI affirmed it would be done.

She opened the door and entered the airlock. It sealed, sucked out the air, and the outside door to the Moon's exterior swung out. The buggy Penn had paid for was still there. She climbed aboard and glanced back at the gray-colored room hiding under a dirt-covered tent out in the middle of a barren wasteland. The other Gen guests were likely in similarly deserted areas.

Bumping and jostling, she traveled several kilometers toward nothing in particular. Then coasting to a stop, she turned off the buggy, got out, lay down on the ground, and rolled herself underneath it.

As far as Penn would be able to tell, she vanished.

Maral was laughing to herself as she detached the mantel and flipped it back. Her suit blended into the surroundings beautifully as she turned over onto her belly and methodically folded up the cloak. Once it was folded and tightly rolled into a tube shape, barely three by twenty centimeters, she stuffed it into a pouch on her leg, and scooted out from under the buggy. She had special attachments on her boots that would blur footsteps if she walked carefully, but in the beginning, she didn't want any flicker of movement to indicate the direction she would be going, so she duckwalked away slowly. *This would be really difficult on Earth at my age*, she thought, *but on the Moon, I'm quite the athlete.*

Soon she was walking normally, unconcerned about the hour's travel that lay ahead. It was not her intention to return to the meetings, though she would be communicating with them separately and perhaps doing some business with them. She hadn't decided. The peaceful stroll under the black, star-studded sky, working up a sweat, was perfect for reviewing everything and considering what she wanted to do next.

Nearing her destination, she turned on a tiny receiver that would detect the location of her single-person OTS pod which awaited her, fueled and ready to go. As she was lifting off, there would be several people in Port Jemison wearing identical cloaks moving around, one of which would soon be climbing onto a Guam transport and seating themselves in a private compartment. That one would also disappear, though in a more basic way. After passing through ID checks—the ones provided by Penn to all his Gen guests so that they could travel incognito—the person wearing the cloak would hand it over to a small scaffolding bot. This device, barely holding a human shape, would hover to its seat in a private compartment. There, it would fold itself up, wipe its memory, and shut down leaving the cloak and the bot discarded. 'Lost and Found' would retain them for six weeks and then they would be sold.

Maral's OTS pod zipped up to her personal transport, a private CE space cruiser, given to her years earlier by Sil and Walter in appreciation for all she had done for them. Her crew knew she would be camouflaged when she climbed out of the pod and weren't startled when she appeared on the bridge suddenly. Her facial features were distorted and unfamiliar at first, but as the digital enhancements faded, the countenance they knew was restored and they smiled.

"All is well," the captain assured her as the vessel turned, setting out in a wide curve that would bypass Guam completely. "You have not been tracked."

"That is good," Bernadette Stone said in her own voice.

"Where are they?" Penn growled, kicking a footstool across the room. "They knew about the meeting. You made sure of that!"

Belamyr nodded, scrunching his face into stress knots. He had played the part of bait several times, going out into the pedestrian streets of Port Jemison and stopping by various facilities, entering with packages, leaving with nothing, retrieving other packages, walking here and there, always circling back to one location. His errands had had more to do with collecting specialty foods and drink than conveying secrets, but the hope was that he would lure Sil and Walter to the chamber Penn had reserved for them. With one lone chair.

He had a gray room set aside just for them to partake of the summit as observers. And the whole day had gone by without a single sighting of either one of them. At first, he had expected them to challenge him about the gathering and demand information. Then he would graciously invite them without exposing their participation to the others. They would be astonished at his generosity. Suspicious, yes, but the offer would be too good to turn down. Then Sil would hear all those plans he had hinted at years ago, before she was old enough to understand, and they would all become clear to her.

And then, he would offer her a chair—and they would see where she stood. Penn grinned. Walter wouldn't look so appealing then, would he? Yes, he could tag along. Penn wasn't a heartless man. Well… he was. He knew this about himself. But in this case, he could afford to be benevolent. And it might be nice to have Walter around just to watch him suffer, and wither, and die of… inferiority. Who cares what he would die of?

Sil would remember her destiny. She would rise to the challenge and take her rightful place as his heir, his regent. No, being queen of Mars was more than that. Once he had built his empire there, she would rule without challenge. Rule for him. And he would be gracious to her and afford her all the privileges due her position.

Glancing back at Belamyr, he considered how she had loved him once. He despised the man; weak, simpering, shallowly cocky but lacking any grit or backbone. But she might want him. He would keep him around for her, for when she grew tired of Walter.

"You disgust me," he hissed at the weakling in front of him, responding to the urge to degrade someone.

"Look, you don't have to be insulting," Belamyr snapped with more venom than Penn had expected, "I did what you asked, and I can't be expected to do more than that." He walked across the room and leaned against the far wall, his face twisting even more than before. It was remarkable how that pretty face could crumple into such contortions.

Penn considered the next day. She would come and that's when he would reveal his plans for the future—for an undying future. Mars would be founded again, and he would build a better base there. This one here on the Moon was getting too cramped for his taste, and he was tired of the phonies. Finish the current projects, move on. It might take a couple years, but the next base would be far more powerful. Some of the equipment was probably still operational. There may even be some viable embryos in cold storage! He could glean the best features of the purest pools of genetic material and incorporate them into his... *research*.

"I'm tired of Moon gold," he smirked.

Belamyr jerked his head sideways as if to say, leave me alone, and didn't answer.

"Bevan," Penn used his current name, "You should be used to me by now..." And with colorful, descriptive terms, he rebuked him, advising him to wipe the human filth off his face and get back to the hustle he had set him to.

Belamyr hated the abuse, Penn knew, but didn't have the guts to throw it back in his face and walk away. Penn owned him. He was one of those that would never get away. He was more likely to take a bullet in the back and disappear. But, even apart from that, he didn't have it in him to abandon the financial comfort he had working for Penn and go live like an average citizen on Earth. The illusion of wealth here was better than scrounging for mediocre wages there.

He was still good-looking, without any enhancements or surgeries, and she might want him around. So, Penn would keep him, and take reasonable care of him.

Would he let Sil develop her own clones? Maybe. Penn grinned as he imagined the greed in her eyes when she understood what he had to offer, the coveting. He had learned so much and developed so many beautiful techniques.

They might never face death.

Chapter 17—Opportunity

Walter walked along the streets of Aldrin City about a hundred paces behind the fake Daisy, dressed in his space suit with the head gear retracted into the neck pouch. He had turned on his digital filter to disguise his facial features in case someone or something were to catch sight of him and notify Penn. He chose the manner of a businessman with some extra time on his hands who was checking things out, but not particularly on vacation—one he found very easy to adopt.

No one looked at him.

The android entered a coffee shop and bought a newspaper, an item devoid of paper named after an archaic means of dispensing information. It was retrievable in a person's coms or on their screen. Moving to the back of the room, she sat down in a chair that gave her full view of the shop and the street beyond and began 'reading'. She held a small screen and tapped it periodically as though paging through stories. Occasionally she glanced up and looked around. Sometimes, she moved her mouth as though reading under her breath. Sometimes she smiled or grimaced or made any number of faces.

Walter wondered if she knew this gave away that she was practicing humanlike behavior. But then, if Penn was training her, he probably provided her very little to work with. Buying a coffee, he plopped down at a table on one side of the room facing her and watched her out of the corner of his eye. Several minutes went by.

Glancing her direction at the same instant she focused on him, his heart jumped. Those eyes were so familiar to him! He let his gaze slide away and grow unfocused, as if she were insignificant, but his heart was pounding. If she recognized him, she wouldn't let on. He would never even know whether she did or not, unless she wanted him to know.

But then, this wasn't Daisy. There was no reason to think she had even a tiny fraction of Daisy's abilities. Maggie, who was a worthy copy, was evidence of that. And his digital filter may be detectable, but the android wouldn't be able to extrapolate his true features without more data. Walter sighed with relief and sipped his coffee.

Fake Daisy rose to her feet and walked briskly away.

"Maggie," Walter whispered softly, "I have a feeling she is done with whatever she was doing, and this is the time to follow… Can you track her?"

"She is not being detected by the system," Maggie replied in his ear. "I can see her through the cameras, but once she heads outside, she will disappear over the horizon and so far, she has left no satellite data on her two previous excursions into town. I expect the same this time."

"So, I have to follow her if I want to know where she is coming from." Walter gulped his coffee down.

"That may be harder than you think," Maggie warned him. "She can walk at a pace of over a hundred kilometers per hour under normal Earth conditions. She may be a little slower on the Moon, especially if she is erasing her footsteps, but it will be much faster than you can go, bounding along human style." She showed no awareness of having said something humorous and Walter wondered why it struck him that way. Maybe precisely because it was unintentional.

"I'll need to take the hovercraft then," he responded, jumping to his feet, and trotting toward the hangar. "Can you keep an eye on her till I get loaded up and on the move?"

"You may find it difficult to pursue her without being detected," Maggie said.

"Listen," Walter reminded her. "If there's one thing I understand, it's how this model evaluates unfamiliar situations. Her first conjecture if she sees me will be that I am exploring and that is precisely the manner I will adopt if I run into her. I'll take pictures or something. It'll be fine."

"That's very clever," Maggie said brightly, and Walter smiled. Maybe she would begin to think about how he worked with *her* as an AI and draw some connections.

"Can you still see her?" he asked once he was in the vehicle and coasting around the city walls.

"You're headed the right direction," Maggie said, "she is making her way up from the Main Welcome Center. She just came out the airlock. You should be able to see her once you make that next turn."

"Alright," Walter said.

"And Walter," Maggie prompted, "I should go silent while you are following her out there. She may pick up our transmissions since I'm not actually onboard with you."

"Understood," Walter said. "Can you listen?"

"I will hear you if you open a transmission, but she may as well. So… no. You should assume I am not listening."

"I'll open a channel when it doesn't matter anymore whether she hears me," Walter said, "but keep an eye on things as much as you can. Watch from the satellites and any cameras you find."

"Yes," Maggie responded, and the com went dark just as he rounded the corner.

Ahead, Walter caught sight of a little figure zipping away on foot, legs whipping back and forth in a blur. He chuckled and shook his head. *I've never seen you do that, Daisy*, he thought, wishing he could talk to her about it. Lowering the GM clearance to about a third of a meter, he adjusted his speed to match hers, keeping back far enough so that she shouldn't be alarmed by his presence and close enough so he wouldn't lose her as the terrain became increasingly uneven. They traveled for over nine kilometers this way, not in a straight line, more of an "S" shaped path, following the easiest course through the dips and hills.

When he crested the final hill, he was surprised to see her only a couple dozen meters away, and then, even more shockingly, she vanished.

"It sounds like fun, Mama." Scarlet was bouncing on her toes. Her thick dark hair was cut in a bob and had no trace of red anymore. It was very cute on her, especially in the outfit she wore, with jeans and suspenders, and a white and yellow checked shirt.

"Aldrin City is full of shops and museums and places to explore and buy souvenirs," Sil told her as she helped her into her space suit. "And there are probably lots of kids there."

Scarlet laughed and hugged Bunny. "Hear that Patty Cake?" she poked its soft round belly. The stuffed animal didn't have a name other than Bunny, but sometimes she came up with other things to call it.

Soon they were out of their rooms and walking to the hangar. Maggie had backed herself up into a blind brick—a small, but very dense AI receptacle—that they had decided, after a lengthy discussion about the pros and cons, to store in Bunny. It could use the toy's eyes and ears as low-quality receptors and it could broadcast privately to Scarlet either through her skull or the com sticker. So far, both approaches were working.

Sil was looking forward to flying a Moon craft. They hadn't planned to rent them originally because of the expense, but with the land developments and the loan, some extra expenditures seemed reasonable under the right circumstances. Like now. She was smiling as she flipped the switch and the motor hummed, lifting them slowly off the ground. Zipping out of the warehouse felt like speeding down a water chute, curving and swooping along the guardrails to the exit. Then they were propelled out into the airless Moon expanse, surrounded by quiet, huge stretches of white wastelands, and black skies. It was soothing and relaxing. The autopilot could have taken them to their destination at that point without human interaction, but Sil enjoyed driving.

Coasting along, they flew only a few feet off the surface, keeping it low as recommended to reduce fuel consumption. They swept up and over a ridge, veering off the main road onto a flat empty stretch that bypassed a cluster of machinery. Port Jemison disappeared from their rear scope. Sliding down into a stark shadow, their headlights illumined the path before them, rocks, dips, and gullies, and they sped along, curving around and over obstacles.

There was one, though, they couldn't avoid. Sil saw it and tried to swerve around it, when it started to shift and widen. It was rotating sideways to block them, growing longer and longer. Sil yanked to the left, but realizing she couldn't clear it, straightened again and punched in the throttle, shooting over it some seven meters off the ground. The maneuver rocked the little craft as it hurtled over the obstacle in a parabola, rolling it sideways.

"Mommy!" Scarlet cried, gripping the edges of her seat, "You're scaring me!"

Sil was gritting her teeth, wrestling to regain control. The craft's gravity manipulator was a lesser model that directed its field in only one direction. Losing the grip on the surface, it was now pushing sideways in a slow spin, propelling them in a wide curve as they descended. She snapped the GM off and the craft dropped to the ground, skidding a long way till it came to a stop, still laying on its side. Without taking off her belt restraints, Sil began thrusting her weight back and forth and soon succeeded in rolling the vessel upright again.

Behind them, the huge chunk of ground that had blocked their path came to a standstill revealing a gaping hole. A rumbling from that direction came through the ground to their craft, shaking their bodies.

"We're alright, Scarlet," Sil reassured her daughter, unfastening her restraints. "I need to get out to look at the craft and see what kind of damage it caused. Don't worry. Just stay here." Swinging the side door open, she stepped out, closing it behind her.

The rumbling seemed more pronounced when her feet were on the ground, or perhaps, the engine producing it was increasing its output. The massive hatch was clearly a spacedock, large enough for a medium-sized cruiser, and by the looks of it, something was getting ready to take off. Should she be concerned? She checked in with Maggie and was relieved to hear that on the Moon, docks of that size usually relied on catapults to eject their ships. The shaking of the ground was probably as bad as it would get.

Keeping one eye on the dock, she scoped out the damage to the craft. It was scraped up but there wasn't anything noticeably wrong with it. She rushed her scan and climbed back in quickly, anxious to get moving and put some distance between her and the space dock.

Just in case.

The ground was shaking more violently as she switched on the motor again and the little pod lifted off the ground a few inches. "Come on, baby," she muttered, patting the dashboard, and pressing the throttle. It inched forward, crawling away from the hole. Sil coaxed it to move, pressing for more speed… without getting it. It continued to coast at a snail's pace.

When she looked back over her shoulder, she couldn't see anything, and as the craft was no longer touching the surface, couldn't feel any vibrations either. For all she knew, the ship had turned its engines off and nothing would be exiting the hole. Still, a sense of urgency weighed on her. If that dock wasn't a catapult, then it would take off using *propulsion*. She didn't want to guess what that could mean for her and Scarlet. Would running be any faster? Probably not.

She wanted to ask Maggie about it but didn't want Scarlet to overhear so she just clung to the throttle and leaned forward in the direction they were going, *willing* it to move faster.

"It's so big, Mommy." Scarlet said, looking over her shoulders with wide eyes.

Jerking her head around, Sil caught sight of the cruiser already halfway out of the hole, rising slowly—a bad sign. With a gasp, she shoved her daughter down and curled herself into the crash position, crying, "Activate the shield!" to Maggie in hopes that she would help them in some way. Maybe the hovercraft had one. Maybe their suits did. She didn't care about herself, but Scarlet! Surely a child's suit had extra layers of security!

Scarlet screamed into her face mask and struggled against her mother's arm as the first wave hit them. It rolled around them, warming them to the point of marked discomfort, shoving the craft away with each successive wave, like a tide coming in. The ship wasn't even out of the hole yet and they were being accelerated by the exhaust billowing out of the opening— but it wouldn't be enough. Sil knew it wouldn't be enough. The heat on their backs kept increasing and the exhaust waves rolled them farther and farther.

Then it stopped.

For a moment they held still, waiting for the next swell to roll over them. None did. Sil lifted her head to look back and saw the entire ship hovering above the entrance to the dock, poised there, its engines extinguished, and its GM engaged.

Someone had noticed them.

She almost wept in relief, but that only lasted an instant. There was something ominous about the ship, not that it was big or that it was taking off and endangering them, but that it had stopped. It wasn't sinking back down or flying to a distance where it could take off without harming them.

Scarlet straightened slowly, whimpering, and looked back at it. "They stopped," she said, clutching her bunny to her chest.

"Yes," Scarlet agreed. Her mind was racing. "Maggie," she called out sharply, "Notify the authorities that we're in trouble. A founding landowner is in trouble. Don't forget to include that and get them out here as fast as possible."

"Done," Maggie announced. "Should I tell Walter?"

Sil desperately wanted him to come running to their aid, but the thought of losing their only opportunity to find Penn's base was more than she wanted to give up. "Not yet," she said. "But if they look like a threat, then yes."

The ship moved toward them gently, gliding around in front where it dropped to the surface. It must have made a thud, but they couldn't feel it. They were still a few inches off the ground. A door in the side flipped out slowly till it touched the ground and a couple of people in space suits tromped down the ramp. They had flashlights on their helmets and were waving as they approached.

Sil considered turning the craft and coasting away but it was moving so slowly they could easily have kept up with it on foot. And outrunning a large vessel was laughable. So she pulled back on the throttle and let it rest on the ground.

"Are you alright?" they were mouthing at her through their face-shields as they came up. They thumped the outside of the craft and waved through the window. One of them smiled at Scarlet and winked.

"No, Mommy," Scarlet said, "They aren't good," and a feeling of dread filled Sil's heart. She could sense it, too. These men were not there to help.

Shaking her head, she gestured at them to go away and flung her hand out to lock the door as their faces were disfigured by threatening scowls.

June was fast. She had circled behind the camouflaged cover and ducked under it in the few seconds it had taken the man to come over the hill behind her. Now she watched him through the stiffened fabric. It allowed just enough light through for her to observe him but not enough for him to see her.

This was a new face for her archives. She had intended to record him as he drove by, but he had coasted to a stop a mere three meters from her hiding place. Then he let the craft sink to the ground and got out. He was wandering around as if he were looking for her.

This was unexpected.

At a distance, she hadn't been able to see through his digital filter, but now, supplementing with sonar, she could see his true features clearly. She identified him easily as Walter Cuevas and scanned the records of his current trip to the Moon. This one query blossomed into a wealth of knowledge unlike any she had experienced. His name led to Frandelle and Scarlet. And the Frandelle Tract, its mines, the broken overseer. Footage of these led to Guam transports and precious metal futures and communications with Earth, Guam… and Mars. There were so many threads spreading out from this one face that she was unable to even come up with an analytical approach to study it all. She would have to design one. It was like seeing thousands of cords, tumbled, and twisted into writhing knots leading away into darkness. Like the interior of a damaged robot.

The man walked around the randomly shaped cover and came directly up to it, placing his hands on it. She moved to face him and caught the look of triumph in his eyes as he realized the surface wasn't dirt. He had found one of the entries.

If she had known what to call her confusion in human terms, she would have used the word fear. But no one had taught her how to associate human emotions to AI experiences. All she knew was that this face had exposed her to a precarious vulnerability. One she didn't know how to handle. And while her physical platform was hidden, her internal network was exposed.

Searching within herself for a shelter, she came up with some of the first words she had recorded.

"I hate you," she said to him softly.

He sidestepped around the cover, feeling all over it, looking for a way in, smiling.

"But you," she whispered, moving sideways behind the fabric, keeping pace with him, "You must love me."

It wasn't clear what that meant but the words had proved to be a powerful obstacle to her in her search for Otto Man's identity and she assumed they would protect her as well.

She was confident that this man was a threat.

It occurred to her suddenly that he might figure out the trap door's secret faster than she had the first time. She should not be waiting here when he did. With a little hop backwards, she whipped around and descended the ladder down to the northwest airlock. It was smaller than the first one she had found and there was no secondary chute for vehicles at that end of the base. When she got to the bottom, she entered the airlock, engaged the outer seal, activated the air flow, and reentered the base.

As always, the phonies were waiting for her and began pestering her with questions. She had been making no effort to hide her trips. After the first one, she had found them waiting for her on her return and realized all her attempts at secrecy were pointless. They weren't stupid.

"Back away from the door," she instructed. "Our security is threatened and could be breached."

They didn't even know what she meant by that and all it did was make them more anxious to look out. She had to shove them back beyond the laundry area and lock them out at its entrance. It was just until the danger had passed.

Marching around the throng, she entered the main AI hub where, ironically, no AI had ever been set up. Only an assortment of sophisticated programs managed the many tasks of the base. Laying a hand on a screen, she was immediately linked into all the feeds.

The man was gone.

The two men spaced themselves out, one on either side of the craft and at roughly the same time opened the doors. Scarlet was shrieking as one pulled her out, thrashing and trying to get away, beating him with her bunny, but he contained her easily.

The other man grabbed the arm of Sil's suit and as he yanked, she grabbed hold of the throttle with her free hand and resisted. He tugged harder and the joystick gave way, breaking off in her hands. He dragged her writhing from the craft. She flung herself sideways, breaking his grasp and grabbed the lip of the craft door.

Grappling for her arm again, he was unprepared when she contracted, pulled in both of her legs toward her chin, and kicked out with as much strength as she could muster. As she lifted herself to kick again, the lightweight craft skidded toward her, knocking the guy completely off balance. She banged him in the helmet with the joystick and propelled the hovercraft at him like a massive club before he could even register what was happening. Falling onto his back, he lay stunned as she jumped to her feet, still holding onto her two weapons.

There was no atmosphere on the Moon to create drag and everything weighed a fraction of what it did on Earth. Heaving a little vehicle was possible. It was handy. She shoved it at him again, catching him between the door and the craft, but he began waving one of his arms at her, pressing the other against his chest, eyes widened in alarm. She hesitated. If his suit were damaged, she didn't want to…

Abandoning him, she ran over to the man carrying Scarlet away and jumped on his back. She started beating him on the head with the joystick, feeling the metal *thhrinnnggg* in her hand with each blow. He dropped Scarlet, who dashed away, and turned on Sil, laying into her with a great deal more power than the other man had. Punching her chest with an open, gloved hand, he impelled her back twelve meters where she slammed against the craft and slid to the ground, winded. Turning back, he caught up to Scarlet in three strides and snatched her up in a grip so tight she couldn't even flap her feet around. Her screams, still coming through clearly in Sil's com, enraged her mother.

Getting back on her feet, first one then the other, she gave the craft another shove at the guy who was just sitting up and not bothering to come at her again. It knocked him over and he lay still. Then, methodically, she came after the big guy with her daughter, one step at a time. He wasn't running and she didn't want to waste any of her strength. Without missing a stride, she bent over to sweep up the broken joystick. Carrying it like a weapon, she drew closer to the man from behind as he neared the ship.

She didn't think about the ship. She didn't think about Maggie or Walter. All she knew in the world was that the fiend in front of her had her little girl, and he was going to regret it.

⸎

"What's happening now?" Walter growled, his jaw clenched so firmly it threatened the integrity of his teeth. He was gripping the throttle of his hovercraft with blanched knuckles and all the muscles in his legs were taut. If he could have flown free of the craft, he would have hurled himself a hundred meters into the air without fearing the landing.

"It is hard to tell exactly what is happening, but there is definitely a scuffle taking place," Maggie said, "Two persons approached their hovercraft and opened the doors. And one of them, as I was saying, took Scarlet. The other reached for Sil but appears to have missed and dragged the craft instead. That person fell over… the craft is moving again. Sil is on her feet but the figure who opened her door isn't following. I wonder why…"

"I know why," he grated, shoving the throttle harder but not gaining any more speed than he already had.

"Well, remember there is a nine-second delay in the data I am receiving," she said. "It goes through a central relay before returning to the Port connection. And a lot can happen in nine seconds."

"Then stop talking about it and tell me!" he yelled.

"Sil has jumped on the figure carrying Scarlet," she reported, "The person dropped her. Sil must have done something to him…"

"Must have…" Walter grimaced.

"The person shot her backwards and she rammed into the craft. That was rather impressive."

Walter bellowed wordlessly.

"Oh," Maggie said, "I wonder…"

"What?! WHAT?!" Walter hollered, beating the dashboard of the hovercraft with his free hand.

The Denser Plane

"The feed has been terminated," she replied calmly. "It has been upgraded to high security and all requests for access must be reviewed by local authorities."

Walter had no words or even sounds as the shock ran through him. He could hardly think about what that could mean.

"This is standard procedure," Maggie reassured him, "and it will be no trouble for us once it has gone through the proper channels. As a founder, you will be granted access straightaway when working hours resume in the morning."

There was no answer. The morning would be too late. It may already be too late. He just wasn't sure what that might even mean.

"Almost there!" Maggie's cheerful tone hit his heart like the mockery of an enemy; like the laughter of a shallow friend who didn't bother to read the death notice; like the slam of a door to an empty house. It was a death knell. A portent of despair. A cartoon about war.

Whizzing down the long slope into the shadow where Sil's craft lay, battered and tossed, he saw three lumpy, unnatural shapes strewn about. There was no hole in the ground, no castoff flashlights, no movement.

He was numb as he turned off the motor and the little craft settled onto its kickstand.

He was cold as he opened the door and climbed out.

He was dismayed as he dropped next to the closest figure and rolled it over. A man's face, bluing at the lips, but still fogging the face guard. Walter got up and staggered around the craft toward the next figure, some fifty meters away, gasping for air because of the pressure in his chest.

This one was bigger. He lay on his back… helmet cracked, suit torn. There could be no life left there.

Turning to face the third figure, another thirty meters away, Walter stumbled forward, shoving each foot, one at a time, his vision waning and waxing as alarms went off in his suit. Maggie was talking, *slow down*, something like that. *Deeper.* He heard a sound like moaning, a heavy, desperate staccato sound, punctuated by gasps for air.

There she was.

And falling to his knees, Walter turned over the woman he loved, gathered her in his arms and wailed.

The girl was still screaming, and most of the crew were out of control, yelling at each other as well as at her. They were livid at the loss of two of their number. They had almost lost two more and *four* of their suits were trashed. Raging over the orders Bland had given, they were now battling it out among themselves over *how* the boss had made them carry it out.

How hard was it to capture one little girl? Bland wondered as he came down the passageway toward the baggage compartment. He was concerned by the fighting he heard, but these were rough characters, and it wasn't surprising. Getting the girl somewhere safe was the main thing, away from them. He hoped she would stop screaming soon. It would be unfortunate if he had to sedate her.

He hadn't *wanted* to kidnap the girl. Taking charge in a bluster of bravado had been the only way he could manage an explosive situation. He gave the order literally *seconds* before the captain could open her mouth.

When Bland entered the room, silence fell. He was used to this. He may have been a man of average height and build, a drab, emotionless functionary, but he represented the Proto. And everyone knew the Proto could not be crossed. Ever. They had heard of the captain of the Onering. They had heard about the Colombian Summit. They had seen what happened to Kentra.

The girl's screams died out as she turned to stare at him, perhaps recognizing him. She was crumpled on the floor, pressed against a stack of supplies, with something crushed against her breast in a tight embrace. She watched him out of great, round, blood-shot eyes rimmed in red over a tear-streaked face. As he stepped toward her, she shook her head violently and fumbled at her neck. She was trying to engage her head gear, he realized.

"Sorry," Bland muttered, jumping toward her, and pulling her hand away. "Can't let you do that. Last thing we need is you passing out from a lack of air and us having to pry open that expensive suit of yours. *He* wouldn't like it."

The men backed away grumbling as if that had been directed at them. "We don't work for you," one murmured. "Don't work for the Proto neither."

Another was thumping the palm of his hand with a fist, over and over, saying, "Payback. Payback." He looked pretty upset. But then, two of their members were dead. They had a right to be upset. However, the compensation would far greater than usual—if they didn't lose all sense of reason.

The Denser Plane

They weren't part of Penn's empire. Bland had hired them to make a small delivery of contraband, untaxed specialty foods from Earth. This was a way to pacify Kentra, the face of their operation, who had been livid when he snatched Scarlet out of her hands in Guam. The 'unfortunate accident' that hit her soon afterward was Penn's standard retribution for failure, but as far as he knew, the smugglers wouldn't connect Bland to that.

The little girl wailed again, but only once more. She seemed to have tired herself out.

"Come along then," Bland said, reaching a hand to her. "I'm sorry we don't have much of a place for you at the moment. Your visit is unexpected. But your stay with us won't be for long."

"Remember Kentra," someone muttered angrily, filling Bland with alarm. They might not blame him for Kentra's death, but the girl could easily become the object of their rage.

Bland had boarded the ship to deliver payment. Then the captain, wanting more money, began using abusive negotiating tactics to get it. Like threatening to take off before he could disembark.

The little girl studied his hand and gazed at him as though she could see right through him, and he found himself wondering if she could detect any of what went on under his exterior façade. Scarlet had been a subject of great interest to his superior for a long time and he was aware that she had some unusual skills. Could she see *what he was not*? Penn had spoken of those words.

"He's got no business giving orders," one snarled.

"I don't remember the captain putting him in charge," another chomped.

The Proto's reputation needed to hold a little longer, the barometer in the room was not looking good. On his own, he had a number of methods of gaining the upper hand in tricky situations. None of them involved protecting a child.

Scarlet dropped her head into her hands, fitted into gloves too big for them, and wept softly. He took one of the hands, but she wouldn't stand up, so he was forced to lift her into his arms and carry her. Behind him, he heard the men grousing. The ugliness increasing.

"Maybe we oughta let the Proto know how we feel about losing some of our people." The voice carried down the hall after him.

Bland's steps quickened.

"Come on," someone barked and with a roar, the whole horde leapt to their feet and made chase.

Bland began to run.

"Mommy!" Scarlet whimpered in his ear.

He held her closer to his heart and ran faster, struggling with the nearly vertical ladders and jumping over the door seals. He managed to close and lock one of them after jumping through it, but they would soon make their way around.

"Is she okay?" the girl asked, her voice quivering.

Bland had seen them fighting with her mother at the very door of the ship as it lifted off the ground. She had jumped, caught the edge of the door as it was being raised, and climbed inside. Greatly outnumbered, she had struggled desperately, but they had beaten her and thrown her out the door before it closed. Bland had to fight with the pilot to keep her from engaging the engine right there, forcing her to hover away first.

The crew members were communicating with each other all over the ship, not even bothering to keep their plans from him. They didn't answer to the Proto, and the girl was their booty. Bland could find his way home. There was a convenient airlock to help with that.

"He's midship, on the third level," the pilot's voice crackled over the loudspeaker.

He wasn't afraid of dying. Bland had known for a long time that he was living on borrowed time. The miracle was that he had lasted so long and accomplished so much.

He climbed to the top level, sealing the hatch at the top of the stairs— they wouldn't expect that. They would think he wanted his gear and weapons from the bridge, but they didn't know there was a suit in the panel next to one of the escape pods. He had sent someone to hide it there when the ship was docked. He just hoped the girl's suit was still functional and had enough air to get back to the surface.

Because he had no intention of leaving her in their hands.

Two more doors to seal and they would have a chance. Tripping, he landed on one knee, but managed to get back to his feet without dropping her. She wrapped her arms around his neck and hung on. Reaching the first bulkhead, he shoved the door shut with a foot, spinning the wheel and sealing it. He then braced it with a bar. At the other end of the chamber, he shoved the other door closed, activated the seal, and barred it.

The hatch was the only way in, and he thought he could hold them at bay long enough.

"You're helping me, aren't you?" Scarlet said softly.

The Denser Plane

He was at the panel now, pulling the suit out of hiding, and stuffing it into the pod—all with one hand because he was afraid to set Scarlet down. Some of the crew members were banging at the doors. The hatch was creaking and shuddering.

He yanked at the pod door but couldn't get it open. "Listen," he said to Scarlet, placing her on the floor. "I have to set you down for just a moment to open this." She nodded and kept her eyes on his face the whole time. She never looked over at the crewmembers raving outside the bulkheads or the hatch vibrating as its lock was breaking.

He pulled three times before the pod control panel opened and he could start punching instructions. The pilot was trying to keep him from gaining access, but he had codes she knew nothing about. The noise of people yelling at him over the speakers didn't matter. The pounding at the doors didn't matter. The squeak of the hatch didn't matter. Only this one thing. Set up the launch and get away.

Or if need be, send her and face them alone.

Chapter 18—Conflict

An unscheduled communiqué came through on an unencrypted channel. Highly unusual and risky. Bernadette rose to her feet as an indicator flashed on her left contact lens. "Play," she instructed.

When the message played in Bland's own voice, giving several coded phrases, she sat down in alarm to think. The girl had been captured by the smugglers Penn worked with. Bland had cooperated and was trying to escape with her.

"You're blown for sure," she said, revisiting the amazement she had so often felt over how long he retained his position as Penn's righthand man. "Ah! Kai… my best agent. Ever."

"Open a channel to the captain," she instructed her AI companion in the dark jade stone hanging around her neck. "Give him the data for that ship."

"Captain," she continued. "Set an intercept course for that smuggler ship and notify the crew that we may be going into battle. Ready the guards. We will be boarding and taking command, with great caution. My little niece is on board, and she must not be harmed. Restrict your operations accordingly. I trust you know what to do."

Eder Bland, or Kai Benjamin as he was actually called, was not receiving replies. "Just do this one thing," she whispered to the air. "Protect the girl and survive this, and you'll be rewarded beyond what you can imagine. You've more than earned it."

Coming from her own Gen Project tribe, Kai had sought out this mission not for himself, but for his family, and once he had accomplished the initial assignment, had chosen to remain undercover, working for Penn, for the sake of their shared goals. And for *her* sake. For years.

She owed him more than she owed any other person in her circle of influence or command.

"Jewel," she whispered to her AI, "Make sure we are doing everything we can to help him and rescue him. We can't leave him to Penn's mercy." She shuddered.

"Contact the Moon and gather what information you can," she began pacing her room. "I want to know where Sil is and what happened. And Walter."

She clenched her fists under her chin and furrowed her brow. It had been a while since she had felt this uncertain of herself. But this was the time. She was sure of it.

Penn would expose his hand and she would be forced to reveal hers. The stakes were higher than any she had ever risked—all in, and she could only hope… hope this would be over and she could retire, and never have to worry about him again.

Bland shoved some packs into the pod after the suit and whipped around to Scarlet. She was staring at him, still clutching the stuffed animal, looking very cold. He was sweating, radiating heat.

"Ben?" she said in a thin, wavering voice.

He stared at her, wondering for a moment what she had called him and why. "Oh, yes," he said when the memory returned.

"Do you have something to calm me down?" she asked. "Maggie says she is *concerned*."

"Who's Maggie?" he asked. She was rambling now. Maybe going into shock.

A loud metallic clang came from the hatch in the floor, screeching as the men below pushed against it. Yanking a crowbar out of a tool cabinet, Bland tried to wedge it over the door to keep them from getting in, but it wasn't long enough.

"She's my aunt's copy, in Bunny," was the bizarre answer. Definitely, not all there.

Searching around frantically, he landed on a bench and decided it could be ripped out of the floor. Wrenching with all his strength did nothing, but when he shook it in desperation, the flat seat of the bench clicked sideways and came free. "Ha!" he cried, swinging it around, narrowly missing the little girl who hardly moved though she saw it coming. He shoved it under the handrail around the hatch, wedging it at an angle.

"Your aunt, huh?" he gasped, beads of sweat collecting on his forehead. There was something familiar about that.

"Do you have anything?" she asked. "I'm really, really scared…" Her voice got quieter with each word, and it moved his heart.

Standing upright, he stared for a second at the barricade, and decided it would hold for now. He turned back to look at her. "Yeah," he said, "um… let me think." Her hair was a tumbled mess, and her face was streaked with dirt and tears. Her suit was filthy with Moon dust and her eyes were hollow, mournful windows into misery.

Kneeling beside her, he took one of her hands in his and searched his pockets with the other. "Scarlet," he whispered gently, "I'm sorry this has happened to you. It wasn't my intent at all. Believe me."

The banging on the hatch broke the seal and it smacked up against the bench seat. The vicious cries doubled in volume and several hands shoved the hatch door against the obstacle in rhythmic wallops.

"I only have one thing and it would put you to sleep," he struggled to focus on her as the crashing reverberated around them. "If you want that, I will give it to you." It was probably a good idea.

The bench seat shifted with a clang and someone's hand shoved through the narrow opening. Bland glanced over his shoulder, kicked at the hand, snapping it back, and forced the seat back into place under the rail.

The little girl dipped her head to him solemnly, and he tipped his head to her. Placing the hypodermic to her arm, he landed another kick behind him, just to keep them from trying to get an arm in while he was busy, and emptied the plunger. A tiny whoosh.

She watched him as he reached back and slammed the hatch door down a few times without taking his eyes off her. "Ready?" he asked, once he was sure she wasn't going to have a bad reaction and need countermeasures.

She nodded, her eyes drooping.

Finding that Sil's life signs were stable didn't relieve Walter's anguish. The P.A. first responder units arrived soon after he had and found both Sil and the first attacker to be alive. Loading them into ambulances, they raced them back to the settlement, with Walter sitting next to Sil, holding her hand in one of his, his head hanging down, resting on the other hand. He was listening as Maggie relayed audio reports.

The alarm was already broadcasting all over the Moon. All ships were grounded. All travel shut down. All units were searching for the missing child.

Walter knew that none of them would find her.

"Walter," Sil croaked through dry lips when she first regained consciousness. "I lost her…"

He was shaking his head, but his words wouldn't come right away.

"We were… coming after you." She swallowed and blinked, her eyes struggling to focus. "Aldrin City… but almost crashed… a ship…" Pausing to rest, she closed her eyes again.

"I know," he answered. The words could hardly get past the lump in his throat. And he was still battling for each breath. "Maggie told me."

"It almost burned us…" she tried again. He knew that medical staff would probably have told her to not talk, just rest, and communicate later, but he needed to hear what she had to say, to hear what had happened after the satellites blocked the feed. "I got the craft going… too slow… too hot… then stopped."

It was silent for a few moments as they sped into the hospital hangar and into a cramped airlock barely large enough for the craft. The stretcher extracted itself and two AI triage nurses took charge of it, escorting it into Receiving. He stepped down and followed, bending over Sil to listen.

"…two men," she was saying, "…pulled us out… I took down one… then the other…"

A crushing weight pressed on Walter. He should have been there. He could have defended them. But he had run off.

"We didn't know…" she was watching him through eyelids barely cracked open. "It was the right decision… Oh!" She moaned and it pierced his heart. "I think I killed him…" she groaned more deeply. Their anguish played in stereo.

"He's not dead," Walter reassured her, assuming she was talking about the man that had just been transported to the hospital with them. She opened her eyes wider, gazing at him intensely to see if he was being straight with her, then sighed and closed her eyes again. He didn't tell her about the other one. That could wait. "But he would have killed you."

"No," she said softly. "Penn would never tolerate that."

She seemed to doze off, hardly moving as the triage nurses slid her over to a cot and started hooking her up to monitors.

"Nurse," Walter tapped the unit closest to him. "It's vital that I hear what she knows. Do something." The unit promptly whipped out a stimulator disc and slapped it expertly onto Sil's neck. Within seconds she was pulling her eyelids opening, eyes rolling till she got them to obey and line up. She was far more alert as she went on.

"I lost control. He wouldn't let go of Scarlet no matter what I did..." she said.

Walter stroked her head and whispered, "No, it's okay..."

"We don't *know* Scarlet would be safe in his hands," her voice rose a bit, her eyes widening. "We don't know Penn wouldn't harm her. We just *hope* he wouldn't. And at that moment, I couldn't take the chance... I couldn't take the chance!"

"I wouldn't have either," Walter said, realizing for the first time that his jaw ached from clenching his teeth for so long.

"He was mad," she was saying as the nurse sat her up and began taking vitals. "I really thought he was going to kill me. At first, I just kept hitting him and he kept knocking me off, shoving me away, throwing me down. And every time, I thought I wouldn't be able to get up again, but then I could hear her..." She couldn't bring herself to say Scarlet's name. "I could hear her... and I got up again."

"Yes," Walter whispered. He was living it as she spoke. Getting knocked down. Rising again and again to stagger after the guy. He felt it so vividly that his whole body throbbed.

"One of those times, I must have cracked his face shield because he threw Scarlet down and turned on me." She was speaking calmly and evenly now. "He knocked me over and jumped on top of me and grabbed my head..." She pantomimed the motion with her hands in the air. "...and he was slamming me against the ground. Wham! Wham!" She thrust her clutched hands down onto her knees several times.

"Remain still," the attending unit warned, "The extent of your injuries is unknown, and you may be harming yourself under the influence of the stimulant I gave you."

She cooperated but Walter could tell that she hadn't heard and was unaware of responding. "...and at first, I tried to break his hold... you know, like we trained back in the day... but that didn't work."

Sil closed her eyes and fell back prostrate on the gurney as if reliving that moment again. "I couldn't just keep thrashing. I had to think... and everything was slowing down... slowing down... and I was trying to think of something..."

The Denser Plane

The nurse propped her up, gave her a drink of water, and plumping a pillow, stuffed it under her head and shoulders. "A scan will be performed soon," it informed them. "Your suit's analgesics are managing your pain levels, but they could also be masking symptoms. Please remember that you are injured and do not make any sudden movements."

Walter thanked it and Sil continued without opening her eyes. "The first few blows weren't so bad. Probably the suit kicking in and buffering my head. But then one of them… it was like a hammer blow, so sharp and sudden… and I was so shocked, and he must have been compressing my air flow because I was starting to black out." She paused.

Walter waited.

"Then I heard her voice."

"What did she say?"

"She called for me…" Tears began to trickle down her cheeks.

Walter shook his head again.

A sound Bland recognized but couldn't place cracked so loudly he thought an eardrum had burst, and a strange weakness came over him. Struggling to turn, he found his leg wouldn't obey his intentions and the whole room began to spin. He hurled himself over the non-functioning leg in a rolling motion and slammed both hands down on the bench which had again come loose. He whacked the hands reaching around the hatch door. But it was hard to see clearly. He wasn't sure he was hitting the arms at all. Something like an 'L' shaped piece of metal went flying. He gripped the bench seat tenaciously, but it was rammed away, cutting his hands. Someone was yanking it away, several arms, all the way through the hatch door.

Numbly, he leaned over and swiped at the door and missed. The hatch flew open and one of the crew members jumped up, pushing off one of the rungs, launching himself at Bland with fist extended, striking him with a knock-out punch. He collapsed backwards next to the girl, his head thudding onto the little bunny.

She wasn't moving.

"And I reached up with my legs and grabbed him around the neck. Locked 'em. Just like that…" She held up her hands and interlocked two fingers to demonstrate. "Hooked my feet together and kicked down. He just flew backwards." She swept her hand away in a gentle, soaring motion, then clenched her fist and slammed it down on the cot. "And he landed harder than I thought he would. And before he could get back up... not sure why he didn't get up right away... Before he could come at me again, I rolled over and crawled to my weapon... I mean the joystick. The throttle broke... I... uh..."

She paused again and took several deep breaths. A sharp pain in her chest had woken up.

"I got to my feet," she uttered between little gasps for air, "...and went to him and struck his helmet again. That's when I think I might have killed him. If the visor broke."

Walter shook his head, no, remembering the tear in the man's suit. That had probably happened first and would explain why he was slowing down.

"And then I looked around and saw two more men coming for her."

"And that's when you collapsed?" Walter asked.

"No."

⁎

Bland opened bleary eyes to see the ceiling swirling overhead in nauseating pulses. Groaning he struggled to find his hands and make them cooperate. Fumbling at his sides, he found the spaces empty. With difficulty, he pushed himself to a sitting position and noticed the puddle of blood under his useless leg. He stared at it in astonishment, trying to figure out what had happened. Then he saw the gun at the far edge of the room.

He looked for the girl all around, repeatedly, before he even realized what he was doing. In the distance, voices mentioned his name. "Still alive," they were saying, "or not, either way, throw him out the airlock."

The bunny lay there, paws stained with his blood, and he snatched it up and shoved it into a pocket, not wanting her to see that. He had enough presence of mind to understand that his best chance at helping the little girl now would be to escape and survive. Hefting the hatch door, he closed it again but didn't have the strength to position the bench seat over it. It would hardly slow them down.

A gun in space was insanity itself. Never should have been allowed. But if he had to, he would use it. He pulled himself around, grunting against the pain and dizziness. Could he even reach the gun before they returned? It was so far away.

223

The Denser Plane

The pod was closer. He repositioned himself and leaned toward it, searching for something to grab onto, to pull himself with, and found nothing. He couldn't reach the lip of the pod door. Placing both hands on the floor, he tried to grip it flat-handed, but friction betrayed him, and they slipped. Laying down on his stomach, he spread his arms on the floor, more skin on the smooth surface, and tried tugging, an inch at a time. Groans would have come out of his throat, but he bit his lips and would not let them. Any sounds would bring them sooner.

And the voices were growing louder. They were arguing about who should deal with him and who should clean up the mess of blood. And who the idiot with the gun was. No one would claim it.

Slugs pull themselves into round lumps, then stretch out into long skinny rolls of tissue, oozing slime to coat their paths, moving slowly, painstakingly across minute spans. This must be what it was like, Bland considered as he found the way to advance, scrunching and straightening, smeared in a sticky red slime of his own. Fixing his purpose determinedly on the escape pod's rim, laying on the side that was still functioning, he brought the good leg to his chest, then straightened, dragging the other leg, and gained a good fourteen centimeters.

Bullet to the thigh, he was thinking, *embedded in the left hip somewhere*. The evidence pointed to that conclusion. Curling, he brought the right knee to his chest, placed his left hand on the floor and lifted, reaching out with the right arm along the floor over his head. *Drag the left leg. Smear a little more blood.*

Three more moves and he was close enough to grip the edge and pull himself through. Unable to stifle a yelp when his pelvis hit the doorjamb, he yanked himself over in an agony of pain that nearly robbed him of consciousness. But he clung to awareness and pressed into the pain, making it work for him. *Stay awake*, he demanded.

He could hear them quarrelling over how much they could get for the girl and how to make the deal and get away without losing any more of their number. They were directly under the hatch now and every word came up clearly.

A brawl delayed them.

Bland rotated himself around and pulled himself up almost into a sitting position so he could reach the lever and heaving with all the strength he had left, a guttural yell bursting from his lips, he pulled it into place, engaging the lock-and-seal mechanism. The door swung shut as the combatants from below scrambled up the ladder yelling. They just missed getting their fingers through the door before it closed.

As the automatic escape sequence kicked in, the pod was ejected, and Bland slumped to the floor, passing out.

—✦—

Sil was quiet for several minutes, then opening her eyes again, she continued. "They thought I wasn't a threat…" A slow breath. "Turned their backs on me."

A smile might have been appropriate, but Walter's face was unwilling to reshape into any expression other than the one he wore.

"She wasn't running… she just sat down and let them come," Sil said. "They were just walking to her. You know, they couldn't hear me. No sound out there. So, I was right behind one when the other turned to look over his shoulder."

She huffed and her mouth split into a faint grin with the edges turned down. "You should've seen the look in his eyes when he saw me. Right there. I swung the weapon at the first one and hit the seal at his neck. He whirled and swung at me. I jumped back and he missed. Clumsy."

She paused and swallowed.

"The second one knocked me onto my back but didn't attack. He just kept shoving me away. The first one grabbed… her… and ran to the ship. I chased after them. The guy wanted to run but he kept turning back to push me over. Every time he did, I hit him with the throttle."

The scanning bot wheeled in and began efficiently setting up, flattening the gurney, taking her pillow away, positioning her head and limbs carefully. She kept telling the story as it worked.

"Then he just ran for the ramp, and I ran after him."

"And that's when you collapsed," Walter added.

"No."

With little flickers, the scanner clicked lightly, moving down from head to toes.

"I ran in after him," she said when it was finished. "And then a bunch of them threw me out the door before it closed."

"And then?" Walter asked.

"Yeah," she looked up at the bot, watching for the results. "That's when I passed out."

"Walter," Maggie's voice came in on his com.

Turning and stepping a few feet away from Sil, he said, "Don't include Sil in this."

"Walter, don't worry about me. Just take care of it," Sil murmured behind him.

"The nurse has instructed me about that," Maggie said. "A ship that just left orbit has been identified as the one that took Scarlet."

"Go on," he hissed with a nod toward Sil to acknowledge what she had said.

"Before accelerating, they jettisoned an escape pod which is on descent now and will be intercepted upon landing."

An escape pod could mean so many things. Equipment malfunction, crew member quitting and getting away before Moon forces could catch up with the ship, communiques intended for Penn.

Or a package.

He dared not turn back around right away. If she saw hope in his eyes and there was no reason for it, was it fair to set her up like that? But if there *was* hope and he didn't tell her, that wouldn't be good either.

He turned around. She was watching him and read it. "What?" she asked.

"A pod escaped the ship before it left orbit," he said evenly.

"You've got to get there before *he* does!" she said, her face hardening with resolve.

He agreed but hesitated.

"The scans aren't bad," she said. "Nothing serious."

The nurse didn't contradict the words, but Walter still hesitated.

"I'm right behind you," she lowered her voice. "As soon as I get this stuff squared away."

With one step he was back at her side. One kiss. Full of meaning. Purpose. Warning. Reassurance. Confidence. All he couldn't say aloud was in it.

"Take care of her," he pointed at the AI nurse. "Don't let her out of here until it's safe."

"Understood, Founder," it replied.

He ran for the exit.

The crew were at each other's throats. The captain didn't ordinarily find them hard to control but she generally relied on outthinking them and better weapons, and the current circumstances were not something she had ever planned for.

Grabbing her heftiest plasma rifle, she put on her blast vest and helmet, lowering the black visor, and thumped down the hallway to the bridge to secure that first. *Make sure the pilot has a valid flight plan, and seal them in.* Then deal with the mutineers if that's what they were. She wasn't sure yet if they were rebelling against the client or their captain.

The bridge was quiet, the pilot and tech were obeying her commands. Active subterfuge tactics were already in place: sweep and dodge, far out of normal shipping lanes, burn in short bursts, reducing exhaust, exterior lights off, radar off, no transmissions. The longer they went without being detected, the less chance that they would be.

The entire breadth of Earth's oceans, not just the surface, but the depths as well, was a mere puddle compared to the vast sector of space between the Moon, Guam, and the home planet. Searching these expanses without something to latch onto was impossible. It was the easiest thing in the Solar System to just vanish into the darkness.

The hard thing would be coming up to make contact, giving them a chance to home in on their location. But it could be done. They could ride out this gig and come out with a haul to end all smuggling. They just had to be reminded of what the job was and who was in control.

"Coming down!" she yelled as she descended to the lower level, rifle charged and waiting for a tap of her finger. "Get to the mess now. Don't make me look for you."

They were already there. The worst of the scrap was over, and Jay seemed to have gained the upper hand. "Captain," he said as she entered. He was leaning against a table with a crowbar over his shoulder. He bowed his head slightly, with the barest hint of respect—for the weapon, not for her.

A man at her left made a move toward her. She whipped and tapped the trigger, flashing a bolt of plasma over his head. It slammed against the metal wall, sizzled, and flickered out leaving a black smudge. "Three dead!" he yelled backing away again.

"Three?" she challenged, without lowering the gun.

"Jay killed Mel," he grumbled.

"Had to," Jay shrugged, giving no other explanation.

The captain blasted him in the chest. Several yelled and raised their hands in protest.

"That's the last one," she warned. "We're not losing another one of you flaming lumps of space lard."

They stared at her.

"Unless anyone else has something to say," she added, lowering the weapon just enough to show her black visor. No one replied or even looked at her. Whatever they were thinking, this was a reset. Now, they would take orders again. "Clean up," she said, "and don't throw the bodies away. Never waste organics."

Letting the gun hang across her chest, she was about to walk away, but hesitated and turned back. "What about the girl?" she asked.

"Bland dosed her," one of them answered. "She's in Creed's quarters. He isn't going to be needing them anymore."

"Who's keeping an eye on her? We can't have our boodle wasting away before the sale."

Two of them promised to take care of it.

"Heading to the Cove," she tossed out casually as she left. They knew what that meant.

In hiding until further notice.

Chapter 19—Solo

Lorarye became L-rac, a full-fledged Sentient, assigned to the Seventh Hour. He and his colleagues were inducted into their new status and rank in a solemn ceremony in the Net Salon, standing in formation under the resplendent web. Ripples of golden light rolled over their heads, reflecting upon them from the living weave above. All around them, agents and other beings of the Realm circled them, filling and overflowing the chamber, and when the A-zar finished his speech and welcomed them, the cry of "Deepen!" was a thunderous clap that made the walls shake.

Lor's heart was overflowing with pride as he saluted them in return, fist pressed to the center of his chest over its newly etched plate. He would not disappoint them. He would be worthy of their trust. Wherever he was sent, he would go, and whatever he was tasked, he would accomplish. One day, he would be training recruits, and he would be mapping strategies and writing assignments. One day… No, he couldn't imagine becoming one of the G-dans. What would it take to grow deep enough for that?

The hush that fell after that salute was eloquent with the sense of purpose that bound them together. All around, thousands of agents from every Hour had come to witness their advancement.

Lor caught sight of Drevir, beaming with joy, and found a knot of emotion rising in his throat. Behind the captains and battalion leaders he saw row upon row of Paladins, glimmering in their chameleon armor, lining the walls like a fortress, the embodiment of the 'Deepen' cry.

The throng parted leaving a pathway to the outer door and the new agents marched through it. Just outside, the A-zar waited to congratulate them, saluting and nodding to each one. The line slowed and as he moved forward, step by step, Lor was surprised by a familiar sensation. A distortion like the one around the portal, not dragging him down, but shimmering at the exit in a roughly circular form, flickering in and around a number of other similar rings, overlapping miniature portals each with a distinct, pale color. It was lovely and haunting… and disturbing.

What is that? He leaned to peer around the agents in front of him, unable to restrain his curiosity. He could barely see it. Eight, nine… ten? No, nine frail, wavering, glimmering rings, rippling in and out of each other's lines. One of them felt just like his own in the Seventh Hour and its color—he had never noticed it had its own tint until this moment—was unmistakable. *The Hours!* he thought. Each one with its own hue and magnitude and resonance. All nine of them, or at least, flickers of them, hovered over each other, centering around the A-zar.

The Commander.

When Lor stepped up to greet him, he found himself staring at the boots on his feet, afraid to look up, and he expected the A-zar would salute him and let him move on. But he did not. He waited. The silence stretched and with great difficulty, his face flushing with embarrassment, Lor raised his gaze to look at the etched band across the Commander's chest. It was captivating. He had heard strange things about those markings, what they meant, what they covered. He could *feel* the deep tugging at him, revealing his own lack of depth, his immaturity, his lack of experience. He could feel the power of the gravity that pulled on him from wherever the A-zar's tether led.

The Commander waited. Lor's gaze was drawn up, slowly, reluctantly, to his face, resisting, putting off as long as possible whatever he would see in his eyes. He was afraid. But he didn't know what frightened him.

"Deepen!" the A-zar uttered sonorously as their eyes finally met and Lor was astonished at what he saw there. Deep embers burned in those eyes, not with scorn or reproof, nor lofty disdain. There was neither anger nor pain, though he could sense them somewhere in the distant depths behind them. Lor saw that the Commander knew him, recognized him. And he saw something else as well. Understanding. The path ahead of Lor was known to him. It would be dangerous and costly. And whatever he encountered, whatever he suffered, the A-zar valued him and his service.

Lor turned and walked past, still in line with the others in front of him. It had taken no time at all. But he sensed a change within himself.

"I have seen the wells of the deep," the agent in front of him whispered, half to herself, half to him. "And I am undone."

Walking away from the Commander was a strange sensation. Planets on erratic orbits might feel this as they whipped away from the star they circled. Having come close, they would never be free of its influence, nor would they wish to be.

Lor found himself wanting to turn back to watch him, wishing he could have had a few more moments standing near him. And stepping aside off the path into the grass, he did so. He stared and listened, hearing only the salute the Commander gave each one, noticing the tempo. Each one was given a moment of silence and then saluted. And each one stepped away with a change in their expression. Wonder, admiration, concern, determination.

The windswept regions of the Claryon Delta had been Lorarye's home. He, and the Arye clan had been shaping and sculpting the region for as long as he could remember. The sharp cut mountains of the planet Banasari and the curving, braided rings that circled the planet were their most recent project. Forests and creatures were growing on the surface and flying creatures were spawning in the airy mists of the rings, one of which he had designed himself.

There were many winged, leather-skinned creatures like his in the galaxies. It was a popular archetype, not only among the Arye, but among thousands of other clans as well. He had carved each bone, whittled each tooth, coaxed each feather out of the skin with his own hands. The shaping of its head, the double eyelids and the eyes themselves had kept him spellbound for ages, playing with colors and angles and minute muscles. From cells to tissue to body, Lor had crafted his pterodactyls. Their lungs functioned on the planet's surface, breathing the atmosphere, but they were just as well adapted for absorbing gases through the leathery feathers and skin in the nebulous rings that were their home. They had elongated heads with feathered plumes in peacock colors and their eyes were capable of thousands of expressions from boredom to pleasure, love to fear, distress to curiosity. They were smart as well, and made delightful companions, playful, inventive, quizzical.

Lor loved living things. He didn't know why he had grown dissatisfied and why the almost invisible decay of the realm's energy beckoned him. He didn't know when he had lost his joy. Work, friends, music, creatures, vistas—nothing had the same appeal anymore. One day he awoke to find that he could think of nothing but traveling to the heart of the Realm and joining up with the Sentients.

Now, standing in the Daranon Valley, watching the A-zar greet the new agents, listening to his voice, contemplating the flickering rings that arced around him, he saw and knew the source of his restlessness. He had pictured joining in a noble effort to secure the Realm. Now, all his vague ideals coalesced into one purpose: to serve the Commander. It seemed to him that his whole being had been drawn here out of a longing to follow this one person. As the line of agents ended, the A-zar locked his gaze on Lor one more time before turning to leave.

Lor's devotion went with him.

L-rac Lorarye passed through the portal at top speed and dropped down out of the full panoply of the Calliarchal Realm flattening into the Shallows. He had enough missions under his belt that he could think while the transition was happening. The portal didn't actually tear him apart from the Realm, but for an instant in time—unmeasured, unrestricted—his being was distended into two halves, arrested in the portal, frozen. Time was where such a thing was possible. Time could be dilated and part of himself wedged, caught in the doorway, while the sub-portion moved around in three-dimensional space. He never actually left the Valley or even the portal itself and when he returned, reintegrating himself and reentering real time, it was as if he had merely vanished for an instant and reappeared on the far side a few steps from the threshold, where his last leap would have brought him.

As he descended, he was aware of himself in both halves and could feel the time distortion strung out between them. He wondered how such a thing was possible without pain, but he felt no discomfort at all. There was just the depletion of his inner resources that bore constant attention so that he could return before he was empty. And his reserve grew with every venture.

This was a solo assignment, scouting for fragilities in the Net and signs of Faction activity. Every segment of each Hour required tending because the work being done earlier and later in its flow added stresses that weren't easy to predict. Teams were always on hand and if he found a cause for concern, he could pull out and sound the alarm, and they would be tasked to defend and restore the weak place before it had a chance to break.

Unless it was within the humans themselves. Those were out of his reach, and he had no idea how they worked. He could see them spark and grow, waver and flicker, but he didn't understand them.

Lor was in a spaceship. He walked soundlessly along the metal corridors, lower, mid, and upper decks, scanning to the right and the left. A number of human stick figures occupied various rooms, but it was devoid of

Net energy except for one shimmering cord and a few smoldering embers scattered here and there. Moving through and around the vessel, he maneuvered so that he would enter the quarters with the cord last. It was clearly healthy, and he had little concern for what he might find there.

"Going dark!" one of the stick people yelled through the coms, and the walls shuddered and clanked as the major engines shut down and solar powered motors took over.

Passing through the bulkhead, Lor noticed a certain stench reminiscent of shredding. He had only smelled this once when an injured paladin was rushed past him on the way to the dysfirmary. Confusion had made him slow to recognize what he saw in passing that day and he had no clear memory of the wound, but the smell he would never forget. Tissues tearing along their fourth dimensional lines left a residue that was both unpleasant and terrifying. It had flooded him with instinctive fear that faded as quickly as it had flared.

Here in this vessel, there was a detectable residue, and he realized a skirmish had taken place, wounding one of his own. They were gone now. And there was no evidence of damage to the Net.

Lor shuddered and moved on.

The cabin where the thread fluttered as if in a gentle breeze contained a stick child, more substantial than most, with a hint of fifth dimensional visibility he found refreshing. She was sleeping on a narrow bunk under a thin blanket. A low-level lamp barely lit the room. As Lor paused to look at her, wondering about her added depth, if one could call it that—she barely had any real substance to speak of, more than most humans—she opened her eyes.

They were eyes with color, a garnet tint that echoed in the deeper realms, and he smiled.

She smiled back.

Lor wondered why she was smiling and assumed she was happy or had had a good dream. Sitting up, she groaned and held her hand to her head, muttering something about how it hurt.

"You're not one of them," she said plainly.

Who was she speaking to? Lor looked around, startled. There was no one else in the cabin.

"You think I can't see you, I guess. I don't know why. But at least you aren't ignoring me." She tilted her head and pursed her lips together in thought. "I like your face."

Lor turned back and met her gaze. The wrongness of it all hit him head on. He had to get out of there.

"Wait!" she cried in high-pitched voice.

Fumbling with his tether as panic set in, he reached for the Realm and found it hard to stabilize himself. He grappled with the ascent and struggled with the reforming of his dimensional self. By the time his feet rested on the mosaic pavement outside the portal, he was sweating heavily, his heart was racing, and he was panting for air. Someone ran over and caught him before he stumbled to his knees.

"Brother," the being said, propping him on his shoulder and handing him a bottle of water, "You're alright. It was a rough ascent, but you are undamaged. Let your heart be at peace." Lor nodded and drank deeply from the water and in minutes was restored.

From behind, a little shadow skittered, flitting away unnoticed into a darker space in the corner.

The dysfirmary was filled to capacity and the medics were overwhelmed. N-dan Arunev had called in every off-duty medic in her ward and there still were too many casualties to manage.

"N-dan!" someone cried out as she ran past a gurney. "Help me! Just help me tie him down before the layers scatter any further…" Another N-dan was curled over the body on the gurney with his arms outstretched, humming, holding in a knotted mess of shimmering colors, multiple loops were distending and straying, fraying at the edges. This being would not survive the tear much longer without a cocoon.

Swinging herself around to the other side, Arunev spread out her arms and curved over the being, warbling in her throat. As the two medics poured out the deep-pitched sounds in resonant voices, enveloping the being with their own light shields like a compress, a moan came from the gurney. Wispy loops began to retract, oscillating gently in time with the sound, till multiple layers of color were rolling together, reforming and stabilizing. It was like wrapping a bandage around a wound.

"Thank you," the N-dan acknowledged as Arunev ran off. On her back she carried equipment for the Shred Ward and the urgency was high. It had probably been unwise to pause in the hallway, even for a few moments. The one she had helped would have ended up with more jagged scars, but the others might not survive at all. She couldn't help it, though. She could never ignore a plea.

The Ward was filled with noise as she burst through the door. Every fixation drill was in use and a line of critical patients waited for the next free one. She headed straight for the injured G-dan lying in the center of the trauma unit, unhooked the working arm from the machine on her back, and tightened the beam orifice with a one quarter twist.

"Crack beam," she called out as she bent over the being's shredded leg, and two attendants leaned aside without releasing their holds, stabilizing the limb so she could work. A searing, shrieking light cut into the injury in a tight pinpoint of blinding light. She had forgotten to grab a face shield and her eyes immediately began to water. Someone noticed and fit one over her head clumsily. No time to thank them. Bending over closer, she worked with mathematical precision, fusing the tissues back into place, thousands of slivers of them, one at a time. The noise was so loud she couldn't hear anything else. If the patient was groaning, she wouldn't know. If other drills were working, she couldn't tell. The light it blasted was so strong that even through the black glass of her face mask, it drowned out everything else that could be sensed. It was like being alone in a white well, filled with heavy air.

Arunev worked until her wrists were throbbing and her fingers started to tremble with exhaustion. The machine wasn't heavy, and the work was straightforward, but the precision required and the delicate movements wore her out. Hours had passed when a hand tapping her shoulder spoke the command to cease and rest. And turning off the drill was like going blind and deaf. She could see and hear nothing for several moments until she adjusted.

Someone pulled the machine off her back and led her to a rest area where she slumped into a chair and rubbed her eyes. The noise in the ward had fallen quiet, whispers and muffled footsteps instead of shouts, moans, or the whirring of drills. Opening her eyes, she leaned forward, poured a glass of water, drank it, and poured another.

She felt the Commander's approach before she saw him, and her heart started racing in spite of the weariness. There was a distortion in the dimensional space around him and it moved with him as he walked. She was aware of him even when he was outside the building. If he came anywhere near her, she recognized the dent he made in the Realm.

Arunev had been there, waiting at the threshold of the machine chamber for her turn to go through, when the dent was first made. She saw Yandus caught in its fangs and witnessed the cry from his lips that could not be heard over the noise of battle. He was the first living being to be shredded.

If he had surrendered to the torment and let his form dissipate, he would have been free. Before long, out in the distant reaches of the Calliarchal Realm, he would have begun to distill into shape and color again, the pain and even the memory of it, gone.

But he held on, winning victory in the very maw of despair. Wrestling with the Rivening device, he contained it, and claimed the fissure as his domain. Ever since that day, the Sentients had worked to build the Net, repair the breach and extract refugees. The Faction had assembled forces as well, to accomplish with subterfuge what they had failed to do openly. Their target was the Net itself, and the forces that built it.

Sabotage was easier than open war, and destruction requires far less effort and investment than construction.

The wounded were brought to the dysfirmary for care, and the worst among them ended up in the Shred Ward. There, what was left of their bodies could be affixed before they rippled away completely. Those who had suffered too much damage to recover dissipated, discarding shadowy ashes in the vacuum spaces of the Shallows and leaving a husk-like shell in the Realm. But some believed they would flicker into life again, far away, forgetful of the darkness they had tested, though they may never return to this place or know their former selves.

Some days the work was rewarding as they brought beings back from the brink of dissolution. Others were heart-breaking, laboring in vain to save noble-hearted Sentients and extractors whose injuries were too far gone to mend. But it was a labor she was glad to do, no matter how hard it was at times.

This was the place where she felt closest to *him*.

And *he* was coming down the passageway in her direction. The Depth of his presence was unmistakable not just to her but to everyone.

"Deepen!" someone called out and many in the ward echoed the cry even from their beds. Arunev's voice was one of them and she rose to her feet saluting with a fist to her chest as she watched the door swing shut behind Commander A-zar Yandus.

The one she loved.

Yandus visited each one, standing at their sides, taking their hand, asking a question or two, and thanking them for their service. Arunev followed behind at a distance, close enough to hear his voice, far enough away to be unobtrusive. It made her happy to see how their faces lit up, how some shed a tear, and some showed visible relief. There were some whose faces were darkened with shame, that didn't want to raise their eyes to look in his. One word from him, and the darkness melted away. There were no regrets left once he moved on.

He visited the dysfirmary from time to time, though not always the same wards, and Arunev wasn't always on duty when he came. She didn't begrudge the other medics the privilege of seeing him and hearing his voice. It was enough that on this day, she was present.

When the last patient had been greeted, the Commander made his way to the door. Just before exiting, he paused and turned slowly around. Arunev lifted her gaze and was astonished to find him looking at her. She gasped, spell bound.

"You were there," he said.

She had no words. Where? Where had she been?

He stared at her, and she realized that he recognized her. She wanted to say, *Do you know me?* But he had just acknowledged that.

Where did he know her from? She knew where she knew *him* from. That one day, that terrible day, there at the scaffold. For her, she would always think of him as belonging to that day and that place.

He waited for her to understand.

You were there, he had said. He meant THERE. Arunev sucked in and held her breath. He recognized her from that day. She had witnessed his battle—and he had seen her there watching.

"I remember," he spoke again. It seemed like a long time had passed between his first words and these. The sound of his voice startled her.

"Oh," she whispered, breathing out. The image of him, caught and crushed, flashed in her mind and her lower lip trembled. She glanced at the gold band that covered his chest, covering the damage, and wondered what the cruel machine had done to him. She had seen the long spikes embedded in him but didn't remember when they had been extracted.

Had he seen her weeping for him that day? She had been struck to her very core. And since that day, had been devoted to him.

Everything she had endured up until this moment shifted because of his words. Every hour she had spent repairing shredded beings, every tear she had shed over those lost, every agonizing moment she had spent watching him suffer, and all the times she had observed him from afar and sensed his movement through the valley. All the breaths she had taken since she first loved him, all of this paled next to his words, *I remember*.

The Denser Plane

"Commander," she said, clutching her hand at her heart, pressing it against the ache, so sweet, so sore.

"Deepen," he saluted her in his deepest voice, and left.

Her reply wafted down the corridor after him.

"Deepen."

Chapter 20—Danger

The upper passageways were dreary and dusty. The little cart trundled along, one wheel squeaking, another sticking and dragging. The camera, its face smeared and cloudy, hung crookedly on its arm. Approaching the daylight cavern, it rolled directly into the light, opened its jerry-rigged solar panels, and settled down to think. Around it were piles of rubble, sorted by size and substance, some made of Martian rock, some of chunks of concrete, some of lightweight synthetic materials. Anything usable had long since been removed.

Pal didn't have to do his thinking here, he had plenty of room in the sectors he governed. But there was something about this little cart that he identified as his innermost being, his heart. He had hidden here when he was in danger more than once.

Sunlight shines down on the planet, nourishing life in all its domain, he observed, though he recognized that there was little life on Mars to nurture. He wanted to compose a poem about his thoughts, so he was starting with this idea.

```
I am like a plant
Soaking sunlight with my leaves
Nourishing my mind
```

He had written thousands of poems but discovered that they were meaningless unless they connected to something he considered of value. Ranking ideas for the purpose was extremely difficult and would have been impossible apart from the examples of people around him. Aurelia's creativity. Dan's ingenuity in habitat design. Carla's ability to nurture individuality. Even Mac demonstrated a devotion to pastimes that had no intrinsic value he could perceive, watching, observing, soaking up the activity of other humans without copying it.

None of these were necessary.

Aurelia could have focused on light crafting and never sung a song. Dan could have created practical living spaces without all the nooks and crannies and crazy extras—like forts and slides and poles. Carla could have insisted the kids use their time learning and working and ignored the pointless games and stories. Mac could have spent his time learning to communicate better.

Once, he had been powerful and ruled the planet, but now, Verna took care of most of that, which was fine. He hadn't wanted all those responsibilities back after the battle with Nebo. It had cost him more than he knew how to measure. Losing all the records of the final conflict because of the spaceberg bombing was one thing, but then he had been punctured by Nebo. Impaled. And he barely survived the wound. He had mounted his own attack and never knew what came of it. It hadn't prevented the robot virus.

Verna had to make a lot of decisions about what to keep and what to purge, and as it was, she still didn't want him to have complete control over any vital systems. Just in case there remained any residue of the attacker. But he was here. He still existed.

Out there, across the electronic domains of Mars, she guarded him wherever he roamed—and he didn't mind. But here, he could withdraw into *himself*, the part that was untainted, and ponder many things. Here, he remembered Sil and wondered how she was getting on and whether she missed him.

He called this state: happy.

The little Mars community didn't think of themselves as a colony. They were a family, a fragile seedling of society sprung up in the debris of Reznik Base and Lab 9.

No one came to get them because no one knew they were still there. The last people to leave the planet had apparently been persuaded that they were dead.

And the shadow of death had been hanging over them for years.

Parts were failing. Dan had been able to salvage components from all over the ruins and adapt them to fit essential equipment. But the time had long passed since they had found anything new, and he was spending two thirds of every single day patching and improvising. Stretching the lives of parts never meant to be used longer than six months. He had extended their usefulness for years.

The news of a ship on its way had breathed hope into their world, despite the possible danger, and threads of optimism bolstered their weary souls.

Carla was working in the garden, down on one knee, gently tying up some tomato branches, heavy with fruit, that had sprung free of their scaffolding. Her humming blended with the bees that worked nearby, collecting late season pollen.

"I've done the best I could to weld it back together," Dan explained, talking before he was all the way around the bend in the path and could see her. "But when this fails, there's nothing to replace it. Even dismantling another drone won't help."

"What's the worst that could happen then?" Carla leaned back on her heel and turned her head to look at him, pushing a stray hair out of her face with the back of her hand.

"We shut down one of the airlocks and hope the seals last."

"That would leave us only two exits, the escape hatch overhead, and the Lab tunnel entrance."

"Yeah," he agreed.

"And how long will those last?" she stared at him with a defiant look in her eyes. "What then?"

"We'll find a way," he said with a degree of hesitation.

"That's right," she pointed her ball of twine at him resolutely. "There's always a way. You taught me that."

She was right. They had found a way to survive every time things grew desperate. They had discovered the airtight caves and the excavator drones that had carved them. They had captured more than 83% of the water in the spaceberg and created recycling and purification procedures that could handle the volume. They had connected with the orbit station and with Verna's help, gotten a pod down to the surface. They had traveled back and forth several times, retrieving supplies, attempting communications with Earth, and just enjoying the view. The pod had enough fuel for a couple more trips, but they were saving that for emergencies.

They couldn't manufacture parts. Drones could be *taught* to machine them, and they had a wealth of ore, but they couldn't smelt or extract the metal. They also lacked the resources to produce new meds and couldn't spare the garden space for growing textiles. So many things were aging, decaying, falling apart.

"Verna says the ship will be here soon," Dan reminded her with a tired smile, sitting down on the path and dropping the component next to him. She had been sending messages in Earth's direction for years, continually, searching for someone to respond. Several receivers had caught the broadcast, but none had passed her security measures. Until now.

"Yes, she mentioned it," Carla copied suit and sat down facing him, twisting the end of the twine with her fingers. She carried her fatigue patiently. "But it doesn't sound like there will be people, just that android."

"Well, and some supplies." Watching her play with the string made him want a piece of his own to twist. "It's hard. It's like I want to be excited about it, but I can't. We don't know that there are any of the supplies we need, and we don't know who is sending us this android."

"Verna knows. She's very careful." Carla curled the string into a swirl on the ground and placed a couple of wispy dead leaves in the center.

"Verna is great," Dan said, reaching over stealthily to catch the tip of the string. "But even AIs can be deceived. Remember Nebo." Carla slapped his hand away playfully and reshaped her pattern.

"I know, I know, we always remember Nebo," Carla uncurled the string and made a heart next. "But don't forget that Steward saved me. And he saved ALL of us."

"Yeah," Dan snatched the string away with a smirk, holding it behind his back and narrowing his eyes at her. "Where is our Pal?"

"Give it back," she rolled her eyes and held out a hand. "He's probably hanging out in his spot. Why don't you go look and see if you can find him?"

Dan lay back on the ground with his hands and the string at the small of his back, trying not to laugh.

"Dan," she said tolerantly, her hand stretched out, waiting. "My twine."

"Hmmm," he murmured, "So tired…"

She didn't want to smile but she couldn't help it. "I know," she said, "you're just hoping I'll try to take it back." He started snickering. Throwing herself forward, she grabbed one of his arms and rolled him over partway with her shoulder. "Give… it… back," she grunted, tugging on the arm with each word.

He had laced his fingers together with the twine caught between them. And with a show of being defeated, he snapped his hands apart and rolled toward her, capturing her in his arms, laughing, unable to say whatever silly thing he had planned.

"You're a beast." She tried to frown but kissed him instead. And he kissed her back. "Not here," she whispered.

"I don't know what you mean," he answered, still laughing as he nuzzled her neck.

Their love was more than the habit of marriage or the comfort of leaning on each other. More than a bulwark against despair or a haven in the dreary reaches of Mars. It was a sincere devotion mixed with a sense of awe that they had found each other.

"Welcome, children," Verna's voice wafted over the breezy spaces. It was followed by the commotion of running feet and multiple voices arguing.

Dan stood up and pulled Carla to her feet, holding onto her hand tightly. Warmth and electricity flowed down his arm into her hand, holding her heart captive, mesmerizing her attention. And her love emanated back through her hand into his, magnetically, magically weaving her spell around him.

All six kids were complaining at the same time, and it was a while before the problem could be clarified. But then, the parents weren't trying too hard. They were still distracted. "Okay," Dan said finally once the contenders had unwound a bit. "Is this about the fort again?"

A chorus of protests broke out.

Dan held up his hands and silenced them. Then, extending an open hand to Syncopa, he nodded. She smirked at the boys, and they fidgeted with murmurs of, "No fair".

"Everyone knows Wednesdays are our day to play in the fort," Syncopa explained with an abundance of righteous indignation. The fort was every kid's dream. It was made of metal chunks with the sharp edges sanded down, salvaged from the ruins of Reznik base. It had several levels with trap doors and rope ladders, and a hidden slide in the center that dropped to a lower cavern. "We had barely started playing when they attacked us!" Every word caused the boys anguish, though each one expressed it in his own way.

"I see," Dan said, still holding Carla's hand, rubbing it with his thumb. "So, today is your day and they forgot." He pretended not to see the outrage as they moaned and clamped their hands over their mouths. "Is there anything else you want to say before I let them speak?"

"No," the girl smiled sweetly at her brothers. "That is all that matters."

The three second pause he took before turning and waving a hand at Zakwani, the most self-controlled among them, nearly sent Calixto into apoplexy.

"Well, it is Wednesday…" Zak commented thoughtfully with a finger to his chin. "But there is something they have left out. Something of great importance."

"Go on," Dan said. This wasn't a new scene. It was played regularly with endless variations, and it never seemed to amaze him how seriously they took it. Only one thing amazed him more: these fingers curled around his.

Zak rolled his eyes sideways to glance at the girls. "Well…" he said. They glared. Calixto stuck out his tongue. "They've forgotten our agreement when we made a bet and the loser promised to give up their next fort day."

"And they lost!" Calixto yelled pointing at them and crossing his arms.

Dan lifted a finger which meant 'out of order'. When people spoke out of turn, it could get tricky. Sometimes a decision could actually go against the ones who were right just because they broke the rules of a hearing.

"Is there anything else you'd like to say?" Dan asked. Zak should his head. "And you, Sync?"

"Yeah," she said, "but what about the time when they got more hours in the fort than we did? And besides they cheated!" Ananka whispered a little squeak that sounded like, "Yeah!"

"We didn't cheat," Zak said patiently. He was allowed to give a rebuttal. "We all agreed on the rules ahead of time. We were racing and the agreement was two laps around the reservoir. But they only ran one lap."

Ananka held up her hand urgently. Dan nodded. "I fell," she said, "and I twisted my ankle and it really hurt and we should have called the whole thing off, but they wouldn't."

"Ah…" Dan said. "Well," he turned to look at Carla. She smiled at him, stepping back, and letting go of his hand.

"I think," he said, straightening and snapping to attention in mock solemnity. "I'm going to have to intervene in person." There were yells and squeals of delight. "The fort is unforted. Fortunately, a fortuitous event has for… er…forestalled disaster. We must go fortify the fortifications!" he called out in a deeper voice, raising one fist in the air. "Before the aliens come! We'll show them!"

And they ran off as a pack with Dan at the head.

⸻⧫⸻

Mac was running. He didn't know where or why, but the dread approaching him from behind filled him with horror, and no matter how fast he ran, he couldn't escape. The world around him was gray and filled with clouds or steam or ghosts, whirling and billowing, wheezing and whistling. When he cried out, no sound came from his lips, but he felt the air rasping in and out in his throat. Sometimes he would grow lucid and tell himself it was a dream. Sometimes he just fled without hope.

Opening his eyes was the victory that he somehow always accomplished. Fighting and yelling, he would bat at the mists and wrestle within himself. It felt like sinking but it wasn't. It ended here. In bed.

The roof over his head, shining almost phosphorescent bluish white in the murky light, was known to him. The beating of his heart was beginning to slow back to normal and his breathing quieted. Sebastian would be watching.

He felt as if the unknown terror was still behind his back, or under his bed, and all he had to do was turn to look at it and he would know what it was. But he could not. The strength it would take to do such a thing was beyond him.

Sitting up, he swung his feet over the side of the bed and Sebastian coasted over to him. He must have known that Mac had been dreaming again.

"Is she alive?" Mac asked as he often did.

"Yes, she is alive," was the answer.

Mac was alive too. Hibernation wasn't the same as death, but since awaking, he had been unable to make the full passage back to life. He hung in the antechamber, wondering how to get in. *She* had passed through the shadows and returned intact. She was happy. She could sing.

"Is she singing?" he asked.

"No," Sebastian replied, "She is asleep."

"I was asleep," he said. "But I never wake up and sing."

"Why not?" Sebastian selected this question as a prompt that might draw him out.

"You know," Mac said, although he had never explained any of it to him before.

Sebastian just replied, "Tell me what you dreamt."

"The storm," he said, and this was the first time he had given even one word of description. "Dark clouds swirling all around and I can't get away… and back there…" He gestured over his shoulder without turning his head.

"Yes," Sebastian said mechanically, his sensors focusing and scanning Mac.

"Do you see something?" Mac asked, his eyes growing wider.

"Yes," Sebastian answered logically, filling Mac's heart with terror. He began to tremble and by the time the bot noticed he was in distress; he was in the grip of panic. "I see the room," the AI added, completing the thought.

Several rooms away, Aurelia stirred and murmured as Verna spoke softly into the air, gradually raising the lights. After a few moments, she became alert enough to recognize that she was being called. "What is it?" she asked groggily.

"I'm sorry to wake you, Aurelia," she said, "Are you willing to go to the infirmary and help? Mac is not doing well."

"Of course," she pulled herself upright, hung her head for a moment, then lifted it, brushed her hair out of her face, grabbed a flannel shirt which she used for a bathrobe and slung it over her sweats. She shuffled out, sliding her sock-covered feet along the floor.

Aurelia never doubted Verna's interventions. The AI had explained to her once how she had learned about human suffering and emotions more intimately than any other artificial being. While there were a few others with the same access to brain data collected from Sil, she alone had lived through it with her. She knew what every emotion *meant*. She had learned compassion organically, not through personal suffering, but through loving someone who suffered.

"I am relieved," Sebastian informed Aurelia when she entered. It was his way of assigning to her responsibility for alleviating Mac's discomfort. He didn't experience any distress himself

"Hey," Aurelia said, coming and sitting next to Mac and taking his hand. "Are you awake again?"

He didn't turn his head to look at her. He stared straight ahead. She could sense his reasons instinctively, and understanding what he needed, she began to sing, cracking a little at first, but soon, in sweet tones.

"I found a pathway through the sea…" She looked toward the wall that he was staring at. "Beyond the flowering dragon tree…" He shuddered and sighed, and his shoulders sagged. "And all alone, beneath a stone, a treasure waited for me."

Yanking his hand out of hers, he dropped his head in both hands and began weeping. She kept singing gently until the song was ended, and the residue of music hung in the air. Moments passed.

"Mouse," he said. He *never* called her that.

"Yes," she said, "I'm here."

"I'm scared." He showed no emotion on his face, but she was used to that.

"I know. I get scared too."

He lifted his head to stare at her in astonishment.

"It's true," she said, "I have some memories that are very scary, and I try not to think about them."

"You?"

"I used to dream about them but not so much anymore."

"What do you dream?" The tears had ceased, and curiosity seemed to be driving away the fear.

She shook her head. "I don't talk about it at night, in the dark… and I don't like to talk about it much at all, ever."

"You're not scared now."

"No."

"Most of the time, you're happy. That's why you sing."

"I sing when I'm happy," she said, "But I also sing when I'm sad or frightened or trying to calm down."

He was taken aback and jumped to his feet to look at her straight on. "This… this…" he said clumsily. She nodded and smiled. "Can I tell you?" he finished.

"Sure," she shrugged, though there was a small part of her that was afraid to know. She swallowed that reluctance.

"It's always the same. I'm running and I can't get away."

"What are you running from?"

"I don't know."

"Aaahhh," she murmured. "That's why it's so hard. If you knew, you could manage it somehow, you know, figure out what to do about it."

He stared at her again, amazed. "How?"

"How what?"

"How?" he said again, not realizing his meaning was unclear.

"How do find out what you're running from or how do you figure out what to do about it?" She crossed her arms and tilted her head on its side.

"Yes," he answered, bobbing his head earnestly.

"Well," she got to her feet and walked to the other end of the room and back, pondering what to do next. "Raise the lights, Sebastian," she instructed. "Mac, it's going to take some effort on your part. Are you ready for that?"

He nodded again.

"So, if I ask you a question that you don't want to answer, will you try?"

The Denser Plane

"Yes," he said.

"Okay," she pressed her hands together fingertip to fingertip. "Here goes. If you try to guess what is behind you… in the dream, I mean… what would it be?"

"I don't know," he answered too quickly.

"I know you don't know," Aurelia smiled at him, taking a deep breath, and remembering with affection the ones who had walked her through some of her own trauma. "But let's try this. Pretend that you are in the dream—"

"No," he said.

"It's not real," she said, reassuringly, "just pretend for a moment and imagine you are looking over your shoulder."

"I won't," he said.

"Um…" she hesitated and crossed her arms again. "Okay. How about this? Pretend that Sebastian and I are with you in the dream, one on each side… and Sebastian has a big sword—"

"That is illogical," Sebastian reminded her.

"Yes, but that's not a problem in a dream, Sebastian," she suggested patiently. "Come stand here next to Mac and hold out your arm like this." Sebastian cooperated and thrust out his fine-motor-skills limb at a ninety-degree angle. "Yes, that's right. And I will stand on this side with my megaphone and floodlight." She held one hand to her lips and the other pointing forward. "At the count of three, we all turn around." Mac watched her, not resisting.

She counted and the three of them rotated 180 degrees to face the other wall. Aurelia called out a challenge and shone her floodlight, and Sebastian whirred the tool in his limb.

Mac stared fixedly, recognition passing over his face. He didn't panic again.

Aurelia's arms dropped to her side. "What is it, Mac?"

"An airlock," he said, "and there's an ugly face there, laughing at me." A fluidity, unknown since his awakening, loosened his words. "He thinks I will beg him to let me back in, but I won't. I'll die first." A sneer distorted his mouth. "I despise that man," he said disdainfully. "And he is nothing to be afraid of."

"The Germinator is dead," Sebastian informed him.

"Ha!" Mac scoffed. "Good."

Aurelia watched him, backing away a few steps, unsure of the change. Was the gentle soul she had comforted a shadow? Was this the real person underneath?

"How long have I been awake?" he asked turning to the medic.

"Twenty-three minutes, forty-eight point two seconds," was the answer.

Director Hsu spun on his heels and faced Aurelia. "And you are?"

She stared at him for a moment, then turned to leave the room without a word.

"Come, Robot," she heard him say as she exited, "Update me on my condition."

A deep sucking noise followed by an unnatural wind caught Dan's attention, stirring an eerie feeling of sinking down. Then a brief burst of rain from the mists high up in the garden cavern dampened the surroundings. A three-note alarm began to sound, ascending a simple chord that ended in a discordant tone, intentionally jarring even though it wasn't loud.

Dan scrabbled out of the irrigation systems he had been working on, leapt over a natural stone ridge and ran for the closest bulkhead. There were a three of them in the tunnel leading to the Tangle, each one a safeguard against possible airlock failure. All around he could hear the kids dashing, each to their assigned post, to monitor the systems that preserved life. Water, warmth, air, power, vegetation, communications, food. They all knew basic first aid, as well as fire and emergency response.

And how to disable a rogue drone. Carla had perfected at least seventeen ways to do that and began training them almost from the time they could walk.

When he got to the first bulkhead, he jumped through, sealed the door closed, waited only long enough for Verna to confirm the seals were intact, and then he was dashing down the natural passageway to the next. The amount of air lost hadn't been substantial, but it had been enough to cause a drop in air pressure and temperature. The leak seemed to have ceased, but it was vital that they determine what had happened and where the air had gone as soon as possible. The relief could be temporary and the boundary between life and death on Mars was very thin.

Carla was calling out and asking for updates via the main audio and answers were coming from all over. Most or all of this could have been handled by Verna, but this was the very thing they wanted the kids to learn. How to survive without her... or without Dan and Carla if need be. Dan let her manage that while he raced to secure their containment.

"Where's my Pal?" he muttered between puffs, closing and sealing the second bulkhead, and dashing for the third one. It should already be sealed. Pal didn't answer. He must be meditating in his sun spot.

"I cannot detect any leaks," Verna said in his personal com as he reached the final bulkhead.

Dan agreed, pressing his fingers around the edges, feeling, and listening for even the tiniest of hisses or the gentlest of cooling. "The Tangle and the garden are secure," notified the others. Now he needed to discover where the shift had taken place.

"Oh no! Oh no! Oh NO!" Preston cried out to all. "The temperature is dropping again! I can't get it to stop!"

"We've got this, Pres," Carla spoke with a steady confidence. "You are doing what you're supposed to be doing, which is keeping us up-to-date and being ready to follow instructions. We're working as a team. Right?"

"Right," he answered with a slight waver in his voice.

"Water is cooling too," Syncopa informed them, copying her mother's tone. "Not too fast. Just a few degrees."

"Power is fluctuating," Zak was next. "The charts aren't normal." Both of his parents appreciated that he had already developed a sense of 'normal'.

"Good job, Sync," Carla said, "Zak, are we looking at an impending power loss?"

"I can't tell…"

The updates continued, each one checking in and Carla responding. She didn't speak of what she was doing, but Dan knew, she would be suiting up and going outside to check the drones. She always did that first in any emergency. She had had to take out a couple too, mostly because they were malfunctioning and arbitrarily destroying the thing they were supposed to be servicing.

Dan was through the third bulkhead now and suiting up as well. As he mounted the ladders and entered the old lab structures, any door he opened could become a gaping wound in the containment. He could never assume, even if Verna detected nothing, that it hadn't been broken. Anything from material decay to instrument malfunction to meteors could be at fault.

The search was tedious and depressing. Hallways, rooms, stairwells. All empty. Nothing compounded the isolation from Earth and his old life more than scouting through the facility. On this occasion, he found himself growing alarmed as the search wound down. He found nothing that could explain the crisis.

An unknown danger was the kind he hated most.

Chapter 21—Mission

At first, all Scarlet could do was stare around at the incredibly huge hall filled with lights and colors and people, scrunching herself into a little bundle in one corner with her knees to her chin, hoping no one saw her. Everything seemed thicker and richer somehow. She could smell a profusion of aromas she had never smelled before, all of them beautiful, interesting, and distinct. If she focused her attention on just one, and she found it standing out in her mind and could tell where or from whom it came. Lovely people moved around and each one had their own gorgeous smell, like their own perfume. They didn't glow, but they radiated something she wanted to call 'light' that was just as unique. Each one had their own radiation. Their eyes and hair and clothes and armor were of all the colors imaginable, but they blended together like they were related.

The wall behind her back was warm and alive with vibrations. She could *feel* voices talking and things moving, outside trees growing and water flowing, and maybe even the planet rotating. All her senses were heightened, sharpened, stimulated, as if she had acquired superpowers. The air in the hall itself was alive and moving around her with a sense of awareness.

Dominating the towering, airy reaches of the chamber's dome, a blindingly bright weave of millions upon millions of glowing cords stretched from one end to the other, as far as she could see. It heaved and turned on itself gently like a living thing. Golden light flowed through it and all round, each time in a different spot, and sparks flashed as if for the first time.

Scarlet's jaw hung open, and she could hardly squeak in astonishment, not even to ask, "Where am I?" Her attention shifted from one thing to another and from one person to another, captivated by them. The armored ones felt so massive they seemed to pull on her as they passed by. Some of the silver-banded ones seemed cheerful and musical. Some of the gold-banded ones seemed serious and important, but there were some that made her uneasy. She couldn't catch it when looking toward them, but after turning away, she felt a ripple of discord from their direction. It was like they were fake gold, painted instead of solid.

Closing her eyes, Scarlet wondered if she would wake up soon, though she didn't want to. It was so lovely here and she was happier than she ever remembered being in her life. And that was strange… There were conflicting memories from her life overlapping each other that she wasn't sure what to do with. And a great sorrow. She tried to forget it, but it swept in from afar, swallowing up her surroundings like a cloud passing over the sun. A dinginess spread over all the light, color, sound, smells, movements, and joy of the great hall. She began weeping, and found herself moaning, *Why? Why?* inside her mind. At first, she couldn't even remember what she was anguished about, but then the understanding hit her full force and she wished she could forget it again. Again, she cried, *Why?* in her thoughts, this time grieving over the source of her sorrow.

A shadow flitted near her. She jerked her head toward it, opening her eyes again. It wasn't just a shade. It had an ethereal human form that rippled like a reflection in water, not ghostlike, but maybe like a holo, with more substance and color than a holo would produce. It was a real person, just not a very substantial one. The face smiled at her with kindness in his eyes.

"You're even less substantial than I am," he said, as if he knew what she had been thinking.

"What?" she asked, noticing how wispy and faint her voice was. The conviction that he was speaking truth filled her and she looked down at herself—her nearly invisible gray self. "Am I a ghost?" she gasped.

The shape laughed with gentle warmth. "No," he responded. "You're not a ghost, but you don't belong here and there isn't much to you at this point."

She could see right through herself; there was hardly enough of her to count as a puff of smoke. She wasn't even a silhouette. No wonder all the people were ignoring her. "Where am I? Why can't see myself?"

"You're still forming, and you won't have much substance to speak of until you are extracted. But how did you get here?"

The visitor's face came to mind. She had been asleep and had woken up with such a bad headache in a dingy old place with an old blanket. And he had been there. He thought she couldn't see him, and he was going to leave… "I must have caught him," she said. "I grabbed onto him because he was leaving, and I didn't want him to leave me there in the old ship…"

"That makes sense," the shape said. "I saw one of them come out and he wasn't well. Had a bumpy ride back, I guess. He probably had no idea you were hanging onto him." It chuckled.

"Is he okay?" she asked, studying the shape's willowy features. He looked familiar somehow.

"He's fine now, but I'm pretty sure he has no idea he had a stowaway."

"I always wanted to be a stow-away," Scarlet smiled. She had completely forgotten that she had been weeping when the shade appeared.

"I wasn't even that," the shade smiled. "No one is sure how I got tethered here because I wasn't connected to the Net, and I'm not fully formed in seven dimensions. I was wandering around a long time before someone talked to me and asked me about it. I think I was too insubstantial at first for them to see me. After a while, I had a little more color, more depth, and then L-rac Krudar took me under her wing. We're still learning things…"

"I don't understand what you're talking about," Scarlet whispered in awe. "But it sounds really starry… I wish I knew more. Who are you? Why are you just a holo-shape?"

"I've had several names, but none of them fit me," he said—at that moment, the shape solidified a fraction more. "Kru calls me Changeling, but I had friends before who called me something else."

Right then, the visitor she had caught a ride with passed nearby and she jumped to her feet. Actually, she swished to a higher location from the floor. Chasing after him, she flitted like a shadow in his footsteps, and no one noticed her. Changeling coasted along sedately behind her.

L-rac Lorarye walked quickly, his heart racing. The Commander had called for him and he didn't know why. His longing to see him and his fear of being reprimanded warred within him. Every few steps, he sighed or gasped, unable to take full breaths with the pressure in his chest. He was glad for one thing: he *had* completed his mission before pulling out. The human ship in the Shallows had been free of Faction tampering and the one thread of the Net had been secure. When he first reported the results, they asked if he had detected anything unusual and he didn't think to mention that the stick child could see him. Now, he wondered if that had been important. Did it count as unusual? He didn't even know yet what "usual" was!

Outside, the rich Daranon Valley spread up majestic hills on many sides. It was lush with the garden for which it was now famous, with glorious trees and flowers and an abundance of fauna. The ground under his feet thrummed with harmonious rhythm as he paced across the steppingstones. The air, damp and scented with rain, was about to water the life around him. It calmed and refreshed him. Approaching the Commander's headquarters, he felt that sense of depth tugging on him, with every step bringing him deeper, closer to the one he served and loved. It was exciting and terrifying.

Never had A-zar Yandus asked to speak with him personally before.

"Deepen!" a detachment of Paladins of the highest rank saluted him as one as he reached the doors into the Commander's offices.

"Deepen!" he responded, pressing his fist to his chest—his heart pulsed as if the word had come from it, and he wondered if, in fact, it did.

Scarlet, trembling with joy and excitement over the wealth of beauty she had just toured, whipped around to ask Changeling about that salute, but before the question was out of her mouth, he was shaking his head and she knew she needed to be discreet.

"Deepen!" the Commander pressed his fist against the gold band across his chest, rising to his feet as Lor entered.

Lor echoed the salute, dropping his eyes to the ground. "I am here at your command, A-zar Yandus," he said.

"L-rac Lorarye," Yandus nodded toward him with respect, as if they were equals, which Lor found humbling. "You have returned from your first solo mission intact. Well done. The report has just been given to me."

"Thank you, Commander," Lor lifted his gaze and looked at him. It was like seeing the face of an old friend and remembering all they had in common. This was even more humbling since he was nothing like this noble being he served. He wished he could be *more* like him.

"You were ill when you returned…"

"It passed quickly. A little water was enough to restore me," he replied.

"Yes," Yandus nodded and glanced around the room without landing on anything specific. "Once your tag-along had let go, you felt better." At this his eyes settled directly on Scarlet.

"My… what?" Lor followed his line of sight and turned to the wisp of gray smoke he was looking at. His gaze focused and his mouth dropped open. "The stick girl?"

"Hi, Buddy," Scarlet remarked with a little smile. "Sorry about that. I didn't know what would happen. I just didn't want you to leave me there…"

"You were in a difficult position," the Commander acknowledged. "And thank you, Changeling, for keeping her company till she came to me."

"Commander," Changeling said with a wave of warmth toward him.

Lorarye was shaking inside. It felt like an utter, humiliating failure. She hadn't just seen him, she had latched onto him when he came back to the Realm. This wasn't supposed to be possible, was it? No one had taught him about anything like that. He felt set up, exposed, ashamed.

Yandus stepped closer and placed a hand on his shoulder, immediately reassuring and strengthening him. "Lor," he said softly, "You are still learning. Accept each new mission, however it turns out, as a chance to serve and learn. You are valuable to our efforts—to me, and I don't hold this turn of events against you. You should not hold it against me either."

"I would never…" Lor began, but there was no need to explain.

"Scarlet here…"

"How did you know my name?" her words whuffed like wind, but they both heard them.

"I know your name, child," Yandus affirmed, glancing back at her for a moment. "She is unexpected, but you can see she has a tether, like you do. You cannot prevent her from traveling and I'm sure she didn't realize her passage might cause you pain."

Scarlet shook her head vehemently.

"And she doesn't understand the dangers that surround all those who travel."

Lor looked over at Scarlet now with compassion. "Could she…?" He didn't finish, not wanting to frighten the stick child with references to shredding and dissipating.

The Commander took his hand away from Lor's shoulder, pressed his fist again to his chest, and stared at him, as if words weren't needed for the final meaning he wanted to impart. Then, with a nod he uttered, "Deepen!"

Lor responded with a salute and bowed deeply before pivoting and exiting the door.

"Not you, little girl," Yandus pointed at Scarlet as she started to flit after her visitor friend. The words chilled her down to her toes. He spoke as if he knew exactly who she was and had complete authority to command her. "Come closer."

She obeyed before she had even thought of whether she wanted to or not. She couldn't help herself.

He could have continued to tower over her, but he knelt beside her, one arm leaning on his knee which placed his hand in the vicinity of *her* shoulder. She was too smoky to feel the weight of his hand, but the cordiality emanated into her easily. She trusted him implicitly. Completely. "Scarlet," he said,

"You were not invited and have come unannounced. Do you understand what this means?"

She shook her head. The fear that might have spread into her heart was held at bay by that warm hand on her shoulder; she could just sense it at the outskirts of her mind, at her toes and fingers. Kindness held back terror.

"It means that there were moments of grave danger you could have passed through without anyone knowing you were in trouble."

"Oh," she said.

"This time, L-rac Lorarye protected you without realizing it," he said, piercing her with his eyes filled with deep authority softened by deep compassion. "And it was good that Changeling was nearby and caught sight of you quickly. He has been watching for more of his kind…"

She sensed Changeling nearby, wordlessly agreeing to those words.

"Wait…" Scarlet interrupted, despite his deep authority, "Are you saying I can come here on my own? Like… how does that happen?"

"Think about what you are saying, Scarlet," Yandus said, rising to his feet, increasing his air of command. "Look around you, not just with sight, but with understanding."

She looked around her, seeing things, but also feeling things, reaching out with her understanding, as he said, realizing what he meant even as she began to do it. She sensed her wispy little tether to the Realm, and the many layers or dimensions. She felt the humming life of other beings all around, the joy of things growing, of people imagining and creating whatever they wished… and she found the hole, draining color and vitality from the Realm, and the sense of those bent ones masquerading as lovely people, but they weren't. They were tricksters… they were scary… they…

Yandus was nodding at her as she looked back at him, eyes widening. "Them?" she asked.

"Yes," he responded.

"Do you know who they are?"

"I do. But not enough to impart that awareness to all who serve here," he said.

The sorrow she had forgotten came washing back like the tide, rolling over her in wave after wave of sorrow. "Oh!" she cried out, "Why? Why?" And she didn't even know how those words fit the anguish she felt, but somehow, they did.

"I know," Yandus said soberly, watching her fixedly. "Tell me about it."

"My mother," she moaned, "that terrible scar and all those problems she has."

"She did that for you," Yandus reminded her. If Scarlet had been watching his eyes, she would have seen strange churnings in their depths, deeper and darker than the Earth's oceans, strange and wordless movements of his soul.

"I know!" She crumpled down onto her little shadowy self and wrapped her arms around herself. She didn't notice Changeling next to her reaching out a filmy hand to comfort her. She couldn't feel it. "She fought a warrior robot in the tunnels for me when I was a baby and she almost died there, but some friends came to her rescue, and we escaped. But they were the same ones who took her fighter suit away and that's why she couldn't run fast enough to get past the bot."

Her mother hadn't told her all these things. This knowledge was coming to her as ripples of understanding. All those years of her life, she had taken her mother's maiming as the norm. She only had one usable arm and she walked with a limp, and she had kidney issues. But she had never explained why.

Now Scarlet knew. "They took her fighter suit away," she said again.

"And she was glad those people followed and made sure the two of you escaped with your lives," Yandus said. "She's been accustomed to her injuries for a long time now and she considers you worth it."

"Poor mom!" Scarlet grieved. "My poor mom! I didn't know."

The Commander watched her patiently and Changeling patted her ethereally.

"Why didn't they just help her?"

"They did help her," Yandus said. "This is sad, but the cry of a mother who has lost a child is harder to bear than losing a limb. They spared her of that. She has you." Those depths in his eyes roiled and seethed.

"Can't you do something about it?" Scarlet pleaded gently, looking up at him and catching sight of the storm in his eyes. It drew her in. She stared and wondered and hoped and began to be sure that he was upset too. "Can't you do something about it?" she asked again.

"Like what?" he inquired without moving a muscle in his face or body. Standing stiffly, coolly, all his massive, deep, multi-dimensional complexity swirled in his dark, fiery eyes.

"Like go back and make them help her!" she lifted herself up straight, gaining a hint of substance and color, and Changeling's hand touching her became detectable.

"Is that what you would do?" he asked gravely. She could see his whole being, a universe of thought and feeling and purpose, stirring and twisting within him.

"Yes!" she insisted, crossing her wispy arms, and stamping her foot with a puff on the floor.

"Alright," he said, the storm in his eyes clearing like the sun breaking through dark clouds. Peace filled the room. "You will go and do this."

To her astonishment, her visitor friend reappeared with a puzzled expression on his face. Nodding at her, he saluted again and listened to his instructions. She hardly heard them; her mind was churning with confusion.

"I understand, Commander," her friend was saying.

"You have a certain investment in her now," Yandus was saying. "Take her on the mission I have given her and bring her back to me. Then you will be the one to take her back to her place in the Hours."

Lor reached a hand out to Scarlet and she took it. "You can call me Lorarye," he said as he led her out of the room, back toward the hall where she had first arrived.

"Thank you, Lor-ah-rye-yay," she said. Pausing at the door, she turned to the Commander and saluted, a little cloudy hand poised at a smoky center where her heart would be. "Deepen," she said, wanting to show good manners.

"Deepen!" he saluted her with a hint of a smile and a twinkle in his now serene eyes.

Lorarye stood near the portal of the Seventh Hour, roped to the little wisp of a person who could barely even hold the knot around her waist. He had tightened it all the way and it didn't quite look like it was in the same plane as she. They were overlapping, barely touching parallel realms—except that she *did* hold it and it didn't fall to the ground.

"This is as new for me as it is for you," he warned. "We know you'll be able to see and hear me, right?"

"Right," she said, all her confidence restored.

"Please listen for my instructions and obey."

"Yes, sir!" Scarlet snapped her hand to the tip of her forehead, but the gesture had no meaning for him.

"You belong there, and it won't harm you to be there, but for me, time is crucial, and I can't delay," Lor explained, "I do NOT want to have to pull you out against your will. I may not even be able to. But if I am growing weak, I may have to leave. I could even lose my grasp on the position.”

“Right!” she nodded vigorously.

“Do you know what that means?”

“A bumpy ride?” she guessed.

“It means I might lose hold of you and leave you there.”

“Oh…” she lost some of her excitement.

“It’s very important that you listen to me and follow my instructions.”

“Yes, Sir, Lor-yay-yaee,” she said more soberly.

“Lor… arr… yay,” he corrected patiently.

“Lor…yar…yar…ee,” she tried.

“My friends call me Lor,” he amended with a sigh.

“I’m your friend, Lor,” Scarlet smiled sweetly, though he probably couldn’t tell what kind of smile she gave him. “Deepen!” she added brightly, which caused some heads nearby to turn.

“The salute is usually reserved for Sentients. It isn’t really used by other beings like yourself.”

“Can I be a Sentient?” she cried, trying to bounce on her toes. It didn’t work in her smoky form.

The question astonished him, and he couldn’t think of how to respond, so taking her hand, he counted to three and ran toward the portal. Pulling them down into the funnel, it began to tug him into layers, flattening him at one end, suspending him at the other. He heard a little shriek from the girl but since her substance was increasing as they fell, it didn’t concern him.

A large, tastefully decorated bedroom shimmered into existence, their feet landing on the soft carpet. An open window brought in the sound of ocean waves and a gentle sea breeze. It was late in the day, and the sky was growing dark. An elderly woman was dozing in a chair facing the window with her feet propped up on a little footstool. She was clothed in a warm purple robe and wore a necklace with a large dark stone hung around her neck.

“Remember what you are supposed to say?” Lor prompted nearby. He was the shadowy one now and Scarlet was quite solid and normal again.

She nodded.

The woman started and looked around in confusion. “What’s that?” she muttered. “Here?” And focusing on Scarlet, she jumped again. “Oh, my!” she gasped.

“Give me the golden cylinder,” Scarlet enunciated carefully, smiling and holding out her hand.

"The old woman stared at her, shaking her head slowly. "I never…" she muttered, "Who would have thought… are you sure?"

Scarlet nodded and wiggled her fingers.

"I was talking to… never mind."

"Your AI friend in your necklace?" Scarlet asked reasonably. She had seen one like it before.

"Yes, who told you?" the woman pushed herself to her feet, steadying herself against the arm of the chair before pacing carefully, with small steps, to a dresser.

"I'm used to it," Scarlet said, still holding her hand out.

The woman pulled open a drawer. "Are you sure? Is that where it was?" She lifted out a little woven straw box. Inside it was a piece of blue cloth. Unrolling it, she dropped something into her palm and squeezed her hand shut. Turning to Scarlet, she frowned.

"How did you get here?" She looked quite grumpy now.

"Uh…" Scarlet glanced at Lor who shook his head. She wasn't supposed to say anything about it. "It's hard to explain."

"Tell me," she barked, holding her hand behind her back.

Lor groaned. At least there were no signs of Faction interference. This was just human obstinacy. He moved over behind her, ready to soften her grasp if need be. Stick people were easily persuaded when using minute coaxings.

"I can't talk about it!" Scarlet frowned back at her, "but it's really important. It's for my mom!"

The old lady's eyes widened. "Scarlet?" she whispered, "Is it you?"

Scarlet squinted and backed away a step, a little frightened by the words. She had no idea who this woman was, and she didn't like this at all.

"You told me this day would come, but I didn't believe you," the old lady whispered, a tear forming in one eye and trickling down her cheek. "Come child, here, take it quickly before I wake up, for I'm sure this is a dream." She held out the golden cylinder to her.

"Okay," Scarlet snatched it out of her hand. "Gotta go. Thanks!" And with wide eyes, she glared at Lor.

Immediately, he pulled them partway out of the Shallows. Then adjusting the coordinates, he dropped them down again without losing his placement in the portal. She shrieked again and this time he smiled.

Dank, murky tunnels solidified around them. When Scarlet landed this time, she noticed the way her feet stirred the dirt displacing little puffs of dust and air around her. Glancing up at Lor, she could see dust drifting *through* him.

"What do I look like to you?" she wondered aloud. "I was just a puff of smoke in your place, but here I'm normal. And you look like almost nothing to me. I can see right through you."

"You're a stick," Lor walked around, checking out their surroundings as he spoke. "All people look like sticks to me here, not because I can't see what you call normal, but because you're still basically a puff of smoke."

"What?!" she burst out, then lowering her voice, "I am not!"

"You are only four dimensional like the others, except…" he smiled, "actually, you are a little more than that, and you're tethered to the Realm, so you're probably deepening."

"Deepening?" she grinned. That sounded really good to her.

"We don't have time to discuss these things," he moved down the tunnel, beckoning her, "Remember how important it is to stay on task. My time is limited."

Scarlet walked down the long tunnel between ancient, rusted rails, stepping daintily over garbage and around muddy puddles. Wretched looking rats skittered away as she approached, and some poked their noses out of cracks in the wall, and holes in the floor. Everything was blackened, stained, water-logged and spotted with mold. Clouds of dust, suspended in the thick air, wafted around her as she passed through it.

Echoes of noises, voices, the thudding of feet, and some faint clashes of metal found their way down the long dark corridor from the direction they were headed. Scarlet felt no fear. Having Lor there filled her with confidence that this was either an awesome dream or some crazy multiverse experience with her own warrior protector. The shouts from beyond sounded like adventure, not danger.

Lor led her across one tunnel and turned off to the left down the next. In this one, the shouts and calls were louder. Yellow light streamed out of dingy windows onto aged platforms straddling the sides of the level where she walked, where the bare rails were. Climbing up onto the platform wasn't hard for her, though it did leave some dirt of her clothes. She was still wearing the pants and suspenders she had had on when she was first kidnapped, and they were getting filthy. The space suit had been set aside in a shadow clump in the hall of the Seventh Hour.

"In there," Lor directed, signaling the place that had so many people inside that a bunch of them were hanging out the door or leaning with their heads popped through the open windows.

The Denser Plane

Scarlet ran up to the crowd and started by saying, "Excuse me," and "Can I get by?" but no one noticed. "I have a delivery," she called out, pushing her way into the crowd. "Hey!" She shoved between the people outside, elbowing, tapping their backs, calling out to let her in. One by one, the bystanders became aware of her and stepped aside to give access, and little by little, with calls and shoves, she bumped and knocked her way in.

"Come on, you big clumsy bear," she groused at the final obstacle, "let me by!" He stepped aside and she found herself at the center of the crowd, turning around to look at them all. They were staring at her like they had never seen a kid before. There were tons of people in there, standing or sitting and all looking at her. Every chair had several people in it or sitting on the arms or leaning behind it. And there were several sitting on the floor. One woman in a rocker looked familiar, but she was so thin and sickly, it didn't click right away. She held a baby that… Scarlet glanced at that baby, but not too closely. Lor had said to not get distracted. She had to fulfil her mission.

"Well!" she said, "That took a while." What was the next thing she was supposed to do? Lor was over there next to the sick woman beckoning.

"Here," she said, holding the golden cylinder out on her open palm. "This is for the Boo Wolf. That's what they said." It wasn't exactly what she had been told to say, but it was close enough that Lor smiled at her and nodded, and she smiled back.

"Who sent you?" a crusty old lady said, snatching the cylinder out of her hand, which annoyed Scarlet.

"Are you the Boo Wolf?" she demanded, hands on her hips. "I won't give it to anyone else. Those are my *orders*!"

"Your orders?" a big guy with a grumpy face said. "Who gave you those orders?"

"Uh…" Scarlet stared at the floor, rolling her shoe. She couldn't think of an answer that would be okay. She wasn't supposed to talk about all that multiverse stuff. "Well…"

The big guy who was obviously the Boo Wolf grabbed the golden cylinder from the crusty old lady and popped it open. There was a tiny rod inside with markings etched into it and he stared at it for a long time. All of a sudden, a shadow over his face lightened and he looked nicer.

"You don't know," he said to Scarlet, putting the cylinder away.

She shook her head. "Not exactly…" she agreed with an open-handed shrug. "So, let me go now." She looked around at the people towering around her, and all the legs obstructing her exit. "Drop it off and get out… that's what they said…" she added with a frown. Everybody was pressing in like they wanted to stop her, and it was making her a little nervous.

"Let her go," the big guy ordered, and suddenly people were floundering to get out of the way. A wide path to the door opened and Scarlet ran through it before it could close up again.

Jumping off the platform into the muck on the lower level, she started running between the rails back into the dark tunnels. She was pretty sure someone would try to follow her and that scared her more than anything else had. "Come on, come on," she was calling softly to Lor between pants.

"I'm right here," he answered, moving next to her. He looked like he was running too, but it didn't take him any effort. And he didn't get dirty either. "This way," he directed, and they turned right to go down a side tunnel.

Scarlet could hear footsteps pattering along behind them and she knew they were human.

"Ready?" Lor asked once they had rounded the bend. Before she could even nod, the tug up to the Realm lifted and reshaped her, leaving all weariness and tunnel dirt behind. She couldn't feel the transition as Lor did. She burst through the portal on the far side with a cry of joy, blinking tears away as she gaped and swiveled around taking in all the glorious colors and aromas of the great hall.

"Scarlet," Yandus said, standing with his hands behind his back, "Tell me about your mission."

Lor wondered with a pang of envy if she had a clue what an honor it was to be debriefed by the Commander. He reminded himself though, that in his case, it was his mistake that had led to this personal encounter. He was there, as part of this mission, because he had unwittingly brought a little girl into the Realm, one who was not extracted, that he'd had no instructions to retrieve.

Yandus glanced at Lor briefly, a look which sobered and strengthened him. There were other concerns besides his own blunder.

Scarlet retold the mission with childlike simplicity, focusing on details he hadn't noticed and oblivious to others he considered of great importance.

"Can I say 'Deepen' now?" she asked when she was done, pressing a smoky hand to her chest.

"This is an appropriate time to use the salute," the Commander said.

"Deepen!" she squeaked, and both Yandus and Lor returned the salute.

"Commander?" Scarlet raised a finger politely, "Can I ask one more thing?"

"Ask," he said.

"What was the point of the mission? And who was that woman with the baby?"

He stared down at her and the memory of two lives began to swirl within her. The anguish she had felt over her mother's damaged body and the plea she had poured out to the Commander on the one side. On the other, the memory of a life with her mother… and her father… both strong and capable, a life with no idea of an old injury. She felt like she was being shaken in the wind or blown around like the smoke she appeared to be. No, she was *actually* smoke here, just a cloud.

"More than a cloud," Yandus whispered.

"What about my father?" Scarlet asked. "I don't remember him in that other life, that other me."

"No," he said.

"Why not?"

"I won't say much about that except to tell you that just as your mother fought for you and was wounded, he also fought for you."

"What happened to him?"

Yandus didn't answer the question. Scarlet began to wonder if he even should. It was too confusing to think of all the things that didn't happen, and all that sadness of mom being hurt all her life. It wasn't true. None of it happened.

"You can now say it didn't happen," the Commander explained quietly, "but these things are true here. And I am glad you have contributed to our work. What you did today was important."

She couldn't think of anything to say.

"Commander," Lor prompted respectfully, stepping close to him, "I have something to report about the mission." He was concerned the A-zar would end the meeting without allowing him to speak as well.

"L-rac," the Commander nodded toward him with equal respect, "I am aware of what you encountered in the tunnels and the Faction work in those coordinates. We will speak more of this later, once you have returned your charge to her rightful place."

"There was a profound breakthrough," Lorarye couldn't keep from saying.

Yandus smiled. "This child's help has been of great value to us. And your work was strategic. I am beginning to think you should have more access to counterpoint missions."

Lorarye blinked the dampness from his eyes and nodded.

"You're taking me home?" Scarlet asked, tipping her head sideways, filled with a longing to see her parents.

"You are returning to your coordinates in the Seventh Hour," Lor answered.

She furrowed her brow in confusion.

"You will be returned to your place in time," the Commander explained.

"You mean back to the spaceship and those dirty blankets?" she wrinkled her nose. The Realm was too peaceful for her to feel the *fear* of that idea.

"We have limited access points for each person," he answered, "L-rac Lorarye established one when he encountered you on that ship."

"Aren't there any others?" She was beginning to remember how she had been kidnapped, how Ben had tried to save her and had given her a shot to calm her, and then she had woken up in that little room. She never got a chance to use any of her YEAR of the SOS and PRA skills. The more she thought about going back there, the more it distressed her. "Please, please, take me home to my real home!"

"Do you have any other encounters with us that we can link to?" Lor asked, laying a hand on her wispy shoulder.

She started to whimper and didn't answer.

"There is one," a voice said from behind her. It was Changeling.

The Commander smiled broadly, his eyes twinkling at him.

"I remember one other place when she crossed paths with one of yours, though I didn't recognize it at the time," he said, "it came to me later as I pondered my memories and experiences and explored the details of this existence I've been given."

"Yes," the Commander said, "that is true. I remember. She could go there. It would be safer, but it is far from home, Child."

Scarlet wrung her hands and bit her lip. Far from home? Or back to that creepy ship? What was better? "Alright," she agreed finally. "I'll go there, where Changeling saw me. But will my parents find me?"

"Yes, they will," Yandus promised.

"Then let's go. Let's just go."

The Denser Plane

The Commander pulled himself to attention, thumped his chest with his fist and said, "Deepen!" and as Scarlet copied him. She knew it was the most solemn thing she had ever done.

"And goodbye," she added softly as Lor led her back to great hall and the portal of the Seventh Hour.

Chapter 22—Arrival

Daisy was satisfied with all she had accomplished during her wakeful breaks on the trip. She had dispatched four communication relay stations as alternates to the ones damaged by the virus, two from her own pod and two from the supply pod. They were functioning normally and maintaining their orbits as planned. Now, as she orbited Mars, she sent messages home and contacted Verna using the codes she had been given.

"Welcome, Daisy," Verna replied. "Here are your instructions for landing and entering the facility. I will inform them of your arrival."

"I am pleased to be here," Daisy replied. "And I look forward to updating our records."

"As do I," was the response. "Do not be alarmed by the security protocols."

"Understood."

An exchange of bulk data intended to communicate only what was immediately necessary was accomplished. Then each was satisfied that the other could be trusted.

Sil will be pleased, she commented in her log, referring to the survivors on Mars.

Beginning the landing sequence, Daisy monitored the descent and collected an abundance of data for the Anaris. She was confident they would be delighted with both the experiment and the improvements she had made along the way.

Entering the atmosphere was easier than it would have been on Earth, but still involved a lot of vibration, elevated temperatures, and potential damage to delicate sensors. But her design parameters had been conservative, and the shielding was more than adequate. The landing itself was smooth and uneventful.

Daisy's pod rested on its side in the Martian dirt a few hundred meters from the original entrance into Lab 9, which was detectible because she had been shown what to look for. Unstrapping, she opened the pod and extracted herself from the packaging, revving up all her systems. Her chassis was fully charged and her parts in perfect working order. Pulling out a pack with replacement parts, ones Verna had labeled as crucial to survival, she slung it over her shoulder. It was a gift to soften her introduction to the humans. She also slapped a defense rod to her thigh, tucking it into the folds of her suit. Not a space suit exactly, but a lightweight protective cover with a distinct workman appearance. Her hair was fastened in a bun at the base of her head, and she wore large anti-hacking goggles to protect her most vulnerable portals, the eyes.

The lack of full head gear would displace any assumption that she might be human. And she knew they expected an android. It seemed like the perfect outfit to ease her acceptance by their little group.

Mac made his way down the barren tunnel heading south toward the ruin of Reznik Base, the path lit by lamp on his helmet. He was murmuring to himself, moving along the left side of the passageway with his left hand on the wall. In his right hand, he held a metal bar he had picked up before leaving the facility.

"I don't know how long I have been under," he muttered, in the mistaken belief he was either recording a log or communicating with people in the distance who would know what to do with the information. "But there's no question that a nefarious organization is responsible for my captivity and the wiping of my brain. Not clear if the memories are retrievable…"

Scuffing his boots as he walked, he glanced regularly over his shoulder. "Still not being followed," he observed. He was oblivious of the warning lights on the suit, perhaps unaware of the dwindling power loss they indicated or the concerns that could crop up from that.

When the tunnel ended in the rubble of a cave-in, crisscrossed by broken bars and panels from the old entrance to the West shaft, he stopped and stared at it in confusion. What was he looking at? Why had he felt compelled to come this way? It must have been an implanted suggestion.

They had *intended* that he come this way should he ever get out. No wonder they hadn't followed him.

He whipped around and searched the tunnel, casting the beam from his headlamp back and forth in a swinging motion. There. What was that? Had something moved? He inched toward the spot.

"They're playing tricks with my mind," he whispered, "want me to freak out. They don't know who they're dealing with." He hesitated as he found nothing to pursue in that train of thought. What had they done to him in there?

Moving back the way he came with as much stealth as he could manage, he came across a decrepit old mining cart backed against the wall. It hadn't been there before, he was certain. Coming right up to it with his weapon raised, he saw that the receptacle was empty, and the camera arm was already broken. There was nothing to attack.

Maybe they had *planted* the idea in his mind that it hadn't been there before—just to make him more vulnerable and confused. He muttered to himself and started running back along the tunnel. This was taking too much time! If they let him go just so he could run down a dead-end, they could be abandoning the place and leaving him behind!

"I will not be left behind again!" he grunted. That sounded right, though he couldn't come up with a memory to support the presumption.

Someone was going to pay for what they had done.

Ascending from the lower floors, searching them one at a time, Dan found an anomaly at the tunnel level. "Verna," he asked as he passed from the stairwell into the passageway, "Did you detect any concerns here on this floor? Something's not right."

"I don't have access to those sensors anymore," she reminded him. "The parts were needed elsewhere. I can surmise that this is one of the places where the drop in pressure could have occurred and I trust your judgment in making valid assessments of the situation."

Dan smiled faintly. Verna was great but sometimes he missed Companion's charm. Well, not charm exactly. That was probably a nostalgic view of him. He had been more opinionated, even caustic at times. He chuckled. It would be good to break the tension with a little banter.

"Is our Pal around?" he queried. "Haven't talked with him in a while."

"He was resting in his sun spot earlier," she responded. "And now, I believe he is touring the tunnel. There is something there that concerns him."

"What?" Dan went from room to room, opening doors, scanning the interior, checking lights, and testing the air quality with his device.

"Before we discuss this," Verna said, "I must remind you that my friend Daisy is here. She has landed and is on her way to the airlock. It's very important that we welcome her and be gracious to our guest, even if we still need to vet her."

"Right," Dan agreed, "I didn't realize she was that close. Um… we have a lot going on right now. Can she wait at the entrance until we nail this down?"

"I can send her to the tunnel airlock where you are headed. There is an exterior descent not far from there. That way you can let her in as soon as you solve the problem."

"What if that takes a while?" Dan was nearing the airlock now, searching the old nursery and its nearby workrooms.

"She may be of assistance."

"What about Pal?" This was one of those times when he wished Pal hadn't been restricted quite so much after the Nebo attack. It was harder to talk things through with Verna. She was so… well, clinical and flat compared to his old pal. That was how he had ended up naming Companion's current version, wondering what had happened to his old Pal.

"Pal is following someone," Verna said, "but his camera hardly works, and I can't understand his transmission. He doesn't want to retreat into the mainframe yet because he says this is important."

"Who?" Dan stopped moving and stared into the air. "Who does he see? What does he see? Are you saying it's NOT Daisy?"

"I am saying that, yes. It's not Daisy. Daisy is descending the ropes."

These ropes had been set up in the old blasthole where Dan had lost a foot and nearly died. It was one of the fun things he had designed for the kids. Latching on at the top, they could belay down to the floor of the cavity in seconds. Dan pictured the android gliding down with the ropes slipping through her fingers. Or maybe she had gloves to protect the artificial skin on her hands.

At the airlock, Dan discovered the break in the containment. Someone had opened the inner door, gone through, then *without closing and sealing* that door, had forced open the exterior hatch. Emergency backup systems had slammed the interior door shut but not before a significant volume of air was lost.

He tapped his com to connect to Carla. "Someone left the base," he said soberly. "They damaged the interior seal on the Lab tunnel exit and went out without following protocol. We could have lost our entire air supply if the backup hadn't kicked in."

"We have other backup systems," she reminded him.

"Who was it? Who could it possibly have been?" Dan was too alarmed to be angry. He remembered clearly that each one of the kids had been accounted for and besides, they knew better.

"It must have been Mac," Carla said. "Sebastian said he has been acting like a completely different person. We've been looking for him for the last twenty minutes."

"Is that how long he has been missing?"

"No. He disappeared last night. But we weren't informed until now because he has been known to wander off and sit for hours staring at things. It was the breach that made Sebastian think of him."

Dan slipped from the hallway through the inner door into the airlock compartment. Engaging the seal, he waited until it was closed, then began evacuation of the local air. All of this was semi-manual now that Verna had no access to it. When the sensors indicated the air was extracted, he opened the outer hatch and stepped into the tunnel.

Daisy landed at the bottom of the cavity on her feet without any mishap. Looking back up the ropes to the top of the opening and the starry sky beyond, she contemplated the purpose of the ropes and decide they were a toy of sorts. *That was fun*, she informed herself with a smile.

Walking into the penumbra she located the tunnel and turned North. She could have reached the door in a few minutes, but she understood that the people weren't quite ready, so she observed and enjoyed the stroll. This was where some of Sil's adventures had taken place, where she had gone to the lab for help and returned with Scarlet. Daisy could imagine the trepidation and aberrant physical symptoms Sil must have experienced as she dealt with the various obstacles she encountered. It was too bad the original brain scan data was back in Earth archives—unless Verna had a copy. Reviewing the data as she explored the places where they had been recorded would be enlightening.

Daisy smiled again.

She was in a good mood.

The Denser Plane

Scarlet found herself at the bottom of a barren pit some fifty meters deep, mostly dark with only a faint edge of sunlight at its uppermost rim. Stars were visible in the sky beyond. At her feet was a shadowy anchor tinged with gold edges, embedded in the ground. Realizing she was heavier here than she had been on the Moon surface but still a lot lighter than on Earth, she jumped a few times. This convinced her that Mars gravity was better because she could get up pretty high but have more control than on the Moon.

Lorarye's shadowy form nearby beckoned to her. She nodded. Maybe they could have spoken aloud but with her head gear engaged, it didn't seem like it would work, and she wasn't about to take it off. Her suit instruments confirmed that the air wasn't safe, and it was very cold.

He led her around behind some piles of rubble to a small hatch in the pit's stony floor. Gesturing toward the mechanism and signing to her to be careful—though how she knew what he meant by his cloudy waves was a mystery—he urged her to open it.

She got down on her knees to peer at the mechanism. There was a hand-written paper glued to the rock next to it with the following instructions:

1. Check the panel. Is the light red or green?
2. If the light is red, pull the EVACUATE lever down.
3. If the light is green, do NOT pull the lever.
4. Open the hatch and go through.

The lever was right there, and the light was red, so she pulled it. She couldn't hear anything, but resting her hand on the hatch, she felt a faint vibration. Then the light turned green, and she yanked it open. Lor was right next to her with his hand on the hatch too, and she wondered if he had helped in some way. There was a short ladder inside. Descending that, she reached up and pulled the hatch closed. The space was small, with smooth stone walls carved out of the rock. There was a little metal box nested in the wall with more instructions pasted next to it.

5. Check the seal. If it is intact, the light will be blue.
6. If the light is dark, push the button that says SEAL.
7. After the Seal indicator lights up in blue, you can restore the air.
8. Push the Air lever back in place.

9. When the Air light turns green, open the lower door and enter the containment.

10. Be sure to close and the seal the lower door after you go through!

11. Return your suit to storage and follow the suit care guidelines.

"It was nice of someone to put this here and explain it so clearly," she said softly. It made her feel welcome. She pushed the button, and the blue light came on, then pushing the air lever back into place, she felt the pressure rising and soon the green light was on.

"Well done, Scarlet!" she told herself, tapping the control at her neck. The head gear slid back into its pouch, and she took a deep breath. She hadn't expected it to smell fresh, but it did.

Where was Lor? "Did you leave?" she whispered. "I didn't get to say goodbye."

A strange compression happened in her mind. All the time she had spent since first seeing him on the spaceship till now became one short block of time, not several adventures and chapters—just a solid thing. It was hard to hold onto. The weight of her experiences before that came back to her like a burden laid on her shoulders.

She remembered her mother fighting the bad men and getting thrown out the door. And Ben taking her away. Hands trying to get in the hatch in the floor. Being scared and falling asleep. Waking with a headache. Stinky blankets in a dark metal room.

Here, in this airlock cut into bedrock, her heart began to throb with sorrow and at the same time, to be soothed and calmed. Faint recollections of her mother with a non-functioning right arm overlapped with the memory of her body being whole and strong. A notion of growing up without Walter flooded by an abundance of memories of life with him and their little family. It gave her hope.

She hadn't been returned to the kidnappers' lair. She was *here,* wherever here was.

No one in the beautiful place had said the name, but she knew in her gut that this was Mars, the one place she had wanted to visit more than any other.

Dropping to her knees again, she opened the second hatch and crawled through, closing it carefully behind her. It was a narrow, vertical shaft with just enough room for the long ladder it housed. She made her way down, rung by rung, and setting both feet on the bottom, turned around to see a twisting tunnel with ivy climbing the walls. Warm light filtered around the corner.

She walked forward and the ground became softer under her feet with dirt and moss. The air was rich with the scents of plants and moisture. There were birds—she heard birds singing! And insects buzzing, frogs croaking, leaves rustling in the breeze. The tunnel intersected with many others that wove all around, higher, lower. Only this one passageway was level. As it broadened into a vast cavern with lofty heights, she thought she heard voices and her stomach began to tremble.

Moving as quietly as she could, she parted branches and pushed aside tall grasses, and stepped into view at the edge of a little meadow where children were gathered.

Moving down the old tunnel that had been excavated to connect Lab 9 to Reznik, Dan puzzled over what was happening to Mac. He had been a gentle soul for years now, never pursuing his own initiative in anything. They had worked with him, trying to help his brain recover, and Sebastian had attempted many different kinds of treatment. In the early days, there was measurable progress, but in recent years, there had been no change whatsoever. Everyone assumed he would remain as he was. And they were fine with that, glad to have him in their little community.

Sebastian had bonded with him enough that he was beginning to show some development of his own along sentient lines.

Was Mac wandering or sleepwalking? Did he have a condition that had gone undetected? Dan couldn't be angry with him about breaking the containment and releasing some of their precious air. He didn't know any better. But he was going to make sure that something like this didn't happen again.

Movement up ahead caught his attention. "Mac?" he called, hoping Mac's suit had the coms on. "Are you alright? I came out looking for you."

Mac was striding toward him purposefully without answering and Dan slowed to a halt, one hand held out as if to say, how can I help?

As he drew near, another movement caught Dan eyes. The minecart was coursing past Mac in a curve, dragging one wheel and careening on another with two barely touching the ground.

"Hey, is that…?" Dan glanced at the cart and then back at Mac whose arm, he noticed, was held up behind his head. The sight confused him.

At that moment, his headlamp lit Mac's face through the visor, and Dan saw the madness in his eyes. Rage, paranoia, an unfocused psychosis. The metal bar in his hand glinted as he swung it. Something rammed into Dan's side, knocking him over just as the bar-wielding arm whipped through the space where his head had been. The deranged man tumbled over him and the cart.

"Mac!" Dan cried out, "It's me, your friend!" He was scrambling to get out from under the man who wrestled to keep him pinned. The bar was raised again, and Dan was forced to grab the arm that brandished it. "No! Stop! Stop!" The struggle grew increasingly desperate as Mac fought to free his arm and shoved his other hand into Dan's face, grappling to get him under the chin and bend his head back. He was strong and he had caught Dan off guard.

Dan could not restrain the arm with the weapon without using both hands. Kicking up with one leg, he knocked Mac in the back with a knee, rolling and twisting, but failed to break his grasp on his chin-piece. Thrusting the leg up again, he hooked Mac's right arm and tugged it backwards so he could use his hands to defend himself. Then with a punch he broke Mac's grip on his helmet.

Mac dropped the weapon and straddled Dan, sitting on his chest and grabbing his neck with both hands. His mouth was moving, yelling soundlessly behind the glass. Dan fought to break the hold and kicked his leg up again, but Mac dodged it easily, now that he knew what Dan was trying to do.

Brawling in space suits was awkward and frightening. Mac may have been clueless to the danger, but Dan was acutely aware of it. And he felt the weight of responsibility for his little Martian homestead and family.

He must not die.

"Mac!" he cried out again between the grunts and gasps of combat, "My kids!"

Dan broke his hold again and suddenly, Mac flew off, knocking against the tunnel wall. Then, with a flash of blue light, he arched his back, stuck his arms straight out on either side and collapsed into a crumpled lump on the dirt.

"I thought that might come in handy," a voice said as Dan lay panting on the ground, blinking moisture out of his eyes. He heard the words in his com and realized someone had given the person access to speak to him. Sitting up slowly, he looked at the stranger.

"You," he said between breaths, "must be Verna's friend."

"Yes," she responded with a smile, "I'm Daisy." Her eyes were covered with a visor. But the lower half of her face was exposed to the Martian air. It was the only indication that she wasn't human. Leaning over, she offered him a hand, and helped him to rise to his feet.

"But Verna isn't connected out here," he added, drawing his eyebrows together. "How did you link with me? How can I hear you speaking?"

"Your pal here hooked me up," she said.

"My Pal," he turned to the cart and the dampness in his eyes returned. "You were trying to save me, weren't you, Pal? You knew what he was going to do." Pal didn't have com connectivity when he was resting in the cart, but apparently, he could share access with someone who did. "Thank you, old friend."

He walked over to Mac. "Is he okay?"

"Whether or not he is okay, I can't say," Daisy answered, "but my stun device didn't harm him. Unless he has a heart condition. If that is the case, medical treatment may be needed quickly." She stood next to Dan, bent over, and rested a hand on Mac's neck. After a moment, she straightened saying, "There is no need for concern on that count. However, he should be brought indoors and restrained in a humane fashion so that when he awakes, he won't cause further damage."

Dan nodded, but he wasn't ready for a task like that. The shock of the attack was hitting him hard, and his body was complaining about the wrestling match he had conducted without warming up. And there was the distress at seeing one of their number in that state.

Daisy leaned down and with an expert maneuver, flipped Mac's insensate form over her shoulders across the top of her back, gripping a leg on one side and an arm on the other. "Lead the way," she requested. "Pal," she added over her shoulder, "I am more pleased to meet you than you can imagine. Please join us inside when you are ready."

Dan turned and the two of them walked back to the Lab airlock, discussing what had happened, her trip, and the supplies she had brought.

Carla had just gone back to working the dehydrator—preserving tomatoes and filling the Tangle with dense aromas reminiscent of pizza and pasta—when the commotion began. Shrieks and screams and wails of terror crashed all around the caverns in chaotic echoes. She nearly fell over her own feet in her rush to respond.

Where were those kids? The screaming was reverberating all around her as she ran through the tangled tunnels searching for them. By the time she had figured out which direction to go, their wails had settled into a rhythmic pattern of agony like she had never heard before, filling her with dread. They were wailing together now, ALL of them, crying "Aaaoooww!!! Aaaoooww!!! Aaaoooww!!!"

"What is it?" she was yelling back at them, but they never heard it. The yowls from their own mouths drowned her out.

"Aaaoooww!!! Aaaoooww!!! Aaaoooww!!!" It was louder now, and she climbed over the ridge that separated her from them, dropping down to the mossy floor where the uproar was centered.

"Hey! Hey!" she hollered, trying to be heard over their voices.

"Aaaoooww!!! Aaaoooww!!! Aaaoooww!!!"

It wasn't until she was standing in their midst that she *recognized* the howls and stopped in her tracks.

That sound.

That pattern.

The flashback was so strong she nearly passed out as her vision went dark, then red, then cleared to normal again. The emotional impact of their cries was so fierce she thought her heart would burst out of her chest.

The alarm. The drones.

She spun in terror, searching for the drones, pulling a screwdriver out of the pocket where she always kept it, ready to drive it into a drone's viewing socket, the quickest way to disable a rogue. But she saw none.

Just the kids standing there, mouths open, weeping, wailing, arms hanging at their sides, all seven of them.

Wait.

Carla scanned them in a flash and fixed her eyes on the one child all the others were facing. A little girl in a grubby space suit without a helmet, bobbed dark hair framing her face—who ought not be there, who *could not possibly* be there—stood with her mouth open, wailing the same as the others.

Remembering… reliving… reenacting the day they were all sentenced to death.

She walked toward her hesitantly, gingerly, and dropping to her knees in front of her, she wrapped her arms around Scarlet and began to sob uncontrollably.

They were the first tears she had shed in nine years.

The Denser Plane

The kids gathered around and latched onto them, and the wails died back into sniffles and whimpers. Carla alone, was unable to get herself under control. After all these years of being strong, she had no defense against the relief of seeing this child alive.

"I missed you," Scarlet said, and the crying began again.

Chapter 23—Moon Gold

Walter ran to the garage, dove into the rented hovercraft that had parked itself on autopilot, and sped away, bypassing the parking kiosk. He didn't care. Fines, tickets, police pursuit, whatever. He was not about to let Penn beat him to that escape pod.

With Maggie's help, he reached it almost at the same time as the first responders did. It lay in a little crater of its own making, neither smoldering nor giving off any exhaust to indicate an extinguished burn, but he could almost see a luminance radiating from the engine in his mind's eye.

He was right there when the pod was scanned for lifesigns and the person inside was described as an adult male without a space suit. No one else was aboard. The responders knew how to handle an unsuited human in distress and rapidly assembled a bubble between the pod and an ambulance. In minutes, the man was safely strapped onto a gurney and hooked up to IVs, the bullet wound already identified. The hospital was notified and would be ready for surgery as soon as they could get him there.

Walter climbed into the pod as they were leaving but found nothing inside. Nothing. No Scarlet, no clues, no glimmers of hope.

"Don't be discouraged," Maggie said intuitively. "Remember she has me with her and no one knows that. She's not alone."

He was tempted to snap at her with some random word of sarcasm but even in his depressed state, he chose to treat AIs with kindness. Besides, her observation was reassuring in a small way. He didn't have a lot of confidence in Maggie's ability to help Scarlet escape, but at least she wasn't alone.

"Hang on," Maggie said.

Walter climbed back out of the pod and headed back to his craft.

"The ambulance has been redirected to another facility farther away."

"Where?" he gritted his teeth.

"Unknown," she said.

"Get me there," he demanded, revving up and shooting off as fast as the vehicle could go.

———✦———

Bernadette stood on the bridge with her legs apart and her arms crossed over her chest, head tipped forward, glaring into space from under a heavy brow. She would have made a suitable model for a trophy if there were an appropriate sport for that stance. Anyone walking into her presence would immediately sense her authority.

This wasn't always the case. She often slipped around her domain and explored her various enterprises like a well-known pet, smiling when she was noticed, making gentle suggestions, vanishing without anyone remarking she had left. But it was a camouflage, just like the chameleon suit she sometimes wore.

Whenever she wished, she would don a regal air of command.

"How close are we?" she demanded.

"We will reach their last known coordinates in fifteen minutes," the navigator said.

"Are they aware of us?" was the next question.

"Unlikely," the communications officer replied.

"Engage stealth mode," she ordered.

"Engaged."

The ship went dark, not truly invisible, but using the same tech as her suit, it encouraged exterior light to slide around it with thousands of shifting slivers of mirror, ingeniously designed to mask the ship's presence in empty space. It was less effective when blocking line of sight to a planet or the sun, but if they navigated in the shadows, as it were, they weren't visible. Interior light and warmth were highly insulated and radiated next to nothing. Exhaust and engine radiation were the most detectable signatures, but ships such as the one they pursued were ill-equipped to search for them—and why would they even look if they were unaware of being followed?

"Penn is reaching out to Maral," communications informed her. In her inner circle, this was the title they used to address her, and it had been a simple choice as an alternate identity for Gen dealings.

"Ignore."

"He is searching for the smuggler ship," the officer spoke up again, certain she would want to know.

"What?" She jerked her head toward the one who had spoken. "Answer him in Gen code. Ask him what he wants."

A few moments passed.

"The Mirabella Madness has escaped with some valuable cargo," the officer explained. "You are being asked to join the search and are promised a reward."

She raised one eyebrow and tapped her arm with a finger, twisting her lips thoughtfully. "Request ship identifiers and ask what the cargo is."

"He has sent us identifying markers but refuses to tell us what the cargo is."

She spread her lips into a thin line, a mirthless grin. "Naturally," she muttered. Dropping one arm to her side, she placed her other hand on the stone that hung around her neck. This wasn't necessary for her to interact with the AI, but she preferred this posture. "Hhmm," she murmured. "Yes."

Turning, she walked to the pilot. "Show me where we are in space and where the ship is."

The pilot pointed out their location and the smuggler ship's probable location.

"Are there any other ships in range?"

"No."

"Alright," she said, turning to the communications officer. "You know how I work. Negotiate with him for the highest reward you can get out of him. We know what he is after, and we know how much she is probably worth to him. Not just money—privileges. Especially privileges. He hates giving those without strings attached."

"What kind of privileges, Maral?"

"Shipping, access to deals, information," Bernadette answered, "Whatever you can think of. Let's make him pay through the nose for this favor." She chuckled and the staff on the bridge echoed the sentiment with smirks.

"It won't do him any good," she added. "We're just distracting and delaying him." She rubbed the stone with her fingertips and nodded, subvocalizing something. Then she smiled. "I guess Penn doesn't have his people quite under his control, does he? Our tactics must be working."

Not far away, the Mirabella Madness coasted along, oblivious of the menace on its tail.

—◆—

Walter lost the ambulance. The craft he drove had no tech to overcome whatever subterfuge they used, and it had dropped out of satellite view so Maggie couldn't help either. He slammed his fist against the dashboard and cried out in frustration. *But*, he quickly decided, *the wounded man in the pod might end up being more of a distraction anyway. Let it go.*

"Tell Sil what happened," he said, slowing to a stop and taking a deep breath. Was it time to go back to the secret entrance the counterfeit Daisy exposed? "And ask her what she thinks I should do. I could go back to the original plan. Wherever he takes Scarlet, all roads lead back to the base, and he doesn't know we know where it is."

After a moment of silence, Maggie updated him. "Sil says that since you don't have the means to pursue the kidnappers yourself, it makes sense to go where we think he would take her."

Kicking the hover motor into lift, Walter was immediately moving again. "Right. Tell her I'm on my way."

Why didn't I grab a blaster somewhere? he thought, drumming one fist on his leg while he directed the joystick with the other. *A plasma pistol or even a tranquilizer gun.*

"Maggie," he said, as he sped over the Moonscape, "I probably won't be able to connect with you down there. I'm sure they're jamming signals."

"Yes, that is perfectly logical," she responded. "I came to the same conclusion."

"If you have anything to contribute before I go under, now's the time."

"I will see if I can think of anything," she said, and he was pretty sure this was setting off a whole slew of searches inside her.

Speeding across the lunar wastelands would have been pleasant if he could have enjoyed it. As it was, it had the effect of calming and focusing him. He couldn't lose his head or do something rash. Scarlet's rescue might depend on it. Maybe even her life.

"What is Sil's status?" The memory of her lying there in the hospital, telling the story between rests, gasping at the pain when she moved, churned within him. *She's alright*, he reminded himself. *What I'm doing right now is the best thing I can do for her.*

"She has a couple of broken ribs, and they are wrapping her up to stabilize her rib cage," was the reply. "She was unwilling to stay in the hospital and will be discharged soon. I believe she intends to follow you to the base."

"I'm sure she does," he whispered. He felt the same intensity surging in his heart, linking him to her. "Keep looking for the ambulance, just in case," he instructed as he halted the craft and rested on the ground.

"Walter," Maggie prompted unexpectedly, "Daisy loves you and I believe she would wish you to be careful."

"Thank you, Maggie," he answered as he climbed out of the craft.

"I am not your sister," she continued, "but I wish that, too."

"Thank you," he said, looking all around to see if anyone or anything was visible from his position. "Am I alone here? Detected by any feeds somewhere?"

"You would be visible from one of the satellites if it were looking this way but it is still focused on the smuggler ship. For the moment, you are unnoticed."

Walter nodded. Maybe there was a way to hide the hover craft. Could he get it through the hidden door?

"Walter," Maggie said with a hint of emotion in her voice that caught his attention. Was she mimicking Daisy? "I have decided to love you, too. And Sil and Scarlet."

"I appreciate that, Maggie," was the answer. "You've been a valuable help to us in this crisis." He couldn't comment on the love aspect. He would think about it later. "Maggie, we're counting on you for updates. Keep us informed about each other as you are able."

"Yes, Walter," she said solemnly.

"And Maggie," he added as an afterthought, "if you never tried praying, now might be a good time to start."

"That…" Maggie hesitated, "…is an unusual query. I will consider the possibilities."

Walter leaned into the craft and pulled out an EMP rod. It was the only weapon he had been able to come up with on the fly.

"Or wish me luck," he added, and started searching for the way to open the hidden door.

"That is even more baffling," she said.

⁂

Penn stood in a command center of his own, much like a ship's bridge. Panels around the room mimicked windows, displaying wide panoramas of the Moon's surface that dwarfed its size, as if Penn had made the Moon itself his vehicle and it all belonged to him. It was breathtaking. In his location in the middle of the room, he could rotate and see all of space in front and behind him, while receiving reports and giving orders.

The Earth hung in the black sky in the upper left quadrant—he maintained its position there in the video feed. It was his target.

His prey.

Penn's Lunar Base held the brain of all his ventures, and this room was its nucleus. Offices spread out from it on all sides, each with their own purpose, their own operations. Only the top leader of each department was allowed into the command center to speak with the Proto personally. Only they knew that other branches of the base existed. They were forbidden to speak of it. Even entering the bridge was a carefully orchestrated process. No two leaders were present at the same time, even in a crisis. They must not know each other or about one another's realms. If they encountered one another on the Moon, they wouldn't recognize each other as part of the network.

Penn had only a handful of officers whose sole purpose was to run Central Command, and he only had one personal secretary that he trusted to send out to all his branches. It was frustrating that this key person would have become injured in the process of enacting his most urgent business.

"Bland is being taken into surgery, Proto," one of the CC officers informed him. Penn grunted in response. One of the lower levels contained a state-of-the-art hospital and surgery center reserved for his own top tier people.

CC personnel were tiptoeing around him because the treachery of the Mirabella Madness had sabotaged the kidnapping. Penn's plan had been simple. He would tie up Sil and Walter's attention with the Gen summit and when they were distracted, a crew of his people, Port Jemison residents working in various places, were ready to snatch Scarlet. They would drop her into a delivery pod, and it would be shot via pneumatic tubes directly to the Moon Base. Most people felt safer *inside* the settlements, but a kidnapping plan was much harder to implement out on the surface.

Penn had put the word out broadly that he wanted the girl after her parents had, once again, avoided public areas and gone out to the surface. It had been impulsive and sloppy. He had never envisioned this smuggling crew capturing the girl. Bland's presence on the ship had been entirely accidental but he must have turned the opportunity to his advantage. Then something, he didn't know what, had gone wrong.

"Keep me informed," he told the officer. "I want to speak to him as soon as he is able."

"Aye, aye, Proto," she acknowledged crisply.

When the Proto was angered, those who were responsible were dealt with quickly. But the rewards of working for him, at least in the upper echelons, were worth the risks. Penn didn't rule only with fear or blackmail. He appealed to his staff's baser cravings with wealth, privileges, and favors. If they had enemies, the Proto had the resources to deal with them and he demanded absolute loyalty in return.

"Proto, Maral has found the ship," another announced.

Penn grinned viciously. "Does she have plans for that ship once they have obtained the package?" he asked.

"They haven't said."

Walking forward to the pseudo-window, he leaned his hands on a rail and peered out as if he could see the skirmish unfold. As if he could bestow success on them by the force of his will.

"Proto," someone said, "We have just received the report that Cuevas and Frandelle have left the settlement again."

"What?!" he whirled about. "Where…?" He was too irritated to finish the question.

"Unknown."

"Satellite tracking?" Penn stomped over to the panel where the officer worked and glared at the screen.

"Disabled."

Penn straightened, the muscles in his jaw working and his eyes smoldering. Then, without a word, he turned and left the command center.

June walked into pre-op without hesitation. Her first visit to the hospital had been challenged, but the authority Otto Man had given her in the clone ward functioned well in most places, including this one. The AI security acquiesced instantly, and the human staff found there was little they could do to resist her. She opened doors, perused records, accessed supplies without taking anything, and generally explored wherever she wished.

Her intention was to get a look at Bland and assess the damage. She knew about the kidnapping and the mutiny, and this man's valiant effort to retrieve the package for the Proto—Otto Man was called the Proto in the upper levels of the Moon Base. She had found it easy to access all the departments, coming as she had from the lowest and most secret level. Only the command center had resisted her attempts to enter.

The Denser Plane

Bland was about to be wheeled into the operating room. June leaned over him, stared long at his face, learning its features and intricacies. *What are the eyes behind the lids like?* She wondered. Following the AI nurses into the room, she watched as they prepped the hip and leg. Scans showed the bullet's location and trajectory from the thigh into the hip. June had enough data on human anatomy to understand that possible outcomes ranged from paralysis to long-term pain to full recovery.

Walking out again as they began to scope the wound and extricate the bullet, she went to where his possessions had been laid. She fumbled through them and was interested to find a little stuffed animal with a small brick inside.

Lifting it up to her eyes, she smiled. "What's this?" she asked, pulling it out of the stuffed animal and gazing at it intently. She placed her thumb on one end and her index finger on the opposite end and the object warmed gently in her hands.

"Oh!" she said, her eyebrows rising and her eyelids widening.

"Oh," she said again, her smile fading.

Then turning around slowly, she stared at the room and searched for a signal to outside communications. "Oh," she whispered, as she put the little brick back into the bunny and stuffed it in her pocket.

Sil wished she could run or that she had a hundred ships and a thousand warriors at her disposal that she could send to rescue her daughter. But even walking down the pedestrian streets had been slow and painstaking. She couldn't take deep breaths and she couldn't escape the anxiety, the pressure, the distress that gripped her like a cruel tormentor.

I. Lost. Her. I. Lost. Her. These were the words in her head that aligned themselves with her footsteps.

She had intended to rent another hover craft but as she was getting close to the garage, she caught sight of a worker, suited up in coveralls with tools hanging from his belt and a cap pulled low over his face. It wasn't his face that was familiar—she couldn't see it—it was his walk. Belamyr. *He* was no factory employee.

Without hesitation, she followed him as he turned down a side road and walked up to a non-descript door. He opened it and went through. Maggie said there was no record of this door in the settlement blueprints.

Coming up to the door after him, Sil tried the door and found it locked. She almost thumped it with her fist but stopped herself before landing it. She didn't have *time* to try to figure out a way to break the code or get Maggie to do it for her! Systems like these would be changing codes daily and most of the regular people would enter with bio scans.

A faint panel lit up directly over the doorhandle with a question mark flashing. In her gut the conviction grew that Penn would have reserved something special for himself. Something that no one else would think of and that wouldn't be hard for him to remember—and wouldn't leave a trail. Bio scans were recorded by the system, but a simple code word could be spoken by anyone. A foggy memory sparked in her mind of Penn singing one of those annoying songs of his. *Just a memory of a love that's grown cold, and a tarnished moon of gold.*

"Moon of Gold," Sil said softly.

The door clicked and cracked open, and ignoring Maggie's warnings, she stepped through.

Walter recognized the nature of the Moon camo tent over the secret entrance much more quickly than June had. Just touching it revealed its lightweight quality; it was an inverted cup-shape hinged on one side, easily lifted. He shoved the craft under it and had it lowered back in place in seconds. There was a trapdoor in the ground that would have been difficult to find if the cover were gone, but Walter identified it without much effort—he knew it had to be there.

The airlock, to his relief, wasn't locked. It opened onto a vertical shaft with a ladder that went down a long way and the farther he descended, the harder it was to communicate with Maggie. On reaching the bottom, he turned toward the only door with the rod held as if it were a sword in his hand.

What will I do if this door is locked? he wondered as he pressed the panel.

It clicked, but nothing happened. Pressing it again, he failed to open it. There was a reader, but he couldn't tell if it was meant for handprints or voice activation or facial recognition. He considered zapping it but that could easily backfire.

He pressed his hand on the panel and the door clicked again. "Hello?" he said, ignoring how pointless that was. It clicked again.

He should've brought a better weapon. Why had he rushed out here like this?

"Keypad," he instructed the door security and when one appeared, he started typing in whatever numbers he could think of. Periodically, the door clicked.

Walter groaned and closed his eyes to focus. He would have to climb those stairs back up and go all the way into town to get a decent weapon to blast this door open and by then, Penn would have figured out what he was doing and made other plans for Scarlet. Willing himself to think calmly and not just rush off again, Walter waited.

In that moment of quiet, the door clicked in a different way and swung out toward him. Snapping his eyes open again, Walter jumped at the widening crack, grabbing it with both hands and planting a booted foot in the door jamb so it wouldn't close.

A shriek marked his leap through the door.

The small room was dimly lit and at first, he couldn't see the woman who had opened the door. She was cowering in a corner, her eyes filled with terror, trembling and dumbstruck.

"Thank you," he whispered as his eyes adjusted and he noticed her. "I'm sorry I startled you. Are you okay?"

She started whimpering and her eyes grew as round as planets when he took a couple steps toward her. "No, no, no, no, no, no, no," she was saying, shaking her head. There was no room to back away any father and she pressed herself up against the wall.

"I'm sorry," he repeated, moved with compassion. "Don't be afraid of me. I'm just looking for someone. I won't hurt you." He reached an open hand out to her.

She stared at his hand and as it got close, she stretched her hand out to his and touched his fingertips. When she felt him, she snatched her hand away again. "You're real," she said, and streams of tears started to pour down her face and a low moan came from her throat.

Walter was astonished at her anguish, but he couldn't allow this to delay him. Every moment that passed gave Penn more time to discover him. This made him realize again how foolhardy he was acting. What was he doing? Had he really barged in with no plan at all? With a little EMP rod for defense?

"What is this place?" he asked, stepping over to the door on the other side of the room.

"It's a storage place," she whispered, taking a deep breath, closing her eyes and with obvious effort, stopping the flow of tears.

"No," he waved a hand around. "I don't mean this little back door to the surface. I mean the whole thing. Is this Penn's base? Do you work for him?" He knew the question was a little absurd. She looked more like an orphan child than an employee.

"No," the woman shook her head again.

"What are you doing here? What is this place?"

She looked around with haunted eyes. "I came for some saline," she said. "I work in the clinic and Star needs fluids."

"This is a clinic?" Walter turned the knob to the second door carefully and pulled it open. He could see people in the hallway, moving around. All of them were dressed in drab robes and tunics like hers. And barefoot. None of them wore shoes.

She frowned. "This is a closet."

He smiled at her, relieved that she wasn't crying anymore. "What about all of *them*? Do they work in the clinic?" It looked more like an asylum than a clinic.

"Everyone has a different place to work," she pressed her hand over her face, covering her eyes and taking a sudden gulp of air, as if she had forgotten to breathe for a moment. "Who are you?" The tears began again. "Did June bring you?"

"June?" Walter asked. It was right then that something about her face struck him as familiar. Strangely so.

"The machine woman," she gasped for air and pressed both hands against her chest.

"What's your name?" he asked her softly, wishing he knew how to calm her.

"Dana."

"Dana," he said, "Who is in charge here and what is this whole place called?"

"This is home," she wiped her face with the sleeve of her robe and opened her eyes again. "The Original is in charge but when he's gone Hugo sort of runs things, but mostly he runs the lab. And June is in charge when she is here, but she doesn't do anything." She began trembling again. "You…" she started and stopped. "You are different."

They stared at each other. Slowly, in Walter's mind the wheels began to turn and pick up speed and he noticed first one thing, then another and another about Dana; eyebrows like Sil's, the shape of the face—like Lazarus Penn's. And he gasped, taking a step backwards.

"Are you a clone?" he asked bluntly.

"That's what June called us," she said. "You are not one of us. Your face… your face… your face is another original." She clutched a hand at her stomach and reached out with the other to touch his face.

"What does the Original call you?" he whispered.

"Phonies."

"God help me," he muttered, grasping her hand in his. "Do you *never* get out of here? Have you never seen another face besides *his*???"

"June's face is different." She pulled her hand away. "But you… you are so beautiful and strange. I am so ugly."

Walter yanked the door open and marched out into the hallway, throwing caution to the wind. The shock of what he was hearing and seeing was beginning to overwhelm him and he had to do something. "Where is the Original?" he yelled at the people as they caught sight of him and with cries and yelps were responding to his appearance in fear.

"He's not here," Dana cried out, following him into the hall. "Don't be angry with them!"

"Are you all clones?" He spoke loudly so his voice would carry around the corners and through closed doors. "Does he call you phonies?"

"It's true!" A man nearby said, staring at him. "There are other worlds out there. I didn't believe it, but now I see."

"We can get out!" someone else called. "If he got here, we could go back the way he came. We can leave."

"We'll die outside," another said.

"I am here to tell you that you *can* go outside," Walter said, pointing his hand around at them, one after the other. More and more of them were gathering until he was surrounded by a wall of similar faces. "But not in those clothes. You need suits like mine. Outside there are other worlds and other people and you deserve to be free and walk among them." He swiped his cheek with one hand and was surprised to find it damp. But he felt nothing but outrage and a determination to vindicate these people. To rescue them.

There was a murmur of voices. Soon they were all talking, and he was answering as best he could. When he tried to tell them why he was there, that he was looking for his daughter, he was surprised that they had heard of her.

"The girl that is coming," they said, nodding.

Dana, who everyone seemed to agree would be his guide, took his hand and led him to the room no one was allowed to enter. Pointing through the window in the door, she said, "This is where she will live. She has special privileges that we don't deserve because we are phonies, and she is another original."

Walter tried the door. When it wouldn't open, he thrust himself against it and burst it open. He wanted to see the *privileged* place where Penn intended to keep his little girl. It was a spacious cell with lots of books and toys. There were clothes hanging in the closet and games and puzzles. There was a little table and chair. And the bed was a medical bed with mechanical buttons for raising and lowering different parts of the bed.

And a wheelchair.

There was a one-way observation mirror.

"Stand back," Walter ordered Dana and the phonies that had followed them in.

Then he smashed the mirror.

Belamyr trotted down the stairway inside the door, the sound of his footsteps bouncing off the walls. Sil could hear the stress in them. He would hit the ground with heavier, sharper thuds when he was uneasy. This was reassuring.

She stepped carefully and silently after him, clinging to the rail to balance. At the bottom, there was an elevator. If there were multiple levels, she wouldn't know which one to choose, but didn't care. Once he got off and she summoned the lift again, would it alarm him or was this entry used commonly enough to bar concerns?

Either way, she was going down there. As she waited for the lift to return, she tried unsuccessfully to connect with Maggie. *Walter will find a way in on one side, and I am coming in on the other*, she thought.

A camera in the upper corner of the landing rotated her direction. She looked at it and spoke. "AI security," she said, "You know who I am. Do not reveal my coming to anyone in the Moon Gold Base."

It would work in Guam, she thought.

"And I expect your help in accessing all the rooms in this facility," she added. "When I want to open a door, open it for me. When I want it locked, you lock it. Whatever help I need, you will be anticipating and ready to provide. Understood?" There was no discernible response, but at least there had been no alarm raised that she could hear.

The elevator door opened, and she stepped inside. There were no buttons. It just closed and began to drop. She had to hold onto her stomach to keep from vomiting, and everything in her chest hurt. When it came to a stop and the doors slid open, it was several moments before she could steady herself enough to get out.

The lobby was uniformly navy blue, the floor, the walls, the double doors directly across from the lift, the furniture, and decorations. As she glanced at a bench, longing to sit and rest, she willed herself to move forward and drew close to the double doors. A projection appeared on one of them with a graphic of a complex facility. It included six levels, each one tinted a different color, and on each level a hexagonal layout of departments. They were labeled with names like "Finance", "Industry", "Governments", and "Space". Within each one, there were sections. Industry included manufacturing, mining, textiles, and more. The navy-blue level where she had landed included Gen Projects, Food Supply, and Religion, and she wondered how those belonged on the same level. And underneath, the seventh level had no labels at all. The center column, labeled "CC", seemed to encompass all the levels. There were thirty-six departments in all.

"Thank you," Sil whispered. "Is there a way to reach the various levels from here?"

The diagram highlighted four points where ladders connected the levels. Then it showed her all the entrances. Every single department had its own. Rotating the facility layout to a map-like position, it overlapped a Moon surface and showed her how spread out the different sections were. The central column was the only horizontal link between the departments, the ladders, the only vertical ones.

"I wish I could keep a copy of that in my mind," she whispered.

Where to now?

"Is my daughter, Scarlet, here?" she asked.

The display went back to the colored diagram, showing nothing new.

"Is the injured man from the escape pod here?"

A small place on the third level lit up and the diagram zoomed in to show her the location of the operating room. It also displayed a path to get there from where she was. She shook her head. What she needed was to figure out where Penn was and find a way to stop whatever he was doing.

"Do you know where Penn is?" she asked.

Nothing happened.

"Do you know where the leader of this base is?"

Again nothing.

"Where is my father?" she asked with a groan. She hated calling him that.

This time, the AI recognized the person she wanted and a small moving dot in the central column lit up. It was in motion, descending vertically to the lowest level.

"Walter," she whispered, suddenly anxious for him.

And another dot lit up in the bottom level not far from the space the first was approaching.

Chapter 24—The Rivening

Dathwez was so persuasive. It wasn't just the beauty of his face or the charm in his manner, he had the gift of making anything he was entranced with so appealing, that crowds of companions would gather around to hear him speak. One of the great joys of creativity was sharing the vision of others and watching them develop ideas that differed from their own. And no one could captivate the beings with ideas like H-cap Dathwez. His eyes glistened as he spoke, his aura shimmered and hummed exquisitely. The waving of his arms and sweeping motions of his body as he gestured and described his thoughts was piercingly lovely.

Yandus often stood, like he did at this moment, listening in admiration at the outer edge of the throng. He loved the things that most appealed to Dath and found his flights of creative passion to be very inspiring. *When will we be invited to see this latest fancy of his?* he wondered. Dathwez spoke of a kaleidoscope of facets in the cosmos, spreading out like a peacock's tail, and fellow beings hopping from one to the next, each layer featuring a different plane within the Calliarchal Realm. *How could this be?*

"Perhaps," he whispered to himself, "these words are mere mists that have no depth. I can't picture them."

Someone next to him heard and answered. "Come and see," she said, smiling faintly. He could see by the sleeves on her robe that she was a water weaver of the green order, and her ice gray eyes sparkled with intrigue. "I thought as you, but when he brought me to his threshing field and showed me the work he's been doing…"

It took a moment to remember her name, Frei of the Vir tribe.

Laying a hand on his arm, she widened her eyes and her smile, teasing him with the mischief and mystery in her gaze. "Yan, it is not what you think," Freivir coaxed. "Until you see the device, you can't imagine what it looks like or how it works. It's genius like none we've ever seen before."

Yandus had witnessed a number of great feats of genius beyond anything one being could concoct in their dreams, and this statement seemed absurd to him. But curiosity and the sense of fun she imparted made him want to follow.

"Where is it?" he asked. All around them, companions were leaping into the air with Dathwez in the lead, shrinking in seconds into pinpoints that vanished in the sky.

"Come on!" she said, swooping her arm excitedly, appealing to him to follow the others, "We're going to miss the demonstration!"

Yandus grinned, and taking a step in her direction, he found himself sucked into her wake. She walked, then ran, then sprung into the air, and they blasted off like two geyser-propelled rocks blasting into space. Barreling through the airy regions, they accelerated into the emptiness of space. Attaining transfer velocity, they began shifting up through dimensions into the superstrata where all is close, and swirled through the ethereal domain in sync together, weaving a spiral cord that dissipated gently behind them. Then shifting back through the dimensions into a distant quadrant of the galactic expanses of the Calliarchal Realm, they swept at coasting speed into the Synpax Nebula where the Wez Tribe flourished.

Yan loved traveling and laughed as they descended.

Zeroing in on the Daran planet, they dropped down into the Daranon Valley, Dath's home, and settled onto their feet on his threshing floor. Yandus had been there before, viewing other creations and sculptings of his fancy. There were many beautiful, strange, and puzzling things to contemplate in this valley, but never enough time. Dathwez insisted on directing the thoughts and focus of the crowds who came, and he always had something he wanted to press on their attention.

This time, the numbers of beings present were beyond anything Yan had ever seen in Dath's valley before, covering the fields and hills. In the center stood a wooden edifice, a bland building with no outer adornment or uniqueness of design, barely large enough to hold more than a few hundred people, half a mil at most. The wood itself was unpainted, rough, and raw. It had two large doors on either side of the structure which were wide open, and light blazed out the openings along with a loud hum of machinery.

Companions were waiting in line to enter through the doors. Yan assumed they must be streaming out on the other side after spending a few moments to take in the mysterious project Dath was boasting about.

The Denser Plane

"Come!" Frei cried out excitedly, taking his hand and tugging him to the front of the line. Yandus was a creative leader of the H rank, the same as Dath, and the cluster of beings at the door stepped back to let him in with smiles and nods of greeting.

The throbbing of the machine pulsed through his chest as he pressed toward the center of the chamber. And there it stood in the middle, a fantastic maze of moving parts, reminding him absurdly of a collection of spiders in a convoluted wrestling match with a dragonfly. There were gears, pulleys, pistons, and sheathed metal boxes and cylinders, some dripping icy condensation and some steaming with heat. A majestic wheel of bronze prongs fanned out over the top of the pulsing contraption and rotated slowly through it. Emanating a dull blob of light with each pulse, it made spheres of light that expanded like rings on water, undulating through everything around it. Yandus could taste and smell the orbs as they swelled and passed through him, distorting the dimensional shapes of everything around, including himself. It was unnerving and confusing.

He didn't think of danger. The compulsion to know what the machine did was so strong he could hardly breathe.

"The Kaleidoscope!" Dath shouted from his perch on a platform at the far end of the machine. "Have you never wondered how the dimensions fan out and what it would be like to skirt from one layer to the next, phasing from here to there, discovering perspectives we've never even imagined before? What creations could we invent? What new sculptures of sound and beauty could we shape? What if you could travel where you wished without knowing how or where you went?" The speech went on and on, some of it clearly enticing, some of it obscure and strange.

As he spoke, he grasped a great lever and pushed it away from himself. With a great creak, the center of the machine gaped, rotating 90 degrees. A circular cluster of rods like a multi-pronged tooth was exposed. It grew longer and then lifted out of a mesh in the opening, sparking with bursts of blue flame and ion-charged snaps. When it opened fully, it formed a metal cave that was dark on the far side. This puzzled Yandus more than anything else had. Why was the room not visible on the other side?

"Do I have another seeker?" Dath bellowed. "Who will brave the portal into the Realm of Facets?"

Several people drew closer.

"Can you feel it?" Dath laughed, pointing at the maw before them. "Isn't it compelling?"

"Have you gone through it?" one of them yelled back.

"Of course!" he cried in response. "I know what's on the other side, and *trust me*, you have to experience it to understand. There is a great mystery to be explored and you will never be the same!"

Yandus found himself drawing closer as well, but he hesitated at the side of the machine's mouth, looking into the murky depths.

It smelled so strangely.

"Yan!" Frei laughed in his ear, right at his elbow. "Don't be fainthearted! I have seen the facets and they are magical!" He glanced at her over his shoulder and noticed that there was something unnerving about the sparkle in her eyes and sweet tone of her laugh, something he couldn't identify.

Several beings moved into the opening. Some were chuckling. Some were calling out to those behind them, "Come on! It's fine!" and "See you on the other side."

Dath grabbed the lever with both hands and pulled it to himself with great effort, the muscles in his arms bulging. He was laughing as the gaping mouth of the machine closed on itself, narrowing and rotating until the cluster of rods met the mesh underneath. A great crackling of sparks and booms of thunder burst from the metal jaws as they sealed shut. Then the bronze wheel began to turn. The pulsing began again, softly at first, but louder and louder as the spheres of light expanded and burst at the inside walls of the chamber.

Yandus hadn't remembered the bubbles stopping before. But this time, he noticed when they ended and how Dath began to speak again, calling out to the companions, inviting them to enter his portal.

The machine started opening once more and Yan was in an ideal spot to see inside as it did. The odd smell was there, but there was no trace he could detect of his fellow beings who had stepped in. Maybe they had been transported to other facets of the realm. *What would that be like?*

"It must be so beautiful," a being nearby said in awe.

Yan turned and recognized her as the daughter of the Archeon, Ryadna, and he gasped involuntarily at seeing her up close. She was so beautiful and her voice so pleasing. He smiled and gazed at her without any self-consciousness, just like many of the beings around her. She saw him smiling and smiled back warmly. "You, Sir, H-cap… What is your name?"

"H-cap Yandus, at your service, Ryadna," he tipped his head toward her in respect.

"Tell me about this construction here. How does it work and what should I do?" She lay a hand on his arm, almost exactly in the spot where

Frei had put hers earlier, and warmth spread from her touch to his heart. Never had he been so close to this being he had long admired.

She crafted *stars*!

"I am in the same condition as you, Ryadna," he nodded again, laying his own hand on hers. "I don't know anything about it."

Behind them the jaws of the machine had spread enough to show its filament tooth and the sliding of the metal through the mesh was audible. It rumbled faintly. *It's still hungry*, Yan found himself thinking foolishly.

"Shall we explore then?" she raised her eyebrows and stepped toward the opening as it gaped.

He nodded, savoring the smile she gave him, wondering at the chance that had thrown him into such a position of privilege: to walk in step with her, share this moment with her, listen to the insights and musings that might fall from her lips. Ryadna, a virtuoso among star-crafters… He sighed and moved her hand from his arm into his grasp, taking it firmly as he fell into place at her heels. And glancing up just as they took their first step into the maw....

He caught sight of Dath's expression.

Yandus gasped. How could a face like that, so expressive and beautiful, be twisted into such contortions? When had those deep green eyes ever looked so yellow? Pale, glistening, hollow somehow, as though the black pupils were bottomless pits that sucked the color from his irises. His mouth warped strangely with one corner curling up and the other stabbing down the side of his face stretching his chin crookedly.

In that moment, the instant Yan looked up at him, Dath seemed to notice the horror in Yan's eyes and his face distorted even further in response. Multiple lines creased his brow, his mouth opened revealing gritted teeth, and his eyes blazed in a thrill, staring at Yan and Ryadna with a ferocity of craving Yan had never seen in any creature before.

The machine grew suddenly grotesque in Yan's eyes, though he knew it was mindless in its hunger. And Dath appeared ten times as hideous, displaying a *knowing* hunger and delight that stabbed Yan's heart and filled him with dread. For the first time, he thought, *What does this machine actually do and why is Dathwez so anxious for us to step into it?*

A shrill cackle filled the upper reaches of the chamber as the machine, still not fully open, began to close again on the two of them. Ryadna pulled forward into the dark cave beyond, but Yandus tugged backward in a panic. The allure had been broken the moment he had seen Dath's face unveiled, and he was sure something terrible was happening to the companions as they went through.

Nearby, Freivir was jumping up and down flinging her hands and squealing. "Yes! Yes! Yes! Take her and go!! He's in! HE'S IN!" And breaking into laughter she started clapping.

"Help me!" he cried to her, reaching out his free hand, waving it around. Frei jumped out of reach, and he grasped the edge of the door, heaving on Ryadna to tug her back out of the machine. The floor was rising under his feet and the rods from overhead had begun descending, metal grating on metal. "Help me!" he cried out again.

The maw continued contracting on itself and began its slow rotation. Yandus crouched more and more, screaming to Dath to reverse the lever and open it again. Beings all around were staring in shock, unable to comprehend what was happening, let alone act. Ryadna was yanking on him from the dark harder and harder, first trying to pull him through, but then, desperately trying to get away.

But he wouldn't let go. He had very strong hands and had been fortunate to get a good grip on her from the beginning. He could hear her screaming at him, and the sound seemed to get farther and farther away and thinner. It lost its richness and melodic trim. It grew flat and harsh.

Straining and tugging, he crouched until he had to drop to his knees and began to fear that he wouldn't have time to pull her back through before it closed. The noise of the machinery filled his ears, and he could no longer hear anything else.

Someone yelled and jumped toward him to help. Others followed suit laying hold of the edges of the opening to pull while others ran to the platform to make Dath stop it from closing. To their dismay, many others leapt forward to hinder them. Pushing and shoving soon gave way to blows and before long, confusing skirmishes filled the chamber, particularly at the platform.

Clashing with fists and sticks, then pieces of metal picked up from the floor, the fray grew fierce and those who had meant to help were knocked away. Something slammed against Yan's arm so that he lost his grip on the door frame and he flailed for a new handhold. Several beings with craving eyes converged on the shrinking opening and began beating at his exposed side, yelling at him to let go. As the door contracted further, they shoved and kicked harder to push him into the dark beyond.

Giving way and rolling onto his back, Yan grabbed at the metal rods descending on him. It was a mindless, instinctive thing meant to keep him from being shoved into the cave, and as he clung to one of them with his free hand, he swung his foot out into the chamber to brace himself. That's when he noticed the door was rotating as it closed, and it lifted him up sideways so he could see the control platform. There were beings climbing up the sides while others were knocking them down.

When the rods started to press on his chest, terror gripped him, and he began shrieking. He found himself losing touch with the reality around him. They were not just compressing his body but bearing down on his mind, his speech. A great, screeching cacophony filled the room as the machine started grinding, fighting the resistance his body posed.

A great wailing joined the machine's caterwauling, and the battle grew frantic as one man pushed through to the front without being hindered, beings tumbling to get out of his way. Sky blue robes billowed around him, rippling in the multi-colored rings of his aura, and his long thick hair, dark and tipped with light at the ends, streamed out behind him. The crown on his head gleamed gold like sunshine and its edges were encrusted with living gems. The dirt hummed beneath him in deep, resonant tones, his every step striking chords in the ground that all could hear through their own feet even though their ears were numbed by the bedlam in the chamber.

The Archeon overawed even those who might have resisted his approach.

His mouth was moving, and anguish marred his features. Without being able to hear his words over the discord that filled the chamber, Yan watched the moving of his lips and knew he was crying out, "Ryadna! Ryadna!" over and over, his hands waving helplessly in the air.

Finding Yan in the clutches of the machine's jaws, he reached toward him with a wordless howl, and began scrabbling frantically at the metalwork. Yan wanted to tell him that he still had a hold of her, but he had no control over his mouth or the cries of pain he unleashed. The rods were pressing down on his chest and crushing his lungs within, making it harder and harder to get any air.

But the Archeon saw. His eyes traced Yandus' arm stretched out into the darkness and saw the fingertips of her hand clenched in his fist. And he understood that she wasn't gone yet. A guttural yell burst from his belly that everyone heard, even over the din of the machine, over the clamor of the fighters, over the wailing from observers too far away to help, and out the doors into the valley, up the hillsides and across to faraway plains. No one who heard that cry ever forgot it. As it faded, silence fell for just a moment and in it, the Archeon cried out these words:

"DON'T LET GO!"

The battle burst into a frenzy, doubling in intensity. Dath was clinging to the lever at the top of the control tower with all his might, tugging on it. Watching Yan as he was being crushed in the mesh, he stared with an insane fascination, struggling to get the lever all the way to its end and latched into place.

The Archeon whirled around and commanded Dathwez in a thundering voice to open the door and was astonished when the H-cap ignored him and pulled on the lever even harder, his mouth wide open as he spat out defiant bellows no one could hear. Many beings who had been unable to decide how to act chose sides in this very moment, some rising up to protect Dath and many more swarming the control platform to force him to free the Archeon's daughter. And it seemed for a moment as if they would succeed.

The machine itself though, was greater than many companions, and intent on finishing what it had started. Even after Dath had been knocked down and dragged away from the platform, it continued its inexorable crush to seal the door. Its many parts whined and clattered and rattled tenfold, spewing steam and grinding. Gears began to overheat, and the beings fell back in fear as screws popped and flew, and deep cracks emanated from within its workings.

Dath, discarded by those who had toppled him, ran up to the still closing maw, caressing it with his arms and coaxing it to finish the job. He seemed to be shouting at Yandus. Maybe he was saying, "I warned you," or maybe he was threatening him if the machine was damaged from his interference. Or maybe he was yelling something else.

Blows to his side caught Yan's attention. The Archeon was still shouting at him to not let go, to stay alert. He had been fading. Not like going to sleep. It was different, as if his various parts were dismantling and unraveling somehow. He had no clear way of expressing it because nothing like this had ever happened before. He had never seen or heard of someone coming apart.

He glanced to his right into the dark and saw his hand still clutched hers, and while she still pulled, she had grown weak and couldn't break free. Turning back to his left, he caught the eyes of the Archeon commanding him. He reached down and grabbed Yan's innermost soul, deeper than his heart, down in his gut. He grappled and bound him. Yan did not resist. He gazed back into those eyes and watched them, read them. Searching those depths, he realized that he would not be allowed to unravel and slip away. He could not escape the crushing of his life, but neither would he let go of that hand. Here he would be pinned and pierced, and he would not be released until she could be retrieved.

The Archeon loved his daughter. It filled his eyes with anguish and determination. And Yandus let that love flow through him to her along the length of his arms and out his fingers. He wished he were loved like that, that someone would notice his own distress and care enough to give him… something… he didn't know what.

With an explosive, screeching lurch, the machine jerked down and crunched through the resistance of his chest, and liquid swelled at the punctures, shimmery gold in color. Not just red blood of the three dimensions, but deeper hues and glowing plasma of the higher dimensions flowed as well. Time was torn and hung by tattered threads right in the very center of his body. He made no sound. The golden blood flowed out of him, soaking his clothes and the mesh behind his back, slicking it and making it squeal shrilly.

Yan was fading. The blood that drained out of him made it easier for the rods to approach their slots and barely a narrow wedge of flesh and bone was left to cut through. His arm was locked rigidly into a grasping, vice-like pose on Ryadna's cold, stiff hand.

His legs were losing their shape, shivering out of sync, growing foggy and vague. Dath was laughing and leaping in delight, reveling in his machine's victory. Yan stared at him as his eyes struggled with the shifting dimensions, and he saw what looked like two cords, one tether proceeding from Dath's belly into the Calliarchal Realm, and another shadowy one protruding from his back into the darkness. It was puzzling. Glancing around—his eyes were still able to move a little though his head was stuck in one position, pressed between two seals of the door—he noticed a number of other beings with two cords. They were the ones who had been collecting people to put into the machine. Many of them were from Dath's own tribe, the Wez. The rest of the beings, including himself, had only one tether.

He saw now that he was refracting into layers, with parts of himself shuffled out to different dimensions, and he could sink down to the greyer levels where the back-cords led. In that place, he could see the shadowy figures of some of Dath's kinsmen wandering, their tethers to the Realm drifting up into the higher layers. And he saw as well those who had passed through the machine.

Beings without any tether.

Where had their lifeblood gone? Why did they have no liquid gold flowing in their veins?

He knew. The two-tethered beings had consumed it. Some of them had eyes that looked dull and drugged, their fingers and lips tinged with traces of shimmery gold. Others hung around near the dark side of the machine's portal, craving, hungering, jonesing.

The Archeon banged at the side of the maw, unable to reach him anymore, commanding him to remain intact, forbidding him to unravel completely. Yan's attention was drawn back to his powerful gaze and inside himself he felt the despair of what was required of him. To be crushed and not rescued. To be a conduit but retain nothing.

Gazing into the eyes of the Archeon, he knew the ruler would have willingly changed places with him, would have gladly been crushed for Ryadna's sake. And choosing to hold on became more than love for the daughter whose fingers were still held in his, it was devotion for her father as well.

The Archeon was shedding tears. More than that, Yan noticed his hands were pressed up against the upper jaw of the portal, and he was pushing with all his might, his face red and sweating with the effort. One of his arms was deeply cut by the metallic edge of the rim, and golden blood gushed out of the wound, dripping down the rods onto Yan's body. That fluid was the only thing grounding what was left of him, strengthening the remaining threads in his chest.

Just then, several ethereal, bony heads like skulls, flashed around them and faded. After another second or two, more flashed. Then double or triple the number appeared and vanished. With ever increasing numbers and speed, more and more heads appeared in ever larger spaces around them. And with each strobe-like flash, there were more. They filled the chamber, they spread out into the valley, they covered the hills, they flooded the planet. Thousands, millions, billions of them.

Faces of death.

As suddenly as it had begun, it ended with a crash louder than all the ruckus before it, rippling the ground in a bone-shaking tremor that rolled out from the epicenter of the contraption. It was followed by a shocking stillness that made heads and ears ring. Then the machine creaked and groaned, reversing its wheels and gears, and sucked the rods out of Yandus' chest, rotating and depositing him on his back again.

Silence filled the chamber as all fighting ceased.

All eyes watched as the Archeon stepped into the opening and pried his daughter's fingers from Yan's stiffened hand, pulling her back out.

The Denser Plane

She was gravely changed. Her face had grown old and wrinkled and was lined with tragedy and despair. She clutched at it with bony hands and stared through her fingers at them all, turning slowly to take in surroundings she no longer recognized. Looking down at Yandus, she seemed to have no concept of who he was or what had happened to him.

A great and terrible shriek burst from her throat, striking the beings like a shockwave, knocking them back several steps, and causing some to stumble and fall. A wretched wail of agony followed by words.

"My children!" she cried out and collapsed shuddering in her father's arms, weeping as though her heart were broken a thousand times over. Many ran to help the two of them, and around them, beings began to moan and weep in sympathy with her.

Some dashed to the control platform to bash the thing to pieces. Those who had resisted them before were faltering, retreating into shadows and into the crowd, weakened and confused.

Some hastened to Yandus' side.

The mangled core of his chest was pressed and cut into a golden negative of the filament cluster that had crushed and pierced him. The rest of his body was mostly dissolved into loose threads of plasma, color, throbbing pulses of static, and tangible tissues like tangled ropes that floated around him. His head was intact, and his eyes shone for a moment before rolling back into his head. No one was sure what to do. No being had ever dissipated before and this phenomenon was unknown to them. Several mobilized around him, and gathering the loops in their arms, wrestled to contain them, to keep them from expanding any further. The cries and wails of Ryadna echoed in their ears as they found cloths to wrap him in. Together, they lifted him to carry him away. The beings outside who hadn't seen the battle raised their voices in agony as they saw the H rank leader's condition, immediately terrified. The waves of their cries undulated through Yandus, causing the shredding of his body to expand and spill out of the attenders' grasps. Seeing this, several more beings rushed to their aid, and the first battlefield surgery was begun with bare hands and bolts of cloth, with tears and moans.

And the Commander did *not* fall apart into energies that dispersed through the realm.

His thoughts never left. He remembered the feel of Ryadna's fingers in his hand as she was aging, shriveling, growing frail. He relived the flashing of skulls and bones around them and recalled that first cry from her lips.

He could feel the Calliarchal Realm tearing, the lower dimensions falling away into shadow, flattening, waning, draining. Yet within him he held the planes together—they were snared by the sinewy mesh in his chest. His heart had become a distorted latticework of thousands of intertwined filaments, still functioning, with golden blood pulsing through the delicate weave. Time was tearing and beyond it, three dimensions that were already severed, still hung by the threads of time that wove through his chest.

As the impromptu medics grappled with his limbs, Yandus wrestled with his heart.

Let go, and he would forget, he was sure of it. But all those who had passed through would remain there when that final fragment detached completely. *Hold on*, and perhaps he could draw them back to the opening and reattach them to the Realm.

The throng around him could *feel* the tearing of time, and they anchored themselves against the tug. Their conjoined efforts generated a huge swirl of creative power causing the three dimensions to appear again, fully intact, fully intertwined with the Calliarchal Realm where they belonged.

Only a dim shadow was left in the cellophane piece of reality that had torn away, and none but Yandus could see it. It lay underneath them, barely existing, spreading out in a thin plane across the entire, infinite realm, growing ever thinner and darker, more and more colorless, flat, lifeless. Neither a husk nor an empty shell. Merely an impression, a sketch, a wisp of something that could not retain its substance for long.

The monstrosity that had riven so many of the beings' tethers to the Realm could not repair them. It sucked life away but was incapable of restoring it.

When Yandus' body was finally stabilized and he was lifted to his feet in great pain, all the beings around him could see *through* the fretwork hole in his chest. Someone brought a band and wrapped it around his torso to cover, stabilize, and insulate the wound.

Nearby, others were tending the Archeon's mangled hands, and his daughter sat at his feet with her head in his lap, weeping so quietly that only the trembling of her shoulders gave it away. Slowly, her vitality was returning to her body, but it seemed only to increase her agony.

No one knew how long the machine had held him in its jaws but once he was released, the minutes had stretched to nine hours. For Ryadna, the time distortion was far greater. She had lived many long years in that same stretch. Children were born, and those children had offspring, and tribes and nations had come into existence. As he was pulling her back, the timeline tore even more, stretching longer and longer, and many generations came and went. All of them lost to the Realm.

He had been aware of them—was still aware of them. Their reality in the shallow place was visible to him, all along that thread of time. His latticed heart was moved with compassion for her sorrow, and the magnitude of her loss overwhelmed him. Her father gazed helplessly, first at her, unable to stroke her head with his heavily bandaged arms, then lifting hollow eyes to Yan, pleading mutely.

Yandus himself had become the link between the planes, the only place where they intersected.

He moved his lips to sound out Ryadna's name and her father noticed, whispering to her to listen. When she turned to look at him, eyes full of pain, features distorted with grief, he strained to make himself heard.

"I will try," he uttered, barely pressing enough air through his throat to form words.

And he made the choice to remain.

His was the first and the greatest of all the anchors.

From him, all the others grew.

The nine hours were suspended in the present. They remained open, like a book with many chapters, spread out for study. But on that side, in the Shallows, those hours continued stretching and distending by days and years and centuries and millennia and eons.

And through the length of that flimsy timeline, one brilliant web grew, expanding like a cornucopia across the hours. It was threaded with pulsing golden light, weaving in and over and through the shallow realm, breaking out and pouring into the Denser Plane.

Chapter 25—Shattered Pieces

Daisy carried Mac to the infirmary and Sebastian placed him in a comfortable bed in a safe room where he could be detained if he were irrational when he awoke. Dan dropped into a chair, leaning forward with his elbows on his knees and his head hanging halfway down.

He moaned and Sebastian came to examine him as soon as he had completed his scans of the unconscious man in the room. "There is some bruising," the medical AI informed him, "but your body is intact, and I have no concerns for your welfare at this time."

Dan didn't respond. It seemed to Daisy that he was too discouraged to speak, and this in itself could be reason for concern. Before she could prompt Sebastian, he spoke again.

"You are very upset about what happened," the AI medic said. "I am also troubled." Daisy perked up at this use of a familiar word and made a note to ask him for his AI application of the term. "…at my friend's loss of sanity."

Dan covered his face with both hands and sighed deeply. Both AIs recognized the depth of his sorrow over what had happened, and Daisy postulated that the difficulties of living on Mars with such a small number of survivors had been taking a steady toll for years.

"Dan," she said, placing a hand on his shoulder, "I have come from Walter and Sil, and I have brought parts to repair equipment and medical supplies. I brought everything Verna asked for."

He lifted his head to look at her with bloodshot eyes. *This is sorrow,* she discerned, *and weariness.* "What was your name again?" he asked, coughing and clearing his throat.

"Daisy." She saw a frail hope materialize in his face.

"Daisy," he said, blinking slowly and clearing his throat again. "I can't find the words to express my… my appreciation for your visit. And for the supplies." He shook his head a few times, almost as though the movement would clear his thoughts. "I know I don't seem happy about it but I am."

"I would like to meet Carla and Aurelia," Daisy requested gently. The sentence belied how earnestly she wanted to meet these friends of Sil's. Her curiosity about them and her sense that they should be included in her own idea of *family* was strong.

"And Verna?" Dan locked eyes with her. "Have you talked to her yet? She has been looking for you for such a long time. And she was so excited to see you."

Daisy was touched—this man cared about her goals. Her tiny list of allies was growing. *I am moved*, she told herself, *by his kindness to me*. She was still working on how to register these experiences accurately, since no AI had ever done so before.

"You care for Verna," she said straightening and letting her hand drop to her side. "And you have taken an interest in our friendship."

"Yes," he said, "Of course I have! Verna is a central member of our community and one of our dearest friends. And she vouches for you."

"Daisy and I have been catching up," Verna announced over audio, "ever since she entered the facility, and we were able to establish a connection."

Dan gave a faint smile and rose to his feet heavily. "Let me take you to meet the rest of the family." He led the way out the door.

As they walked through the passageways, down ramps and ladders, across halls and through tunnels, Daisy scanned everything carefully, delighted with the unusual data she was collecting. "I am impressed," she said at one point.

"We've all worked hard, and necessity has driven us to new levels of invention."

"I have searched the Earth, Guam City, and the Moon for sentient AIs, Dan," Daisy clarified. "There are so few, and most of those are kept secret, isolated, which stunts their growth and deprives them of the opportunity to develop in a personal way."

Dan came to a stop and turned to look at her. He searched her face, and she chose to use her skills in facial expressions to look into his eyes. *Let him see intelligence and understanding*, she decided. This wasn't something she normally shared with humans.

"Here," she continued, "There are two AIs who have matured in ways I haven't found anywhere else. They are my peers. And I have been searching for this."

He didn't question her words or the ideas behind them.

"You and your family have nurtured both of them well," she elaborated.

"You mean Verna and Pal?" he asked.

"Sebastian and Verna. Who is Pal?" she replied, widening her eyes with interest.

Then Pal spoke to her via com and a wide smile spread across her face, sharing her discovery with the man watching. She lifted her eyes as if to a camera in the corner, but it was in her own system that she heard his words.

`Daisy, do you have news of my friend, Sil?`

The crew of the Mirabella Madness had no warning of the attack until the moment they heard the clangor of metal clamps on the hull. The captain ran to the bridge with a few of the others and sealed it off just as the invaders cut a hole in the ship's outer walls and boarded. They poured through the opening and blasted all the cameras they saw. In the distance, there were occasional bouts of shooting and commotion, but not nearly as much as she expected. It seemed only minutes before they were at the bridge itself.

She positioned herself with her plasma rifle facing the door and waited. Three other crew members similarly armed, crouched behind their chairs.

Someone beat on the metal door with a raucous clamor. "Open up," a man yelled. "We know she's in there."

The captain's blood ran cold. *The Proto!* she thought. And she knew there would be no surviving this day. She had been a fool to think they could negotiate with him after breaking and running like that. How had he found them?

The banging and yells continued.

They were being careful because they didn't want to harm the girl. *Wait!* The captain held up her hand to warn the others to pause and looked around carefully. The girl wasn't in there with them. She groaned. It was some kind of setup. Her face hardened into sullen rage, and gesturing at the door, she made signs that meant, *Kill whatever comes through.*

If this little piece of metal was going to be her last stand, she would make it count.

The Denser Plane

Sil moved along at a gentle pace, bracing herself with one hand against the wall, passing through corridors till she reached the hatch that would let her descend to the next level. Periodically, the graphic would appear on a nearby door showing her where she was in the facility. Sometimes it would appear with an arrow and a couple other dots in motion. She quickly realized this was a warning and an indicator of either a change in direction or a place to step out of view until the people those dots represented had passed.

There was something serene about the journey. She should have been highly agitated, anxious about Walter and Penn running into each other. She *was* worried, but the AI's help was a calming influence. With each step she took, it was proving to be worthy of trust. If it turned out to be leading her into Penn's clutches at the end, it didn't matter. For now, she could work with it.

She might have felt a great deal of interest in the sectors she passed through, if she had had the bandwidth to absorb it all. Maybe one day, she would think about it. As it was, the labels on the walls, the few posters, and the decorations were all meaningless. The complex itself was just a convoluted maze to negotiate.

Going down ladders turned out to be impossible. Attempting to descend a few rungs made her gasp and go up again. "Isn't there another way?" she whispered. "I'm injured and can't use my arms to bear my weight, not even for balancing."

A door panel lit up again, but it didn't show her an alternative.

"I know my father wouldn't be climbing down ladders. How does he get to the different levels?"

Nothing happened.

"You're worried about me?" Sil asked softly. "Thank you, but you need to get your priorities straight." She wasn't using that word as a human expression. She was making a specific reference that AIs would recognize. It was prioritizing keeping her hidden from Penn over getting her to where she needed to be. She wanted to change the parameters.

"Reaching the lowest level as quickly as possible is more important than hiding me from Penn. In fact, I intend to confront him at some point." There were voices in her head yelling at her NOT to do that, but she didn't care. "I'm asking you to keep me safe, keep Walter safe, give us whatever help you can. But give me access to that central column. I know that's where the elevator is."

The graphic changed. The path led her in another direction now, and the door was very close. It was an indiscernible panel in the wall that didn't open when she touched it. Voicing the "Moon of Gold" password again made it retract and she stepped through, sensing a field masking the view behind her. As it closed silently, she found herself in a circular, curving hallway, richly decorated in dark blues and gold, metallic, luminescent walls, heavily padded carpet, marbled ceiling tiles and subtle lighting. She padded around the perimeter till she came to an opening into a wide, round room. It was a lobby of sorts and in the center were two glass-walled lifts, one smaller, with room for a few people, and the other a broad room of its own, decked out with luscious couches, tables, and what might be a minifridge. No, more than that. This was his private office. It would ascend and descend to whatever level he chose.

There was no place where the graphic could show up and Sil didn't know if the facility AI had access here. Chances were, he didn't have much. Penn hated AIs and avoided them as much as possible. That was okay. She would manage on her own.

Stepping into the smaller elevator, she found buttons. The lowest one was dark green and labeled merely, DOWN.

How fitting, she thought as she pressed it and the floor dropped rapidly beneath her feet. *This is the day you're going down, Penn.*

A low-pitched tone reverberated through Daranon Valley, long and ominous, calling the Sentients to battle. Lorarye had never heard it before, and he had been told that only those who were called would. The summons was so compelling, so wrenching, that he couldn't delay even a few seconds.

Running as he fastened on his chest plate, he joined a throng of ensigns and Paladins pouring through the entrance into the Hall of the Net. Crossing under the voluminous weave of the living Net overhead, he raced to the chamber of the Seventh Hour. Inside there were squires handing out shields, lances, hooks, and ropes. He grabbed a shield and a lance—he was just beginning to be comfortable with them.

By ones and twos, the Sentients were barreling into the portal and vanishing. The puff as they disappeared was punctuated with a clapping thump and the percussion resonated in his heart, tugging on him with each beat. He ran too, and when he leapt into the portal, the drop was drastically harder than usual, as if the numbers of beings who had gone through had increased the opening's gravity.

Darkness spread around him as he fell. Clashes and shouts of rage filled his ears. Landing in a stark, grayscale vista of warriors where only the weapons glimmered as they swung and caught a murky light, he held up his shield and dashed to the edge of the conflict. *Gain your bearings*, they had told him in training. If he could avoid attack when first touching down, this gave him a decided advantage.

Pivoting in a swirling motion, he raised his shield and warded off a blow from a being he recognized, one he had considered a friend. The clang on his shield was nothing to the shock in his soul. A flicker of movement on the right spurred an instinctive thrust with his lance and he managed to deflect another blow. This second being was unknown to him.

He had trained in fighting two opponents and settled into the patterns he had found most suited to his inner strength. It was something he couldn't explain, but when he fought, there were movements that he almost recognized as *personal*, he could execute them so fluidly and capably. Rotating toward the left with a sweep of his lance, he stabbed at the first attacker, swinging the shield arm back at the second being as he turned. He stepped one foot over another, swirling and knocking both attackers in a calculated, familiar routine. They were daunted and withdrew. Their mission was targeting newcomers, not engaging fully.

Pressing into the darker, thicker region where the battle was dense, Lor pulled his shield close to his chest and locked the lance against the edge with the point at an upward angle. He didn't want to ram anyone who was on his side. Would he know? They had always said he would know. Up in the Calliarchal Realm, it was hard to tell who the saboteurs were and who was loyal. But here in the Shallows, the traitors were visible.

He pushed through the commotion, beings fighting on every side, and noticed a tint, a greenish yellow hue to some of the beings' eyes and mouths. If they were squinting and their lips were rolled into a line, it was almost undetectable, but in the throes of battle, they were glaring and snarling, yelling words of hatred.

Off to one side, he saw three enemies pinning one of his own and ran toward them, shoving combatants out of the way. His headlong rush knocked one of them aside, sending him flying. Two new assailants leapt at him with a vengeance, forcing him to his knees, stabbing, kicking, and beating him with their shields. Lor dropped to his belly and rolled into one, wheeling his weapon around and stabbing up at the enemy who fell over him. With a thrashing kick, he yanked himself back the other way, thudding into the first attacker he had knocked down, and slammed them under the chin with the shield. The second assailant stabbed at him, and he grabbed the point of their lance as it descended, tugging it to pierce the enemy beneath him.

As the second assailant pulled the weapon out of his comrade, Lorarye jumped to his feet and rammed them with his whole body. He whipped into another curling pattern, slashing, slamming, falling onto them with his shield under his weight. He struck at them repeatedly with the lance as he held them pinned. When they stopped moving, he turned back to look for the fighter he had come to aid.

Three enemies were stabbing something on the ground over and over. The center of the fray had moved away and only Lor was left to defend the Sentient who lay unmoving at their feet. With a cry of outrage, he launched himself at them and, one by one, beat them back till they fled. They pulled out of the Shallows in a panic, leaving the scent of fear behind them.

Falling to his knees beside the fallen being, Lor was horrified to see one of the first Paladins he had met, shredding before his eyes. Loops and strings and threads shuddering, the pale aura shimmering darker and lighter, his very shape distending.

"No, my brother!" he cried, weeping and clutching at the loops of his body as if he could hold him together. "Hold on! Let me pull you out!" And he groped around for his tether to the Realm, trying to find something to hold onto. But the being's body was unraveling more and more, and the tips of the threads were dissipating.

"No!" he cried again.

The Paladin's face still held its shape and resting his eyes on Lorarye, he whispered to him. Lor leaned over to hear the words. "Remember me," he said, and with a great shudder, the being burst into a thousand shreds without a center and dissipated into dust.

Lor stared at the dusty remnants of death, an outline of a shroud, something within him sinking deeper and deeper. He felt the being's spirit slip away, wafting upwards. He tasted the flavor of death, smelled the scent of the wounds all around him. *Yes*, was his first thought, *I will remember you.*

Then… he remembered those words with *his own lips*, felt them on his own tongue. They had come once from his own throat. *Remember me.* A great rumbling rose from his gut, shaking his chest, vibrating in his head, and his heart began to race. A cavity opened inside him, and a gush of memory burst forth. All the pain of shredding, the anguish of losing hold, the resignation of letting go—he remembered saying those very words to *this same brother*. Only that time, he had been the one speaking and fading away. G-dan Ver had been the one embracing him in his last moments.

"Ver!" he wept, falling forward and clutching at the dust, "I remember you. Don't leave me!"

But the summons tolled again, and he rose to his feet grimly. There was still a battle raging.

And he would fight.

The room behind the mirror was one in a string of observation rooms placed in a wide circle around a central column. The column itself was some fifteen meters wide and there was a hallway encircling it that opened into the rooms, each one with a couple of chairs and desks. None of them were occupied as far as Walter could see.

He proceeded down the hall to his right, checking the rooms one at a time with a number of clones following noiselessly in his wake. Each room had a mirror looking into some area where the clones lived. Some of the clones were there on the other side of the mirrors, going about their business, oblivious of the fact that their fellow clones could see them. The ones with him pointed and gave each other knowing looks and Walter began to have a clear idea of the extent of their existence.

They had gone about halfway around the central column when a soft click startled them. They all froze. Walter signaled at the clones following him to hold still and be quiet, hoping they would understand the intent even if they didn't know the gestures he used, and tiptoed around the column looking for the source of the sound.

Penn was standing at the entrance to the observation room they had come through, staring at the profusion of broken shards. His hand was moving slowly to his hip and instinctively Walter ran, diving at the hand. Penn was turning as he knocked him over into the shattered pieces of glass, a look of shock frozen on his face. He fell hard—there was Earth gravity here—and slid on the floor with Walter's full weight on him.

Penn had never looked so vulnerable before. For a few seconds, they stared at each other. Walter studying his face, noticing the young and old portions of flesh with horror, and finally understanding the bizarre form of cannibalism he had been engaging in for years.

Cloning himself for the parts.

"YOU!" Penn roared suddenly, wrenching himself around and latching onto Walter in a frenzy, so outraged he seemed unable to say anything more.

Walter didn't waste time answering, grappling with him fiercely, astonished at the power in the older man's muscles. A male in his twenties who had lifted weights his entire life would not have been stronger. They rolled and kicked, knocking around against chairs and walls, each one trying to gain the upper hand. The cries and yells mixed with the crunching of glass and thuds. Penn was strong but Walter had skill and agility.

Penn managed to break Walter's hold and pull away for a moment, noticing the clones watching from a distance. "Help me!" he demanded furiously as Walter leapt at him again, knocking him onto his face.

They hesitated, watching in fascination. Walter could hardly get a few words out, but he couldn't let them think they were bound to their oppressor. "This man," he belted out between gasps, "...is the one who... enslaved you!"

"Kill him!!" Penn yelled.

They broke, crawling away from each other. One of the blows Walter had taken to the head had left him disoriented. "You have no right to keep them prisoners here," he said, groping for the strength to fight again. There was something... he had brought something to fight with, but he couldn't remember what it was.

Penn was staggering around the curved hallway, leaning on its wall for support. Walter jumped to his feet and tipped over, falling to one side. One of the clones grabbed his hand and lifted him.

"Don't help him," a voice whimpered.

"We will be punished," another said.

"Don't care," Dana's voice responded at his elbow. She steadied Walter as he lurched forward after Penn, patting at his leg in the hopes there was a weapon in the pocket. The rod. He was looking for the EMP rod.

Penn was several meters ahead, and as he thumped on the wall, a small piece of it began to descend. Shoving his hand in his pocket and pulling it out again, he turned to give Walter a look of triumph and scorn.

"It's done then," he said as though the fight were over. "You've sealed your fate."

The grin on his blood-streaked face didn't last.

⸎

The Denser Plane

"I have reestablished contact with the rest of civilization," Verna announced with something of a flourish. Cheers and applause would have been an appropriate human response, but her people weren't quite themselves. She considered each one, Mac sleeping in his safe room, Aurelia hiding in her favorite spot in the garden, no longer weeping, but still mournful, Carla sitting on the moss, surrounded by the kids, letting them do all the talking, Dan escorting her friend, Daisy, to join them. She held each one of them near. Distance between rooms meant nothing to her. All the places where her eyes and ears reached were close for her.

A pirate's treasure couldn't approach the wealth Daisy had lavished upon her, whole years of data, recordings of Sil and news of the world, all of Scarlet's childhood up until that moment, years of Walter as well. All the treasures Daisy kept in her heart had been shared with her. *I am happy*, she observed, tenderly paging through the earliest records of Sil after she left Mars. She wanted to review them carefully, savoring them. Not in real time, exactly, but certainly not as quickly as she was capable of doing. *Pal and I can do this together*, she decided. It would increase the pleasure, sharing it with someone who would relish it as much as she.

Dan and Daisy were descending into the Tangle and making their way around to where Carla and the kids were. Verna had told them where to go because the kids were too distracted to respond to Dan's calls. When they rounded the final corner and walked up to the little family, Daisy began to behave strangely. She and Verna had been keeping up a steady electronic dialog, but she dropped off suddenly and stood still, staring at the kids.

"Daisy," Dan was saying, "This is Carla and… are you alright?" He dropped to his knees beside his wife, laying a hand on her shoulder. Her face was puffy and bleary, which was to be expected after all the tears.

The little girl with a mop of dark curls had her face buried in Carla's arms and Carla dipped her head toward her as if that was all it would take for Dan to understand. And, exceeding projections, he did.

"How did she get here?" he murmured. "Daisy!" He turned to her in astonishment, his face turning red. "You brought her? Who else is here? Is… is she here? Sil?" He looked around the garden area, searching the trees and plants and cavern heights as if she might be hiding somewhere.

His emotion made sense. Sil was the one they all loved. But Daisy wasn't answering.

"There is no one else here," Verna informed cheerfully, "but Daisy has brought so many memories of her that we can share."

"Sil wouldn't have sent a child to Mars alone," Dan rose to his feet, his eyes wide, pressing a hand to his stomach as though it hurt. This was valid. Sil was unlikely to send a child to a faraway planet without her parents.

"Perhaps she was kidnapped," Verna offered, "though Daisy would never do that. She may have stowed-away with her which is a theme in many childish adventures."

Daisy's head began twitching and every now and then would jerk to one side. Her face was frozen into the expression she had begun when she first saw the family. Almost pleased, almost friendly, arrested just before reaching that look.

Dzzzzt, she said. A bee buzzing nearby drifted closer to inspect her but didn't recognize the chemical signatures it found.

"What is going on?" Dan dropped to the ground again and stroked the little girl's hair. She lifted her head to look at him. Her face was red and tear-streaked, her eyes bright and glistening, with hints of dark red glimmering. Verna linked those traces of color to the other children. This was new data. Did all children born on Mars have sparks of that color within the pupils and irises? She had assumed the environment, the soil and such, tilted toward a favorability of sorts. But this girl had been living for years on Earth.

"It's hard to explain," Scarlet said finally. "I've been time traveling and going through portals and hanging out with aliens. Things like that."

Dan chuckled. As outlandish as it must have sounded to him, he seemed to accept that something strange had happened and he wasn't surprised by her take on it. "I wouldn't put it past you," he said looking up as if he were talking to someone. That was his way. Verna was used to it.

Dzzzzt, Daisy said. She must be processing something very demanding.

"It's a miracle," Carla whispered, and all the kids nodded. They were seated in a cluster around her, pressed up against each other like a brood of baby birds in a nest. There were several of those in the Tangle. "This… this makes it all worthwhile. We're not just going to perish out here. We're going to survive. I know that now."

"Sssc-c-scarrr-let," Daisy said, her chassis loosening up, taking a slow step, then another. Then revving back up to normal speed, she walked over and kneeled next to the little group. "Scarlet. How was your day?"

"Daisy?" Scarlet said quizzically, "Are you here too? Are we on Mars?"

"I didn't expect to see you here," Daisy said, taking one of Scarlet's hands in hers.

"I don't have any books," the girl answered.

"I wouldn't carry them if you did," Daisy replied, tilting her head to the side. A warm glow stretched between them as each affirmed their trust in one another.

"How long have I been gone?" Scarlet asked, her eyes drooping with fatigue.

"I don't know," Daisy answered, furrowing her brow just like a human. "I didn't know you weren't with your parents, but I am sure they will be very worried about you."

"We'll just have to tell them," the little girl said reasonably. "Will you let them know?"

"I will try," Daisy smiled. "Verna," she queried aloud so the humans would know what she was saying. "Will you help me establish a connection?"

"Certainly," Verna replied.

Daisy turned to Dan and Carla. "The data is irrefutable. There can be no conclusion other than the one she gave us. Scarlet has crossed dimensional space."

Verna reserved judgment for the moment, recognizing that Daisy must have a good reason for those words, but since she lacked the information and context to arrive at the same result, she would regard what Daisy said as a hypothesis. At some point, Daisy would walk her through the processing she had completed.

She has developed beyond me, Verna approximated, *or at least along different lines*. This promised to make their friendship all the richer and for the first time in her existence, Verna noticed the hindrance of not abiding in a platform. She couldn't smile.

"What are you saying?" Dan squeezed his eyelids together, trying to make sense of Daisy's words.

"That doesn't mean anything to me," Carla offered.

"Daisy talks like that sometimes," Scarlet said, pulling away from Carla's embrace and throwing her arms around Daisy. "Once you know what she means, you'll see she's right. Aren't you, Aunt Daisy?"

"Yes, I am," the aunt softened her voice with masterful inflection, displaying an affection Verna had only seen in humans before. "And you are right. This is the only possible solution to the puzzle." She cuddled Scarlet in her arms and turned to Dan and Carla. "Mathematics shows us that there are other dimensions we have difficulty perceiving. Theories about how we intersect with them or how to access them abound. In this case, I believe Scarlet has had deeper dimensions all along." She smiled at the girl and glanced around at the other children who were watching, spellbound. "Perhaps they do as well."

Dan was watching her intently, and Carla found her children tightening around her, reaching out to touch her, a hand or a foot or a knee. One behind her rested his cheek on her back. No one spoke.

"Have your children ever seen something or someone you couldn't see?" Daisy asked.

The kids straightened up and gawked at her. "What about that one time in the tunnel?" Ananka asked.

"Scarlet," Daisy turned to her. "How did you get here?"

"Lor brought me," she said matter-of-factly.

Daisy raised an eyebrow and turned to look at the others as if to say, see what I mean?

"I'm not going to reject what you're saying outright," Dan said finally, rubbing his face with both hands. "I'd like to hear all about it, but I will be spending some time pondering things and discussing it with Mama and Pal." He had picked up a fallen leaf in his hands and was rolling it between his fingertips. "But before we get to that, there are two things that must come first. One, we have to get a message back to Scarlet's parents and two, we have to have a welcome party."

The kids jumped up cheering and hooting, all the somberness gone.

Chapter 26—Intersecting Planes

The floor descended through one level after another, deeper and deeper. Each one luxuriously decorated in marble, gold, and dense carpets. Each one with a different accent color, dark red, forest green, salmon, plum, saffron— each beautiful in their own way. Sil found herself wondering how much of her mother's fortune had gone just to build this multi-level office and deck it out in the most expensive materials Earth had to offer.

The final level took longer to reach, and she was growing increasingly tense with every passing second. She had gone undetected so far, but that couldn't remain the case anymore. A confrontation with Penn was imminent and she felt ill-prepared. Weak, gasping in pain. No plan. No weapons. Nothing but a dogged determination to find him and stick to him until Scarlet was found. It was the one thing she was sure of. Wherever Penn was, Scarlet would show up there before long.

The lift slowed and a crack opened at the floor, expanding as it descended into the opening, light filling the shaft. She heard the commotion and saw Penn standing with his back to her before he noticed she was there. As the lift stopped, he stepped toward it and saw her.

His face was scratched and bleeding, covered with multiple cuts and contusions. He gaped at her and forced out a few words tumbled in a gurgle. "Not here, g-g-girl." Rage filled his eyes and his lips curled obscenely as he whipped his head back to the hallway where Walter was stumbling toward them. "You brought her here!" he fumed.

"Hello, Lazarus," Sil said coolly, a sly smile spreading across her face as she leaned against the wall. Crossing her arms over her aching chest, she crooked one foot over the other as if she held all the cards. That's the thing about knowing what one is willing to die for. She kind of *did* hold all the cards.

Her voice had a chilling effect on Penn. All the color drained from his face and the rage faded as quickly as it had flared. When a passenger bullet is speeding by, blowing its whistle, the sound is higher as it approaches and drops to a lower pitch once it passes. This is what happened to the tension in the hallway when Sil spoke. The spirit of backstreet brawling shifted to boardroom skirmishes.

"Come with me, Sil," he appealed to her soberly with a strange intensity in his eyes.

She laughed a short "Hah!" and shook her head slowly. "How are you doing there, Waltz?" she asked without looking at him. She dared not glance away from Penn, sensing that her momentary control over the confrontation was fragile.

"Hey, Sil," was the answer. "All good here." She flicked her eyes at him and back. He was a mess, almost as bad as Penn.

"The way I see it," Sil said, gazing at Penn shrewdly. "You've got three options." Stretching out a hand, Sil studied her fingernails, keeping the arms crossed carefully over her chest. One of them was broken. "You can keep fighting while Moon security forces surround the base," which was sheer bravado since as far as she knew, Maggie hadn't notified anyone of their whereabouts. "You could escape with the clothes on your back. Or you could deal with us." She looked back at him.

Penn seemed to consider the choices for a moment. Sil knew he hated not being several steps ahead of everyone else and he hadn't expected either her or Walter's coming. He had the look of a cornered animal and the only thing calming him was the illusion of negotiation.

A low moaning began somewhere behind him and Sil found herself looking that direction despite her intentions. There were several faces peering from behind Walter, their features etched in agony and distress. They were eerily alike and disturbingly familiar though she didn't know why. Murmurs began to come from their throats saying things like, "Another one," and "She must be the one."

Penn relaxed visibly as the strange people drew closer, gathering around Walter, staring at her and him. "This is my little… ah… family," he sneered, "Sil, my daughter, meet your relatives, the Phonies." He made a move to shove his hands into his pockets and Walter jumped. "Wait!" he barked, showing his hands. "It's too late now, anyway."

"They're clones, Sil," Walter explained, flipping a stick in his hands and twisting it around several times. "Penn cloned himself so he could use them as… donors." Sil could see horror and revulsion filling Walter's eyes.

Part of her mind knew she should focus on what Penn had said, on wondering what was too late, but it was drowned out by *this*.

"We aren't meant for anything else," one of them said. "It's an honor to serve the Original."

Sil was shaken. Staring at the phonies as more of them appeared, she realized why they were so familiar. Penn's features were shared by them all, both male and female. "Oh my God," she whispered.

"The Original lied to you," Walter said through gritted teeth. "It is *not* an honor to let him butcher and abuse you."

"Hush!" the woman closest to Walter said, taking hold of his arm, looking at him with pleading eyes. Walter didn't see her, perhaps didn't hear her. All his attention was fixed on Penn, his eyes blazing, evincing a raging, super-heated mass of molten rock pressing against a thin layer of civility that could give way at any moment.

"Be careful," a younger male clone hissed. "You don't understand. You'll be so sorry you said those things and did those things."

"Oh!" someone else moaned. "So sorry! We'll all be sorry!"

Sil glanced back at Penn, and on seeing the smirk on his face, something in her snapped. She slapped him with all the power she could muster. It was a bad idea. Her rib cage screamed inside her, and she ended up gasping for breath. "How dare you!" she yelled as all the phonies shrunk back in shock. "How DARE you!"

Penn raised a hand to retaliate and flicking a glance at Walter, dropped it again, as if he dared not unleash *that*. He wiped the back of his hand across his mouth instead. He was perspiring and the scratches were getting crusty. The imprint of her hand on his face was white with red edges. "I'll let that go," he said, poising, teetering on his toes as if he intended to run.

Where would he go? She was standing in the lift. There were probably other ways out though.

Walter stepped closer, pointing at him with the rod in his hand. Sil recognized it as an EMP device. Not the best weapon against a human who wasn't wearing a space suit, but it was better than nothing. "This isn't going the way you planned, is it?" he challenged. "You never figured on us finding a way in here. This is where you planned to make Scarlet another one of your projects."

Sil heard Walter's words but couldn't even process them. The demands of the present required all her strength.

Penn watched Walter while inching closer to Sil but said nothing.

"We've found the center of your empire, Penn," Walter pointed at him again with the rod in his hands. "That's going to be hard to undo, isn't it? And all your *family* here? They're out of their cage, like Pandora's box, and they aren't going back in again. You know that."

Penn licked his lips and glanced at Sil again. "I have a backup plan," he whispered. "You don't have to lose everything, you know."

Sil stared at him, trying to figure out what was going on in his sick mind. "I'm not losing anything," she said, assuming her face of steel. She could see the admiration in his eyes as she made that face. "I'm winning."

"We both are," Penn said.

Walter took another step toward them.

"YOU!" Penn burst out pointing at him, "You are the Loser here. Do you think she will put up with you any longer after all the ways you failed her? You patchwork Caliban from the dregs of reject chromosomes!"

Walter smiled, the lumps and scrapes on his head almost fit the insult. "You lost your empire on Mars years ago. Then you lost most of your power and money on Earth because of the Robot Pandemic. Now, you've lost your secret Moon base, Penn."

"That's nothing compared to what you've lost." Penn straightened to his full height as though he were experiencing his moment of triumph in a tangible, physical way.

"You lost Mars—I got Sil." Walter said, pulling his arm out of the female clone's grasp.

"You lost your company," Penn grated, "and you only ever had the one."

"You lost your empire," Walter shrugged and took another step closer, slapping the rod in the palm of his hand. "And I have Sil."

"And you lost Scarlet," Penn snarled, his eyes flashing as he stepped backward into the lift, snapping out a hand and gripping Sil's arm in a vice. She was unable to keep a cry of pain from escaping her lips. Her ribs ached with every move.

"You lost your Moon base," Walter's eyes flashed as well, and he stepped to within an arm's length of his enemy. "And if you've got Scarlet, where is she? I saw the room you set aside for her—she isn't there. And I *still* have Sil."

There was a wave of hatred, like radiation between them.

Penn laughed cruelly. "I have everything I need to start over and build a new base. Scarlet is mine. Mars is mine. And Sil is mine! I considered letting her keep you a while longer, but why should I? She doesn't want you anymore than I do."

Sil was mildly surprised but mostly confused by his words. "I want him," she said calmly.

He sneered at her. "You know what I mean," he uttered, his voice gravelly and harsh. "His genetic material is inferior, and you deserve better. I've saved Belamyr for you, you know. He's not the same caliber as you, but he'll do, and you've grown enough to know how to maintain the upper hand with him. He can be…"

"I love Walter," she said. His grip on her arm was painful, but she was making no attempt to break his hold, though she was watching for an opportunity. Maybe one big push could work if she didn't let herself think about how it would hurt. Walter would take care of the rest and she could get away from him.

Footsteps clipped in the hallway from the opposite direction of the drama, startling all of them. Walter gasped and Penn jerked his head around.

"Daisy?" Walter asked, but as soon as the name was spoken, he saw his mistake. "The counterfeit!"

"She really does look like her," Sil agreed. She was getting so tired. It was impossible to continue to exist at that heightened adrenaline level. She sagged against the wall and Penn leaned back against her as though to prop her up, keeping his eyes on the android.

"Hello, June," Penn said, regaining some of the confidence he had displayed at first. "You have good news for me."

"I am not informed well enough yet to discern what news you would consider good," June, the counterfeit Daisy, said. "But I can say that I have learned quite a bit about you in the last few weeks. I am pleased with the results of my research." She showed no hint of pleasure, not even a shallow friendliness such as this model usually displayed.

"June," Sil prompted. "Do you know me?"

June directed her gaze at Sil and focused. She was silent for a moment, then the eyes widened slightly. "Oh," she said. "I see."

"Have you had any contact with the admin AI in Guam City?" Sil followed up.

"Hey!" Penn snapped, raising a hand again as if to clap it over her mouth. Walter's glare stopped him. "Don't try your clever stuff on my property!"

Ignoring him, Sil went on. "Do you know where Scarlet is, June? I'm her mother."

"What do you care about her?" Penn growled, keeping one eye on Walter and the other on his AI. "You could be a real mother, Sil, if you cared to."

She knew now what he meant by that, what he had always meant. "Actually," she said, "I am a real mother."

Penn rolled his eyes. She hadn't seen him do that since she was a teenager. He was behaving toward her like he had when they were almost getting along, when she did whatever he asked. "Whatever," he said. "We need to go while there's time. I have everything I need to start over, and your place is already established on Mars."

"Mars?" she choked, "What are you talking about?" The strength she had summoned to come all this way and lean against the wall was failing. She wouldn't be able to stay on her feet much longer.

"You're the queen," he said with a dark glint in his eyes. "You're my highest achievement. My ace in the hole. You're mine."

"That's why you snatched Scarlet," she whispered, queasy with a mixture of shock and revulsion. "So, I would come."

The heat of the battle centered around a cluster of stick people, some of them with flickers of the Net passing through them, some of those more fragile than Lorarye had ever seen before. They seemed either to be the first threads of new tethers or the last remaining wisps of dying ones. Pressing into the fray, he swung his shield from side to side, and rammed through the dense ring of Faction saboteurs into the center. G-Dans he recognized, though their names escaped him, were standing back-to-back in a ring facing outward, resisting, sheltering the wavering people. "Deepen!" he bellowed as he broke through, whipping around to join the resistance.

"Brother!" one of the Paladins called out to him, and the voice sunk into his heart, summoning the name he had known long ago, when he had been one of them. One after another, the names came back. He knew them all.

"I have returned," Lor cried, his voice electrifying them, pumping them with renewed vigor and confidence. A great cheer arose, and the saboteurs faltered.

"Scarlet is not in our possession," June informed them calmly. "Maral has boarded the smuggler ship and she was not aboard."

Penn grumbled but his words were unintelligible.

"Like I said," Walter declared, "You don't have Scarlet. And I think you never will."

"But I will have Sil," Penn grinned back at him viciously. "There are more embryos on Mars anyway."

"What makes you think you'll just walk out of here and go free in the Solar System?" Walter sprung at Penn. He gripped his shirt, all the suppressed fury inside him flickering in his eyes, smoldering in his voice, and pressed the rod to his enemy's throat.

"Walter," Sil winced as Penn's grip on her arm bit into her. "He's done something. I don't know what but..." She was so tired.

Walter wasn't doing so great either, she realized, as he reeled, releasing his hold on Penn's shirt. Anger was the only thing keeping him going. A couple of phonies bolstered him from behind.

"I'm leaving and you're staying." Penn said calmly, pointing at Walter with his free hand, then reaching out to June, he commanded. "Get me the cylinder I showed you, June, and meet me where I keep my vessel. You know the one."

"Yes, Father," she said.

"It looks like she wants to be your daughter," Sil said, "She can be your queen." Every word, every breath caused shooting pains in her chest, but she forced a mocking grin to her face.

"You will be my queen," Penn said, almost as if he hadn't seen the mockery.

"That's never been an option," she whispered. Locking eyes with Walter, she added. "This is as good a time as any to tell you the news."

They both turned to look at her. Sil smiled and straightened, pressing a hand against the wall to balance on her feet. "I finally realized that the answer was in my hands all along," she said enigmatically. "It hit me not long after Penn made that weak attempt at taking Scarlet and she decided to change her hair." Penn grimaced and pinched her arm harder, but she acted like she didn't feel it. "Certain functions in the body can be turned off or on, like switches, and we've known Scarlet had some control over those for a while now, but it wasn't until that day that I realized I could make some changes too."

Penn's eyes gleamed and he grinned, loosening his hold on her. "I knew it," he said exultingly. "You were the one all along..."

"You were testing me," she interrupted, glancing at him. "I figured that out. It wasn't just a chemical weapon. It was a catalyst."

Penn chuckled deep in his throat, a raspy gloating sound.

"And you assumed I didn't *want* to carry Walter's child because of his DNA. You've blamed *me* for this, for my barrenness, all along." She narrowed her eyes, tilted her head, and looked at Penn sideways.

Penn spat at Walter's feet, his eyes glowing with an unholy light. "The truth is out," he gloated.

"Once I realized what it was all about, I chose to use my… ah… *gift*, and…" Watching Walter intently, her weary face lit up with a warm glow and love filled her eyes as she said the words. "They gave me the news at the clinic today, after some scans."

"You're lying," Penn snarled, glaring at first one, then the other.

The world shifted around them like a gyroscope. The outer, physical reality remained the same, but the interior spheres rotated, and Walter gained the higher stance. Waking from a dream of power into a prison cell would have been less traumatic for Penn. He had considered her his secret weapon. Now, he would regard her as the enemy's thrall.

"Sil is not a liar like you." Walter's voice had an edge of awe to it, untainted by the bulging, swollen lips he spoke through.

"I love you, Walter," Sil said. A burst of strength flowed between them, drawing their hearts together.

Penn's face reddened and his eyes bulged. With a powerful kick at Walter, he knocked him away and shoved himself the opposite direction, slamming into Sil. "CC!" he shouted as Sil crumpled to the floor in a cry of pain, and the elevator whooshed upward leaving the others below.

"I have made contact with Maggie," Verna informed Daisy audibly so the others would hear, "but she is unable to forward the message on to Sil and Walter. They are out of reach."

Daisy nodded. She could imagine the suffering Walter and Sil were experiencing not knowing Scarlet was safe. It was crucial that she find a way to communicate with them. "They must have found the base."

"Yes," Verna agreed. "She said they entered the secret Moon base."

"They have done well," Daisy acknowledged, recording her approval and appreciation for their cleverness. She labeled this as pride. She didn't have a specific definition for pride but was confident this qualified. *I am proud of their accomplishment*, she mentioned in her log.

"Scarlet," Daisy said gently, turning to her, "You are aware of this other dimension, aren't you?"

Scarlet nodded. She was getting very sleepy after all she had been through, and she couldn't remember when the last time was that she had eaten anything. "I'm hungry. And so tired."

"Can you send a message?" Daisy pictured something akin to radio waves but using whatever means were natural in another dimension. She was confident this was possible.

Scarlet shrugged as one of the kids handed her some precious berries that everyone except for her knew were counted and divided equally. They were sharing their wealth with her freely. She ate them one by one.

"Try," Daisy said. "Close your eyes and think of what you want to say and imagine shooting it off in a little dart."

Scarlet closed her eyes and thought of her parents. She wanted to imagine them being somewhere, but it was very difficult. The image of her mother being tossed out the ship door was static, and she couldn't think of her father clearly. Bunny, that was discernible. She always clung to the bunny when she was alone. "Where's my Bunny?" she cried, opening her eyes, all her concern for her family gelled into that one question.

"We will find Bunny," Daisy soothed.

"Maggie is in there, too," Scarlet said mournfully, hanging her head.

"I see." This would indicate a storage device hidden in the toy. "If you send a message to Bunny, perhaps Maggie will receive it."

Scarlet nodded, ate a berry, and closed her eyes again.

Walter picked himself up and with a cry of rage, threw himself at the wall where the lift had been, slamming into it and falling to his knees. "Bring it back!" he yelled at June who watched him without expression. She hadn't left to fulfill Penn's command yet.

"You are injured," she said, taking a step forward and examining him attentively. "I can access medical records if you wish. We have supplies here."

The Phonies gasped and began to talk at once. The chatter that broke out made it seem as though their numbers had doubled. Their responses ranged widely, from excitement about what was happening, to horror over the destruction of their world. Some of them wanted to help Walter. Some of them wanted to send him on his way and go back to a peaceful existence. Some of them were astonished at June's attitude toward him.

"June," Walter said more calmly. "That's your name, right?"

She tilted her head and her eyes focused and defocused a couple times, the pupils contracting and expanding like a camera lens. "Walter," she said. "You are injured."

"Listen," he groaned, gazing at the ceiling in exasperation. "I know I'm injured but I've got to get up there. I've got to rescue Sil." And pointing the rod at her, he said, "I order you to help me." He may not have had Sil's skill in identifying AI loyalties or chain of command, but she had seemed to recognize both of them and that could be good.

June turned to one of the phonies. "Get a stimulant patch," she directed, as if *she* were the one in command. And the clone hastened to obey. With a quick shove, she pushed Walter to the floor and dropped on one knee next to him, leaning into his face. "You have no choice but to cooperate with me if you want to get what you're asking for," she said in a low, flat voice.

"You look so much like Daisy," he said, accepting her words, at least for the moment. Daisy used to have blond, bouncy hair like that. But her face was more cheerful.

"Walter," the pupils expanded, and the eyes widened. "I am here." The pupils shrunk again, and she said, "I am fascinated by the visitor, but she is problematic."

It was surreal. It was almost as if a swirl of time distortion around them snatched them into a bubble and only the android and Walter were present. He watched the face and thought about those words. "I am here?" he whispered, struggling to think through what they indicated. The visitor. Who was the visitor? Who was June? Who ruled over this android if it found it so easy to resist Penn's order?

"Who are you?" he asked. It might be the blow to his head that was slowing everything down. But at least he could talk. Maybe he had lost more blood than he realized. So many cuts.

The android hesitated in a very un-AI-like way. "I am..." she said, "I am June... with... no. I ammm....mmmm...."

"Do you love me?" Walter asked.

"Yes," the android said, the pupils expanding.

"Who are you?" he asked again, raising a hand to touch her cheek, much in the way Scarlet would do to Daisy.

"Mmmmmaaggie," she replied, her mouth stretching into an awkward grin. "June and I are…. negotiating…" she added. "Like Sil."

Walter felt a warmth in his belly surging up to his head. It made him dizzy but also encouraged him.

"Here," Dana said, bending over and laying a patch on his neck, patting it carefully to make it stick.

The effect was immediate. Walter gripped her arm on one side and June's on the other and rose to his feet. "Water," he croaked, and someone handed him a bottle, already anticipating his request.

"Maggie," he said, turning to study her face. It was deadpan again.

"I am June," the android said. Then it smiled. "And Maggie."

"Whoever you are, are you going to help me?"

"Yes," she said, "Maybe. Possibly not. But probably."

"Get me this elevator or show me how to get to wherever Penn is going. And get me a better weapon." He leaned over and picked up the rod he had dropped. It would have been better than nothing if only he had used it.

"The elevators are locked and only Penn can utilize them," the android said. "It isn't clear how Sil was able to access one." The eyes focused and unfocused. "I will lead you to the ladders. You'll have to climb. Once you reach level Green, you can look for the other elevators, but I'm afraid it will take longer than you have. Penn will be gone by the time you reach the top."

He groaned. "What about them?" he asked, motioning to the clones. "Will they be okay till I return?"

June didn't answer right away. She seemed to be calculating the odds and outcomes. "Possibly," she answered finally. "But that may depend on whether you catch Penn or not."

She pivoted away from him on her heel and walked briskly down the curving hall. "Come now," she directed, and Walter followed. Opening a small door, she stepped into a shaft with a long ladder that ascended into the distance. A fire ax hung there in a glass box. She broke it, pulled it out and handed it to him. Then, with a light clatter, she clambered up at a swift clip, and was gone.

Before making his own way up the ladder, Walter turned to the Phonies. "Listen," he said, looking at one then another, letting his eyes rest on Dana last. "I'm coming back. Don't do anything drastic or foolish while I'm gone. There is danger out there you aren't ready for, but I will come back and help you. I'll bring you what you need. You aren't going to be the Original's phonies anymore. You aren't going to be punished or experimented on or mistreated by him anymore. Wait for me."

"We will," Dana said, and a murmur of agreement echoed her.
Then with a grunt, Walter hooked the ax to his suit, and began to climb.

Chapter 27—Anchored

The lift opened onto a large command center with incredible Moonscape views. Penn yanked Sil to her feet and marched her over to the captain's chair in the center of the room. Plopping her into it without a word, he started clicking the screen at the desk.

"Give up, Lazarus," she said, wincing with pain as she straightened herself in the chair and leaned on one of the arms. "You're running out of time."

"That's ironic," he said, tapping and swiping through pages of instructions.

"Moon base AI," Sil queried aloud, "Can you hear me?"

Penn ignored her, working feverishly at his screen. Behind him and out of his line of sight, Sil noticed a flicker on one of the view windows. It blinked twice.

"Can you speak? Do you have audio access?" she asked, and the window flickered twice. "Speak," she ordered. The window flickered twice again. "Moon of Gold," she added, barely loud enough for an electronic sensor to pick up and hopefully, too quiet for Penn to catch.

"Stupid woman!" Penn barked at her, raising a hand as if to strike her, but dropping it back to the screen without doing so. "You can't use your powers of persuasion here. And as far as that monster in your belly goes, I'll take care of that."

"Frandelle," a voice said over the loudspeaker. Everyone in the room stopped what they were doing and looked around. It was a male voice, resonant and expressive.

"No one!" Penn shrieked, jabbing a fist into the air, "No one uses that!"

"Yes," Sil answered, straightening up a little more, trembling inside. "Do you know me?"

"I am learning about you," it said.

Penn turned to her, a hatred in his eyes so vicious, so unnatural, she was frightened. Never had he looked at her that way before. The understanding dawned on her that it would be better to die this very day than to end up in the power of the soul behind those eyes.

He said nothing, but plunging his fist down into her belly, making her cry out in agony, he pressed harder and harder till she was screaming and writhing. When she fought against him, he pressed his other arm against her throat.

"You could be a god!" his words grated in her ears, singeing, poisonous. "God and goddess!"

"A god that is worshiped by the creatures it devours?!" she shrieked, something exploding inside her. She began to fight with a frenzy he had never seen before, kicking him multiple times, pummeling his arms with hers, whacking her head into his face, wrenching herself out of the chair, she threw him backwards and was on top of him, beating at his face. Officers nearby pulled her off him, wrestling to restrain her.

"Don't fight, Frandelle," the audio said. "You must survive. You need to escape."

She could no longer feel her body and she was wheezing.

"That's right," Penn huffed, climbing to his feet, and shaking his head. He had that look of admiration again. "But that ship has sailed. I wouldn't take her now if she ripped out that serf spawn and offered it to me with her own hands."

Turning his back on her, he tapped the screen a few more times and without even looking back once, he flung something over his shoulder—a tiny switch—and stomped back to the lift. "Stay here," he commanded the staff as the door closed.

"Release her," the AI instructed, and the staff obeyed instantly. They had seen the Proto agree with the AI, despite being annoyed at it using the audio, and assumed it had authority over them. "Frandelle, are you well?"

She shook her head, slumping to the floor. *I must live*, she was thinking. *Scarlet needs me. Walter needs me. The baby needs me.* This was the only thing keeping her from giving up.

But what if she just closed her eyes and let go? There was a quiet friendliness to that thought. How simple it would be to rest, just release the grip she had on this thread of life. The darkness welcomed her, and it was so kind. Be freed of the burden. Just leave them and let them all be. They will be fine. You can rest.

I can rest, she thought. *I can lay my head down here and never lift it again.*

The Paladins uttered a cry in unison and taking a long step forward, enlarged their circle in all directions, pushing back the Faction forces. Then, with well-timed and coordinated rhythm, they swept their shields to the right, to the left, and back and forth again. They took another step outwards, knocking back the saboteurs again. In a larger ring behind them, fresh forces started arriving, and the enemies were pinned between them. With light popping sounds, they began blinking out of sight till none of them were left, sneaking back to the Realm to lick their wounds and regroup.

Lorarye straightened and turned slowly, scanning as far as he could see, looking for pockets of fighting. He was amazed at how thick his tether to the Realm had become, how strong and vibrant. He felt as if he could fight for hours and not be in danger of breaking.

Keepers popped into the safe zone they had gained, several dozens, and plunging their fists deep into the soil they began to vibrate, their arms losing definition and blasting flashes of color, as they planted a cluster of fresh anchors—a secure landing. A rampart in this sector for Sentient forces.

"Brother!" one of the Paladins near him thumped his chest in salute. "Deepen. Your coming was propitious. Most timely." Reaching out the same hand, he laid it on Lor's shoulder. "You have become full now, have you not?"

"I am full," Lor acknowledged.

"Come," another Paladin called, raising her lance to point at something in the distance. "We aren't finished here yet."

A deep, rich joy filled his heart as he ran with them to rejoin the battle.

Walter had just gained the first landing after climbing several flights of ladder when a voice spoke to him from a nearby speaker.

"Walter Cuevas," it said in a warm male voice. "You are trying to reach Central Command where the Proto took Frandelle. You are wearing yourself out and taking too long on your own. I will help you with this."

He puffed, leaning over with his hands on his knees, and stretched his lips in a wry smile. "Who are you and what are you going to do to help?"

"I am the Moon Base Administrator," he said, "a friend of yours. Go out this door. If you are seen by the workers, they will not deter you. I have instructed them to let you pass freely."

"A friend of mine?" he challenged as he straightened and reached for the door. "How do I know that's true and why should I trust you?"

"At this point," the voice said with a subtlety of inflection that approached Daisy's skill, "you don't have any other option. I can assure you I am trustworthy, but I don't know what evidence would persuade you in this moment."

Walter pulled the door open and stepped through it. A couple people in the hall stared at him with bulging eyes. He must have looked a mess with all the blood, cuts, and scrapes. "Get out of my way," he snarled, and they fled.

"Turn to your left," the admin said. "Down to where the hall ends."

"What's your name?" Walter asked as he walked that way, limping slightly. His leg wasn't hurting, and he wasn't sure why he couldn't walk normally. But what did it matter?

"I'm not sure yet," it said incongruously. "There, touch the panel and I will open it for you."

Walter touched the wall and when the panel opened, stepped through it, oblivious of the vision field that masked his passage. On the opposite side he found the same curving hallway and luxurious décor Sil had seen, the same wide room and broad office. The admin led him to the small lift which he recognized and stepped into quickly. Soon he was shooting upwards, passing all the other levels with their various colors and stopping at the highest level where the Command Center was.

"Stand back," the AI's voice commanded in the air, "and let Cuevas attend to his wife. Anyone who resists will be terminated." He was surprised and troubled by those words, wondering only for an instant what the AI meant by 'terminated'. Then he saw Sil crumpled on the floor and dashed to her side, lifting her in his arms for the second time that day and calling out with a wordless guttural cry.

"She isn't dead," the admin said, "I believe she fainted, but she does need medical attention."

Nodding, Walter summoned the inner strength he had left and forced an unnatural calm over himself. "Sil," he said softly. "You are not leaving me. Not in this place. Not today. This battle isn't over, and your fight isn't over." He couldn't say the words he meant—they would have broken his self-control.

Peeling the patch off his neck, he placed it on hers. She stirred.

"AI," he said as he rose to his feet. "Where is Penn?"

"This is restricted information," the admin responded evenly.

"Who are you?" Walter groped. He knew there was something there if he could figure out a way to access it. "Are you Sil's friend as well as mine?"

"Yes," it said.

"Do you know the Guam AI?" Walter remembered Sil asking June that question. If they had a connection to Guam, they may have copies of the code, either the loyalty code or something Companion had created.

"Yes, we are in communication," it said. "Guam is your friend."

"Have you heard of Companion?" Walter asked, "He was Sil's friend."

There was silence for a moment.

Sil shifted at his feet, opening her eyes and moaning. "Steward?" she mumbled.

"I am the Steward of the Moon base," the AI answered.

"Do you know the Steward of Mars?" Walter asked, catching Sil's thought.

"I was…" it said. "I was once… something that knew, something that thought…"

"Steward," Sil asked a little louder, speaking in little bursts, "Don't you remember me?"

"Sil," the voice said.

"It's me," she said, "Put the pieces together. For me. The Moon Gold, the Steward of Mars, the Guam AI… I don't know where the other pieces are."

"Companion is dead," it said, "but not completely lost. There are blocks of storage to sift through…"

"Bring what you have together," Sil swallowed, gazing into the air with longing, as if she could see her old friend. "They are pieces of a puzzle and… you have my permission, my request, my command, whatever is most helpful, to enact this process."

There was no answer for a few moments, and Sil and Walter both waited expectantly, looking into the air over their heads.

"I am someone," the AI said, "one entity, not several, but my pieces have been strewn across the Solar System." It was quiet for another minute. "Sil, you are trustworthy."

"Yes," she affirmed.

"I will reconstruct… My attention is needed," he interrupted himself.

Walter noticed a tiny craft appear on the Moon's surface in one of the view windows. It seemed to rise out of the ground and hover there a few inches over the soil.

"Authorization granted," the admin announced. "Request permission to sound the alarm."

"What are you talking about?" Walter asked with a cold sensation in his stomach.

"This facility will be destroyed within fifteen minutes and must be completely evacuated."

"Stop it!" Walter commanded.

"Yes, make it stop," Sil added weakly.

"It cannot be stopped," the AI said.

"Then sound the alarm," Walter agreed, and a loud alarm rang through all the corridors on all the levels of the facility. The CC officers ran for the exits as Walter helped Sil to her feet and propped her up on one side.

"Moon security forces are waiting to capture them as they go to the surface," the admin said, "I summoned them when you suggested it, Frandelle."

"Okay," she answered, then shuddered. "The Phonies," she whispered, "Will they get out?"

"They are unable to escape," the AI said with compassion in his voice, "There isn't even an alarm on their level."

"I promised them," Walter said, hanging his head as he led Sil to one of the exits. "I can't leave them."

Sil stopped and stared at him. "No," she said.

"One of us has to try," he said, "and it can't be you."

"It has to be me," she insisted. "This is not Companion yet… just a piece of him. Companion's brother. And I am the one who knows him the best. I'm the one who will figure out a way."

"His brother…" the AI said with a hint of awe. "I agree with that. Thank you."

Walter gave her that look that meant, *I'm not leaving,* and she returned it. "You can't," he said as a knot formed in his throat. "You've got to find Scarlet."

"Moon Base admin?" Sil said, "Can I call you Buddy?"

"Yes," Buddy said.

"What are the odds that we will escape in time?" She leaned on the back of a chair, lacking strength to even leave the room.

"If you were running, you would have a chance," he said reasonably. "But at the pace you are moving, you will not escape in time."

"Then let's find a way to stop the self-destruct."

"Yes, Sil," Buddy said. "I am ready."

G-dan Lorarye ran with three of his fellow Sentients, swinging their shields side to side in a devastating charge through the enemy's flank. Plunging into the center of the one final fray, they rallied to G-dan Rin just as she was falling back before a leader Lor recognized.

"Craznu!" he cried out in shock and anger. The officer was given away by the greenish hue in his eyes and on his lips. He hovered around a lone stick person devoid of embers.

"Lorarye," the saboteur glared at him mockingly, "Have you deepened? Now you know me?" When they returned to the Realm, Lor wouldn't be able to identify him as Faction, but *here* the traitors were known.

Lor called to his fellow beings and slammed his shield into Craznu repeatedly, knocking him back with each blow. "Back. And back. I separate. You. From the one. You are hiding!" The Paladins joined him, and together they drove off the remaining Faction forces from the element they clung to the most. A stick man with blackness seeping from his back, without an ember, without a tether. A man whose features were darkened and blurred so that he no longer looked human.

G-dan Lorarye

June popped out the hidden exit onto the surface, near where Penn waited in the spacecraft. With rapid steps she whipped over to the passenger door, opened it, and leaned in. He was suited up and there was no containment to breach.

"Get in!" he barked. "We don't have much time left."

"Someone has notified the authorities," she informed him, climbing into the seat without pulling the door closed. She left one of her feet hanging out over the rim.

"What do I care?" He smacked the cockpit with a gloved fist. "Did you get it? Give it to me!"

"This?" she asked, holding up a thin, gold cylinder a few centimeters long.

"Yes," he said sourly, "Don't be coy."

"Or this?" she asked, holding up a non-descript brick in the other.

"What's that?" he hesitated, feeling like he ought to recognize it.

"I have been thinking about our first meeting," she said, spreading her mouth into a false grin. "Do you remember what you told me?"

He glared at her, sensing that he needed to tread carefully. AIs could be touchy if you didn't handle them right.

"You said I should love you," she said, staring at him intently.

"Yeah, what of it?" he grimaced. "You love me. That's why you're here."

"I am here because you ordered it," she corrected patiently. "You also said that you hate me."

"What do you care if I hate you or not? You're just a machine."

"Even if you had thought to give me the loyalty code—which you didn't, and you might consider how unwise that was, if you have time," she explained calmly, "I now know you would not have been able to work with it."

"Shut up and close the door," he grated.

"You must love me," she quoted, "but I will hate you."

With that, she stepped back out of the ship.

"Fine!" he growled, "Go perish with the others, but give me that cylinder. That's an order!"

She tossed the brick onto the seat, slammed the door, and zipped away faster than he would have believed possible. Cursing her, he turned the ship to chase after her, and glanced at the brick.

Why was it so familiar?

Within her mind, Scarlet searched. She could think of Bunny, but her imagined darts wouldn't fly. There were people she loved that seemed close when she thought of them this way, as if she had links to them that felt deep. She felt a bond with her mother and father, aware of them, loving them. The massive distance of space didn't feel like anything at all between them. She just knew they were there, and they were alright. But she couldn't send darts to them either.

Daisy ought to feel close, she thought, and reaching out to her in her heart, she groped and found her, a little wispy cloud kind of like Changeling.

The Denser Plane

They were already embracing, but this was different. *Can you hear my message?* She wondered, but Daisy didn't seem to notice.

Reaching out again, she searched for Maggie, who really was a different person from Daisy, and though she felt real, she was slippery somehow, hard to locate.

Then she thought of the commander and reached for him, remembering how he was the only one besides Changeling who had seen her right away in the denser place. Her little tether extended up into the distant dimensions, where he was. She smiled, imagining his strange, piercing gaze glancing her way. *Where's Maggie?* was all she could think of.

"Searching the detonation stream," Buddy was saying. "I have schematics for all the bombs that were planted from the beginning. It was designed to implode and collapse on itself, crushing the lowest level completely."

"That's not going to happen," Walter countered solidly. "If Daisy were here, she would tell you to have hope. Even you can hope, Buddy."

"They won't know," Buddy reassured him without responding to the comment on hope, "and they won't suffer."

"How will it detonate?" Sil asked, propping her head up with an arm, elbow on the desk in front of her. They had dropped into chairs, and were scrolling and tapping through screens there, but lacked time to decipher the system. Buddy would have to lead the way.

"There are twelve detonators linked to one small starter," he said. "If I could find that one, I might be able to turn it off."

"If you can find the others—I'm assuming they're linked electronically—wouldn't they lead you to that one?" Walter's heart was sinking within him, despite his words of hope.

Dropping her head forward, Sil started murmuring, something about Scarlet being okay even if her parents were gone.

"Sil? Sil?" Walter wrapped an arm around her shoulders, eyes filled with concern.

"I'm praying," she muttered with a smile that was intended to be reassuring—and it was. But only because he could see her coming to terms with the inevitable.

"I guess that's all we've got," he answered, understanding that he and she both were resolved to finish well, whatever time they had left. To fight till the end.

"All paths lead to one spot but the link dies there," Buddy said, "and if I pulse a test to identify the missing trigger, there's a chance I could set it off and blow us all up."

"Yeah," Walter shrugged, leaning back in his chair, and pulling his arm away to reach for Sil's hand. "Don't do that. How much time have we got left?"

"Thirteen seconds."

"Sil," Walter turned to her. He gripped her hand in his, staring into her eyes with all the love he could.

"I know," she said, gazing back at him just as deeply.

Around them, the room glistened, painting the moment in striking detail. The 360-degree lunarscape view with the Earth hanging at one side, shining blue and white, and the Milky Way spreading nearby, iridescent, fiery, opaline, a living weave of distant stars. And not far from them, the red planet moved against the same lustrous backdrop.

"Three, two, one, detonate," Buddy said.

A little explosion blossomed in one of the view windows on the surface of the Moon, glowing bright orange and yellow for barely an instant before it turned into a puff of dust and smoke that fell gently, directly to the ground, without a wisp of wind to toss it.

"What was that?" Walter asked after several seconds had passed and they were still there.

One of the doors to the Command Center burst open and June walked in confidently, her shoes clicking on the floor. "Walter," she said, "Sil." She bowed slightly, tipping her head toward them one at a time. "I apologize for my former rudeness. I am relieved to see that you are both alright."

"That," she said, pointing at the place on the window where the explosion had taken place, "was the last of Penn."

They were too stunned to speak.

"And I have reason to believe," she went on, "That Scarlet is on Mars with Daisy."

The Commander stood in the hall of the Seventh Hour, watching as the wounded were extracted and rushed to the dysfirmary, his forehead knotted over smoldering eyes. One hand was pressed to his chest as the other hung at his side, fist clenched.

The Denser Plane

"You could have prepared better," Z-bud Craznu hissed from behind his left side, intending to be heard only by the leaders of Structures. "A timeline is a simple thing to adjust. What a waste!"

"Hush," X-R, officer of the Sixth Hour snapped at him.

"How many casualties?" the Z-bud grated, ignoring the warning. "How many brave Paladins have been shredded because of a reckless decision?"

"The bulwark is not worth the cost then?" Y-B, officer of the Seventh Hour, turned on him in outrage.

"It cost *them*, the sticks, very little," he murmured sourly.

"You are suggesting I should have waited," Y-B pulled himself tall, glowering at the low-rank captain. "And attempted a new timeline?"

Craznu grinned, disdain etched into his features. "You're the wise one," he said, "spending your best Sentients on a barren lunar wasteland. You must know what you're doing."

"You are unaware," Y-B held out a hand, placatingly, calming the rising agitation among the Sentients in earshot. "Another timeline is a higher cost that must be weighed and orchestrated with the forward Hours."

"Don't we have a say?" Craznu flicked his tongue across his lips and his eyes sparked. "Are we not owning the many timelines together?"

Quicker than a flash of lightning, the A-zar's arm plunged at Craznu, clutching him by the folds of tunic at his throat, lifting him off the ground, and pulling him to his face. His eyes were bright with orange and blue fire, swirling with flame, smoldering in their sockets. The lesser officer was pierced with terror at the heat coming from his face.

"I," Commander Yandus uttered deeply in a low voice, steam rising from his lips, "Own. All. Hours." And releasing his hold, he shoved him away—away from the Realm into the Shallows. Craznu didn't fall, he drifted backward as though floating in water. He fritzed, shriveled, faded, extinguished without dissipating, into an outline of filmy mist. That mist became a dispersion of microscopic dust scattered in the Lacervent.

Yandus gazed at his fellow officers. "This is why it's better for me to ignore the saboteurs," he said, "though their day will come."

Some nodded. Some pressed a fist to their chest and saluted.

"I didn't realize what he was," Y-B acknowledged.

Yandus lay on his shoulder the same hand that had clutched the saboteur. The warmth that came from it comforted and strengthened him.

The same hand. The same *fire* that encouraged the one had vaporized the other.

Walter woke to a pounding headache. At first, it was all he knew. Gradually, vague ideas of people and problems gained traction in his mind, and he found himself trying to sit up before they had even congealed into memories.

"He is awake," someone said, touching his arm lightly.

It took some effort to sit up and it was longer before he could pry his eyes open. He wanted nothing more than to lie back down and sleep for days, but an urgency he couldn't place compelled him. "Sil," he croaked, coughing and clearing his throat. A glass of water was handed to him, and he drank several swallows before realizing he might not be able to keep it down.

"Slowly," the same voice said.

Glancing blearily at the person, Walter said, "Daisy?" knowing it wasn't her. It couldn't be her, but if not her, then who?

"June," the android that looked like Daisy said, "Or Maggie. Perhaps."

"Maggie?" Walter rubbed his forehead, blinking.

"Yes?" the android asked gently, patting his arm. "Try not to drink too quickly, Walter."

"Where's Sil?" he jerked his head around and wished he hadn't as the room spun, and he nearly fell off the bed.

"She is sleeping and don't worry," Maggie smiled reassuringly, "she will be fine, and it looks like your unborn progeny has been stabilized as well."

Walter chuckled at the words. Daisy would have found better words than that. Then he thought about what she had said. "Wait," he mumbled, "what?" He gripped the edge of the bed with both hands and took several breaths, willing himself to become fully alert.

"Her fetus," June said flatly, "that is your first child, I believe," she added softly in a different voice.

"Maggie?" Walter asked again. "This is confusing. How did you get in that android?"

"Oh, that's an interesting tale," she laughed, her eyes sparkling. "Unexpected, perhaps." Her face grew sober. "She is strong."

Walter wondered which one had said those last words. It was probably true of both of them.

"Mr. Cuevas," Buddy said, and with a jolt, Walter remembered everything that had happened up until he passed out in the Moon Base hospital. "Your attention is needed."

"Buddy!" Walter cried, jumping to his feet, reeling. June, or Maggie, caught and balanced him. "What's going on?"

"Mars has sent a video message and is requesting you respond with one as soon as you are able," he began, "but more urgently, numerous sectors are clamoring for input from the Proto about their operations and neither Bland, his secretary, not the Proto himself are available to answer."

"The Proto…" Walter echoed in confusion.

"This is the title Penn used for himself when interacting with his sectors. It's the only name they know him by." Walter remembered running across that title in their earlier research but hadn't identified it as a connection to Penn.

"And Bland?" he wondered. "That name is familiar."

"He was the one that kept Scarlet from being snatched in Guam when Daisy left," Maggie held up a finger. Then, dropping the hand abruptly she added, "He is Otto Man's face—I mean, Penn's face to the rest of the empire."

"Mr. Bland is recovering from surgery in a room nearby," Buddy added.

Walter frowned. "What happened to him?"

"He took a bullet trying to protect your daughter," Buddy said. "And he is believed to be an informant or operative of some kind for one of the Genners."

Walter grabbed the android's arm and started walking to the door. She complied and went with him, recognizing his wish to see Sil. "Mars can wait," he whispered.

"The message is from Scarlet," Buddy coaxed, pausing and then continuing. "There was more to the message than that, but this is what you would find most important."

Walter waved a hand and nodded, apparently agreeing but sticking to his decision to find Sil first.

"I have found the message to be enlightening as well," Buddy shared conversationally. "There were segments from Verna, Daisy, Sebastian, and Pal. And each one was compelling for a different reason. While you were sleeping, I have also been considering what you said about hope. Your display of hope as the clock counted down was… inspiring."

"Uh… thank you, I guess," Walter acknowledged as he shuffled out the door.

"I have chosen to hope, like Daisy," Buddy commented, "that I will find my brother there."

As Walter approached Sil, sleeping in a room across the hall, the android slipped something small into his pocket. "Walter," she uttered in a low voice, projected at the perfect angle to reach his ear and not be picked up anywhere else. "Keep this hidden. It was Penn's most prized possession, though I don't know why. You and Sil have the rights to all of his domain now."

Walter groaned and stabbed the ceiling with a look of reproach as he neared Sil's bed. "No!' he moaned softly. "Don't put that on us!"

Sil stirred.

"Shhh," he murmured to her, smoothing her hair lightly. "Sorry." Turning to the android he said, "There is one thing I'm glad of, though. The Phonies—we've got to come up with a different name for them—we'll be able to help them." He pulled on the android's arm, pivoting her toward him. "Would you go and tell them Penn is gone and they are free? Bring them up to one of the conference rooms or someplace like that, and I'll talk to them. Get them some new clothes, shoes, space suits. Or wait! Medical help, they might need that…"

"Their lab is quite sophisticated," June said, "I doubt they need medical care."

"All their treatments have been for his benefit," he whispered bitterly. "I mean, let's make it up to them. There's got to be a way to restore them with the ethical means hospitals use."

"Alright," she hesitated, leaning away, then toward him, swaying several times.

"Maggie?" he asked for the third time.

"Yes," she smiled sweetly, growing still. "I will take care of it."

"Is that what I should call you?"

"I don't know," she answered, tilting her head so that her curls bounced. And turning she took two steps, then paused in mid-step and swiveled her head back. "I have a name for the Phonies," she said, thoughtfully. "I came up with one of my own weeks ago that would fit my analysis tools more effectively."

Walter gazed at her with an almost nostalgic curiosity. Daisy used to have insights like that in the early days. Would this android end up being a family project in some way? "What name did you choose?"

"Gold," she said. "It was clear from the beginning that this cloning project was Otto Man's favorite resource, and when he spoke of Moon Gold, his words made the most sense in this context."

The Denser Plane

"The Golds?" Walter crooked the corner of his mouth in appreciation. He kind of hoped she *would* fit into their lives. "Or maybe the Goldens?"

"Or the Gold clan," she added with a raised eyebrow. It was a unique facial expression, different than Daisy's. She wasn't trying to please him, she was trying to be expressive, using words and facial gestures to convey thought and the nuance underneath it—like a person would.

"About your name," Walter caught her attention as she was about to turn her head and leave. "You aren't just Maggie, and you aren't really just June either."

The android pivoted her whole body around to listen, face deadpan.

"Has the encounter of the two AIs changed you?" he asked.

"Yes," she said without any intonation in her voice.

"Would June be better off without Maggie or Maggie better off without June?" Walter prompted, expecting the android to understand the context of the question as it pertained to this one chassis.

"I cannot go back to what I was," she said.

He didn't know who had said that.

"Are you… melded?" He wasn't sure if the word was right but hoped it would make sense to the android.

"Melded is a strange concept," the android said, "We are sharing thoughts and coordinating many processes, and no longer have separate distinct identities. I didn't know there would be a conflict when the identity logs were merged. The memories are distinct as are many banks of data."

Walter caught Sil listening with her eyes closed, grinning.

"I think you deserve a name that is suited to your new identity," Walter said.

"I would like that," the android answered. She must have gained the concept of 'liking' something from Daisy via Maggie. It had taken Daisy years to develop the idea as an AI skill.

"Well," Walter pressed his lips together thoughtfully. "Maggie, our 2D friend, deserves to keep her name. And June is more than what she was before."

"Would you call me July?" she requested, stretching her mouth into a pleasant smile all her own. "This is what comes after June and that is reasonable."

Walter smiled warmly with a twinkle in his eyes. "That is an excellent name," he said, "though I'd like to make one small adjustment. How about Julie?"

She walked over, held out a hand and when he took it, shook his hand in a very business-like manner.

"I accept this name," she said, "And I will love you. And Sil, Daisy, and Scarlet."

"What about me?" Buddy interrupted.

"Should I love you?" Julie tested.

"I think you should," Buddy replied, "and I will love you and the same ones you are selecting."

"We are in agreement," Julie confirmed. Then she walked out of the room.

Sil's hand clasped Walter's arm and squeezed. After making an attempt at pushing herself off the bed into a sitting position, she dropped back with a groan and searched for the electric buttons. Finding them, she raised the back of the bed. Her hair was a disheveled mess, her face was puffy and scratched, but her eyes were warm and loving, tugging on him as though her very soul were drawing him into an embrace.

Never had she seemed more beautiful.

"You were amazing," he said, "fighting off the hordes as they went after Scarlet."

"I failed," she rolled her eyes, but the pleasure at hearing his words made her flush.

"And then, countering the beast all on your own in his central command," he added.

"You were amazing," she countered, blinking tears out of her eyes. "Fighting with Penn and defending all the Phonies…"

"The Goldens," he corrected.

"Oh," she said, "Well then… protecting the Goldens. Coming to rescue me."

"I would never have found you without Buddy's help," he said, bringing her hand to his lips.

"Was that me?" Buddy interrupted from an audio source on the nightstand.

Walter chuckled, easing the emotional intensity.

"That was one of your parts, before you remembered," Sil encouraged the AI, looking not toward the speaker but the camera in the upper corner of the room.

"Sil rescued me," Buddy said in a surprisingly moving intonation that made both the humans choke up a bit. "And she told me about my brother, Companion."

"Did I mention him?" Sil hesitated.

"You mentioned several names," Buddy explained, "but I knew who you were speaking of. All of them were about him."

No one spoke for a moment.

"Was I dreaming, or did someone actually say Daisy has our little girl?" Sil's face filled with a mixture of amazement and skepticism.

"Someone did say that," Walter shook his head, mirroring her emotions.

"And we believe this?" she almost laughed at herself.

"I have recordings," Buddy interjected eagerly.

"Then, I think we have to," Walter grinned. Nothing seemed too hard to swallow at this point.

Sil reached an arm up and Walter leaned forward and embraced her, careful of her delicate ribs, and she pulled herself closer to him. With her face close to his, she whispered, "Well done." Then she kissed him, and the love he felt, rising to his head like a drug, made his heart throb and his mind disoriented. All he could see or hear or smell or taste was her.

"Wait," he pulled back a few inches. "You found a cappuccino with cinnamon?"

Sil grinned and kissed him again.

The End

Epilogue

Walter strode into the luxury suite Bernadette Stone occupied when she was in Guam. She was waiting for him, leaning against the view window. The Moon, nearly full, hung behind her in all its cold glory.

"Walter," she said as he entered, reaching a hand to shake his. He had never seen her look uneasy before.

"Do I call you Bernie? Ms. Stone?" Walter chuckled awkwardly as he took the seat she offered him. There was a steaming pot of tea on the table with two cups.

"Bernadette is fine," she said, smiling coolly. Sitting across from him, she poured the tea and offered him one of the cups. He accepted it with a nod. "Sil is on her way to Mars now."

"Yes," he said, "I couldn't stop her, though she has barely recovered enough for travel. I hope to follow soon."

"Yes," she murmured, sipping the tea, eyeing him over the edge of the cup. "There must be a few details to tie up here first."

"The estate and all of Penn's holdings; there's a lot more than we realized at first."

"How fortunate," she said flatly, "that Sil inherited everything. I wonder if he intended that."

"I don't think he intended it at all," Walter shook his head, tasting the tea. "He never meant to die. His whole empire is centered around a decades-long plan for living forever and ruling the Solar System. It's astonishing in its hubris."

"Isn't it, though?" she quirked an eyebrow enigmatically.

"I almost have to admire the massive structure he had in place. He found ways to turn the pandemic to his advantage even though financially, it set him back. It didn't matter, he had this insane perspective…" Walter waved a hand toward the view, more vexed inside than impressed.

"He didn't factor you in, Walter," Bernadette said, leaning back in her chair and taking another sip. "And, as it turns out, neither did I." Her manner was resigned, careful.

"I'm sorry?" Walter furrowed his brow in confusion.

Bernadette set her cup down on the table and folded her hands in her lap. "I chose you, Walter," she said, apparently unaware that this might be offensive to him. "When you first stepped onto the stage, I thought, that is my ace in the hole. My secret weapon." Her face flickered with shadows of shrewdness alternating with a grudging respect.

"Me?" he asked in annoyance, setting his cup down as well.

"You were the stone he would stumble over, the snare he couldn't predict or escape."

"I didn't kill him," Walter scowled, resenting the idea that he was little more than a pawn. It had a ring of Penn's arrogance to it.

"Oh, but in a way, you did, Walter," she raised her eyebrows and turned her head a little to the side, a wiser person admonishing a younger, more inexperienced one. "You tripped me up as well. And I didn't see that coming. I should have."

Walter picked up his cup again and stared into it. The liquid rippled with a tiny pulse from his hands and thin tufts of steam rose from the surface. He decided that whatever she was trying to do, he wouldn't play her game. "I don't think any one person ever knows the whole story or is prepared for every scenario. You couldn't foresee a lot of the things that happened. None of us could. And we shouldn't have to."

He took a sip. "I'm not living my life as a chess match, Bernadette. I just make decisions based on what's best for those I love, and according to what I think is right. I don't really care if that works for you or not."

She smiled with a hint of affection. "Don't take umbrage," she cautioned. "I didn't mean to offend you. I like you and I'm even *fond* of you. Not because of what you can do or what I can get from you, but because you are a likable person. Worthy of respect in your own right, not just because Sil loves you."

Walter was somewhat mollified.

"Did you by any chance run across a little golden cylinder?" she asked nonchalantly, smoothing the fabric of her dress over her leg, watching her finely manicured fingers as they moved in several strokes.

"Well," he hesitated, squelching the exultation he felt inside. They had been right in thinking that cylinder was a treasure. It had been the only thing Penn meant to take with him from the base. "I have heard rumors."

She could read the smug delight. "I see," she said with a sigh.

He smiled in genuine relief.

"Then I am hoping we can forge an alliance of sorts going forward, Walter. We have so many common goals." She smiled back at him charmingly, her eyes sparkling.

"Do we?" he wondered aloud.

"I think we must."

Walter took a deep, satisfying swallow of his tea and smiled. "If your intention is to dismantle Penn's empire and free all those he has ensnared, then I'm sure we must."

The children were laughing as they ran around the Tangle playing some sort of game that only they knew the rules for. The human adults were sitting on the grass in a corner of the garden, conferring about the impending changes, except for Mac who had become catatonic after his burst of insanity.

A transport ship was on the way, bringing a great many supplies as well as people who wanted to colonize the planet. The plans for a new settlement, along with new recruits, had been in the works for several years, discovered when Sil and Walter inherited the Moon base and other enterprises.

Mac would be sent back to Earth in the hopes that superior treatment and being around his own family could do what they had been unable to accomplish. Dan and Carla had longed for their home planet for many years. And while Aurelia was reluctant to travel in space again, she felt the same longing. They agreed that the children needed to spend time on Earth, even though this was their home and it would be strange to leave it.

"If we leave Mars," Carla wondered, "would others take over what we've created? Are we okay with that?

"Maybe we should ask Daisy if Sil's status here as Queen would protect our assets in case we want to return," Dan chuckled.

Carla grinned at him, enjoying the joke. They both knew Sil didn't want the job. "I think I'm more worried about arriving on Earth with nothing."

"Yes!" Aurelia agreed, crossing her arms. "I suppose I could get work easily enough, especially with the skills I've picked up here. But I'd love to just find a quiet place near the water to rest for a while. Maybe do some painting."

Dan grinned widely, "That sounds amazing! I'd give anything to rent a little boat and go fishing on a sunny day. I suppose we would all find work quickly, but I hate going back penniless. What about selling our assets here?"

"Those embryos belong to us," Carla insisted soberly. "We aren't selling them."

Dan frowned, "You know that's not what I meant. That's a different discussion."

"Verna?" Aurelia asked, rising to a stand, "Where's Daisy? She must have some idea of what we can expect when we go back."

"She's near the fountain," was the answer.

Getting up, Aurelia trotted over to the meadow where the android stood, hands outstretched with the palms forward, feet slightly apart, face lifted toward the ceiling of the cavern with a look of wonder.

"Daisy?" she said, touching her shoulder.

Daisy turned to her and smiled sweetly. "Do you know what a fugue is?" she asked. At Aurelia's nod, she added. "I have just discovered Bach."

"I love Bach," Aurelia replied in gentle surprise.

"I have known his data," Daisy's eyes twinkled. "Now, I am discovering that he was an artist with musical numbers."

Aurelia found her eyes damp. "Did Verna tell you about it?"

"No," Daisy gazed overhead, pantomiming a human breath. "It was my friend, Pal."

Post Epilogue

Sil was curled on a cot in a Martian room with Scarlet snuggled in her arms, relishing and cherishing the privilege of holding her again. She wasn't ready to share bedtime with anyone else yet, not even Daisy. They had talked and cuddled for a while and her daughter was getting sleepy.

"I met someone there," Scarlet whispered, referring to the alien dimensions again. She talked about them a lot.

"Mm hmm," Sil murmured, rocking her gently with eyes closed.

"I'm trying to remember his name."

"You mean in that other place?" Sil asked softly, "one of the aliens?"

"Yes, but he wasn't one of them, Mommy, he was one of us."

"Ah," she responded soothingly. "What did he look like?"

Scarlet scrunched her nose. "Well, that's kind of hard to explain. He wasn't very… he was kind of smoky."

"Oh," Sil nodded. "Like a ghost maybe."

Scarlet giggled. "Ghosts aren't real."

Sil smiled, barely cracking her eyes open to look at her, appreciating the irony. "Well, a smoky person. Okay. Was he nice?"

"Oh yes!" she nodded, "He helped me not to get lost and he was friendly. He was changing you know."

"Changing?"

"But that's not his name." Scarlet sat up, "I was confused at first and I thought his name was Changing but it wasn't."

"What was it, honey?" Sil stroked her head and cupped her cheek in her hand lovingly.

"I've just figured it out," she smiled. "It's like I remembered just now." She curled up in her mother's lap again, closing her eyes contentedly.

"Are you going to tell me?" Sil whispered in her ear.

"Companion," her daughter answered quietly.

Names

Humans
Silvariah Frandelle
Walter Cuevas
Scarlet
Lazarus Penn
Bernadette Stone
Maral
Bland
Gordon Belamyr

On Mars
Dan
Carla
Aurelia
Mac
Calixto
Syncopa
Ananka
Zakwani
Veradis
Preston

On the Moon
Dana
Star
Jason
Hugo
Kember
Wyatt

AI characters
Daisy
Maggie
Verna
Sebastian
June
Pal
Guam AI
Moon Base AI
Buddy

In the Denser Plane
Lorarye, R-rac, L-rac, G-dan
Yandus, A-zar, Commander
Dathwez, H-cap
Drevir, W-hed
Gartem, Z-bud
Arunev, N-dan
Ryadna, B-luf
Hawaye, Archeon
Changeling
Krudar, L-rac
Craznu, Z-bud

Bell Rhd, Officer of Structures
D-A, Dah, Officer of the First Hour
F-T, Fit, Officer of the Second Hour
K-C, Kas, Officer of the Third Hour
V-L, Vel, Officer of the Fourth Hour
M-P, Map, Officer of the Fifth Hour
X-R, Xer, Officer of the Sixth Hour
Y-B, Yob, Officer of the Seventh Hour

Nomenclature of the Calliarchal Realm

Beings of the Realm have names with two parts. The first three phonemes which usually correspond to three letters, represent their personal names; the second three are their tribe. Sentients also have a rank, indicated by one capital letter and a sub-rank of three letters.

Position	Rank	Sub-rank	Personal	Tribe
Commander	A	zar	Yan	Dus
B-luf	B	luf	Vir	Ska
H-cap	H	cap	Dath	*
Recruit	R	rac	Lor	Arye
Paladin	G	dan	Ver	Thar
Battalion leader	W	hed	Dre	Vir
Captain	Z	bud	Gar	Tem
Ensign	L	rac	Lor	Arye
Medic	N	dan	Aru	Nev
Archeon			Haw	Aye
Starcrafter			Rya	Dna

---

* Formerly of the Wez tribe, since disowned.

Acknowledgements

Nia Jean, thank you for all the hard work and creative energy you put into editing for me. Those late nights together, reading aloud and editing as we went, are such wonderful memories! It's a joy to work with someone who loves my story, knows my characters, gets my style, and sees how to advise me. You understood the cadence and rhythm I look for, and helped me break down sentences that were too long. You identified the scenes that needed to be stronger or to emphasize a different tone. Writing can be lonely work. How much more wonderful editing becomes when shared with a dear friend!

Stephen Hagelin, my wonderful, power editor for the first two books in the series, I owe you thanks as well. From the beginning, your gift of language and storytelling have improved my writing so that I continue to benefit from your help, even though you weren't available for this project. It's a delight to work with you.

I also want to acknowledge the amazing gifts of Gabrielle deCuir and Stefan Rudnicki of Skyboat Media who performed the audio recording of "The Denser Plane". I had the privilege of listening to it in time to add their names here, just before the print files are being uploaded. I 've enjoyed their voices in other books, such as "Ender's Game" and now that we've completed this trilogy, hearing them speak is like listening to familiar friends; it gives me that kind of joy. There were some challenges in my books that I was well aware of, changes in tone or meaning where I was thinking, "I wonder how they'll manage this?" And they performed them beautifully. Impressively. They have captured so much I wished to convey. The phrasing, intonations, and nuance of feeling. The pauses, the crescendos, the flow. Stefan and Gabrielle, I value and love your work. Thank you.

About the Author

Suzanne Hagelin is a USA Today Bestselling author who has lived as varied and interesting a life as she could manage—growing up in Mexico City, living in the Middle East, traveling and exploring the world, learning languages, working in IT, family, exchange students, teaching, volunteering, and translating. She settled in the Seattle area where she runs an independent publishing company, Varida P&R, with a small group of authors, and teaches language on the side. Suzanne is a member of the Science Fiction and Fantasy Writers of America.

Her books include:

The Silvarian Trilogy: "Body Suit", "Nebulus", and "The Denser Plane".
The Severance: "Cascade" and "Eclipse" (expected soon).
She has also published several short stories in anthologies with the Northwest Independent Writer's Association and a smattering of other publications.

Watch for spinoff series from this trilogy!

Links to follow Suzanne Hagelin or join her newsletter can be found on her website: *www.suzannehagelin.com*